I0645674

THE
TRAGEDY
OF THE
TRAITOR

copyright © 2022 Mandi Grace
ISBN: 978-1-957620-06-0 (Paperback)
ISBN-978-1-957620-07-7 (ebook)
First Edition November 2022

Cover by Stone Ridge Books LLC

Mandigraceauthor.org

THE
TRAGEDY
OF THE
TRAITOR

FORWARD

Since publishing the first of these rewritten novels I have gotten into the habit of adding a forward to explain the history of the book in your hands and how it came to be. That first forward flowed from my fingertips with ease...but to be honest, each subsequent forward has been harder to write. I am bound to repeat myself, but I will hope it isn't too redundant for those of you who take the time to read these words.

I was seventeen when I first became entangled in this Robin Hood world of my own creation. Seventeen when I first dove into the realm of self-publishing with no idea what I was doing.

To those of you who might have read the original series, I say the biggest and most heart-felt THANK YOU. I will always be floored that anyone took the time to fall in love with my characters as I had. To those of you who have no idea what I am talking about, let me explain...

When I started my self-publishing journey, I did so under the name Amanda Grace. The series I lovingly refer to as the OG Robin Hood series, five books in total, were all under that name. Allen's book was, and is, book four of the series.

Eventually I switched over to writing under Mandi Grace, but I left my old books behind me for several years. The sequel Robin Hood series (Return to Sherwood) was my only Mandi Grace work. And then one day I decided to move all of my books under one name—and while doing so, revisit and rewrite the old ones to give them a more polished story and brand new covers. This is what you hold in your hand today.

Rewriting Allen's story was more fun than I should probably admit, giving how I tortured his character so much more this time around. But it's true: I had a blast rewriting this book. His story, his *tragedy* is not a particularly happy story but his struggle to let go of the ghosts from his past and the memories of the fateful fire that destroyed everything was one that broke my heart, and I hope will break yours, too.

to the girl fighting ghosts
to The Tragedy of the Traitor

Prologue

The wind was screeching outside, making the wooden frame of the house shudder. The frigid air caused Robin to pull his hood tighter around his shoulders. The fire crackling across the room threw a cheery light into the darkness, leaving friendly shadows dancing along the walls. On the floor in front of the hearth opposite him sat two children and an elderly woman.

At the table next to Robin, his wife Marian lifted a mug of steaming tea to her lips and smiled at him. "It could be worse."

"Yes." Robin pulled his cloak even tighter around himself, trying to ward off the cold. "We could be living in the forest in this weather."

Robin glanced toward the other side of the room again. His daughter Mari-Lu was pressed up against Aunt Lucy, undoubtedly her favorite person in the world. Aunt Lucy was actually Robin's grandmother, but she answered to 'Aunt Lucy' to several generations of children who grew up in Nottingham and the surrounding villages. Robin had adopted the title as everyone else had. Aunt Lucy stroked Mari-Lu's hair as they both watched the other child–Edmund, a family friend–drawing a likeness of Aunt Lucy.

Edmund bit his tongue and leaned forward slightly, enough that his curls fell into face. As Robin watched, Aunt Lucy reached out and ran a withered hand through Edmund's hair as he concentrated on his drawing.

"Will you tell us a story?" Mari-Lu asked, turning her head to look up at Aunt Lucy's face as she leaned against her shoulder. "Please?"

1

A familiar smile crossed Aunt Lucy's wrinkled face and she glanced toward Robin. He had yet to make any move toward putting his daughter and Edmund to bed for the night, and undoubtedly Aunt Lucy was gauging whether there would be time for one of her long tales.

Robin gave her an encouraging nod and Aunt Lucy winked at him.

"Alright. I will tell you both a story." Aunt Lucy shifted position and Edmund set aside his drawing, moving to snuggle up beside her as Mari-Lu was.

"Which story will you tell us?"

"Which story would you like to hear?" Aunt Lucy asked, brushing Edmund's curls from his face again.

"I want to hear about Dusty!" Mari-Lu said.

Robin smiled at his daughter's enthusiasm. There were few who didn't enjoy sitting and listening to Aunt Lucy wax poetic about her days fighting alongside the famed Robin Hood and band of outlaws, but no one loved her stories more than Mari-Lu.

Marian shifted next to Robin, taking another drink from her warm beverage. "What story do you think she'll choose?" she whispered. Robin grinned at his wife and shrugged, turning back to watch the trio by the fire.

Edmund remained thoughtful for a moment, and as Robin watched Aunt Lucy tilted the boy's chin up to see his solemn face more clearly.

"Have you decided, my young friend?"

Edmund nodded.

"Well?"

"Could you...could you tell us about my great-grandfather? About Allen of the Dale?"

2

"Oh do!" Mari-Lu clapped her hands. "We haven't heard that one!"

Aunt Lucy closed her eyes for a moment, lost in her memories. It was always the same with her whenever she told one of her stories– she would sit for a moment, pulling all the memories to the forefront of her mind, and then her tale would begin.

Aunt Lucy had become the keeper of the family histories, and as the last surviving member of Robin Hood's gang her stories held a great deal of weight–both within the family, and without. Robin suspected she was training his own daughter Mari-Lu to become the next keeper of the stories and it warmed his heart to see the two of them reposing together. His daughter couldn't remember the rest of the gang– most had died before she was born, and those that hadn't had died before she was old enough to retain memories of them. Aunt Lucy was all she had, and though she likely didn't know the importance of every precious moment spent together, Robin cherished the memories for her.

"Alright," Aunt Lucy said, opening her eyes and looking down at the two children who stared up at her with wide eyes. "I will tell you about Allen of the Dale. Yet you must be warned, this is not the happiest of tales…"

"But it has to have a happy ending," Mari-Lu said. "They all do."

"You will see…"

Part 1

The Innocence

Chapter 1

London, England. September, 1188.

Allen walked along the busy street, his hood up and covering his face. The people around him all seemed to have a purpose. Merchants moving with confidence toward their establishments, soldiers swaggering with pride as they prepared to fight for their king, nobles walking along the street with light feet and bright smiles.

There was a fortress of pain between Allen and the sense of purpose he saw in the people on the street. He could not share it with them, locked as he was behind his own defenses.

William had left for France two weeks earlier and Allen was alone in the world.

Not that he minded. He hardly deserved companionship.

As the sun made its way across a blue sky dotted with clouds, Allen paid for a room at a local tavern and settled by the window in the common room downstairs to watch the happenings on the street outside.

Women were scurrying by with baskets over their arms or children trailing behind them. The men were marching up and down the street going about their business. People were smiling, laughing. Living life as though nothing would ever go wrong for them. As if they didn't know it could all change in an instant.

Allen grimaced as he brought a mug of mead to his lips; he had lived like that once, taking it all for granted.

Allen scowled as he plunked his mug back onto the table. William was right; the Crusades were a good idea. Allen needed to distance himself from this grief, this lifelessness, this useless existence. He needed a change. If he was lucky—which was unlikely given the curse he no longer doubted—he could die an honorable death fighting for the King of England.

Allen listened to conversations in the dining room of the tavern, sipping from his mug and scowling at anyone who dared make eye contact with him. He didn't want anyone to talk to him, but he tuned in to specific conversations around him, in particular those pertaining to the Crusades and Prince Richard's army.

From the talk around him, it seemed he needed to go to Dover eventually, a port along the English Channel. It was there young men would sign on to sail with the King's fleet to march on the Holy Land to take back Jerusalem. Allen had little interest in the religion or politics of what was coming; he merely wanted an excuse to get away from his past and potentially end his miserable existence in the most honorable way he could.

When he retired to his room that night, darkness pressed on his mind, the shadows of the dark room around him seeming to come to life and twist into the haunting shapes of his wife, his sister, his mother. As he lay in his bed, the rattling wind outside his window sounded no different than baby Duncan's thin wailing cries.

Allen pushed the memories aside, fighting against the gentle smile on Eri's face and the sparkling green eyes of his sister Alice.

He shoved it all down, refusing to acknowledge it for fear of falling to weeping and never being able to stop.

When the weak light of dawn began to filter through his window, Allen gave up on sleep. With weary limbs and heart, Allen rose to prepare for his day.

Hordes of young men came en masse to London in the days and weeks that followed. The onslaught had begun before Allen arrived, and continued long after he'd been there. The tavern where he was staying was soon filled to the brim with them–they spoke cheerfully and zealously of the war to come. Allen could not share in their passion, but he was eager for the war all the same–eager for the solace he might find in death.

Training in London began, which Allen eagerly joined. He knew how to use a sword thanks to his father and William, but there was always space for improvement. And so he trained, his days long and hard, and he went to bed each night more sore than he'd ever been before–and tired enough he wouldn't dream of his family.

The summons finally came and the hordes of young men left London and marched to Dover where the King's fleet would be waiting to take them across the channel. The Crusades were truly beginning.

Scotland. July, 1171.

The sun was high in the cloudless sky, burning down on the field where Duncan was currently leaning against a black cow, trying not to think about his wife.

"Do ye think she is alright?" Duncan asked the cow.

The cow ignored him.

Duncan sighed, brushing a hand across his forehead. "Ye should be more sympathizin'. My good wife, she is givin' birth today."

Still, the cow ignored him.

Duncan surveyed the field in front him; the rolling green hills of the pasture that housed his cattle surrounded him, farther off he could see the waist-high plants of runner beans and beyond that a vibrant vegetable garden. Looking in the opposite direction he caught a glimpse of the wooded area beyond his lands, and closer to his pasture the fruit orchard. To the south were the fields where he would grow barley and wheat depending on the time of year, and then another set of fields for his potato crop. His land was vast, covering a great distance and housing more than one small village of tenants who worked the fields and tended the animals for him. The hills and valleys were many and varied, especially the closer his land drew to Edinburgh.

Duncan was the head of one of the more prestigious families in the area–the Logan clan. He closed his eyes, shutting out the sight of his wealth and feeling the warm air on his face, trying to imagine having a son or daughter at his side the next time he surveyed his lands.

It would never happen.

His clan was cursed.

Duncan opened his eyes, glancing around the open pasture again. The sun was casting its cheerful hue across the field, but Duncan could not find any cheer in his heart despite the fact that his firstborn might be coming into the world at that very moment.

"Duncan!"

Duncan's heart leaped to his throat, his palms instantly going clammy at the sound of his best friend's voice. He turned around, keeping one arm draped across his cow as he watched William approaching.

"What ye be doing here, William?"

"I came to see how your wife is faring." William approached with a smile on his face. He was tall and lean, his face weathered by years and his dark hair bearing hints of grey.

"I cannae tell ye."

"But you are worried, I imagine." William patted the cow's rump and then crossed his arms, smiling at Duncan. "Never fear, my friend. Women give birth all year round."

"Aye, and if they be of the Logan clan they die…or the bairns do. There's no two ways about it: we're cursed."

"So you always say. I seem to recall you having two perfectly healthy parents."

"I was a true blessing child, I was."

"I was here when you were born," William chuckled. "I know what you believe, my friend, but I have faith your little one will be a blessing child, too."

"They all die." Duncan rubbed his forehead, shaking his head. "The bairns or the mothers. They cannae both live, not in the Logan clan."

"Except, as I said, in your case. I do not believe your family is cursed."

"Ye ought to believe it; ye have witnessed it enough."

"Evanna will be fine. Your child will be fine."

"Osla's stillborn seven months past?"

William shook his head, unconvinced.

"Ricard's wife died a year ago; he's raising his wee bairn on his own now."

"I am not saying there have not been tragedies; I'm saying you aren't cursed. I have faith Evanna will be fine."

"Master Duncan, sir!" a small voice cried out.

Duncan and William both spun around at the sound of the child's voice. Nevin, a servant boy, was running up the path between the fields waving energetically. The cow didn't take any notice, but Duncan's heart rate increased exponentially as he held his breath.

11

"What is it, lad?" William asked as Duncan tried to find his voice.

"Ye…yer…wife…" The boy ran up to them, doubling over and gasping for air.

"Och, nae!" Duncan's legs buckled beneath him, and he nearly fell but for William grabbing his arm.

"Steady, man." William pulled Duncan upright. "Let the boy catch his breath. He's winded from running, that is all. Now, Nevin, what is that you have to say?"

"The lady has given birth to a boy," Nevin said, standing up and grinning at Duncan. "You have a son, Master Duncan."

"And the lady herself?" William asked as Duncan wrung his hands.

"She is fine. She has been askin' for Master Duncan. Florie sent me to fetch ye."

Duncan took off running down the path, not waiting to hear more. He could hear William laughing behind him, but that didn't slow his feet as he pounded down the path away from the fields toward the manor house not far from the pasture.

As he ran up to the house, he cried out, "Evanna!"

There was no response, but he didn't slow his pace. Duncan pushed open the front door of his two-story home, only to have Florie–his family's faithful cook and the village midwife–grab his shoulders and push him back outside.

"Nae so fleet, Duncan. Nae, ye dinnae."

Florie was not a small woman; she was far stronger than Duncan and easily pushed him outside without even trying. Her dark hair was pulled back into a tight bun, though curls leaked out here and there, and her grey eyes were flashing.

"Florie, ye best let me through. My good wife, she is in there!"

"Och, I ken that well enough. But ye cannae come in, nae til she be cleaned up, and the' little laddie has had a bathin'."

"Florie–"

"I'll tak' nae argument from ye, Master Duncan. Ye will hold yer horses right 'ere til I say otherwise."

"Nevin said ye sent for me."

"Ye came faster than I imagined ye would."

Duncan sighed. There was nothing he could do to fight her. Florie had the rule of his house and they both knew it.

"Do nae shift from 'ere." Florie gave him a stern look before disappearing inside where Duncan could not follow.

The wait was not long, however. Florie soon reappeared and pulled Duncan into his own house rather roughly. "There now, she is waitin' for ye."

Duncan darted through the open room at the front of the house that contained only a wooden table with stools and benches around it and a hearth along the far wall. There were tapestries hanging on the wall embroidered with the daring tales of his clan, and his claymore was mounted over the fireplace. He ignored all of it as he rushed to one of the three doors that led out of the spacious front room–the one on the right would lead to Florie's kitchen, the one to the left opened into a stairway that led to the second floor. The third door was his target, the bedroom he shared with his wife.

Despite rushing across the room, Duncan paused before the closed door, unable to bring himself to open it. Florie reached around him with a chuckle, opening the door and pushing him inside.

"Do nae be too loud. I expect ye to let her rest. See yer good wife and then git."

13

Duncan moved cautiously toward the bed. His wife was sitting up, propped against several pillows, her brown hair a matted sweaty mess and a sheen of sweat across her forehead. She looked exhausted.

"Evanna…"

She turned toward him, a smile lighting her face. "'Tis a fine wee lad I have for ye, Duncan."

Duncan moved to the edge of the bed and ran his fingers gently down Evanna's cheek as he glanced at the bundle in her arms. "Is it now? Does he have a name, my lassie?"

"Allen, after yer father."

"'Tis a fine name." Duncan gazed down at the small, red, wrinkled babe in his wife's arms and felt a warmth flood his chest.

"Are ye happy?"

"Aye," Duncan kissed Evanna's head. "That I am, lassie."

More than happy. The curse had been avoided. It was a miracle, and Duncan had a blessing child after all.

Chapter 2

Scotland. August, 1184.

Thirteen-year-old Allen looked at the list Florie had written out for him, and then glanced around the busy street market looking for the next vendor he would need to approach. The rolling green hills, sharp crags, and deep valleys that housed the growing city spread out around them but Allen ignored the wider surroundings and focused on the booths in front of him.

His nine-year-old sister Alice shifted the basket in her arm as she trudged along beside him, moving through the busy market at the edge of Edinburgh. "Are we almost done, Allen?"

He smiled at his sister. "Almost. We need a couple more things."

Allen watched as Alice's lower lip protruded as she turned to survey the crowded marketplace–merchants at their stands calling out to attract buyers, women with baskets over their arms and children clinging to their skirts, men with swords at their sides and serious expressions on their faces. The sun was shining down on them all as their voices filled the air with a chaotic hum of activity.

Alice had begged to be allowed to go to the market and Evanna had agreed on the condition that Allen went too. Allen could still recall how Alice's face had lit up with triumph; she had been ecstatic. But now she was tired and her basket was getting heavy, her green eyes falling to a darker shade the more frustrated she became with her predicament.

"We were nae supposed to have to work," Alice sighed, her red curls almost drooping about her face.

"As long as we were comin' we might as well help Florie," Allen replied. He glanced at his list again and then grabbed his sister's hand. "Come on! We're almost done."

Allen led her to another merchant and handed his list to the man so he could fetch what Florie needed. Allen and his sister were recognized on sight by most people in Edinburgh, considering their father, Duncan, was one of the wealthiest and most respected nobles in the area.

When they'd bought the last item on the list from Florie, Allen and Alice weaved through the crowded marketplace headed for home. As they moved through the crowd, however, a woman stepped in front of Alice and stepped on her foot which in turn caused her to jerk away and knock Allen into someone behind him.

Allen righted himself and turned around to apologize. He froze when he turned, however, and not a sound escaped him.

It was a girl, one he'd never met before. She had dark brown hair that was pulled back in a braid and her eyes were a deep blue, like the sky at twilight. She smiled, and a single dimple appeared in her left cheek.

"Sorry about that," she said with a giggle. "The crowds always make me bump into people."

Allen wanted to say it wasn't her fault. He'd bumped into her, not the other way around. But he couldn't speak.

Beside him, Alice started laughing. "Close your mouth, brother, before a bug flies in there." Turning to the girl, she grinned. "I'm Alice. This is my brother Allen."

"I'm Eri," the girl said, her smile widening.

"I haven't seen ye around before." Alice shifted her basket out of the way of a man passing by her and stepped closer to Eri so they could continue their conversation despite the jostling of the market crowd.

"My family just moved to the area," Eri replied.

"Do ye have brothers and sisters?"

"Nae. 'Tis just me and my parents."

"Ye should come to dinner at our house," Alice said. "My mama will nae mind."

"I'll have to ask my parents. What is yer father's name?"

"Duncan of the Dale."

"I'll tell my father. Maybe I'll see ye for dinner. And if nae, I'll see ye here again perhaps."

"I hope so," Alice replied.

Eri smiled, her single dimple coming out again. And then she was gone, skipping off into the crowd, presumably in search of her family.

Allen resumed breathing.

"Why were ye so dumbstruck?" Alice laughed, pulling her brother through the market and toward the road out of town.

"She's beautiful."

Alice giggled. "Oh nae, you are nae fallin' in love, are ye? Florie will nae like that."

Allen grinned. "Father will though. If I'm going to have the land when he dies, I must have a family to go with it."

17

Alice shook her head. "Father is nae dyin' anytime soon. And ye should nae be thinkin' about marriage yet."

"I'm thirteen, Alice. I'll have to think about it soon. Father will undoubtedly already be planning a strategic marriage with the nobles in Edinburgh or beyond."

Alice frowned and stopped walking, her green eyes swirling with emotion. Allen paused beside her, waiting.

"But if ye have a wife...I will nae be yer favorite. Ye will nae tell me all yer secrets or spend all yer time with me anymore."

Allen wrapped an arm around Alice's shoulders. "Ye will always be my favorite, Alice." After a pause, he added, "Next to Florie, of course."

Alice swatted his arm, but she laughed all the same, her green eyes sparkling once more. That was all Allen needed. They resumed their walk home, Allen taking the heavy basket from Alice so she could move more freely.

Eri and her family did not come to dinner that night, which disappointed Allen, but he did not have to remain disappointed for long as they came a few days later.

Duncan fell into easy conversation with Murdoch, Eri's father, and Allen was happy to see that his mother Evanna seemed to feel just as at home with Senga, Eri's mother. Allen was less dumbstruck at his second meeting with Eri and he, Alice, and Eri kept each other laughing throughout the meal.

"How old is yer lass?" Duncan asked Murdoch somewhere in the midst of their conversation.

"Twelve years," Murdoch replied, turning to watch his daughter. Allen tried not to be obvious as he turned to watch the men.

He did not miss the way that Murdoch's eyes lit up fondly as he watched his daughter talking to Alice.

"She's the sweetest thing ye'll ever meet."

"I think ye'll find that honor belongs to my own lass." Duncan grinned as he said it.

By the end of the meal, Allen was more convinced than ever that he wanted to marry Eri, and the way his parents and hers had gotten on so well throughout the evening gave him hope that they might consider it.

Chapter 3

Scotland. September, 1184.

It was nearly a month before Eri and her mother came for another visit. It was a windy day, but in spite of this Allen had taken his wooden sparring sword into the grassy area behind the house to practice various stances and movements that William had been teaching him recently, so he did not see Eri and her mother arrive, but it wasn't long before Alice and Eri came running around the house to where he was practicing.

He stopped when he saw them, lowering his sword. "Eri!"

"Oh do nae stop!" Alice laughed. "Show us what ye can do, Allen."

Allen grinned, and with a sly glance toward Eri he began to demonstrate what little he knew of swordplay. He swung his sword first in a slow and measured horizontal cut, and then again in a downward, vertical motion before bringing it up with another slow measured movement.

The girls both clapped their hands and Allen grinned.

Allen bent his knees and brought his sword arm close to his hip, pretending to anticipate an opponent's next move. Allen then began to move more quickly, as though he were in a real sword fight. He sliced quickly to the right, above what would have been the belt of his imaginary opponent and then swiftly struck to the left. He pivoted slightly and with practiced motion his sword cut to the left, where his imaginary opponent's legs would be and then just as swiftly cut to the right.

Alice plopped onto the grass to watch him as Eri clapped again.

Allen slowed his arm movement and focused on his stance, moving his feet, legs, and upper body into several different defensive positions. Eri seemed quite impressed.

"Ye are quite good."

"Nae," Alice said. "Ye should see father with his claymore. That is an impressive sight."

Allen grinned. "Someday I'll be just as impressive."

"I would believe it," Eri said, her dimple showing again.

"We should get the claymore!" Alice said suddenly, green eyes lighting up with mischief. She jumped up and grabbed Eri's hand.

"We are nae supposed to play with it," Allen replied.

"But father is in town on business," Alice said. "All it would take was distracting mama. Ye could show us what ye ken and Eri and I can do it, too. Ye with the claymore and us with your sparring sword."

Allen thought about that for a moment. He wasn't sure it was a good idea, but Alice's green eyes were sparkling and how could he say no to that?

Slowly, a grin spread across his face. "Ye distract mama, I'll get the claymore."

Alice's eyes were twinkling, but Eri was slightly more appalled. "Will nae we get in trouble?"

"Nae," Alice laughed, waving her hand to dismiss the idea. "Father might scold a little, but mama will stop him. Besides, this way Allen can teach us."

Eri shrugged, finding no other reason to object.

Alice darted around the house and Allen and Eri followed more slowly. Alice went running inside and threw herself into her mother's arms while Eri's mother Senga watched with amusement. Evanna had been sewing, fixing some of Duncan's shirts that had acquired holes, and she laughed when her daughter jumped into her lap.

"Easy, lass. Watch the needle!"

Alice grinned and began chattering away about Allen's impressive sword skills, sliding off her mother's lap and taking hold of her hands. Allen and Eri peered through the doorway to watch her progress.

Alice continued to gush about Allen and as she did so she walked around her mother. With her hands held hostage by Alice, Evanna had no choice but to turn in her chair until she was facing her expressive daughter. Alice didn't let go but just kept giggling and talking. Senga turned to watch Alice as well, seeming amused by her antics.

Once Evanna's and Senga's backs were to the doorway, Allen handed his wooden sword to Eri. He stepped carefully into the room and tiptoed over to the hearth, above which hung the claymore. He gently lifted a wooden chair and carried it closer to the fireplace as Alice continued to chatter away on the other side of the room.

Allen held his breath as he slowly set the chair on the ground near the mantel, trying not to make a single sound. Then he stepped onto it and reached up for the claymore. He gently lifted it off of the pegs that it rest on, and pulled it down. His father's large sword was much heavier than he'd anticipated and it dipped dangerously toward the ground. His heart was pounding in his ears and he held his breath, stepping off of the chair with his father's sword in his hand.

The women continued to listen to Alice's chatter. Allen moved as swiftly as he dared without a sound across the room and out the front door where Eri was waiting. As soon as he was outside, he hurried toward the back of the house as quickly as he could stumble with the weight of the claymore in his hands. Eri followed him.

Only a few minutes later, Alice appeared.

"Now teach us!" Alice beamed.

Allen held his father's claymore in front of him, testing. It was heavy; still, he could probably manage. Allen nodded. "Okay, who's first?"

Alice grabbed Allen's wooden sparring sword out of Eri's hand and immediately swung it as hard as she could in Allen's direction. Allen was momentarily surprised by her sudden attack, but not so much that he couldn't easily bring the claymore up to meet it. The blades met mid air with a loud crack as the claymore bit into the wooden sword.

Not three seconds later, Florie came barreling out of the kitchen's back door. She had flour in her black hair and covering her apron and arms, and the frown on her face and fire in her eyes made Alice drop the sword in her hand immediately.

Florie glared at her and snatched the claymore from Allen's grip. "What do ye think ye are doin', young rascal?"

"Just practicin', Florie," Allen said. Florie glared at him and he cowered before her gaze. "Do nae tell, father, please."

Florie huffed and marched back into the house, claymore in hand. Alice giggled when she'd disappeared.

Eri sighed. "Do ye like to get in trouble, Alice?"

Alice grinned. "I like to get away with it, that's the most fun. But making Florie angry is fun, too."

"Nae, that is false," Allen sighed. "I hate making Florie angry. She'll complain to William and then he'll...talk to me."

"Ye do nae like William to talk to ye?" Eri asked, confused.

"It is nae that," Alice laughed. "He just wants William to look at him like an equal, man to man." Alice rolled her eyes, as though she thought this was the most ridiculous thing she'd ever heard of. "He hates when William scolds."

"I guess we're done for the day," Allen said.

The three of them were nervous when they went inside for dinner that day, but neither Senga nor Evanna said anything, which made Allen believe Florie hadn't mentioned the incident to them. The claymore was hanging in its spot above the mantel once more. Duncan greeted them cheerfully when he saw them, and when Florie served the food, her conspiratorial wink made Alice grin. It seemed she hadn't told any of the other adults.

Allen smiled to himself, stuffing a bite of Florie's food into his mouth to hide his delight. Florie might fuss and wail, but she wouldn't betray their secret. How she got the claymore back in its resting place without his mother noticing was something he could hardly guess, but for now at least trouble seemed averted.

In the months that followed the claymore incident, Eri became almost a permanent fixture at Allen's house. She came for many a visit, and more often than not her mother came as well. Eri and Alice got along splendidly, but being closer to Allen's age Eri enjoyed his company more, or so Allen thought. Still, the three of them were nearly inseparable.

Chapter 4

Scotland. November, 1185.

Allen couldn't sleep. Not because he wasn't tired–he'd fallen asleep almost immediately after crawling into bed late in the evening after a long day trying to assuage Alice's concerns while also catching Eri's eye. Alice and Eri were friends, but sometimes Alice made it clear to Allen that she felt he was replacing her and she did not appreciate it.

It was a lot to balance and he'd been emotionally exhausted by the end of the day. Yet though he'd fallen asleep so easily, now he was wide awake once more.

He could hear low voices in the room next door, his father's room where his books and maps were kept. The voices he heard were those of his father and Eri's father Murdoch. Allen assumed that was what had awoken him.

"...is of age now."

"And for the dowry?" Duncan's muffled voice asked.

"The two fields...discussed..." Allen strained to hear what Murdoch was saying, but his voice was even more muffled than his father's through the wall.

Allen sat up, his heart pounding as he stared about the darkness around him. The moon was casting a slight light in one corner of the room as it spilled through a window, but otherwise it was all darkness. Allen leaned against the wall, hoping to be able to make out their conversation better. They were discussing a dowry, a wedding.

That meant father was preparing to marry off either Allen or Alice, and considering he was speaking to Murdoch–whose only child was Eri–it seemed clear whose wedding they were making plans for.

"...agreeable?" Murdoch asked.

"Aye," Duncan replied. "I'll speak to Evanna and then to Allen tomorrow."

"We'll set the betrothal for later this year, and the marriage sometime after?"

"Aye. It is a blessin' they are already friends."

"Indeed."

Allen pulled away from the wall.

His father and Murdoch had just come to terms for his wedding.

Allen plopped back on his bed, staring at his ceiling in the dark room. A slow grin spread its way across his face.

Marrying Eri was exactly what Allen wanted to do.

The next day Duncan told Allen the news, and he did nothing to hide his excitement. Later that day, however, he found Alice crying in the pasture with the horses.

Allen sat down beside her, wrapping an arm around her shoulders. "Ye love Eri, why are ye upset at havin' her for a sister?"

Alice buried her face in her hands. "I do nae want you to forget me."

"That would nae happen." Allen kissed her forehead. "Ye are my beloved sister and that has not changed."

"Ye'll love her more."

"I'll love ye both deeply; differently."

28

Scotland. April, 1186.

The sun was partially hidden behind a few fluffy clouds, but the day was bright and clear and to Allen's mind seemed to match his feelings perfectly. A little nervous, but eager and excited as well.

When he'd gone for a walk that morning to release some of his excessive energy, the grass had been growing green and tall in front of the house. His mother Evanna's flowerbeds, so carefully tended, were beginning to bloom. Sheep were bleating somewhere in the near distance. The day was perfect in every way.

Now, however, he wasn't outside enjoying the perfect weather and the feeling it ignited in his chest. Instead, he was inside the house, surrounded by a group of people that had gathered to share in the most momentous occasion of his life to date.

Despite the warmth of the day, a fire was burning in the hearth. Allen's father Duncan was standing in front of the fireplace, his claymore not on the wall but rather hanging at his waist as he wore his best clothes. Allen's mother Evanna stood beside him, wearing a new dress of a deep purple. Senga and Murdoch stood nearby, and William was there in his chainmail, his sword on his belt, looking every bit the knight that he was.

Allen took a deep breath to try and keep calm, though he felt ready to burst out of his own skin. He glanced around again, noticing Florie standing by the kitchen door–not on equal footing with the rest of the guests, perhaps, but present for the ceremony regardless. She'd braided her black hair around her head, and her eyes were shining with tears.

Allen looked away from the tears and toward his siter Alice who was beside their mother, in a new dress of deep green. Her first "grown-up" dress, cinched at the waist and with sleeves that were tight until the elbow where they opened and draped nearly to the floor. Her fly-away red curls had been slightly tamed by being pulled back with a green ribbon.

Alice flashed him a grin, and Allen felt himself relax further. He stood in the center of the group with Eri, and next to them stood Friar Roderick who'd been sent for from his abbey on the outskirts of Edinburgh.

Allen was in a new set of clothes. His hair had been brushed, and Florie had scrubbed his face half a dozen times so he was as clean as could be. Florie and his mother were insistent that this day be perfect in every way, but to Allen's mind it would have been no matter what he was wearing or what he looked like.

Eri, like so many others, was in a new dress. It was violet colored, similarly designed as Alice's; cinched at the waist and with tight sleeves that opened and draped from the elbow. Her gown was also adorned with intricate needlework of golden flowers and trees along the hem and the sleeves. Her hair was pulled back into a braid and there were flowers woven into it.

She was the most beautiful thing Allen had ever seen.

Allen caught Eri's eye and grinned, and she shyly returned his smile.

It was the day of their betrothal ceremony. The wedding would take place later in the year.

With direction from Friar Roderick, Allen pulled a simple silver band from his pocket and slipped it onto Eri's middle finger. She would

30

receive a new one at the wedding. This was merely a symbol of their betrothal.

Eri's hands were shaking as Allen placed the simple band on her finger, and he clasped both her hands, squeezing gently in the hope of calming her nerves.

As they held hands, Friar Roderick spoke a blessing over them. Allen was impatient for the formal ceremony to be over so he could say he was betrothed to Eri. The words of the blessing, the rites being spoken that day, meant nothing to him. All he cared about was Eri.

After Friar Roderick was finished, Duncan and Murdoch shook hands, and that was that.

Florie brought food from the kitchen and a small feast commenced. Allen's joy never abated. He dug into his food heartily, and continued to grin whenever he caught sight of Eri beside him. She remained quiet throughout the meal, though occasionally she returned his grin with a smaller smile.

William clapped a hand on Allen's shoulder. "I suppose congratulations are in order, young man."

Allen grinned, glancing toward Eri. "Never thought I'd beat you to it."

Something that looked like sadness flashed across William's face as his gaze darted toward where Florie was serving food at the other end of the table. Whatever it was seemed to pass and he grinned at Allen. "Having watched your father grow up and get betrothed and then married to Evanna, and now you…I am beginning to feel I am finally getting old."

"You don't look it," Allen said.

William shook his head. "Perhaps not. Listen…cherish every moment with her, Allen."

"I intend to."

When the meal was over William accompanied Friar Roderick back to Edinburgh. Duncan and Murdoch went upstairs to Duncan's study to discuss the finalization of Eri's dowry.

Alice ran her hand along the smooth surface of her dress, giggling. "Ye should get betrothed every day, Allen. I love gettin' new dresses!"

"And that one really is gorgeous!" Eri said.

Evanna and Senga got up from the table and went outside, deep in discussion about Evanna's flowerbeds. The three youngsters remained at the table as Florie cleared the remains of the meal.

"Yers is pretty, too," Alice told Eri.

Eri fingered the needlework on her sleeve. "'Tis the most beautiful dress I have ever owned."

Allen glanced between them, wondering what he could add to such a conversation.

"Ye'll likely have an even better one for the weddin'!" Alice said, excitement permeating her voice and face.

"I didn't know it would be such a fuss and bother," Allen chuckled. "The betrothal and the wedding."

"That is silly," Alice said. "Of course there's a fuss and bother. It's a marriage!"

"Do ye like our new dresses?" Eri asked.

Allen shrugged. "They look nice. You are both beautiful."

"I'm happy ye will be kin," Alice slung an arm around Eri's shoulders.

"I'm happy, too," Allen said. "Are you happy, Eri?"

"Of course I'm happy," Eri said softly, though she barely met his gaze and her cheeks grew pink with obvious embarrassment.

Allen bit his lip, unsure what to make of that. Was Eri not as excited as he was to be betrothed?

Chapter 5

Allen leaned against the doorframe of his house, watching Eri and her mother walk down the path away from Allen's home. They had come for a visit and were headed home now, the sunset hues of lilac and orange spreading across the horizon behind them.

Eri had been quiet during the visit. She had never been as exuberant as Alice, perhaps, but she used to engage in conversation more. Allen had spent the whole visit trying to get her to talk to him.

Alice crossed her arms and leaned against the opposite side of the doorway, glaring at Allen. "That was an interesting visit."

"Why are you giving me that look? What did I do?"

"Ye spent the entire night glued to Eri."

"She seemed out of sorts and I was trying to get her to talk to me."

"Well I was trying to get ye to talk to me."

"What do you mean?"

"Ye seem to be forgetting these days that I am yer best friend."

"Eri is going to be my wife."

Alice rolled her eyes, glaring at Allen once more. Allen sighed, reaching out to put a hand on her shoulder.

"What do you want me to say? You are my best friend, but Eri will be my wife. I can't ignore her just to spend time with you. And anyway, I see you every day and Eri only when her family visits ours. I have to make the most of every visit–particularly on days like today when she is out of sorts and I don't know why."

Alice's lower lip protruded in a pout and her green eyes shone with unshed tears. Allen didn't know what to do—why was she so upset?

"Alice…"

Alice spun away from him and marched into the house and to her bedchamber. Allen watched her go but didn't follow after her. They'd already talked about this before and Allen didn't know why Alice couldn't let it go.

In the weeks that followed, Allen noticed two things: Alice continued to be jealous of his attention toward Eri, and Eri remained more shy and hesitant in their friendship than she had been before the betrothal. He wasn't sure what to make of either situation, so one day he asked for William's advice.

They were walking along the path that led between the various fields and orchards on Duncan's estate, the sun high in the sky and the wind blowing across the hills.

"I don't know what to do about either of them," Allen sighed after explaining the situation to William.

"It seems to me Alice is just worried you won't care about her now that you have a wife. I think it is understandable for her to fear such a thing. You have always been her favorite person, and she yours. Now that the dynamic of your relationship is changing, it makes her nervous."

"But of course I still love her! She shouldn't worry about that."

"Yet she does worry about it, Allen."

"So what do I do?"

William looked thoughtful for a moment before he answered. "Find ways to continue to show your affection and reassure her. It is true that your relationship may change now, but let her know that it won't end."

"Telling her I still love her doesn't seem to work."

"Then don't use words, my young friend."

Allen sighed, pausing in their walk to lean against an apple tree covered in white blossoms that would later become fruit.

"What about Eri?"

William crossed his arms, studying the apple blossoms for a moment, and then turning back to Allen. "Women are fascinating creatures that I am still trying to understand."

"But when Florie is upset and won't tell you why, what do you do?"

"I *know* Florie. I understand her very soul–if she is upset, chances are I always know why."

"I don't have that with Eri."

"You will."

"Okay, but I don't have it yet. So what do you think could possibly be wrong? We were all good friends, but since the betrothal Eri won't banter with me as she used to, and Alice is always angry with me. I thought this marriage would be a good thing, that I could merge the two families I love so much, but it seems to only bring trouble."

"I cannot say for sure what is bothering Eri, but from my perspective–what I have seen is a shy girl who likes you."

"But she won't talk to me."

"Be gentle with her; she's a delicate thing. I do believe she cares for you, Allen, and that is part of why she feels so shy around you now."

Allen sighed. "What am I supposed to do then?"

"Just keep being yourself, and keep convincing her you care."

They stood in silence for a time, listening to the summer birds chirruping around them. Eventually, Allen broke the stillness.

"Why won't you marry Florie?"

William winced. "I cannot."

"But why?"

"I don't wish to talk about this, Allen."

"But–"

"It's none of your concern!"

"Okay, okay. You don't have to shout."

William sighed, taking a step away from Allen and running a hand down his face. "Sorry."

For a moment they were both quiet, and then William cocked his head to the side and stared at Allen with wide eyes.

"What?"

"I've just noticed...your accent."

"What of it?"

"You seem to be losing it."

Allen bit his lip, glancing at his boots. "Yeah..."

"Are you intentionally not speaking like your family, like a Scotsman?"

"Yeah." Allen glanced up. "I wanted to talk like you."

"I'm English, Allen."

"I know."

"And you're Scottish."

"I am aware of that."

"It's important to know who you are, my young friend, to hold onto your roots. A tree can't survive without them."

"I'm not a tree. And you're...well, you're William."

William raised his eyebrows, his eyes twinkling. "Oh?"

"I just...I respect and admire you and I want to be like you when I become a man."

"You're already becoming a fine man, and one I am proud to call friend."

Allen nodded, feeling heat radiate from his face. He kept his gaze on his toes.

"I am flattered you wish to emulate my speech as well as my character. Just don't lose yourself, Allen. You don't need to be William; you need to be Allen of the Dale, heir to Duncan of the Logan clan."

"I think I can manage to be myself and still learn from you."

"I'm sure you can."

Chapter 6

Allen plucked a blade of grass from the ground, slowly ripping it to shreds and letting all the pieces fall back to the earth. He was sitting in the open pasture behind his house with Alice and Eri, both of whom were sending furtive glances his way.

He'd hoped today's visit would be simple; everyone would get along like they used to and they'd get up to antics like the day they'd stolen his father's claymore. He was disappointed to discover that the tension building between the three of them was not assuaging, no matter how much he tried to reassure both girls that he cared for them.

Allen wanted to talk to Eri, to get to the bottom of her shy behavior, but he didn't want to bring it up in front of Alice, who flatly refused to leave his side while Eri was visiting.

Allen grabbed another blade of grass and began tearing it up.

"Why are ye bein' so aggressive with the grass?" Alice asked, crossing her arms and watching Allen shred another blade of grass.

"The truth? I am trying to relieve my frustration."

"Why are ye frustrated?" Eri asked, her face glowing bright red as her gaze dropped to where she was wringing her hands in her lap.

"We used to all three get along so well, but ever since our betrothal things have changed–and not for the better."

Eri's wringing hands stilled, though her gaze remained lowered.

"I want us to be as we were, all three of us. Yet we are not, and nothing I do seems to help and I am feeling frustrated."

"I want things to be as they were as well!" Alice said.

"Then why do you act as you do?" Allen ripped up a handful of grass. "You mope and you whine and you cling to my side like you believe you'll be abandoned."

"I do not!"

"You do though–it's been going on for weeks!"

"Well I guess I won't spend time with ye after all, brother." Alice hastily stood, marching away from Eri and Allen and around the corner of the house, out of sight.

Allen sighed. "That is not what I wanted either."

Eri said nothing.

"What about you?" Allen turned to her. "How can I offend you?"

"Ye do nae offend me."

"Why aren't we friends anymore?"

"We are."

"It doesn't feel like it."

"I…" Eri took a deep breath, her blush returning.

Allen scooted across the grass to be closer to her. "What is it?"

Eri's hands began their anxious movement again and Allen reached over and laid his hand atop her clasped ones, hoping to ease her discomfort.

"You can talk to me, Eri. I'm going to be your husband."

"Does that bother you?" Eri asked, finally lifting her face to meet Allen's gaze.

"What?"

"Being my husband."

"Why would that bother me?"

"We were friends, but everything got weird after the betrothal…"

"That's exactly what's been bothering me!"

"But I thought…I mean…did it get weird because ye wanted to be friends, nae…nae my husband. I ken our fathers arranged everything…ye did nae have a choice."

"Of course I want to be your husband! Don't you know I care about you?"

"I…I was nae sure…"

"Eri." Allen cupped her face in his hands. "Nothing pleases me more than the fact that you are going to be my wife."

Eri's blush deepened, but she smiled up at him, her eyes sparkling. "Truly?"

"Truly."

Edinburgh, Scotland. September, 1186.

It was a rather dreary day, the sun hiding behind dark clouds hanging low in the sky. Allen kept a wary eye on the storm clouds as he stood on the steps of Friar Roderick's abbey. Friar Roderick was beside him, standing before the doors of the abbey as they waited for Eri and her procession to arrive. Allen's parents were standing to one side of him, as well as Alice.

Allen looked away from the storm clouds to where Alice stood, her green eyes watching him thoughtfully. He wondered when that storm would break, and if clear skies would ever shine over their relationship again. Things had been strained for months. He missed his carefree sister.

William stood beside Alice, smiling broadly. He'd seen Allen's father married, and now it was Allen's turn–Allen was curious if

William would live long enough to see Allen's own children get married, too.

Various members of the Logan clan were gathered outside the church waiting for Eri's procession, as well as different friends and connections of Allen's father. Today was a momentous day.

Allen heard singing, and turned to watch the street leading into Edinburgh proper. He could see Eri now, sitting atop a horse that her father was leading down the street. She was wearing a gown of satin–one Alice had been eager to talk to her about, the one thing the girls never failed to discuss despite rising tension within the group–from what Allen could see of her as she approached, the gown had fitted sleeves to the elbow which then fluted to her wrists where they draped open. The bodice was decorated with delicate hand beading of glass beads and pearls that ought to sparkle in the sunlight, but there was none today as the low dark clouds hung over everything. Her skirt flowed in elegant waves from her waist to the ground like a shimmering waterfall.

Following behind Eri on foot was her mother Senga, grandmothers Gormelia and namesake Eri, and various cousins and distant relations.

The procession made its way swiftly along the road toward where Allen and his family stood waiting, the women singing as they walked behind Eri.

When they reached the front steps of Holyrood Abbey, Murdoch helped his daughter off of the horse and he and the rest of the procession joined the gathered onlookers. Eri took her place on the top step with Allen and Friar Roderick.

After ascertaining that there was no legal reason that Allen and Eri could not marry, Friar Roderick then turned to Allen. "Do ye, Allen of the Dale, take Eri daughter of Murdoch to be yer wife?"

"Yes," Allen replied with a grin.

"And ye, Eri," Friar Roderick turned to her. "Do ye take Allen of the Dale to be yer husband?"

"I do," Eri said, lips trembling and tears dangling on her lashes.

Friar Roderick then spoke a blessing over the two of them. After the blessing, he instructed Allen to take off Eri's betrothal ring which he promptly did. Her hands were trembling and he gave them a squeeze to reassure her.

Friar Roderick handed Allen the wedding ring.

"Now, as we practiced," Friar Roderick said softly, for Allen's ears alone. Allen straightened shoulders and went about placing the ring on Eri's finger. He began by putting it on her right thumb and saying, "In the Name of the Father," and then he moved the ring to her index finger "And the Son," and once again he moved the ring to the middle finger. "And the Holy Spirit. Amen."

Allen took a deep breath, taking a moment to remember the words Friar Roderick had instructed him to say next.

"With this ring, I thee wed. This gold and silver I thee give. With this body I thee worship. And with this dowry I thee endow."

The crowd then erupted with hoots and cheers and Friar Roderick led everyone inside where he then conducted a short service.

After that the whole procession, all of the family and other guests, made their way to Duncan's home where Florie, with help from hired cooks, had prepared a great feast. Tables were set up outside the house on the lawn, away from Evanna's flowers so they wouldn't be trampled. Each table was piled high with food–cock-a-leekie soup, lamb, herring in wine sauce, salmon in a walnut and garlic sauce, roasted chicken, various kinds of cheese, freshly baked bread, stewed cabbage, pies stuffed with spinach, onions, or mushrooms, shortbread, cinnamon and sugar cakes, fritters, oatcakes, fruit pies–more food than Allen had ever seen in his life before.

There were also baskets filled to overflowing with flowers on the tables, and garlands of flowers strung up on poles all around the field along with ribbons of every color that blew in the breeze. The sky was still dark with clouds that threatened rain, but no one noticed.

"Oh, it is heavenly!" Eri gasped when she saw the feast and the flowers.

"Do ye think we'll even be able to eat all that food?" Alice asked, eyeing the tables warily. The guests had begun filling up the tables and digging into the mountains of food. Allen and Eri, with Alice in tow, took their places at the head table.

"Where do we even start?" Eri asked with a laugh.

Allen grinned and shoved a fritter into his mouth. "Anywhere."

The feast lasted for several hours. Everyone ate and chatted and ate some more. When Allen couldn't eat another bite, he leaned back in his chair and glanced at Eri; his wife.

"Are you happy, Eri?"

"Very happy, Allen."

Eventually everyone made their way to their various homes. Florie and the hired servants set to work cleaning everything up. Murdoch and Senga were the last to leave, saying a tearful goodby to their daughter.

And then Eri was left alone with Allen and his family.

Chapter 7

Allen listened to the birds singing around him, breathing in deeply the sweet smell of the apple orchard. He was seated in the branches of one of the apple trees, enjoying the day. His father Duncan had been making Allen do more business with him—visiting merchants and nobles in Edinburgh, going over ledgers in Duncan's study, speaking with the farmers and tenants of the land to keep the estate running smoothly. Even meeting with various members of the clan now and again to deal with the strife and tension that sometimes arose with disputes. He was going to be the lord of the lands eventually, and it was past time he learned how.

His days were busy, but he always got to come home to Eri's dimpled smile and gentle embrace and that made everything worth it.

Hearing footsteps crunching through the grass, Allen looked down from his perch in the tree and saw Alice approaching. She swung herself up into the apple tree beside him and leaned against the trunk of the tree, studying him.

"Do you need something?"

"Only to apologize."

Allen raised an eyebrow. "I don't recall you offending me recently."

"Recently." Alice rolled her eyes and elbowed him. "But I've been driving ye batty since the day father agreed to marry ye to Eri."

Allen shifted so he could see her face more clearly. "Aye."

"I'm sorry." Alice shrugged, her green eyes serious instead of sparkling for once. "Since the wedding…ye've been here; still my

47

brother, still lookin' out for me. And now I have a sister to spend my days with, too. I should nae have been so concerned."

Allen bumped his shoulder against hers. "Is this an appropriate time to say 'I told you so'?"

"Nae." Alice grinned. "But I'll allow the gloating."

Scotland. July, 1187.

Allen slumped against the wall, running a hand through his unruly blond hair. He was exhausted from all the pacing he had been doing in front of his house. The sun shone down on him and a gentle breeze tickled his cheek.

"You remind me of your father," William said, coming to lean against the wall beside him. "He could never stand still when his wife was in labor either."

Allen glanced at his friend and smiled. "My father would still be pacing if he knew that Eri had gone into labor. He's lucky he's in town on business today."

"True enough. You have nothing to worry about, though. Florie is the best midwife in all of Scotland."

"High praise, but perhaps biased."

William chuckled at that.

"Why didn't you ever marry her, William?"

William sighed. "That is not a discussion for today, Allen."

Allen wanted to press his friend, but William was always defensive when Allen brought up marriage with Florie, and today he had more pressing things on his mind.

"Do you think Eri is alright?"

"Women give birth every day."

"Not in the Logan clan."

"Oh here we go." William rolled his eyes. "I haven't had to hear about the famed family curse in over a decade, Allen! Don't start now."

Allen chuckled. "I don't actually believe in the curse like father does."

"Ye should!"

Allen and William both turned to see Allen's father Duncan come striding toward them, his business in town apparently completed.

"Why are we discussing the curse today?" Duncan asked as he came to stand in front of them.

"Eri has gone into labor," Allen said.

Duncan's face paled. "Och, nae. Is it early? I ken it is too early."

"It's not too early," William said, placing a firm hand on Duncan's shoulder. "Don't scare your son. The curse is not real. You have two healthy children and a bonnie wife as well."

Duncan shook his head. "The miracles I have been given make it all the more likely the blessings will not last."

Allen crossed his arms, picturing Eri writhing in pain as she struggled to give birth to his child. What if father was right?

"There is no proof of your curse," William said. "And Allen and Alice were healthy and happy, and have grown to adulthood all while your wife still lives and breathes."

Duncan seemed unconvinced and began to pace in front of the house.

A frail cry was heard from within the house and Allen shot off the wall. William grabbed his shoulder as he started toward the door. "Hold on! You know Florie won't let you in there for a while yet."

Allen sighed and started pacing in front of the door in tight little circles as his father made a longer path from one side of the house to the other, trampling the grass as he went.

Allen's heart was pounding more loudly in his ears than he'd ever heard it before. He wiped his sweaty palms on his trousers as he paced in front of the door, wondering what might be going on inside. He could hear his child crying, but what of Eri?

It was only a few minutes before Florie opened the door. "Alright, young Allen. Ye can see yer good wife."

Allen charged past Florie and bounded up the stairs to his room where his wife lay on their bed. Her hair was a mess and her skin gleamed with sweat, but there was a smile on her face.

She was alive.

She was staring in awe at a little bundle in her arms. Evanna sat on the edge of the bed, staring with tears running down her cheeks at the child in Eri's arms.

Allen moved slowly closer to the bed, crossing the room with hesitation. The women hadn't seemed to notice him.

He was close enough to see the little bundle now. A tiny little face, red and wrinkled, was resting against Eri's shoulder, nestled in a warm wool blanket.

Eri turned, and caught sight of Allen and her smile broadened. "Look, Allen! We have a son."

"I see that." Allen knelt beside the bed, putting his face close to the infant in his wife's arms and feeling his heart bursting inside his chest. "What is his name, Eri?"

"Duncan of course, after yer father."

Allen grinned. "Of course."

Little Duncan screwed up his nose and let out a tiny squawk. Allen grinned even wider, placing a hand ever so gently on the small red head.

"He's hungry," Evanna said, watching little Duncan's mouth open and close as he searched for a source of food.

Eri obliged her ravenous son and Allen moved to sit on the bed beside her. She lay her head on his shoulder and they both watched the tiny boy eating.

"He's perfect, Eri."

"I ken that well enough. Are ye happy, Allen?"

"Yes. I'm more than happy."

Alice came bounding into the room a moment later. "Do ye have a child yet?"

"Look," Eri said, lifting little Duncan up slightly. He squirmed and squawked his displeasure at being removed from his source of food.

Alice grinned and jumped into bed beside Allen, leaning over him to watch little Duncan feeding. "Oh he is perfect!"

"We certainly think so," Allen replied, laughing.

Scotland. November, 1187.

It was a dark night, not a star to be seen in the sky above Duncan's house. The clouds dumped their loads of snow over Edinburgh and the surrounding villages and farms. The frosty air seeped through the wooden frame of the Logan home and into the bones of the family gathered there.

They were huddled about the fire, Evanna wrapped protectively in Duncan's arms as they leaned close to the heat of the flames. The room was dark but for the light from the fire in the hearth casting flickering shadows to dance across the walls, the flames reflected in Duncan's claymore above the hearth.

Eri was safely tucked in Allen's arms. Blankets were pulled tightly around Allen's shoulders and by proxy, Eri's as well. Alice was huddled close beside her brother, and he spared an arm for her. In Alice's lap was her nephew.

Only a few months old, he couldn't understand the discomfort of the cold and wailed continuously. Florie was busy in the kitchen, making soup and hot drinks to keep everyone warm.

Allen tried to keep his wife, sister, and young son warm by sheer will as they leaned into him for warmth and he watched the flames eating log after log in the fire.

After a minute or two, Florie entered the room, bearing a tray of mugs. Allen reached for one, as did everyone else, sipping at the warm drink appreciatively. The mug burned beneath Allen's cold fingertips, but he ignored the pain in favor of getting the warmth inside him.

Eri used her blanket as protection for her hands, wrapping it around her mug and holding it carefully from outside the shield of the blanket.

"I'll be back with food for ye," Florie said. When she spoke, Allen could see her breath in the frosty air.

"Why is it so miserably cold?" he asked no one in particular.

"It will pass," Evanna said.

"Hopefully sooner rather than later," Alice said, bouncing little Duncan slightly, hoping to calm him as he continued to wail his displeasure.

The steady snowfall outside began to change into a drizzly rainfall.

Florie entered the room again, bearing a platter with soup bowls. Steam rose in tendrils from the surface of the soup, gently twisting and swaying in the air. Florie passed out the bowls, and mugs were set aside as the family began to eat.

Eri took little Duncan from Alice's arms and held him close, juggling him and a bowl of soup for a moment until she settled the bowl on her knee.

"How long do ye think the storm will be?" Evanna asked.

"There's no tellin'," Duncan replied. "We'll just have to wait and see."

"'Tis the worst storm I've seen in twenty years," Florie said, before she retreated back to the kitchen.

"It's rainin' pretty hard," Alice commented as a boom of thunder echoed across the sky.

"Strange that," Allen replied. "It was snowing a moment ago, and hard."

As Allen spoke another burst of thunder split the sky. The house rattled on its frame; they could hear loud crashes from upstairs, probably Duncan's books falling off their shelves in his den.

Sparks flew from the fire into the faces of the family gathered there as another crack of thunder rolled around them and in that moment Florie let out a shriek from the kitchen.

It was a sound that would haunt Allen of the Dale for the rest of his life.

Chapter 8

The sparks from the fire had Evanna and Alice jumping up, throwing off their blankets and stomping on the places where the fabric had caught fire. Duncan had made a dash for the kitchen as soon as Florie's scream had been heard. It still echoed in the thin air, or at least it felt like it was still hanging there to Allen's ears.

Another booming clap of thunder reverberated through the shaky house and more sparks flew from the fire as the logs there shifted from the movement of the house, causing more fires to catch on the blankets on the floor that Evanna and Alice were trying to put out.

Allen pulled Eri to her feet.

"We have to get outside."

"But the rain! And the wind! Little Duncan should nae be out there!"

"I know, Eri, but look!" Allen turned her around by her shoulders to see the hearth and his mother and sister. Alice and Evanna were still trying to put out the small fires that the sparks had started on the blankets. Behind them, the fire was starting to lick its way out of the hearth and across the wooden floor. The flames were getting larger with every passing second.

"Surely ye can put it out."

"Maybe I can, but you should be outside until I do."

"Allen!" Eri stared behind him.

Allen turned.

The door to the kitchen was engulfed in a dark fog of smoke, though flickering yellow and orange could be vaguely seen through the smoke.

"Florie!" Allen dashed toward the kitchen. "Father!"

Allen was coughing before he'd crossed the threshold into the kitchen. He couldn't see anything. His eyes were burning and tears were leaking down his cheeks. The smoke was too thick. How could a fire have gotten so out of control so quickly?

"Florie?"

There was no response from the darkness.

The flames were licking up the walls and across the ceiling, but the smoke was so thick he could hardly make anything else out.

As he pressed further into the room, he could vaguely make out more flames. The table where Florie had so often prepared meals, the oven, everything was completely engulfed. The heat was oppressive; Allen staggered backwards. He tripped over something and fell onto the floor.

The air was a bit clearer down there, if only a little. Allen rolled onto his stomach, coughs wracking his frame. His chest was burning.

Everything was burning.

Allen felt by his feet, trying to find what he'd tripped over. His hands found an ankle, the skirt of a dress.

"Florie?" Allen crawled toward her, found her face.

He couldn't see much in the smoke and with his burning, tear-filled eyes but as he leaned over her, he could tell that there was no life left in that beloved face.

Her eyes were open, but there was nothing in them, no spark of recognition or pain or fear.

"Florie!"

More tears were cascading down his cheeks, this time not from the irritation of the smoke.

Allen grabbed her around the waist and started dragging her toward the back door. She was larger than he was, and much heavier than he'd expected. Foot by foot, stopping for a breath, inch by inch, pausing when he was overwhelmed with coughing, he dragged Florie toward the door.

The fire was all around him now. There was no escaping it. It ate up Allen's clothes and burned his flesh. Still, he dragged Florie.

When he reached the door he turned slightly and kicked it, as hard as he could. The fire had weakened the doorframe enough, the wooden door popped right off its hinge and fell outside.

Allen dragged Florie over the fallen door and out into the yard behind his house.

He lay there in the grass panting for a moment. The rain extinguished his burning clothes, the cold seeping into his bones; steam rose off of every inch of him as raindrops pelted him and put out fire around him.

Allen turned to look at his house.

The flames still appeared to be on the bottom level, they hadn't moved upstairs yet. They were headed in that direction though, eating up the wood frame despite the constant rain. Smoke billowed out of the kitchen doorway.

Allen stared in horror for a moment before he remembered the rest of his family. Bolting upright he charged straight back into the kitchen.

He wasn't watching where he was going, and he tripped over the fallen door. Pain shot through his wrists as he tried to break his fall. He still ended up smacking his nose on the floor of the kitchen.

Everything went white. Allen put a hand to his face, rubbing his eyes, trying to see through them. Slowly, ever so slowly, the world swam back into view.

He was engulfed in thick, black smoke. His eyes began watering again.

Allen pushed to his feet, but a coughing fit overcame him and he doubled over, his lungs rebelling against the smoke.

He had to get back inside.

His mother. Alice. Eri. His son. They were all inside.

Unless they'd run out, like Allen had tried to get Eri to do. Eri would listen to him. And Alice and his mother were smart. They would get out.

Allen backed out of the kitchen, tripping over the wooden door again. He fell on his back this time, toppling over the still form of Florie.

Allen struggled to his feet and ran through the rain toward the front of his house. He slipped in the wet grass and hit the ground face first.

With a grunt, Allen got back on his feet and rounded the corner. It was hard to see in the dark, and the rain, but he didn't see his family.

"Eri! Alice!" The only response Allen was given was a thunderous clap from the sky.

Allen scanned the yard, and then turned back to the house. They must still be inside. Why? Why hadn't they come out yet?
Allen took a step toward the house.

And then he watched in horror as the lower level walls gave out, crumbling, crashing to the ground.

The second floor of his house slammed into the ground, sending a shiver across the yard that knocked Allen's legs out from under him and he hit the ground once more.

He pushed up on his elbows, watching the flames start to engulf the rest of his house.

He couldn't do anything.

He couldn't run forward to try and put out the fire, or dig out his family.

He couldn't move.

Allen lay there, his lungs burning, his skin still hot enough that the rain continued to turn to steam as it splashed down from the sky and pelted him.

The rain had lessened.

It would stop soon.

It wouldn't put out the fire.

Allen lowered his head to the ground and groaned. The groan turned into a moan and then slowly shifted until Allen was wailing. Wailing at the top of his lungs.

His father.

His mother.

Allen was shaking with sobs, screaming at the sky as the cold intensified but the rain slowed.

Florie.

Alice.

How could he live without them all? Allen screamed into the darkness.

Eri.

Baby Duncan.

They were all dead now. He was alone. Utterly and completely alone.

Allen screamed until he was hoarse, as the fire engulfed his family crushed beneath the weight of the house that had fallen.

Scotland. April, 1188.

Allen pulled chunks off of the bread in his hand, but he didn't eat it. He just kept peeling it apart, letting crumbs fall on the table. He had a small army of crumbs there already.

"Eat, Allen," William insisted, sinking into the chair across the table. "Eat."

"I'm not hungry."

"Neither am I, but that doesn't change the fact that you have to eat. You'll die otherwise."

"Good."

Allen watched the bread falling to pieces in his hand, darkness weighing heavily on his chest.

Tenants of his father had seen the flames on that fateful night and come to help put out the fire. Word spread among the Logan clan, more had come–William had to drag Allen away, still screaming.

The bodies had been found the next day as William and the others dug through the charred rubble. Allen had only seen glimpses of them, unable to stomach the sight of their blackened skin. He'd retched at the first sight of them and then run away.

William had had to deal with the funerals and everything else as Allen sat in William's home, not doing anything unless forced.

"Allen." William put his face in his hands, sighing heavily. "I understand. I do. That was my family, too."

Allen didn't respond. He just kept peeling apart the bread in his hands.

"Five months, Allen. At some point, you have to be a man. I can't keep force feeding you for the rest of your life."

"Then don't," Allen barked. "My life is over."

"I know, I know." William's eyes were dark with emotion and shimmering with unshed tears. "Trust me, Allen. I know. I understand."

"Why didn't I die, William?" Allen asked, anger lacing each word. "Why?"

"Because you had the wits to leave the house."

"Oh, so I'm the coward who abandoned his family to burn in that fire."

"You did what you could, Allen. You tried to save them."

"No. I tried to save Florie…but she was already dead. I did nothing for the others." Allen was quiet for a moment. "I should have died, William."

"But you didn't. You are right, perhaps you should be dead with the rest of them. But you aren't dead, Allen. So do something with your life! Quit sitting here having a pity party."

"I'm not–"

"Yes, you are. You can mourn and grieve, Allen. You *should*. I am, believe me. But you can't waste what is left of your life. You only have one."

"Whatever."

"Allen, I am serious. It's been five months. Find a new purpose."

"You don't understand!"

"Me? *I* don't understand." At the sound of William's cold, hard voice Allen's gaze rose from the crumbling bread to see William's flashing eyes. "I suppose that wasn't Evanna who died in the fire, was it? My sister in all but blood, a girl I helped to raise. Or Duncan, my life long friend? Or Alice, a girl I've known since birth, my niece if you will, one I adored. Or Eri, the sweetest member of our family. The girl who made Allen, *my* Allen happy. That was *my* family."

William sighed, his head lowering as his shoulders slumped. Allen's heart broke afresh.

"I do understand. That was *my* Florie, the woman I…" William covered his face with his hands, his shoulders shaking but no sound escaping him.

Allen watched, horrified. William was always so strong and sure. For a while, William quietly cried and Allen watched. Eventually, however, William seemed to calm down.

"What do we do?" Allen asked once William's shoulders had stopped shaking in silent sobs.

"I don't know." William sat up, wiping his hand across his face, erasing the tears that had fallen there. "I was thinking about going to France."

"What?!"

"I need to do something, Allen. I can't stay here. I have no life here, apart from you, now."

"But why France?"

"Because King Philip has joined the Third Crusade. It will give me a purpose, something to strive for. I need that right now or I'd wither up and die."

Allen didn't respond.

The Crusade.

Maybe…

Maybe he could join the Crusades. Maybe he would get himself killed.

"Alright, I'll go with you."

"Are you sure?" William shook his head. "You should take time to think that over, Allen. Don't make a rash decision."

"How long have you been thinking it over?"

"Months."

"Alright. I'll take my time and think about it."

Allen was sure he'd go, but he'd give William the time to adjust to the idea.

He had to go. It was either that, or kill himself—which William would never agree to.

"I want to go to France," William said. "But Prince Richard of England took the cross last year and is also mustering an army for the crusades. That would be easier to join."

"Then why do you want to go to France?"

"Because I need to get away from it all, Allen. Scotland, England, my history. I need to get far away."

Allen could sympathize with that sentiment.

Part 2

The Darkness

Chapter 9

Allen stood by the docks, taking in the smell of the sea. The sun shone down from a brilliantly blue sky as he surveyed the ships in the harbor. They were of varying sizes, some of them small fishing boats only a few men could fit into, some of them larger than his house had been before the fire. All of them took his breath away.

He'd never seen ships before, having never had occasion to visit the sea, and so many all in one place! Hundreds of ships filled the harbor in every direction. Seasoned sailors with scraggly beards and muscled arms were moving about the docks hefting large crates and laughing loudly at each other's jokes. Young men, innocent and out of place, wandered the docks as well as experienced soldiers with swords swinging at their sides and grim expressions on their faces.

"Looking for something, boy?" A gruff voice asked.

Allen turned to see an older man, with grey hair and steely eyes standing beside him.

"I am planning on getting a berth on one of those ships," Allen replied.

"A boy wanting the glory of battle," the man huffed. "I'm Sir Adam. I've got a few spaces that could be filled in my company of men if you aren't already assigned."

"Thank you, Sir Adam. I don't have a crew. I did train with men in London, but never found a proper place."

Sir Adam grunted, the frown on his face deepening. "Do you have a name?"

"Allen of the Dale, sir."

"Well, Allen, we sail in four days, on *The Barbara*. I've got a few more berths if you happen to have any other fresh-faced, naive friends who still need a company." And with that said, Sir Adam stomped off down the docks.

Allen watched him go. This was it. In four days, he'd be sailing on *The Barbara* with a new purpose.

What that purpose was, Allen wasn't entirely sure yet. They were going to reclaim Jerusalem of course, but that was hardly important to Allen himself. He just needed to be far away from Scotland. Living in England the last few weeks hadn't been far enough– he was still plagued with nightmares of his family.

Allen found an inn to lodge at near the docks, watching the boarders around him at every meal. Most were young men like himself, eagerly joining up to follow Richard the LionHeart—recently crowned King of England after the death of his father—into war. Some were more seasoned soldiers, watching the young men with grim or amused expressions.

As Allen dug into his porridge one morning, he noticed a new face sitting beside him. He was young, around Allen's own age, with blue eyes and slightly unkempt blond hair. He was with a friend of his, a smaller young man who looked more timid.

Allen watched them quietly chatting for a moment before he decided to take a chance on them.

"Are you joining the Crusades, like everyone else in Dover?" he asked.

The young man looked over, smiling immediately. "Yes, we are. I'm Robin of Locksley, son of the Earl, and this is Much, my faithful servant and dearest friend."

"I am Allen of the Dale. I'm sailing on *The Barbara*. Which vessel do you sail with?"

"I have not arranged all those details," Robin replied. He had rather distinct blue eyes and a mess of blond hair that needed to be combed. "We only arrived last night."

"Ah, well, if you'll allow me, I can help you. There's a few berths left on our ship. I hadn't realized until I arrived that the king had so many ships at the ready, and yet they're all being filled to the brim. Have you seen the harbor?"

A serving girl approached with plates of food for Robin and his companion Much.

"We have," Robin said as Much started eating. "It is quite the sight, especially considering how few boats of any size we've seen prior to this trip. Though I think my friend here is far more interested in the sight of the castle than the sight of the ships."

"It is rather an impressive castle your King Henry has constructed there," Allen said, referring to King Richard's late father.

"My King Henry?" Robin asked.

Allen felt a jolt run through him. "Ours." Allen quickly changed the subject–dwelling on the fact that he was not English would lead to questions about his past and he had no desire to remember his family just now. Luckily for him, he'd been imitating the speech of the English since he was a child. He could hide his accent well.

"Are you finished with your breakfast? We can head down to *The Barbara* and speak to the captain. You arrived in Dover just in time. We set sail in three days."

"Where to?" Robin asked.

"Along the coast of France, I believe, until we reach Marseille to meet up with King Philip's forces. Though I could be mistaken. I have only the rumors to go off of; no captains of the king's army have seen fit to discuss our strategies with me."

Robin chuckled.

Once they had finished eating, Allen led his new companions down to the docks, and then to the ship called *The Barbara*.

Sailors and soldiers were moving about in the same busy manner that they had been since Allen arrived in Dover.

Robin took a deep breath. "Do you smell the sea air, Much?"

Much wrinkled his nose. "It doesn't smell good."

Allen laughed. "You'll get used to it. I assume you haven't sailed before?"

"Never," Much replied.

"Neither have I. It should be an adventure."

"I have never fought either," Much added.

"Oh don't worry, Much!" Robin slung his arm around Much's shoulders. "We're both proficient with swords and bows."

"And I'm sure there will be training as we travel as well," Allen added. "The captain I have chosen to follow is convinced we're all lousy boys who need to be whipped into shape. He's impressively grumpy. You'll enjoy his personality, I'm sure."

Allen pointed out *The Barbara* to his new companions–the name of the ship scrawled in white paint across the hull of the wooden boat. He waved down a sailor to ask if the captain was nearby but the sailor informed him the captain was on business in the city, making preparations for their departure.

Not to be deterred, Allen marched along the street horizontal to the docks searching for Sir Adam, his new companions following along behind him.

They found the lord seated on a stone bench sitting outside one of the many taverns in the city. He was a middle aged man with a wrinkled tan face and a greying beard. He frowned as Allen walked up to him, but Allen was growing rather used to that kind of response from him.

"Sir Adam, may I introduce you to Robin of Locksley–son of the Earl of Locksley–and his servant Much? They desire to join our company."

Sir Adam studied Much and Robin, from their foreheads to their toes and then back up again. "Son of an earl, you say?"

"Yes, sir," Robin replied, his back straightening slightly.

"You could probably lead a company of your own, young Robin. Most noble men in our ranks do, bringing their own soldiers from home, or picking up the strays who don't have a liege or lord to follow, such as this whelp," Sir Adam gestured toward Allen.

Allen hadn't told him he was a nobleman–he couldn't. He wasn't a noble of England, which meant if he had to explain where he came from memories of Eri would rise to the surface and that was the last thing Allen wanted.

"I do not believe I have the experience necessary for that," Robin replied. "And I did not bring more than one man from home."

"Then by all means, you may join mine. Now if you don't mind…" Sir Adam waved them off casually, and Allen led them back down the street.

"Well, that's that I suppose," Allen said. "He'll let the captain of the ship know, no doubt, so you'll be given berths on the ship. And we sail in three days."

"Let the adventure begin," Robin grinned.

Chapter 10

The last three days in Dover passed swiftly. Allen spent most of his time with his new companions, Robin and Much. They were both cheerful fellows and when he was in their company Allen found it easier to forget his life was in shambles and that he hated himself.

At the end of the three days, soldiers were loaded onto the fleet of ships and prepared to set sail. Allen and his new friends stowed their things below deck in a room filled with hammocks, claiming theirs for their journey. Now, however, they stood at the railing above deck watching the English shore disappear in the grey fog of the morning.

"This is it, Much," Robin leaned over the boat's rail, the wind in his hair. "Our adventure is beginning."

"Yes, Robin," Much replied.

"Isn't it splendid?"

Allen clapped Robin on the shoulder, forcing himself to be far more cheerful than he felt. "It is! Can you believe we are on our way to join the King? What a grand time we shall have."

"We are going to war," Much said. Allen glanced toward him and noticed how carefully Much was watching him. It unnerved him. "I do not believe 'grand time' is the best way to describe such a thing."

Allen chuckled, trying to ignore the growing feeling that Much could see straight through him. "Don't be so grave, master Much."

"I am simply worried." Much grabbed the railing and leaned outward–not in the same eager way that Robin had; he seemed far more nostalgic to Allen's mind. "Shall we see this shore again, do you think?"

"Why would we not?" Robin asked.

"Casualties in war are not unheard of."

"Of course there are, but we won't be among them."

Allen turned away from them; he was rather hoping he would, in fact, be one of the casualties.

Not too long after they had set sail for Marseilles, Sir Adam called together the men and the crew of *The Barbara* to explain that he wanted training to commence every day. Not everyone could be on deck at the same time and still leave room for sparring and training–and room for the sailors to do their work–so Sir Adam and the captain worked together to devise a schedule of sorts. Much, Robin, and Allen ended up on the earliest shift, which meant they would be waking at dawn for the remainder of their journey in order to train first with the other unlucky souls whose sleep was to be so interrupted.

One morning after they'd groggily been forced from their beds by Sir Adam and forced to begin sparring on the swaying deck, Allen found himself in melee with Robin.

Allen barely managed to raise his blade in time to block Robin's sword that came crashing toward him. His knees bent as his arm strained against the weight of Robin's attack for a moment.

Allen eventually mustered enough strength to push Robin back and they separated, eyeing each other's defenses.

"Trying to kill me, Robin?" Allen asked casually, hoping to bring Robin to a place of ease before he darted forward for an attack.

With a flick of his wrist, Robin deflected the blow and with his free hand gave a solid punch to Allen's jaw.

Allen stepped back, lowering his sword and rubbing his face. "Ow."

"I didn't hit you that hard." Robin grinned.

Allen shrugged. "You hit me hard enough. Either way, I think I have had enough for this morning. Unless Sir Adam the grump can stop me, I'm calling it quits." Allen gave a deep bow to Robin. "I concede, your lordship."

Allen sheathed his sword at his waist and then moved over to sit on the deck near where Much was standing at the rail. Robin followed.

For a moment they watched other sleepy young men sparring across the deck.

"You're a better swordsmen than I, Robin," Allen sighed. Despite all of William's and his father's training, young Robin was far more skilled.

"I've had years of practice, but I haven't seen any real combat," Robin replied. "I'm the son of an earl, though, and I would be disgracing my Father if I was not good at what I do."

Allen winced, wondering if he was a disgrace to his own father.

He knew he was. It wasn't even a question.

He'd failed to save any of them.

Had he even tried?

"And anyway…I just can't bear not to be the best."

Much laughed at Robin's comment. "That is very true."

"I think you'll come in handy," Allen said, shaking off his darker thoughts and forcing himself to meet Robin's banter. "I doubt any Saracen could get through you."

"They won't even come close if I use my bow," Robin winked. "It's harder to showcase my brilliance in that respect on this boat, but just wait…"

"You keep praising your abilities with the bow and I'll expect nothing but perfection once I see you in action," Allen laughed. He reached a hand up to his jaw once more, wincing slightly.

"Oh come on, I didn't punch that hard," Robin reached over and pushed Allen's shoulder.

"Hey!" Allen shifted across the deck a bit to get out of reach. "That hurts, too, you know. Every muscle in my body hurts when we train. We've only begun this journey and already I am exhausted," Allen sighed, rubbing his shoulder. "This is going to be a long road…"

Sir Adam grunted as he walked near the group, glaring at Allen. "Longer than you know. Don't begin complaining yet. Save that for after you've been stuck in the Holy Land for more years than you care to count."

"Have you been before?" Robin asked.

"Of course," Sir Adam said. "I was a soldier in the Second Crusade."

Sir Adam continued on his way to greet the men rising from below deck for the second hour of training, as those currently sparring came to a stop. Some went below deck, some collapsed along the edges of the deck as Allen and his companions had.

The sun was shimmering across the water as it rose over the horizon. Sunrises on land had been beautiful, but nothing had prepared Allen to see them reflected across the entire surface of the water–two sunrises wreathed in a million shades of pink and lavender and orange.

Robin chuckled as he watched the next set of soldiers begin their sparring under the watchful eye of Sir Adam, who stomped around correcting posture and barking orders.

"They have it so easy, getting up after the sun." Robin laughed, shaking his head.

"It's not as though any of us are sleeping in those hammocks anyway," Allen said.

Not to mention the nightmares…

Chapter 11

The Barbara appeared to be one of the fastest ships in the fleet, and therefore arrived in Marseilles before the rest of the fleet. Sir Adam arranged for his company of men to lodge at an inn, and the captain cared for his sailors as they all waited for the rest of the fleet to arrive.

Their arrival in Marseilles was met with cheers and celebration. The people of the city were enthralled with the idea that their King Philip was joining the Crusades, and any soldier claiming to be an ally was most welcome. Allen was relieved to get out of the adoring crowds and into the tavern where they would be staying–he wasn't a hero and didn't want the people's attention in such a way.

As they settled into their bedrolls for the night, Robin sighed. "It really begins now. When we set sail for the Holy Land, it all begins."

"Are you nervous, Robin?" Much asked, his voice shaking as he was clearly nervous himself.

"I'm more excited than nervous."

"I do hope no one dies."

"Someone is likely to die," Allen said, trying not to make it obvious he hoped he would be among the dead. "This is a war, Much. There will be casualties."

"Just as long as it isn't us," Robin said. "I have to get home to Marian."

"Don't worry, Robin," Allen said. "You'll return a war hero and every woman will fall at your feet."

"There's only one woman I want falling at my feet," Robin replied. "I just pray she'll wait for me."

Allen rolled over, putting his back to Robin. He pressed his hand over his mouth to keep any sounds from escaping as tears pushed their way stubbornly out of his eyes despite his best attempts to control them.

There was only one woman Allen wanted, too, but she was nothing but a blackened crisp now.

One night Much, Robin, and Allen were sitting at a table in the back of the common room of the inn, watching the comings and goings of the others in their company, and various French individuals that they did not know. Robin had ordered a round of drinks for the three of them, and Allen was chugging his.

"What comes next?" Much asked.

Robin shrugged as he leaned his chair back on two legs and rested his legs on the table. "The rest of our fleet arrives, and then King Richard and King Philip lead us to the Holy Land, I suppose."

Allen ignored their conversation as well as he could, pouring more of his ale down his throat.

"Young Robin, we have work to do," Sir Adam said without preamble as he approached their table.

"How so?" Robin sat up, his feet and chair legs hitting the floor with a resounding thud.

"King Richard is too impatient to wait for the rest of the fleet; he has a mission he wishes to accomplish immediately. We'll be setting sail once more."

"When?"

"As soon as the tide goes out. Come with me, we have men to find, a sea captain to rouse…"

"Work to be done," Robin nodded with a sigh. He pushed his half-drunk mug of ale towards Allen. "Finish this off, will you? I'll be back eventually."

Sir Adam and Robin left the tavern, and Allen picked up Robin's mug and began to guzzle his drink.

"You're going to get drunk," Much commented.
"That's the idea."

"We're apparently sailing tonight, and for the King of England no less."

"I heard."

Much stood up from the table. "I'm going to make sure Robin's things are gathered and ready for our departure."

Allen didn't watch him go, but stayed where he was, emptying all three cups at the table.

The crowds cheering for them upon their arrival had set him on edge, and over the course of their stay every time he bumped into a Frenchmen they wanted to thank him–every time the serving girl brought food or drink to him in the tavern she wanted to praise him for fighting in the Crusades, too.

He was no hero. He let his whole family die.

Allen drained the last drop from Robin's mug and then waved down the serving girl to order another.

It wasn't long before Sir Adam and the captain were leading their soldiers and sailors back aboard their ship. The King of England came aboard with little fanfare, staying close by his Royal Guard as preparations were made to set sail.

Allen found himself below deck in the bunk room–filled with hammocks hanging throughout the middle of the room, while along the walls barrels and crates of various cargo were stashed. He was seated on one of the barrels alongside Robin and Much, his head pounding. Perhaps he shouldn't have drunk quite so much…

Sir Adam and other members of the company were swinging in their hammocks nearby as dawn slowly approached. Some of them were asleep, but Allen and his companions were not.

"What does King Richard wish to do in Sicily?" Much asked. They'd learned from Robin that Sicily was their destination for whatever mission the King wanted to accomplish while waiting for the rest of his fleet. "Why are we sailing there?"

"We're sailing there," Sir Adam grunted from his hammock nearby, "because last year William of Sicily died and was replaced by Tancred."

The world was spinning around Allen, and the rocking of the ship was not helping. His stomach lurched and it was all he could do to keep from throwing up.

"Tancred imprisoned King Richard's sister Joan," Robin said. "We are going to Sicily to rescue her."

"It is foolishness," Sir Adam snorted. "The Crusaders in the Holy Land are dying and need our help, and we are stopping along the way to save a silly woman?"

"Wouldn't you take a detour to save your own sister, if you had one?" Robin asked.

Allen could suddenly see Alice, green eyes sparkling with mischief, her face framed by her wild red curls. He turned away from his friends to hide the tears starting to form in his eyes.

"Not when the fate of our army hung in the balance," Sir Adam replied, his expression grim. "We could return for Princess Joan on our way home, if she's so important, we need not delay our journey to Jerusalem."

"But that could be years away!" Robin said. "Anything could happen to her in that time. Do you have so little regard for women, Sir Adam?"

Allen rubbed a hand across his face, trying to listen to the argument over the pounding in his head as he shoved the image of Alice far from his mind.

"You have far too much regard for them," Sir Adam growled. "How many times have I heard you pining over the lass…what is her name? Marian? Wondering if she is waiting for you back home. I will tell you now, do not hope for it. Women are not worth the trouble."

Robin shook his head with a grin. "Clearly, you have never been in love."

Allen jumped up from his perch on the barrel, striding out of the bunk room and toward the ladder that would lead him above deck. He couldn't bear this conversation a moment longer.

Once above deck, Allen leaned against the rail and stared into the swirling water below him. The sun was just peaking over the horizon, lighting both the sky and the sea in a variety of shades of orange and red.

He didn't think of Alice and Eri all night anymore, unable to sleep. He didn't spend his days trying to get the image of dead Florie out of his head. He thought he was, as William would say, moving on.

But they were still there.

Allen closed his eyes.

He'd failed them. Failed to save them. Failed to keep remembering them.

Not that he had forgotten, because he most definitely still remembered. But they didn't fill his every waking moment now, and that bothered him. Yet the fact that Alice had invaded his thoughts a moment before also bothered him.

Allen angrily brushed a few stray tears from his face. The best thing he could do was either die or forget. Those were the options that appealed to him. The fact that he was actually starting to enjoy life again because of Robin and Much was inconsequential.

Chapter 12

For several weeks *The Barbara* sailed along the coast of Italy until approaching the island of Sicily, some miles north of the town of Messina.

Allen stood with Robin at the rail on deck, watching the shores of Sicily come ever closer. It was scarcely dawn, the sky grey, a deep fog permeating the air. Sailors were running about the deck and up the rigging, busy about their tasks. Allen ignored them.

"How do you suppose King Richard is going to get Joan?"

Robin shrugged. "I don't know, but he is bringing an entire army to this little island. The fleet is expected to follow us here. I'm not sure Tancred will have a choice but to give her up."

Not long after they were docked, Sir Adam and King Richard could be seen at the helm of the ship, talking with the captain. More soldiers began to gather on deck and Sir Adam was pointing at various men as he and the King spoke.

"What is he doing?" Allen asked.

"I don't know. It looks like he's choosing soldiers."

"Maybe he's gathering the men he wants to go with him to rescue the princess."

"It's possible. I'm going to wake up Much though. He won't want to miss this."

Robin hadn't gone far when Sir Adam began to move across the deck and start speaking to various men.

Allen sprinted across the deck to follow Robin, scurrying down the ladder to the hold. "Robin!"

Robin turned around. "What is it?"

"King Richard is talking to soldiers now!"

Robin grinned. "Let me get Much."

Robin disappeared down the hallway for a moment and then came back with Much following him, looking less than happy to be dragged from his sleep.

"There you are!" Allen threw up his hands in exasperation as Robin and Much joined him at the base of the ladder. "Come on, he's already talking to people."

Much, Robin, and Allen hurried onto deck where most of the rest of the company were already gathered.

King Richard stood near the stern of the ship, speaking softly to the captain and to Sir Adam but when the latter caught sight of them he seemed to gesture in their direction. King Richard turned and his gaze settled on Robin.

"Do you think he'll come over or just stare at you?" Allen whispered.

Before Robin could respond, Sir Adam and King Richard approached.

Allen bowed, and his friends did as well.

"You're Robin, son of the Earl of Locksley?" King Richard asked.

"Yes, Sire," Robin said.

"I am told you are good with a bow and remarkable with a blade."

"I do my best."

"I have been informed you are better than most."

"I couldn't say, Sire."

"I would like you to come with me on the mission to rescue my sister."

"I would be honored, my King."

"Are these two companions of yours good fighters as well?"

"I would say so, Sire."

Sir Adam shook his head. "They have nowhere near Robin's skill, my lord, although Allen is a decent soldier. This one…I'm not so sure," Sir Adam gestured toward Much.

King Richard looked Allen over, and Allen straightened his spine, trying to look like a competent soldier. This was his first chance for a battle–his first chance to lose his life in a fight.

King Richard said nothing and turned his gaze on Much. "You do look too gentle to be on this ship, lad."

"I follow my master, Your Majesty," Much said. "No matter where he leads."

"Ah, you are Robin of Locksley's servant then."

"He is my friend," Robin put in, "and he follows me as much from loyalty and love as from duty."

"All qualities I can admire," King Richard smiled. "I will take the three of you."

King Richard turned and moved off to speak to other soldiers.

"Go get your weapons," Sir Adam snapped. "We'll be following King Richard to shore shortly."

In what felt like no time at all, Allen and his friends were equipped with their weapons and leaving the boat as they followed the King of England and the other soldiers he had hand-picked onto the island, marching southward toward the town of Messina.

They marched for several miles until Messina came into sight. There was no wall or fortification around the city, which made King Richard's job rather easy–he marched his men right into the city.

Men of the city came to greet him with swords drawn, and Allen gripped his own blade tight in his hand, his blood up, eager for his first fight.

But Allen was to be disappointed. He, Robin, and Much were in the back of the company following King Richard, and though there was a brief struggle between those at the front and the men of the town, the fight was over in mere minutes and no lives were lost as King Richard took possession of the town. There were only a few guards stationed there, and the common people had no desire to fight the King of England–his sister had been their beloved Queen, after all.

King Richard chose a house as headquarters, and Allen, Robin, and Much were stationed outside it to keep watch while King Richard made his plans for saving his sister Joan.

The sun had been up for several hours now, and it was shining cheerfully down on the street. It was a pleasant morning, though Allen wished he could have been a part of the action.

As Robin voiced his own displeasure at missing the chance to showcase his skill in battle, Allen leaned against the door they were stationed outside of, intent on listening to the conversations within.

"Don't eavesdrop," Much said.

Robin leaned forward eagerly, pressing his own face to the door. "What are they saying?"

"King Richard is sending a small group of soldiers to Tancred with a message."

"Who?"

Allen shrugged. "I don't know."

The door opened a moment later, causing Allen and Robin to jump backwards as King Richard came out.

"Robin of Locksley!"

"Yes, Sire."

"I want you and your companions to deliver a message to King Tancred of Sicily. Come inside, and Sir Adam can show you on the map where his palace is located."

"Yes, Sire."

The King gestured them inside and the three of them followed him to a table–a map was spread across it and Sir Adam and other advisors to King Richard were circled around it. Sir Adam pointed out the palace.

King Richard turned to Robin. "You will go there today, deliver my message, and bring my sister back to me."

"Yes, Sire," Robin said.

In no time at all, Allen, Robin, and Much were on their way to King Tancred's residence. The day was pleasantly warm, the air fresh, the sun shining down on them warming their backs. All around the road were vibrant flowers and varying cacti–the sort of flora and fauna that Allen had never seen before. With every hill they crested they could see down to the shimmering blue and green sea. It was all so different than his cold, heather-covered moors of his home in Scotland.

After a few hours walking in the lush countryside, they came in sight of the palace. It was a large stone structure with many towers and high turreted walls. As they neared the front gate, they saw two armed gates at the entrance. When the guards caught sight of them, they lowered their spears menacingly.

They called out in a language that Allen did not understand–he thought it might be Latin, as it reminded him of Friar Roderick. Robin responded in kind, and Allen glanced between him and the guards as a tense conversation he could not comprehend ensued. After a few minutes, the guards called for the gates to be opened and led Allen and the others inside.

The guards led them through several passages within the castle until they came to an ornate door that one of the guards knocked on.

The door creaked open and the guard was admitted, while the second one stood outside with Allen and his companions.

Allen wanted to ask Robin what was going on, what had been said between them, but with the guard still standing next to them he held his tongue and waited.

The guard who had disappeared inside the room came back; he spoke in what Allen still assumed was Latin, and the door was swung wide open. The three of them were admitted into what was obviously a throne room.

The room was long and spacious, with a ceiling set so high above them that Allen would have to crane his neck to fully look up at it. Along the walls were long windows reaching from floor to ceiling and letting in the bright sunlight and a view of the lush landscape.

King Tancred sat on a throne on a raised dias with guards on either side of him. Robin bowed, and Allen quickly did the same.

Robin started to speak, but King Tancred interrupted him and soon enough the two of them were in a tense conversation, snapping back and forth rather quickly. Even if Allen had been able to understand the language that they spoke, he imagined it might have been difficult to keep up with them. Much glanced toward Allen for a moment, and Allen wondered if he was equally as confused by what was happening.

Suddenly soldiers moved forward, grabbing them by their arms. Allen jerked out of the soldier's grasp and was shoved backward toward the door.

The soldiers were closing in on them, and Allen's hand twitched toward the hilt of his sword, but Robin grabbed his shoulder and hissed, "Not now."

After being rudely escorted outside by the guards, Allen turned to his companions.

"Now what? I take it things did not go well, though I understood very little of it."

"Now we return to King Richard and explain that King Tancred has refused to meet his demands. It went better than it might have, honestly. We could have been imprisoned or worse."

The walk back to Messina was a quiet one.

As they walked down the road, Allen was lost in his own thoughts. He hadn't immediately countered Robin internally about wanting to die and that disturbed him. Did he not think he deserved to die anymore?

Allen glanced at his companions. Robin looked cheerful despite the failure of their mission; Much looked nervous and unsure of himself as always. What was it about these two that made him forget his despair and his guilt sometimes?

Chapter 13

When the three of them returned to Messina and relayed their news to King Richard, Sir Adam, and the other advisors, King Richard was furious. He slammed his fist onto the table in front of him which caused Much to jump.

"Refuse me?" King Richard shook his head. "We move out tonight. We'll take his castle and save my sister by force if necessary."

Once the army was mustered, they marched the short distance to King Tancred's castle. The King of Sicily did not put up a fight–it seemed once he saw King Richard's army approaching he chose to surrender.

King Richard stormed into the throne room where King Tancred was still sitting proudly, trying to look as though his castle had not been conquered. Sir Adam's company of soldiers followed the King and his Royal Guard into the throne room, and thus Allen had a front row seat to the action.

"Where is my sister?" King Richard demanded in English, grabbing Tancred by the neck of his shirt, pulling him off of his throne and shoving him against the wall. The veins in King Richard's face and neck were throbbing. Allen shuddered, knowing he'd have done anything for Alice, too.

"She is in the dungeon. I can send someone for her," Tancred replied, his own English perfectly good which surprised Allen. Had he been speaking Latin before merely to assert his power of invaders he might have assumed didn't speak it?

"I'll send my own men," King Richard said. He turned to his Royal Guard, instructing them to bring Joan to him safely. They spun on their heels and left immediately.

As they left the room, King Richard looked over his shoulder–still holding Tancred against the wall. "Robin of Locksley!"

"Yes, Sire?"

"I've sent my personal guard to the dungeons to bring Joan to me, and you and your two companions will act as my guard until they return."

"Yes, Sire."

Allen eagerly stepped forward to stand beside King Richard as Robin and Much did the same.

"I will take your pathetic kingdom today if any harm has come to my sister." King Richard's hold on King Tancred tightened. "And I demand the entirety of her dowry be restored to my family as restitution for the treatment she has received here."

"I don't–"

"I am more than happy to take Sicily if that is preferred."

"No, no. I can send someone to…gather the equivalent of her dowry."

King Richard allowed Tancred to summon one of his treasurers and task him with collecting what King Richard desired.

After the man left, they waited in tense silence for a few minutes, as King Richard glared at Tancred, who was looking much less proud and haughty now.

"Richard?"

Everyone turned toward the sound of a woman's voice. A beautiful woman who couldn't have been many years older than him stood in the doorway in a flowing white dress, with her dark curls spilling around her shoulders, her blue eyes unsure and afraid.

"Joan!" King Richard dropped his grip on Tancred and ran across the room toward his sister. Joan sprinted to meet his embrace, throwing her arms around his shoulders.

"You came for me?"

"Of course I came for you!"

For a moment, Allen thought someone might have thrust a sword through his heart, but a quick glance at himself suggested he had no external injuries. He tightened his grip on his sword, blinking away his unwelcome tears and any memories of Alice as he turned to face King Tancred instead, raising his sword to keep the man in line until given a different occupation.

The treasurer soon returned, with a line of servants in tow carrying chests of treasure to compensate for Joan's dowry.

With Joan and dowry in tow, King Richard and his army retreated back to the sea. There they waited as the rest of the fleet of both King Richard's army and King Philip's arrived. Along with them came a boat carrying King Richard's mother, Eleanor of Aquitaine.

When King Richard went to greet them as they disembarked from their boat, Sir Adam was at his side as always. King Richard had also requested Robin of Locksley be with him, and Much had followed because he never went anywhere without his master. With nothing better to do, Allen joined them. King Richard did not seem to mind, though Sir Adam grumbled under his breath about upstarts forgetting their station.

After embracing his mother, and the young lady who accompanied her, King Richard turned toward the rest of them. "Robin of Locksley, come meet my mother."

Robin moved forward as Queen Eleanor glanced at her son. "Who are these fine young men, Richard?"

"Robin of Locksley, son of the Earl of Locksley. He has been entertaining company on our journey and I think you would enjoy knowing him. This is his servant Much, and Allen is a young soldier in my army." Allen bowed to the Queen Mother.

King Richard then introduced them all to the other woman–Berengaria of Navarre, whom he said was his betrothed.

"But aren't you betrothed to–" Robin stopped, and Allen noticed Much shooting him a look of reproach. "It is an honor to meet you, my lady."

Berengaria laughed, her eyes sparkling playfully. "Oh, he was betrothed, Robin of Locksley. You are not mistaken."

"But I am breaking it off," King Richard said, wrapping an arm around Berengaria's waist. "So that I can marry my beautiful Berengaria."

They were soon dismissed from the group as the King, his mother, bride-to-be, and Sir Adam moved off on their own.

"He was betrothed to someone else?" Much asked as he watched the royals walking away.

"Yes," Robin replied.

"I'm not sure Berengaria is beautiful enough to warrant breaking off another political marriage," Allen said. "Who was he engaged to before?"

"King Philip's sister, I believe," Robin replied. "Princess Alys. I imagine there will be some tension there…especially as we travel together to the Holy Land."

"Doesn't seem wise," Allen shrugged.

"Perhaps not, but did you see the way they looked at each other? If I was engaged to Princess Alys I'd break it off in a heartbeat just to have Marian look at me like that. Love will make a man do almost anything," Robin grinned. "Someday you'll understand."

Eri's gentle smile and bright eyes glimmered before Allen for a moment before he slammed the door shut on his memories.

"Perhaps. Should we return to our quarters until we are summoned again?"

Without waiting for an answer, Allen began moving away from the docks at the harbor and toward the tavern where they were staying. He needed to find a way to keep Alice and Eri from surfacing so easily– they only made him want to scream and cry and curl up in a corner and give up on life. He much preferred the comfortable ease he felt around Robin and Much to the dark memories.

Chapter 14

The fleet was soon sailing again. Once they were under way, Allen went in search of Robin. Conversation with his easy-going friend always gave him the strange feeling that life might still be worth living–and Robin's banter was also a welcome distraction from Allen's own dark thoughts.

He found him on deck with Much, as expected, leaning against the rail on one side of the ship. Less expected were the two women standing beside Robin.

Allen came and leaned against the rail nearby and caught the tail-end of Berengaria speaking as Sir Adam also came to join the group. "…my fiance think so highly of you?"

"I do not know, my lady," Robin replied.

Allen studied Princess Joan while Berengaria and Robin teased each other. Her blue eyes never left Robin's face, and every time he laughed or smirked at something King Richard's intended said or did, Joan would smile as well, her eyes sparkling. Joan seemed quite taken with Robin, or so Allen thought.

"Where is Queen Eleanor?" Allen asked once there was a break in the conversation.

"She is returning to Europe," Berengaria replied with a casual wave of her hand. "But I refused to leave my beloved."

"And I refused to leave my brother," Joan said. "Or I just wanted an adventure after being locked up in a dungeon for so long." Joan winked at Robin and he laughed, causing a smile to break out across her face.

Allen tried not to think about Eri and all the ways he'd tried to make her smile over the years.

Two days after they had set sail from Sicily, a storm overtook the fleet. The ominous clouds broke loose, the wind screeched around the boats kicking up the waves, causing the ships to be thrown about in all directions. The sails snapped, the rain splattered, the hulls creaked, and the soldiers were sent below deck to be out of the way of the sailors.

Allen slipped and slid his way across the deck with Much right behind him. When he reached the ladder to go below he decided to forego climbing the rungs and simply jumped down. Much came more slowly.

As the ship rocked violently to one side, Allen leaned against the wall for balance.

"It's quite the storm."

Much froze on the ladder above him.

"Robin!"

"Much, stay below!" Robin's voice echoed from the deck, sounding thin and far away.

Much immediately began to scramble up the ladder. Allen gritted his teeth and followed, if only to see what Much was going to do.

When Allen reached the deck, the freezing rain pelted his skin like sharp needles and he inhaled sharply. The last time he'd felt rain like this…

Florie's lifeless body flashed before his eyes.

Allen shook his head and chose to ignore that particular memory. Robin was running, as best he could on the slippery deck, toward the bow of the ship. Allen could see Joan there, clinging to the railing.

Robin reached her at last and grabbed her hand. They started across the deck, but as they did a great wave came over the side of the ship and swept over the deck. The force of the icy water knocked Allen's feet off the deck and he fell.

For a moment everything was freezing cold and darkness. Then his head smacked against the side of the ship and the wave washed over him. Allen sat up, sputtering, soaked to the bone as the ship was tossed another direction and the last of the wave dissipated from the deck.

He looked to where he'd last seen Robin and Joan. He could see nothing more than a very white hand gripping the wet railing.

Allen ran forward, stumbling to his knees a few times due to the wet wood beneath his feet and the violent pitching of the boat. When he reached the railing, he saw Robin hanging over the side of the deck, holding the rail for all he was worth with one hand. Joan was wrapped in his other arm and she was clinging to his neck. Sailors nearby were shouting about men being overboard.

"Are you alright?" Allen asked, grabbing Robin's arm in the hopes that he could keep Robin and Joan from tumbling into the turbulent waters below.

"I'm fine," Robin said through gritted teeth, the muscles in his arm straining beneath Allen's fingers. "Get Joan."

Robin tried to hoist Joan up with one arm, and Allen reached over the side of the ship and gripped her by both her arms as he began to pull backwards. With Robin pushing and Allen pulling they managed to tumble onto the deck.

Allen scrambled to his feet to help Robin over the railing next.

"Are you alright?" Robin asked, turning to Joan the minute he was back on his feet.

"Yes, thank you, Robin. Just soaked."

"Allen, take her below," Robin said.

"Are you not coming?" Allen asked.

"Not yet. Much went overboard."

Allen's heart plummeted to his toes. He gripped Joan's elbow and began to pull her along.

Much was overboard.

It was happening again.

He was going to lose someone.

Once they were below, Allen saw to it that Joan had blankets and something warm to drink and then he sat down heavily on a crate near the wall.

Much was dead.

It wasn't fair.

Allen punched the wall in frustration. He pulled his hand back, wincing.

The ship rocked to one side and the crate Allen sat on, along with others, went careening across the room. Allen stumbled back over to the wall for support.

And then he heard a sputtering voice.

"Y-you were g-going over-b-board." Robin ushered a soaked and teeth-chatting Much into the room.

"And you thought jumping over the ship's side was going to help?" Robin snapped, grabbing a blanket from a hammock nearby and wrapping it around Much's shoulders.

"I c-couldn't just w-watch."

"Oh, Much." Robin's arms wrapped around him again, his voice hoarse.

Allen pulled himself into his hammock, watching the affectionate hug with a stab of jealousy, though the far more overwhelming emotion burning in his chest was relief.

When Robin pulled back from the hug, Much rubbed his hands up and down his arms to warm himself up as he leaned against the wall for support. "How is Princess Joan?"

"As wet as anything, but unharmed," Allen said.

"How are you, Robin?" Much asked.

"I am perfectly fine," Robin said, stripping off his shirt and moving toward his pack to get a new one. "Don't try anything so rash again. The whole time I was clinging to that rail with Joan in my arms every bone in my body was telling me to let go and dive in after you."

"Why?"

"To save you, of course," Robin replied. "I couldn't live without you, Much."

Allen groaned, curling into himself in his hammock. There were people he couldn't live without either...but he had no choice.

"Oh, shut up, both of you!" It was all too much to endure–their emotions, his memories. "Why do you have to be so emotional? You're brothers in spirit, you love each other, we get it. Move on."

Robin laughed. "Someday, Allen, you will have a best friend and then you will understand."

Sir Adam grunted from his own hammock, seemingly unimpressed with the conversation around him.

Robin moved toward Much and pulled the blanket from his shoulders. "Come on, you have to be in dry clothes, too."

Much swatted Robin's hands away and began to pull off his soaked clothes.

"I had a best friend," Allen said softly, unsure if his friends could hear him over the creaking of the boat and the muffled shouting of the sailors on deck amidst the storm. He didn't know if he was referring to Alice, Eri, or Florie...but it hardly mattered. They were all past tense now.

"Then you should already understand," Robin said, pulling himself into his own hammock.

"I do understand, Robin..." Allen clenched his fists, trying to keep the tears out of his voice as he spoke. "My friend is dead. They're all dead. I'm alone in the world."

"You've lost everyone?" Much asked.

"I lost everyone." Allen nodded, closing his eyes as he turned his face away. The concern in Much's voice was not helping with his resolve not to cry.

"I'm sorry."

"I don't need the two of you to feel sorry for me," Allen snapped. What he needed was to forget. It would be far better than this pain.

Robin rolled out of his hammock and moved toward Allen, putting a hand on his shoulder. "You may have no one of your own back home, Allen, but you have us."

"Robin, there's no need–"

"Nonsense!" Robin gave Allen a wink and a grin. "I could do with another brother."

"Thank you," Allen said softly as Robin returned to his hammock and Much struggled to climb into his own in spite of the

102

pitching boat. The tears won their fight and he covered his face with his hands as they rolled unchecked down his cheeks.

Chapter 15

Allen lay in his bunk listening to the waves continually crashing into the side of *The Barbara* as the ship tossed to and fro. He nearly rolled right out of his hammock several times as the ship was tossed about, forced to grip the edges of the hammock to keep himself from hitting the floor. How Much was soundly sleeping through the storm, Allen couldn't understand. Maybe the ordeal of going overboard has exhausted him so far that the movement of the boat could be ignored. Allen tried to ignore the pitching of the boat, and ignore the emotions roiling inside of him, and failed at both.

The memories of his family's deaths were bad enough, seeing Alice's shining green eyes and Eri's shy smile and hearing his mother's laugh…the good memories were even worse than the bad ones.

There was a fire burning in his chest and Allen was convinced he'd do almost anything to make it go away.

And on top of the painful emotions his family brought on, there was Robin and Much. His friends. Now his brothers in all but blood. Allen was grateful for them and terrified of them at the same time. If something happened to them, as it had happened to everyone else, Allen was sure he'd die.

While he was lost in this line of thinking, the ship jolted violently. Allen was thrown right off of his hammock. He sailed through the air and crashed into Robin who in turn was shoved to the side and on top of Much. Much, for his part, cracked his head against the floor.

"What was that?" Robin struggled to sit up off of Much, rubbing his elbow.

Much sat up, his hand on his forehead. "Did we hit something?"

"Are you alright, Much?" Allen asked.

"I think so. Are you?"

Allen shrugged, assessing the damage from his trip to the floor. "No broken bones. Should we go see what happened?"

"Do you think the storm has passed?" Much asked.

"I doubt it. Can't you feel the rough waves," Robin replied. "We may have hit a reef or something."

Allen hurried after Robin and everyone else as they scurried above deck to see what was going on. Once he emerged from the ladder, he could see the sky was still full of dark clouds, but they were no longer pouring rain. The sea was roiling around the *The Barbara* and several other ships that had run aground on a reef–just as Robin had predicted. One ship was broken to pieces, large chunks of wood being driven back to the sea as men clung to driftwood and thrashed in the water calling for help.

Sailors were running about as the captain shouted orders, pulling on ropes, shouting to each other, clambering up the masts, or leaning over the side of the ship to gauge how stuck they might be.

"Where are we?" Much asked as he, Robin, and Allen moved to one side of the boat to be out of the way and wait for orders. Allen could see an island just off the starboard bow.

"I'm not sure," Robin replied, watching the chaos of the sailors around them.

"Get your weapons!" Sir Adam's shout carried over the rest of the noise above deck.

Robin's head whipped around and Allen turned toward Sir Adam.

"What is it?" Much asked.

"Soldiers," Robin hissed, pointing toward the island.

"We've run aground," Sir Adam came toward them. "There's a boat of soldiers headed our way, more coming behind no doubt. The captain thinks we're on Cyprus, but he isn't sure. He got turned around in the weather, the idiot."

"How do we know they mean us harm?" Much asked.

"We don't," Sir Adam grunted. "But you don't know they mean peace either, so get below deck and get your sword, soldier!"

Much ran toward the ladder at that order, and Allen followed to fetch his own weapons as many of the other soldiers did the same.

Once back on deck, Allen could see several of the boats that had put off from the island–full of soldiers–were drawing closer to *The Barbara* and the other boats that were grounded along the reef. In another moment, archers from the boats had shot toward them and Allen ducked as the arrows found purchase on deck or in the bodies of fellow soldiers and sailors on board.

Allen whipped out his bow as Robin did the same, both of them taking careful aim and then letting their arrows fly. The first of their arrows sailed harmless into the water.

"It's the wind," Allen groaned.

"You just have to compensate," Robin grunted beside him, taking aim again, though he seemed to be pointing his arrow slightly to the left of the approaching boats. As he let the arrow fly, it shifted course in the wind and struck an approaching soldier, who fell into the icy water with the arrow protruding from his heart. Robin turned to Allen with a grin. "See?"

"Show off."

Still, despite Robin and the other soldiers on *The Barbara* doing their utmost to stop them, the boats reached the reef where their ship had run aground and the soldiers in them began to throw grappling hooks up to the rail of the deck and climbed on board.

Bows were soon discarded and swords brought out. Allen sliced, parried, and cut with ease exactly as William had taught him. Robin was beside him, cutting down soldiers with ease and Much stayed near them...but it was no use. They were soon outnumbered, and one by one King Richard's soldiers aboard *The Barbara* began to fall to the deck, their lifeless bodies bringing Florie's burned corpse vividly back into Allen's mind.

Allen tried to shut her from his mind, but as his sword cut through the flesh of the soldier in front of him, he winced. As the body slumped to the deck, he could see Florie once more.

Allen grunted, gritted his teeth, and shoved the memory aside. There were more swords coming for him—it was kill or be killed and he had no intention of dying today.

The thought surprised him, but he was soon engaged in melee once more and did not have the time to consider his desire to live.

The fight didn't last long. Soon enough, Sir Adam had a sword to his throat and was ordered to surrender. He grunted the order to lower their weapons, and Allen reluctantly relinquished his sword.

Soon the soldiers from the island were tying the survivors up and lining them up along one side of the deck, while others went below and brought up any remaining cargo that hadn't been swept away or ruined from the storm, including Joan's dowry and Joan and Berengaria themselves.

When the princess and future queen were brought on board, Robin took half a step forward as though he wanted to do something, but three soldiers from the island immediately pointed their swords in his direction and he settled back against the side of the ship beside Much and Allen with a grunt.

Soon everyone–Allen, his friends, Joan, Berengaria, Sir Adam, and all the remaining soldiers–were being loaded into boats and brought to the island. It was indeed Cyprus, they discovered, as they were brought to the castle of one Isaac of Cyprus and thrown into his dungeon.

Chapter 16

As luck would have it, Allen, Much, and Robin ended up in the same cell of the dungeon Issac of Cyprus had thrown them into.

It was a small, square stone room with one tiny window set high in the wall, and a large wooden door leading to the rest of the dungeon. For several days they were stuck in that cell, and Allen tried not to let the memories of the dying soldiers from the skirmish bring forth the memories of his family.

Guards would bring them meals, but otherwise they saw and heard from no one in the days that followed their arrest. Robin spent most of his time banging on the door or attempting to kick it down. Allen grew irritated with his endeavors on the first day, and with each subsequent day spent banging on the door the more frustrated Allen became.

"Oh, give it up already," Allen said one day after Robin threw his shoulder into the door–to no avail. It didn't budge. "Banging against that door is not going to knock it down."

Robin heaved his shoulder into the door again. "We have to get out! It is our duty to rescue Joan and Berengaria!"

"We can't do anything, Robin," Allen insisted, seating himself beside Much. "We're stuck in here."

Robin rubbed his shoulder and sighed, moving toward them and sinking to the floor beside Much. "We have to try."

"Good luck with that," Allen said. "You've been banging against that door for over a week and nothing has happened."

"Perhaps King Richard will come," Much said. "He will come and rescue us and the princesses."

Robin groaned at the mention of the king, putting his head in his hands. "I have failed him."

"We were sorely outnumbered, weak from the storm…you can hardly blame yourself."

"He told them I would take care of them."

"And you did!" Much insisted. "You rescued Joan from being thrown overboard and drowning in that storm."

"And now she's captured…" Robin shook his head. "And so is Berengaria."

"And so are we," Allen said. "Don't paint it too black, Robin. It's not as though we left them to fend for themselves when Isaac of Cyprus attacked. We're all in the same predicament."

"I feel responsible," Robin replied. "And we don't know that we're in the same predicament. We don't know where they are being held or what's being done to them."

"We weren't the only soldiers on *The Barbara* or the other boats run aground. Everyone was captured; in a way we're all responsible for failing to protect Joan and Berengaria."

"You are not making me feel better."

"Listen!" Much said suddenly. Robin and Allen quieted immediately; Much rarely spoke with such conviction. "Someone is outside."

A moment later they heard a key in the lock, and all three of them rose to their feet as the door of their prison swung inward and King Richard stood in the doorway.

"Your Majesty!" Robin bowed.

"Now what are you doing in prison, Robin?" King Richard asked with a laugh.

"I'm so sorry, Sire–"

"Never mind, Robin of Locksley, I was only teasing. I've heard all about it from Berengaria and Joan, not to mention from Isaac himself. He's trying hard to appease me after capturing my sister and fiance."

"Surely he will not go unpunished, Your Majesty?" Robin asked as King Richard led the three of them out of the cell. There were more of the king's soldiers in the hallway, opening other cells and releasing the rest of the prisoners including Sir Adam.

"Of course he will not go unpunished, Robin of Locksley. He saw an opportunity to take my ships when they blew off course, and I now see one to capture his island and claim it for England. I will dedicate it to Berengaria, I think. How does that sound? But come, if we are going to capture this island you will all need your weapons."

It appeared the rest of King Richard's fleet, and that of King Philip, had landed safely at Crete to wait out the storms while *The Barbara* and several others had been blown off course to Cyprus. Once the storm had passed, both kings had brought the rest of the armies to Cyprus to free the prisoners and punish the ruler of Cyprus, Isaac. It did not take long before the combined armies swept through the small island and Isaac surrendered.

King Richard was so pleased with his success that he not only dedicated the island to Berengaria, but he also married her once the island was subdued. It was a simple affair, and was soon over.

As the soldiers dispersed from the gathering, and Isaac of Cyprus and other nobles were dismissed, King Richard stood on the hilltop where the ceremony had taken place with Berengaria, calling Much, Robin, Allen, and Sir Adam over to speak with them.

"You are quite the soldier, Robin," King Richard said without preamble.

"Thank you, Your Majesty. And congratulations to both of you," Robin bowed first to Berengaria, and then to King Richard. Berengaria grinned at him, her arm linked firmly through her husband's.

"I have a mind to promote you to my personal guard, you and your two companions," King Richard said. "Berengaria agrees it would be an excellent idea."

"I do indeed," Berengaria said.

"Allen is an excellent soldier as well," King Richard continued, "from what I've seen and heard, anyway, and I know Much would not want to leave your side."

"I would not wish to leave his side either," Robin smiled at Much. "But our company…?"

"Sir Adam will continue to lead his company as he has been," King Richard said. "You will be my Royal Guard."

Later that night, as Allen and his companions were stationed outside King Richard's door, Much asked, "What will happen to his original guard?"

"No idea." Robin grinned, unconcerned. "I can hardly believe our good luck. Do you think Marian will still scorn me when she finds out I am part of the King's Royal Guard?"

"Marian doesn't scorn you," Much replied.

Allen listened to his friends continue their conversation, though he only half paid attention. Robin was obviously quite smitten with this girl named Marian. Allen could only hope no accident would befall her. He knew only too well the pain Robin would then feel and he did not wish that upon anyone, much less his friend.

He shuddered, picturing the dimple in Eri's cheek when she'd smile at him. His heart squeezed inside his chest, and he turned away from his friends as he fought to regain his composure. He couldn't cry;

114

that would only lead them to ask questions to ascertain what was wrong.

Chapter 17

"There it is!" Much leaned far over the railing on *The Barbara* and Allen's heart leapt to his throat. "I can see the coastline!"

"I am eager to walk on firm ground again," Robin said.

Allen grabbed Much's shoulders and pulled him back toward the boat. "I agree with you, but let's not get off this blasted boat until it is actually safe to do so."

Going ashore would be a relief from the cramped quarters and unpredictable movement of being on a ship. Allen wasn't sure he'd ever truly have what the sailors called 'sea legs' and he was ready to be on dry ground again...but what awaited them on the shore?

The port city of Acre was growing closer as they sailed toward the coastline Much was so eager to see up close. According to Sir Adam, Acre was a fortified city on the coast garrisoned by a large force of Muslims who were besieged by a force of Crusaders commanded by King Guy of Jerusalem. As the fleet sailed toward the port, the army camped outside the city walls became visible.

"Those are more banners than just the Crusaders, aren't they?" Much asked, leaning over the rail again.

"King Guy's forces appear besieged themselves," Robin said. "It must be Saladin's army, trying to break the siege of the city by cutting off the Crusading army..."

Allen rested his hand on his sword hilt, wondering if he'd be required to use it as soon as he left the boat. Despite his dark thoughts always being just below the surface, he wasn't as eager for bloodshed as he had been at the start of the Crusades–he certainly wasn't hoping for his own death anymore. How that was possible, he didn't know. He hardly knew Robin and Much, but somehow their brotherhood gave him hope.

William hadn't inspired him to want to live, so how could two relative strangers?

Allen sighed, closing his eyes as he thought of William. What had become of his friend? He'd gone to France to join King Philip's army, so it was likely he was on one of the hundreds of ships now sailing toward the stretch of beach outside the city.

"Why are we headed for the beach and not the port?" Much asked.

"Obviously the city won't be safe for us to disembark." Robin rolled his eyes, clapping Much on the shoulder. "We have to stay out of reach of any attack the city might mount as we bring relief to King Guy's soldiers. I imagine we're also going to have to avoid Saladin's army, too, which might be more difficult."

The Barbara sailed as close to the beach as possible without running aground, and then the small boats were lowered and soldiers loaded into them to row the rest of the way to shore. Much was put to the oars of their little boat, while Robin and Allen were on archery duty, keeping a watch out for Saladin's soldiers as King Richard sat between them.

The other ships in the fleet were drawing closer to the beach as well, letting down their own small boats filled with soldiers. As everyone hurried ashore, Saladin's troops attempted to mount an attack, his archers firing on the fleet as they came up the beach.

Allen shot arrow after arrow toward the enemy soldiers gathered on the beach, trying to keep his balance as he knelt at the edge of the boat. Every shift in movement from anyone on board–Much and the other soldiers with oars, or Robin firing arrows from the bow–

caused Allen to lose his sense of stability, which in turn made firing his own arrows difficult and ineffective. He wasn't sure he hit anyone at all. Luckily for everyone sailing ashore, King Guy's army sent a force to fend off the attackers so the reinforcements could make it to shore.

As soon as their boat was close to the sandy beach, Robin leapt into the shallow water and pulled the boat the rest of the way onto the sand. There were still a few archers firing toward the incoming soldiers, but King Guy's men seemed to be dealing with them so for the moment there was less danger.

Once the boat was ashore, King Richard jumped from the boat and began moving toward the encampment. Allen kept at his side, bow at the ready. Robin walked on King Richard's opposite side, and Much followed behind. It was strange to be in the King's Guard with no training and no explanation. Allen wondered what had become of King Richard's previous guard. He also wondered if King Richard would still want him at his side if he knew that Allen was, in fact, a Scot. Despite the easy friendship between Allen's father and William, there were often tensions between England and Scotland and the King of England was likely more aware of and invested in them than Allen could be, having been raised by both a Scot and an Englishman.

The soldiers disembarking from the fleet hurried toward King Guy's camp and as soon as they arrived, King Richard met with King Guy to discuss the siege. For several days Allen and his friends stood by King Richard as he directed camp to be set up for the newly arrived armies and gave orders to his generals to attack Saladin and strengthen King Guy's defenses.

King Richard did not participate in the skirmishes that took place along the line of defense between the Crusading army and Saladin's. The siege was far enough from the city walls that there was no immediate fear of harm from that direction, but Saladin's forces surrounding the armies laying siege would mount daily attacks and then be pushed back.

King Richard seemed restless with his duties behind the lines, eager for action, but King Philip had convinced him–at least for now–that he would serve the war effort better if he stayed alive.

Allen, as a member of the King's Guard, stayed at his side which meant he saw no combat either. He wasn't sure if he was relieved or annoyed by that. He wanted to fight–but he no longer wanted to die.

Between King Richard, King Philip, and then the arrival of Duke Leopold of Austria with forces of his own, the Crusaders swelled King Guy's forces to an overwhelming number, and after a few more skirmishes Saladin withdrew his army and let the Crusaders besiege Acre without contest.

When the city was taken a few days later, the Crusading forces moved into the city to take up residence and take control over the most strategic and prestigious places within the city walls. Soon King Richard had his standard put up to fly over the wall of the city. King Philip and Duke Leopold of Austria did the same. The main bulk of the Crusading army remained encamped in the fields outside the city walls.

One morning Allen found himself walking along beside King Richard as he took the steps up to the city wall two at a time. Robin was hurrying along behind them. The sun was shining weakly above them; it was a cool day. Not cold, by any means. Allen was shocked at the difference between a Scottish January and one here in Acre–it was practically summer by comparison.

When they reached the top of the stairs, King Richard marched straight across the walkway atop of the wall toward the three flags flapping in the wind. Without hesitation he reached up and ripped one of them down.

"Sire?" Robin watched him with curious eyes.

"I will not stand for this," King Richard responded to his unspoken question. "Leopold may have been useful here at the battle of Acre, but he is only a *duke*! To fly his standard beside those of myself and King Philip, as though he were an equal? It is an outrage!"

One afternoon Allen sat with his friends outside King Richard's tent. He was meeting with various advisors and generals in the camp, as he so often did. Allen's job—and that of his companions—was to ensure no unsavory sorts interrupted or attacked King Richard. Robin wanted to insist that one of them stay at King Richard's side in case the people he met with also turned out to be a threat, but King Richard laughed at him and said he could handle himself.

A glance around the camp within view showed no one suspicious. Soldiers were lounging around, laughing together, without the slightest concern. The city was taken, Saladin's forces departed, and now they were merely waiting for orders to come down from the two kings as to what to do next.

High over the city walls in the distance flew the standards of King Richard and King Philip. It was rumored Duke Leopold was furious his flag had been ripped down and was threatening to leave the Crusades—though he'd just arrived—in retaliation.

King Richard soon appeared at the flap of his tent, calling for Robin.

"Yes, Your Majesty?" Robin sprung to his feet.

"I have been receiving disturbing news from England for several months now. Letters from those loyal to me in England, and from my mother as well. My brother is doing things that I do not appreciate, trying to seize power in my absence. I saw no reason to burden you with such details as they did not concern you. My brother is trying to seize control of England and in doing so is murdering many nobles who are loyal to me."

"I am sorry to hear it, Sire."

"I am afraid I am now telling you of the troubles in England because I have news that does concern you. Your father was one of those nobles my brother has murdered, Robin. Your father has been killed for his loyalty to myself."

Allen felt a jolt of pain stab his chest, his own father's face flashing before his eyes. He looked quickly to Robin and saw his blue eyes darkening, a frown forming on his handsome face.

"I am sorry, Robin," King Richard continued, "You are the Earl of Locksley now."

King Richard soon returned to his tent and Robin sank slowly to the ground. Much touched his arm gently. "I am sorry, master."

"Allen?" Robin looked up at him with tears welling in the deep sadness of his eyes. Allen shuddered at the sight; he understood the anguish written across his friend's face all too well.

"Yes, Robin?"

"We are in the same position now." Robin glanced at Much. "We three are all orphans now and we only have each other."

"Orphaned brothers-in-arms," Allen responded grimly.

"Precisely. We must stick together, we three."

Allen agreed wholeheartedly. This was his family now, and there was no way on this green earth he would let anything happen to them. He would not lose them like he'd lost his first family.

Duke Leopold of Austria soon made good on his threats and packed up his army and left the Holy Land. The days passed in relative calm, camping outside Acre as King Philip and King Richard established their control and planned for their next move on the long journey to retake Jerusalem. King Guy of Jerusalem was eager for the Crusaders to march that direction and take his city back from the muslim forces and Saladin's army that had taken the city from him in the first place, but he was forced to be patient.

Allen's days were spent watching over King Richard's tent or following him to various meetings, and nights were spent sleeping on the rough ground outside King Richard's tent, taking turns with Robin and Much to keep watch every few hours.

Robin didn't speak of his father's death, but Allen knew it weighed on him. He was not his usual jovial self most days and there was a lingering darkness in his eyes that Allen knew only too well.

Allen's own nightmares of the fire returned after the news of Robin's father being murdered in England. He would wake every night in a cold sweat, Florie's burned corpse swimming before his vision.

One night when he was thrust back into the fire–feeling the heat of it on his skin, choking on the smoke, tripping over Florie's prone corpse–he gasped awake and was immediately aware of shouting voices nearby. Allen bolted upright, glancing around. It was dark, but the moon was shining brightly overhead in a field of stars.

Much, who had been on watch, was calmly sitting beside him. As Allen grew aware of his surroundings, shaking off the remnants of his nightmare, he realized it was King Richard who was shouting from inside his tent.

Allen turned to Much. "How long have they been arguing?"

"A little while. King Philip is upset."

"About his sister it seems." Allen rubbed a hand across his face, still trying to shake the horror of his memories as he listened to the two kings argue over King Richard abandoning the princess of France in order to marry Berengaria.

Suddenly they heard King Philip shout, "I will not stay after all this!"

"Then you will dishonor your kingdom! To abandon the Crusades–"

"I'll leave a few thousand soldiers." King Philip's voice seemed laced with poison to Allen's ears. "My honor is intact. It is yours that is in need of mending. You are on your own, Richard."

King Philip swept out of the tent and Allen and Much scrambled out of his way.

Allen sighed. "You'd better wake Robin. He'll want to know."

Much shook Robin awake and informed him of what they'd overheard.

"And once again, our army is weakened," Robin sighed. "We haven't even begun yet, and already two high ranking nobility have abandoned us."

"We apparently have a rather contentious king," Allen said.

With Leopold and Philip gone, King Richard was now the undisputed leader of the entire Christian army.

Chapter 18

King Richard's next move was to march his army down the coast to the city of Jaffa. From there he planned to begin his march on Jerusalem. Before leaving Acre, however, he had Joan and Berengaria set up in a house with all their needs met and soldiers to keep watch over them.

The road to Jaffa was not a peaceful one; every day the Saracens attacked. Small groups of them would ride toward the marching army, shoot a few arrows, and then flee immediately. The first time it happened, Allen was unimpressed.

"What good do they think that will do? Kill a couple soldiers at a time?"

But the Saracens persisted in this line of attack as the army marched toward Jaffa. They were in and out of range so swiftly that very few of the Saracens died themselves, but each day more were added to the number of deceased in the Crusading army.

"It's effective," Robin grunted, watching the horses of the Saracens disappear over the horizon. "You have to give them that."

Sometimes King Richard would order a company to give chase, sometimes they would simply ignore the archers and keep marching. If a soldier fell, the men of his company collected his body and carried it until the army made camp each night–at which point the dead were buried and stock was taken on how many were lost. On one particular day when the list of the dead was gathered for the evening, Allen learned that their old commander Sir Adam had been among those shot down that day.

He had been a sour old man, and Allen was not particularly sorry to learn of his death.

A few days later, Allen was marching along the road beside Robin and Much as they followed King Richard who was mounted on a horse and leading the army forward. They were not near Jaffa yet, but were rather approaching a city along the way–Arsuf, Allen thought it was called. The sun sinking into the Mediterranean sea to their right–the brilliant oranges and reds in the sky reflected vibrantly across the water.

Suddenly Much noticed the glint of the sun on armor on the horizon and King Richard pulled his horse to a stop, calling for his commanders and captains and preparing to arrange the army to meet whatever threat was headed their way. They were still many miles from the army that was approaching from the south, and it took another day of marching before they were able to make out the individuals among the army and the standards flying over the approaching enemy. As King Richard's forces advanced, it became clear that it was, indeed, Saladin's army they were about to face off against. In the distance the rooftops of Arsuf were visible as the sun shone down brilliantly from the west.

King Richard sent the archers forward first, which included Robin and Allen, and Much was given the sole responsibility of staying at King Richard's side and keeping him safe. Allen clutched his bow tightly in his hand as he followed Robin and the other archers as they scurried forward and into formation as Saladin's forces drew closer.

As soon as they were within range, one of King Richard's captains shouted the order for them to start firing. Allen grabbed an arrow from the quiver over his shoulder and took aim, choosing a soldier at random and focusing entirely on him. Allen took a deep breath, hoping to steady his rapidly beating heart, and then let his arrow fly.

126

Robin and the other archers were firing arrow after arrow on either side of Allen, and he quickly grabbed another arrow to keep up with them. Soldiers fell, but the Saracens continued their march forward, ignoring the bodies. Their own archers began to retaliate, and Allen tried not to panic as arrows rained down on the men around him.

The man to his right fell, an arrow stuck in his throat. He gurgled and coughed for a minute before dying and Allen bit his cheek, trying to ignore the sound as he shot another arrow toward the approaching army.

He could hear Eri coughing in thick smoke.

Allen glanced to the side to see the soldier beside him had stopped choking on his own blood and was dead.

He gritted his teeth and focused on the task at hand, but even as he let another fly, he could see Florie's charred corpse hovering in the air in front of his vision.

An arrow whizzed right past his ear and Allen dropped to a crouch, his heart pounding loudly in his ears as he tried to take deep breaths to calm himself.

"Steady," Robin said, clapping him on the shoulder before continuing to fire more arrows toward the enemy. Allen slowly reached for another arrow to resume his position beside Robin.

Saladin's forces were close enough now that Allen could see their faces—which did not help with calming his nerves at all.

Allen tried not to look in their eyes or notice their expressions as he continued to pick targets and shoot them down. Arrows were still flying from the Saracen army toward Allen and his companions as well, but none hit Allen. He didn't know if he was relieved or disappointed.

127

In not time at all, the approaching army was drawing swords, running forward. Allen's heart leaped to his throat. In another minute they would be close enough to reach out and touch.

"Swords!" The captain's shout came echoing down the line.

Allen swiftly strapped his bow to his back and unsheathed his sword as the nearest of Saladin's men came running toward him. He raised his blade to block an incoming blow, and then deftly parried and struck, cutting down one soldier after another. Robin remained at his side, slicing this way and that with precision.

Within minutes, the neat lines of the two armies were scattered and both sides were intermingled in a bloody chaotic mess. Allen kept his back to Robin so no one could sneak up on either of them as they fought off any Saracens who drew close to them.

Time stretched on in a blur of blood and screams, and soon Allen was numb to it all. He didn't see Eri or Florie in his vision, he hardly saw the dead bodies on the field around him. He only saw the swords. A blade would swing toward him and he would almost mindlessly respond in kind. He was vaguely aware of a dull ache in his arms and shoulders, and somewhere in the distance of his brain he was aware of the screams of dying men, but it was all a faraway hum.

The only thing he could focus on was the next sword to block and parry and strike against.

But suddenly, there were no more swords.

Allen took a shuddering breath, his own blade lowering as he leaned over, resting his hands on his knees as he gasped for breath. Suddenly all of his aches and pains were at the forefront of his mind and he longed to lay down and find relief.

"They've retreated," Robin commented, patting Allen's back. "I'd say we did rather well."

Allen glanced down at his sword, dripping with blood, and shuddered. Those bodies around him…they were someone's Florie. Someone's Eri. Someone's Alice.

Allen clenched his teeth, shutting out those thoughts. What good would it do to dwell on it? They were dead now. That was that.

Robin led Allen away from the bloody battlefield toward where King Richard had stayed to direct the battle from afar. Men began to gather the dead to bury and the wounded to care for. Soldiers were hurrying to and fro around King Richard, all seeming to be busy with dealing with the aftermath of the battle. Much stood beside the king, holding the reins of his horse, his other hand on the hilt of his sword. As Robin pushed through the busyness toward King Richard, Allen could see Much visibly relax when he caught sight of them.

"Robin of Locksley," King Richard greeted him with a smile. "Made it through alright?"

"We did, Sire."

"I am glad of it. More than one of my commanders praised your archery to me after the battle. I'd be sorry to lose such talent so early in the war."

"If that is the only reason you'd miss me, Sire, I'll take it." Robin bowed and grinned.

When the wounded had been cared for and the dead buried, the journey continued southward. Within a few more days of marching they finally arrived at the city of Jaffa.

Chapter 19

King Richard took up residence in a house within the city of Jaffa, and Allen and his companions stayed there as well–keeping watch over King Richard's door at night, and staying by his side during the day as he planned with his advisors and commanders for the march to Jerusalem, and potential attacks on Saladin's forces depending on where the Saracens went next.

The port city itself was built on a high ridge, with a broad view of the sea and coastline below it. If King Richard was not in meetings, he liked to walk along the docks–eyeing what remained of his impressive fleet, no doubt. Allen enjoyed the walks as well; the sparkling deep blue water of the Mediterranean sea was beautiful at any point in the day.

One day, as they stood guard outside King Richard's chamber, he called Robin inside to speak with him. Allen unashamedly leaned against the door to listen.

"Our army is unfortunately dwindling," he could hear King Richard saying, "both due to losses in battle as well as some desertion. I was not expecting to have to deal with such a problem to such an extent as I have. We are on a noble quest, that ought to be enough to give men the motivation to remain true to our purpose. I need your advice."

"About anything specific?"

"We could still take Jerusalem with this army, perhaps, but it becomes a more difficult prospect with every lost soldier; the more desertion we face the more challenging taking the city will be. This is only made worse by the knowledge that most of my men wish to return to their homes in Europe as soon as we conquer Jerusalem. I do not feel

I could command them to stay here in the Holy Land indefinitely, but how will we hold Jerusalem after we leave?"

Allen crossed his arms as he leaned against the door, glancing at Much. He knew Much would be among those eager to return home–and Robin likely would, too, given how often he spoke of returning his to beloved Marian. Allen, on the other hand, did not feel he had a home to return to at all.

"You think Saladin will lead his Muslim forces to take it back as soon as we're gone," Robin said.

"I do. Unless I kill him so they have no one to rally behind."

"So what is your plan? Find Saladin before taking Jerusalem?"

"I do not know. I do not think we should take Jerusalem only to have it fall again."

"I agree."

"There is the possibility of beginning negotiations with Saladin, to see if we cannot come up with a peaceable solution to our problems."

"I see nothing wrong with that, assuming the treaty ends with Jerusalem returned to King Guy and the Saracen control given back to us."

"Thank you, Robin. That is all."

As soon as the door creaked open, Allen pulled away from it and feigned nonchalance, but once Robin had shut it behind him Allen punched his arm.

"Look at that! King Richard seeks out our brother for advice!"

Robin laughed and shook his head.

"I can't believe I am friends with the man that the King of England goes to for advice. A year ago I had never seen King Richard in person."

Robin snorted. "It isn't that impressive, Allen. Stop making more of it than this deserves."

In the following weeks, King Richard did, indeed, send messengers to Saladin's army and received messengers in return. Negotiations for peace had begun.

And then one day, King Richard decided to give his new King's Guard a day of rest and called for his original personal guard to spend the day with him.

"Tired of our company?" Robin had teased, which King Richard had merely laughed at as he waved them off. After ensuring that King Richard did have guards stationed near him, Robin suggested they explore the city.

"Moving from battle to battle is an adventure, to be sure, but it is rather a waste not to see more of our surroundings while we have this chance to travel the world!"

Much agreed, as he always did. Allen wondered if he had opinions of his own that he subdued to give deference to Robin, or if he really was as empty of original thought as he sometimes seemed.

"Have fun, you two," Allen said. "I need some time alone."

"Is everything alright?" Robin asked.

"Of course. I just need some space. I'm not used to constantly having an entire army around me." Allen forced a chuckle to keep Robin from asking more questions. It seemed to work, for soon enough Allen was free of his companions and walking down the narrow street alone–the stone buildings of the city encroaching on either side of the confined street, one long line of stone, with the only breaks being the cross streets. Allen picked up his pace, hurrying to be free of the claustrophobic feeling clawing at his throat as he made his way to the city gate.

Once outside the city, he wandered through the tents that were set up to house most of the Crusading army that had not taken up residence inside the city of Jaffa itself.

Everything was certainly not alright, but he couldn't tell Robin the truth.

He couldn't get his dead family out of his head and he hated killing the Saracens and he felt so weak.

Physically.

Emotionally.

Allen hated the way he was feeling. He marched along the lines of tents, kicking up dirt as he went, ignoring the soldiers around him. He just wanted this entire ordeal to be over.

But what would he do once it was? He had nowhere to go, nothing to bring comfort or purpose beyond the Crusade and Robin and Much.

For a moment, William flashed into his mind. Allen wondered where his friend was now. Was he among the soldiers that King Philip had left in the Holy Land when he had gone home? Was he somewhere in all these tents, even now? Or worse, had he been one of the soldiers lost in battles along the way?

Allen sighed. With his luck, that was probably exactly what had happened to William.

With another sigh, Allen turned around and headed back toward the city.

When Allen arrived at their quarters, he made his way directly to the room he shared with Robin and Much, passing the guarded door of King Richard's chamber on his way. He nodded to the soldiers standing outside, but they merely glared at him. As he made his way to his own room, Allen couldn't help but wonder how long they'd served at King Richard's side before he'd so impulsively thrown them aside for Robin, Allen, and Much instead. They likely resented being cast off in such a manner with no valid explanation beyond king's whim.

When Allen pushed open the door to his room, he stopped in the doorway. Robin and Much were there, conversing with another young man. He was unmistakably an Arab with his tan skin, black hair, and keen dark eyes.

Allen's hand twitched toward his sword hilt at the sight of what he assumed was a Saracen, but Robin and Much seemed perfectly at ease with the stranger.

"Allen!" Robin grinned and waved him into the room. "Joan and Berengaria are here!"

"Really?" Allen stepped into the room carefully, keeping his eyes on the stranger. He was a small man–unlikely to be much of a threat should he prove to be foe. A quick glance showed that no Joan or Berengaria were in the room at all.

"They gathered up some soldiers to protect them and came after the king," Much said.

"This is one of those soldiers," Robin motioned to the silent newcomer as he took a seat in one of the chairs in the room. "And she's a woman, but don't tell anyone."

Allen's eyebrows hit his hairline at Robin's news.

"She's joining the King's Guard with us," Much said, dropping to sit on the floor at Robin's feet. The woman eased herself to a seated position on the floor as well, leaning against the wall under the window.

"But her identity as a woman is to remain secret for her own safety," Robin said.

"You were a part of the guard that protected Joan and the Queen?" Allen took a seat opposite Robin and studied the young Arab woman with open curiosity.

"Yes." The woman spoke softly. She had a deep, earthy sort of voice that resonated with power despite how quietly she had spoken. It made Allen uncomfortable, though he couldn't decipher why.

"Really?"

"Yes."

"And now you are part of the King's Guard with the three of us?" Allen could hardly believe it. Firstly, that King Richard would let another random person join his personal retinue when he clearly still trusted the original men who were currently standing outside his door. And second, that he would ask a woman to be among those who protected him.

"Yes."

"Is that the only word you know how to say in English?"

The woman's eyes began to twinkle, but Much looked horrified. "Allen, that was not a kind thing to say!"

"It is alright, Much," the woman said. "He has not offended me."

"Why do you want to fight anyway?" Allen asked. "You're a girl." Even as he said it, he could see Alice demanding that William teach her to fight the same as Allen.

"Do not say that so loud," Robin said, glancing toward the door and then to the open window. "We don't want that getting around to the men."

"But she *is* a girl!" Allen insisted.

"No," the Saracen laughed, turning her keen gaze on Allen. Something about those eyes seemed to pierce straight through his

136

shattered soul. "I am not a girl. I am a *woman*. I am nearly twenty years old."

"That's certainly older than we are," Robin said. "All three of us are eighteen."

"Triplets?" the Saracen laughed.

"We aren't actually related," Much said.

"But we are brothers-in-arms," Robin said.

"I know," the Saracen smiled. "I can see the attachment between you already; bound together by loyalty and love."

"Loyalty and love," Allen repeated, "That ought to be our mantra, Robin."

Robin laughed. "It does have a nice ring to it."

Despite his shock at a woman being in the army, and a part of the King's Guard no less, Allen was intrigued by this new development. She would not give her name–which was odd, but no matter how hard they pressed she would not yield–so Allen and his friends took to calling her 'the Saracen.'

The three of them, along with King Richard, Princess Joan, and Queen Berengaria were the only ones who knew that she was a woman, and they were sworn to secrecy to protect her. The army had been on the road for so long, there was little telling what might happen if the men found out there was a woman in their midst. They couldn't do anything to the Princess or the Queen, but a woman of low birth would have less chance of being given the respect she deserved.

Allen was rather surprised by how well she disguised herself as a man, with her short-cropped hair and men's clothing. She was not as strikingly beautiful as Princess Joan, so it wasn't as difficult to pass herself off as a slightly-prettier-than-average boy.

Chapter 20

In the weeks that followed the Saracen's arrival, King Richard continued to send and receive messages from Saladin as negotiations for peace continued. His Royal Guard, now consisting of four, stood outside the rooms where he met with his advisors and ambassadors from the Saracen army, and they watched over his room when he retired to sleep. Nothing seemed to be happening. No assassins, no battles. Allen was grateful for the calm, but frustrated with feeling like he wasn't doing anything.

Robin and Allen had a great many questions for the Saracen, but though she was not shy and would converse with them easily, she kept quiet about her past and said very little about herself at all. There was something there—Allen could feel it in her silence, in the sharp look in her keen dark eyes. But she wouldn't talk about it.

He knew now why she'd so unsettled him the first day they'd met. She was grieving, as he was. He could hardly face his own pain, so he understood why she refused to as well. But he could see it in those eyes. He wanted to tell her that he could empathize; even if they never discussed details, surely she would find comfort in knowing that he *understood* the pain behind her eyes.

But he couldn't.

One day as the four of them stood outside King Richard's door, he popped his head out to inform them he had decided to give Joan as a wife to Saladin's brother as a gift in order to appease Saladin himself so that the rest of the terms of the treaty could be in the Crusaders' favor. Much was given the unfortunate task of finding Joan to inform her and bring her to speak with her brother.

"It is hardly a Christian thing to do, to force the princess into such a position," the Saracen said.

"Nonsense," Allen shrugged. "They had arranged marriages in the Bible, I'm sure." He did not necessarily approve of King Richard's decision to use Joan as a bargaining chip–she would certainly be upset by it–but the Saracen's argument did not seem valid.

"Have you ever read the Bible?" Robin raised his eyebrows in Allen's direction.

"Nope. Have you?"

Robin shook his head and laughed.

"I still do not approve of this," the Saracen said.

"He's the king, he doesn't need your approval," Allen replied.

Joan and King Richard had a heated argument over his decision, but King Richard wouldn't change his mind. Word was sent to Saladin later that day and soon the peace offering was accepted and plans were set in motion for a royal wedding.

One day not too long after the announcement of the royal wedding and the peace treaty, Allen lounged against the door behind which King Richard was conducting his business. Joan had just come tramping down the stairs from her room, linking her arm through Robin's and pulling him away from the door and Allen watched their interaction with some amusement.

"Come now, Robin, I need someone to entertain me during my last days as a free woman, before my brother so kindly shackles me to Saladin's brother."

"I am on duty, my lady," Robin replied.

Joan sighed heavily, laying her head against Robin's shoulder. She turned her head slightly, letting her hair fall across her face but it wasn't enough to hide the tears.

Joan was fond of Robin, that much Allen was certain of. She might even be falling in love with him. She likely would have balked at another arranged marriage so soon after losing her beloved husband, but Allen suspected Robin's existence made King Richard's decision that much harder for her.

Robin, for his part, remained polite and kind as always, but it was clear in every encounter that his heart was not likely to be touched; he was still eagerly awaiting his return to his beloved Marian back home in England.

"I must have entertainment before I am a slave," Joan said in a surprisingly chipper voice as she lifted her head from Robin's shoulder, briskly wiping the tears from her cheeks. "Come on, entertain me."

Robin grinned and launched into a wild tale about some trouble he'd gotten himself into as a kid exploring the castle in his hometown of Nottingham and slowly Joan's mood improved.

A week or so later rumors ran through the camp that officials of the church had come all the way from Rome just to speak to King Richard. These rumors proved true for soon they were approaching King Richard's rooms and Robin let them in while Much, Allen, and the Saracen kept watch. Angry voices soon issued from beyond the closed door.

"We should not be listening," the Saracen said. "This does not concern us."

"I am sorry, Saracen," Robin replied. "but I want to know what is going to happen to both Joan and King Richard."

Allen could clearly hear church officials threatening excommunication if King Richard married Joan off to a Muslim—peace treaty or no peace treaty.

Allen glanced toward the Saracen. "No offense to you, I'm sure."

The Saracen turned her sharp gaze on Allen. "I am not a Muslim, Allen of the Dale. I am a disciple of Christ."

"Fair enough," Allen shrugged. "Makes no difference to me."

King Richard and the church officials from Rome had several more heated discussions in the days that followed their arrival, but in the end Joan was free. King Richard rescinded his offer to marry her to Saladin's brother.

King Richard summoned Robin into his chamber after he'd made the decision and messengers had gone to and from Saladin as the change to the peace treaty was discussed. Robin left the door open when he went in to King Richard, and Allen unashamedly leaned against the doorframe to hear what was being discussed inside.

"Saladin is asking too much from me," King Richard said. "I feel we need to teach him who is in charge here. We are only suing for peace for the good of the people, not because we couldn't demolish him in an all-out war."

"Whatever you think, Sire."

"That's Richard to you."

"Right."

"I have decided we are going to move out from Jaffa and march on Ascalon. That city was demolished by Saladin and his forces not too long ago, and I feel we could spend time rebuilding it, at least in part."

"As you wish, Sire."

"Why so formal, Robin?"

"It is habit."

"A habit you fall into more often when you are upset with me, I think. What is your true opinion of marching to Ascalon?"

"You said you wanted to intimidate Saladin, yes? And rebuilding Ascalon will prove to Saladin, what exactly?"

"That he cannot destroy cities and lives without recourse."

"And yet," the Saracen's voice was soft, so King Richard was unlikely to hear her, but Allen and Much could, "we do the same here. Destroying cities and lives without recourse."

Allen studied her serious face, her brows furrowed in such a stern way. Given this was her motherland he couldn't fault her for siding with the people they fought–though it had been her choice to join the Crusading army. Allen was sure he'd find it uncomfortable to fight any cause–however just or noble or whatever–against people in Scotland. He wasn't entirely sure he could have brought himself to do such a thing and he wondered what had led the Saracen to such a choice.

Chapter 21

They set out for the city Ascalon early in the morning just as the sun was rising. The eastern sky was a mass of purples and pinks, the air was fresh and clean, and Allen felt invigorated. They were going to Ascalon because that city had been leveled to the ground by Saladin and they were going to rebuild it. Rebuilding a city. Helping people. No killing involved. Allen was feeling good about life at the moment.

Much seemed to be in a remarkably pleasant mood as well, joining in conversation easily and confidently for once, instead of cowering politely behind Robin. It was a good day all around.

Only a few hours into their march to Ascalon, however, Allen's good mood changed.

The road they marched along cut through two hills, and as they wound their way through them a volley of arrows flew from either side of the road. The arrows cascaded into the marching soldiers, some piercing shoulders, necks, legs. Men fell to the ground lifeless as others reached instinctively for their weapons and spun toward the archers who'd dared attack their caravan.

Allen whipped his sword out of its sheath and stepped in front of King Richard as Much and the Saracen did the same, forming a tight circle around King Richard as Robin grabbed his bow and nocked an arrow to the string, searching for a target along the hilltops.

He didn't have to wait long.

As soon as the volley of arrows ceased, the enemy soldiers came pouring down the hillside and into the ranks of the soldiers congested in the road. Allen was once more surrounded by bloodshed and screaming and he sank into the numb places of his mind where he

145

was only aware of the blade nearest him, moving through the motions of blocking, parrying, cutting, in a singularly focused way.

Allen blocked an incoming sword with his own blade, and punched a second assailant in the face. As the fight around him thickened, he did his best to stay beside King Richard. His companions were doing the same, but it wasn't easy.

Another sword came arcing toward him and Allen ducked beneath the swing and put his own blade into his opponent's chest. He winced as he removed his sword, trying desperately not to think about his family, or the possible family of the now dead soldier in front of him.

In the press of the battle, Allen soon found himself a few feet away from his companions. Thrusting his sword into another enemy, Allen sidestepped an incoming blade to his left. He pivoted, swinging his sword in a low cut and knocking the next swing of his enemy out of harm's way with his vambrace. He'd probably have a bruise after that stunt. Allen didn't have much time to worry about that though, because he suddenly heard Robin cry out in pain.

Allen swung around, forgetting his opponent for the time being. Robin was falling to the ground, blood clearly soaking through his tunic and mail shirt.

For a moment, everything around Allen froze.

Florie's unseeing eyes. Alice's charred face.

Baby Duncan.

Allen felt his opponent's blade pierce his shoulder just as he saw the Saracen dart to Robin's side and drop to her knees. The pain in his shoulder brought him back to the present, and Allen turned around and sliced the offending man's head off.

He then heard the Saracen behind him. "Allen! Watch my back!"

"On it!" He called back, rushing through the chaotic battle, shoving aside any soldiers–from either army–to get to Robin. The Saracen seemed to be attempting to bind up Robin's wound, but Allen had little hope.

Robin was going to die.

White hot anger coursed through Allen's veins as he stood over his friends, defending them from the oncoming soldiers. It wasn't fair.

Perhaps his father had always been right about that Logan clan curse. Everywhere Allen went, death followed him.

Allen gritted his teeth. If Robin died, he was going to kill something.

Someone? A lot of someones.

Anything.

He relished the chance to plunge his sword into the neck of an approaching enemy, yanking it out and turning toward the next foe, fury and grief and fear coursing through his veins in a fiery heat not unlike the one that had taken his family from him.

Slowly the enemy was dealt with and the battle came to a close. As soon as Allen was free of any opponents, he quickly cleaned his sword and spun toward Robin in the same swift motion.

Allen placed a hand on the Saracen's shoulder. She was still kneeling beside their fallen friend. Allen's hands were trembling as his knees gave way and he sank to the ground beside the Saracen.

"I believe he will be fine, Allen," she said softly.

The relief that flooded Allen's veins almost made him collapse. He swayed slightly and stared at her, and then at Robin.

147

Robin looked pale, and was breathing heavily, but when he caught Allen's eye, he grinned. Allen shifted to Robin's other side so the Saracen could continue her work unimpeded.

Allen pulled his friend into a sitting position, letting Robin rest against his chest. "Don't ever scare me like that again."

"Apologies." Robin's voice was weak, but it was also filled with teasing laughter.

"Robin!" Much came running over from where he'd presumably been doing the job the rest of them had failed at–protecting the King of England.

"I am fine, Much. The Saracen has cleaned my wound. It isn't so bad."

"You will be weak," the Saracen put in, "and in pain for some days, I imagine. This was not a small cut."

"But I will live, thanks to you."

"The wound is not so deep," the Saracen shrugged, wiping the remnant of the salve from her hands to her trousers before putting her pouch back on her belt. "Perhaps you would not have died from it at all."

"But I was incapable of protecting myself either way, and would have died at the hands of those soldiers if you had not been there. You were magnificent! I've never seen anyone fight like that before; you are quite the warrior, Saracen."

"Thank you, Robin."

Allen could feel a smile forming on his face, despite his frustration and fear over Robin nearly dying.

Robin suddenly shifted his weight off of Allen and grinned at the Saracen. "I cannot continue to call you by no name. You have become a friend in the last month, and now you have saved my life."

148

"What would you call me?" the Saracan asked, her voice as soft and calm as always.

"Warrior," Robin said with a wink.

Allen snorted, shaking his head as he playfully whacked Robin's shoulder. "That is not a name."

"Dustin, then," Robin said. "It means the same."

"That does not seem very feminine." Allen rolled his eyes, feeling tears of relief rising to the surface as Robin's cheerful self made itself evident.

He was going to live. He was going to be fine.

"You seem very opinionated about a name that isn't yours," Robin replied, elbowing Allen as he leaned against him for support.

"Dusty," Much said quietly. "Call her Dusty."

"Dusty…" the Saracen whispered, seeming to feel the sound of it, the weight of it on her tongue. She smiled at Much. "I like it."

"Dusty; the warrior, healer, and friend of mine," Robin said. "I like it, too."

"Dusty it is then."

Chapter 22

After the army's arrival at Ascalon, they set about rebuilding the citadel. As much as Allen had actually looked forward to the work, he ended up doing none of it. He and his companions did nothing more than stay by King Richard as he met with his commanders and made plans for the future while other soldiers were put to the task of rebuilding.

The ceasefire that had been in place while they were in Jaffa crafting a peace treaty was now over, and what came next occupied King Richard's mind a great deal.

"You are not bored again, are you?" Dusty asked one day as they stood outside the room where King Richard was meeting with several captains, making plans.

"Not bored," Allen responded. "Just wishing we had something to do. I would have liked to build the city or do something other than stand around."

"King Richard must be protected. What we are doing is vastly important."

"I know," Allen sighed.

"At least this is better than the killing," Dusty said quietly. Allen didn't respond. He agreed, of course, but he didn't feel like talking about it.

He'd been so horrified by the death they incurred that he spent every battle reaching for a numb place in his mind. Yet the way he'd been almost enjoying the act of killing soldiers in their last skirmish, when he'd been overcome by grief over Robin's apparent death, scared him. He wasn't about to tell Dusty that, though.

151

King Richard's zeal soon led him to change his mind about not taking Jerusalem directly, and he marched his army in that direction. They had not been marching toward Jerusalem for more than a week before it began to rain. The rain continued for days and slowed their progress. Some days it poured, drenching them to the bone and making it difficult to see, and some days it was a slow and steady trickle that was more annoying than anything else, keeping everything from their socks to their hair soaked. The road soon became a slosh of mud that the soldiers struggled through.

Only a few days of this weather was necessary to bring the attitudes around Allen to an all-time low. The rain was bad enough, but Robin scowling instead of carrying his usual jovial smile, and Much complaining when he was usually the least likely person to do so, was more than Allen could handle.

As they slogged through the mud, walking behind King Richard, Allen glanced to his left. Dusty was walking there, a slight frown on her face as she concentrated on getting one foot after the other out of the sticky mud. Allen suddenly felt a strong desire to bring a smile to her face, like he used to always feel around Alice.

And so he jumped.

Mud went splattering in all directions and Dusty looked over with a slightly exasperated expression on her face.

"Allen!" Robin complained, shaking off the mud that had landed on his arm after Allen's jump. "The weather is bad enough, we don't need your help in our misery."

"Robin, my friend," Allen grinned. "Can you not tell that I am trying to lessen the misery? If you cannot have fun then what is life worth?"

152

Robin's eyes began to twinkle and suddenly he was hopping through the mud too. Much just watched with something like tolerance written all over his face. Allen got the feeling he was more than used to antics such as this.

Robin and Allen hopped together, splattering mud all over their companions. Dusty did not join in the jumping in the mud, but she couldn't help laughing. That was all that was needed to brighten the mood.

The dark clouds still hung low over them and the rain still chilled them to the bone, but Dusty's laugh brightened everything around her. Even King Richard turned around long enough to smile in her direction.

Dusty laughing, not chuckling derisively or quietly to herself, but outright laughing was a new thing and Allen made it a personal goal to make it happen more often.

Due to the excessive rain, King Richard soon brought his army to a halt at the city of Beit Nuba. For some days the soldiers of the Crusaders' army shivered miserably in tents set up outside Beit Nuba while King Richard and his guard gathered inside a house on the edge of town. The rain continued, and soon it began to hail each day as well.

In the days spent at Beit Nuba waiting out the weather, Allen kept trying different ways to make Dusty laugh. He did not succeed the way he had when jumping through the mud, but he could get her to smile and that was its own reward.

In the end, King Richard decided to delay the march to the city of Jerusalem because of the inclement weather and the effect it had on morale as well as the health of his army, and returned his men to the city of Ascalon. There were a few more skirmishes between the

Crusaders and Saladin's army in the weeks that followed, but no large-scale battles.

One day Robin was called into King Richard's chambers with his other advisors as they made plans. Allen leaned up against the door and Dusty swatted his arm. "Stop eavesdropping."

"I'd like to know what's happening next."

"Robin will tell us when he comes out," Dusty replied, her glaring at him.

Allen ignored her and pressed his ear to the wooden door, though her frustrated expression stirred the same affection in his chest that he'd once felt for Alice when watching her disapproving face. The thought brought a smile to Allen's face for a moment, for both Dusty and Alice.

Dusty crossed her arms but said nothing further. In another moment, however, the door swung open and Robin stood there grinning as Allen tried to retain his balance after losing the support of the door he'd been leaning against.

"King Richard says you can break for lunch, he's going to call for other guards to stand at your post while you eat."

"I think he knows you like to eavesdrop," Much said.

Allen shrugged. "Lunch it is, I guess."

Robin returned to the room with King Richard after assigning new soldiers to the post outside the door, while Allen, Dusty, and Much gathered a meager lunch–provisions were always relatively scarce in the army, made worse when they weren't near a thriving city–and moved outside to find a place to sit and eat in the sunshine. They'd soon settled atop a wall overlooking the sea.

"It's hardly fair Robin is trusted and we are not," Allen commented. "Besides, King Richard knows he's just going to come tell us what's happening anyway."

"It's possible they do discuss private matters that Robin does not disclose to you," Dusty replied.

It wasn't long before Robin came striding down the street below them and cheerfully pulled himself up onto the wall beside Much.

"I have news."

"Good news or bad news?" Allen asked.

"Just news. We're marching again. Apparently Saladin has captured another city that was under European rule and is now most definitely not, and he wants it back."

"What city?" Much asked. "And how long of a march will it be?"

"It's a city called Darum," Robin replied.

"We are marching to Darum?" Dusty's voice shook slightly as she spoke, and Allen stared at her. For the first time since he'd known her, she looked terrified. She'd gone pale and her lower lip trembled, her eyes wide and unable to rest a single surface for more than a fraction of a moment.

"That is what King Richard has decided," Robin said.

"We're capturing Darum," Dusty repeated.

"Releasing it from Saladin's capture, but yes."

"I cannot go." She drew her legs up underneath herself, seeming to shrink somewhat. She was always confident and sure of herself and what she believed, but now her hands were shaking from whatever emotion she was feeling. Allen wondered if that darkness and grief he felt they shared was somehow coming to the surface.

155

"Why can't you go to Darum?" Much asked, reaching out his hand and laying it gently on her arm.

"I cannot," Dusty repeated, her voice strong despite her physical shaking. She was determined, if nothing else.

"Dusty, what is wrong?" Robin asked, leaning around Much to get a better view of her.

Dusty looked between Much and Robin, then glanced toward Allen. He was shocked to see tears glimmering in her eyes.

"It is…Darum is where I come from. The city of my birth."

"You don't want to fight against your own city?" Allen asked, trying to ascertain why she was so upset and what it had to do with her refusal to ever talk about her past or share her true name with them. "It is only Saladin we are after, is it not? It is possible we won't destroy the town itself or its inhabitants."

"Like there wasn't a massacre at Acre?" Dusty snapped. "But no, it is not that I don't wish to fight my own city. The people of Darum are mostly descendants of the Crusaders from the First and Second Crusades, or like myself have both European and Arab blood in their line. The connections the people of Darum have to England, France, Germany–the Holy Roman Empire as a whole–are strong. That is likely why Saladin keeps attacking that city. Those who are left will not fight against the Crusaders."

"Those who are left?" Robin asked.

"Saladin captured my city when I was eighteen," Dusty said. "He destroyed the politically strong there, devastating the city and the people. So many families' lives were destroyed as he dismantled the power of the Crusaders there."

"That's when you lost your own family," Robin said.

156

"Yes." The single word seemed to hang in the air over the group, heavy and dark. Allen's anger flared, intense and hot. Why did everyone have to lose so much? It wasn't fair.

"I am so sorry," Robin said.

"So am I," Dusty replied. "But I cannot go back to Darum. I couldn't...I haven't been back there since..."

Dusty's voice trailed off, but Allen understood that sentiment. He hadn't returned to his home after the fire. He'd lived with William for a while and then run off on the Crusades. He didn't plan on ever going back to Scotland or seeing the destruction of that fire ever again.

"I understand." Robin spoke to Dusty gently, yet his voice was firm. "But we cannot leave you behind."

"I do not see why not," Dusty said. "I only joined up with your army provisionally, given Joan's insistence. And I do appreciate the friendship the four of us have found together, but I can't go back. I won't. I don't have any allegiance to King Richard; I am not one of his subjects. I don't have to go. I won't."

Much wrapped his hand around hers. "Perhaps going back will help you finally face your grief."

Dusty closed her eyes, a frown forming on her lips as tears slipped down her cheeks. After a moment, she opened her eyes and nodded. "You are right. I will pray for the strength to return to Darum and face my past. Perhaps it will be good for me."

The details of her story began to shift into place in Allen's mind, and he cocked his head to the side as he studied her troubled expression. "I thought you were a Saracen."

Much, Robin, and Dusty turned to look at him, confusion at the change in topic written over all three faces.

"What?"

157

"We all thought you were a Saracen, that's why we called you that before you had the name Dusty. But you said the inhabitants of your city were mostly descendants of the earlier Crusades."

"Yes, they were. I myself am a child of both descendants of the European Crusaders and also native Palestinians. I was never a Muslim, as Saladin and most of his soldiers are, but when he attacked my city I hid my identity–dressed like a man, let them recruit me as a soldier and sympathizer. I lived with what you call Saracens–and then at the first opportunity I joined with the Crusading army. I do not often agree with the decisions of King Richard and those in charge–I do not feel the same fervor that they do in terms of who should live and rule in the Holy Land. Uprooting the people who live here or forcing them to abide by your customs and religions is not the way of life that I would wish to pursue. I wish there was peace. But Saladin himself? He destroyed my people, my city, my family. You are fighting him, and that is enough for me for now."

"Dusty, I am so sorry that this happened to you," Robin said. "It's only been, what? Two years? I understand on some level the grief that you feel, and the anger. My own father was murdered by those seizing power in England during King Richard's current absence. I don't know the details–I haven't gone home yet, I don't know what all happened–but I understand."

"It is alright," Dusty said, straightening her shoulders as her voice grew in confidence. "Do not fret over me. I have been well looked after by the Lord, and now I have you three whom I have come to count on as my second family."

Allen wasn't sure what exactly Dusty thought her God had to do with their friendship. He certainly hadn't saved her family, had he?

"I would be proud to call you my sister," Robin replied.

158

"Thank you."

Allen emphatically agreed. She was nothing like Alice, but he loved her all the same. It didn't matter that they did not share blood, or even a native land. She was the sister he had chosen.

Chapter 23

As they neared the city of Darum, Allen kept a close eye on Dusty. Robin and Much also seemed to be watching her. There was a deep sadness in her eyes, but she held herself together, never showing the break of emotion that she had when she first heard about the trip to Darum.

When the city came into view, Saladin's forces garrisoned there came to meet them and the general chaos of battle plans being drawn up and soldiers put into formation began. King Richard was issuing orders to his captains, the companies of soldiers were rearranging themselves to prepare to meet Saladin's forces, and Allen and his friends stayed at King Richard's side. His Majesty had adjusted his approach to the war after the earliest days in the Crusade—there was no commanding from the rear now. King Richard lived for the battles, wanting to lead from the front and be in the thick of things.

The battle commenced with archery but soon turned to swordplay as it so often did. Allen let his conscious mind drift away from the bloodshed and the sounds of horror around him, narrowing his focus to only his muscle movement as he fought off any opponents.

Saladin's forces retreated for a time, and a rough camp was made for the night, but they were back at it again in the morning. For five days the tide of the battle ebbed and flowed, and Allen tried his best not to see the bodies piling up; every night his nightmares returned.

The first night, Allen awoke in a cold sweat, Eri's name strangled and dying in his throat. He could only hope he hadn't screamed aloud. The second night it was baby Duncan turning to ash and dust in his arms that had him stirring awake long before the sun. He had no desire to try and sleep again after that. He began to insist that he take more watches while Robin, Much, and Dusty slept, merely to avoid more visions of his dying family.

Eventually, however, Saladin removed himself from Darum, fleeing the city with the remainder of his forces and the Crusaders took over the city. Some of the city was still standing, but there were portions of the city that were little more than charred remains as though from a massive fire, and there were many stone buildings that had been torn down and stood in crumbled ruins.

Allen could see his own home, burning. Feel the heat of the fire searing his skin. His lungs were burning from the thick smoke clogging his airway.

His house was collapsing on his family as the rain pounded against him.

His throat was raw from screaming.

Allen shuddered. He glanced at his companions, but no one was paying attention to him. King Richard was eyeing their surroundings thoughtfully, and Robin and Much were watching Dusty with concern.

Had Dusty's family been burned to death like his own family had been? Allen could feel the anger coursing through him again. It was cruel, too cruel, this life.

As King Richard marched down a street in the city with Allen and his companions at his side, he was thoughtful. "There are few left in this city who were not a part of Saladin's forces. What has become of the city's population?"

"They were killed, Sire," Dusty said.

"Ah. That is unfortunate." The nonchalant tone with which King Richard spoke made Allen want to punch him. Unfortunate? Dusty's family had been lost here!

162

"Yes, it is." Dusty's voice was soft. Her eyes remained firmly on the toes of her boots rather than at King Richard or at the surrounding city. When they had entered the city, tears had been visible in her eyes but still she did not break down. Allen silently commended her for her strength. He would not have been so strong.

"I do feel invigorated from this victory," King Richard said, surveying their surroundings with his hands on his hips. "I believe we should try to march on Jerusalem once more. It was only bad weather that deterred us the last time, and the weather is fair now. And more than that, we have Saladin and his army on the run."

King Richard's army began to make camp in and around the city of Darum—most of which was an eerie ghost town since so few of the inhabitants remained. King Richard retired to his chamber to sleep after his long five days of battle, and Allen and Robin took up the first watch at his door.

Allen sagged against the door, longing for a reprieve. Every muscle in his body ached from the exertion of the last five days, and on top of the fatigue of battle, his sore muscles were now feeling the tension of anger and concern for Dusty—not to mention the nightmares plaguing his sleep every night.

"We'll get a rest soon," Robin commented, leaning against the door beside him. The hallway was relatively dark but for a few candles in sconces placed strategically along the walls.

"I have the distinct feeling our king is selfish."

"Perhaps."

"And entirely too callous about the tragedies that occured here. 'Ah, that is unfortunate.'" Allen rolled his eyes, his hands curling into fists at his side as he repeated King Richard's words and tone from earlier in the day.

"He does not know of Dusty's painful past here."

"That is no excuse to be so…uncaring about the deaths here."

"We're fighting a war." Robin sighed, shoving a hand through his blond hair. "I am sorry for Dusty, and everyone else who has lost loved ones in these battles…but it is war, and there will be casualties."

"You are not very good at comforting someone."

Robin shrugged and sighed. "I am tired; I do not have the energy to be empathetic just now."

Within a few days, King Richard and the other leaders of his army were doing as King Richard had suggested and using the momentum of the victory at Darum to march to Jerusalem. This time, they did indeed come in sight of the city, but before they could lay siege to it the various rulers and nobles once more began to bicker.

Within a few days of the standstill, King Richard summoned his personal guard into his room to vent. The army's camp spread out along the horizon in hundreds of tents, and in the distance the city of Jerusalem could be seen shining on the hill.

"I have decided marching on Jerusalem is not a wise decision. I was correct in my initial reluctance. If we take the city we will not be able to hold it. I believe we should march down toward Egypt instead, and invade that territory. We could weaken Saladin's power that way, given that is where he is from and where much of his power is drawn from originally. Once we weaken him–take his seat of power, ensure he has nowhere to run and fewer allies to turn to–we could force him to relinquish Jerusalem to us. Staying here, marching on the city, would mean a lengthy siege and even if we took the city Saladin would simply amass his army and strength and come take it back. Rather than play tug-of-war, we should be rid of Saladin himself."

"The Duke does not agree with you?" Robin asked, referring to the Duke of Burgundy, King Richard's right hand in the war effort.

"No. He believes that a direct attack on the city is the best course of action, despite the tug-of-war that will follow.

"We did come all the way here," Allen pointed out.

"I do not believe attacking the city will accomplish anything in the long run," King Richard replied. "I simply refuse to do so."

"You refuse?" Robin asked. "Wasn't this your idea? What does the Duke say?"

"He has refused to march to Egypt with me. I cannot take Egypt alone, and he cannot take the city of Jerusalem without me. We are at an impasse."

"Surely some arrangement could be made," Robin said. "A compromise."

"I have said I will accompany his attack on Jerusalem but I will not lead the army. I would only go as a simple soldier. So I will not command my mend to lay siege to the city, I will not give them direction to attack at all. The Duke of Burgundy would have to do so."

"The entire army will not answer to the Duke," Robin said. "They won't follow anyone but you."

"I know." King Richard looked rather smug.

"So what will we do?" Much asked.

"If we cannot agree on a course of action, the next step would be negotiating peace with Saladin," King Richard sighed. "There is nothing else to be done. Either we attack the city as a unified whole–which I refuse to do–or we march to Egypt–which the Duke refuses to do."

"You're going to call for a ceasefire and negotiate peace simply because you cannot find a way to agree with the nobles who lead this army with you?" Robin shook his head. "I suppose there are worse reasons to end a war. But you didn't accomplish what you set out to do."

"Perhaps not. Jerusalem may be lost to us for now, but much of the kingdom has been restored to Guy of Jerusalem, and he can set up his capital in Acre for now."

"Until Saladin roots him out."

"Which he will not do because we are negotiating a peace treaty."

"I suppose that's it then," Robin shrugged.

King Richard sighed and then gave a firm nod. "I suppose it is."

The army soon retreated back to the coast to the city of Jaffa and negotiations with Saladin began once more. With the end of the war presumably close at hand, King Richard sent his wife and sister Joan back home. The day they packed up and boarded a ship at Jaffa to sail for Europe and make their way to Aquitaine where the Queen Mother Eleanor was living, Joan had thrown herself into Robin's arms for a last hug and cheerfully kissed Allen and Much on the cheek, before giving a much longer and more affectionate farewell to Dusty and her brother the king.

After the departure of Joan, there was little of interest to interrupt the days of the King's Guard. They stayed beside King Richard as he moved around town and spoke to various nobility and royalty, they watched as he dictated messages to send to Saladin and received messages in return, and they stood watch outside his door when he met privately with his advisors—which often included Robin nowadays.

Allen tried not to think about the future. If the war ended… where would he go? Anytime the question rose in his mind, he shoved it down again.

Chapter 24

Allen studied the Mediterranean sea sparkling in hues of green and blue beyond the harbor filled with ships as he stood beside King Richard; preparations were being made to load the army into a fleet of ships and send them home again. Dusty and Much seemed lost to their own thoughts as King Richard and Robin chatted amiably. Peace was not yet secured, but King Richard felt it was close.

The sounds of shouts and running feet broke the calm a moment later. Allen spun around, hand immediately at his sword hilt, and saw a couple of soldiers come running across the docks from the city.

"Your Majesty! Saladin is coming!"

"I did not know to expect him," King Richard said. "Though perhaps meeting in person will move things along swifter than our missives have been able to."

"No, Your Majesty, you don't understand." The soldiers ran up, breathing heavily, both of them looking wide eyed and afraid. "Saladin is coming with his army. They are mounting an attack on the city walls even now!"

"What?!"

King Richard's hand went instinctively to his sword hilt at his waist. "Show me."

King Richard strode after the soldiers who had brought the news as they hurried back into the city and along the streets. Allen and his companions made haste along beside him.

"What is Saladin thinking, with peace so near?" Dusty asked.

"He has been reluctant to relinquish his power," King Richard replied. "This must be his last ditch effort to assert control so that he can demand a surrender–with terms to his liking, because we would have no negotiating leverage–rather than a peace treaty."

When King Richard reached the city walls, it became clear that there were, indeed, Saracens trying to breach the city gates and archers shooting down any Crusading soldiers who were unlucky enough to show their heads above the wall.

King Richard strode along the wall in search of his commanders and began issuing orders. Robin and Allen were sent to join the Crusading archers along the wall to deter any of Saladin's forces from continuing with their efforts to breach the city.

Allen found a place between two other archers and knelt beneath the parapet to keep out of reach of any of the Saracens' arrows as he pulled his own bow from his back. Peeking around the parapet, careful not to reveal too much of his face as he did so, Allen chose a target down below–one of the opposing archers–and fired into the chaos outside the gates.

The archer dropped to the ground, dead.

Once more Allen let his mind drift away from the violence he was inflicting as he focused on the simple and precise motion of nocking an arrow to his string and letting it fly. Again. And again.

Before too long, King Richard's armed forces–including Much and Dusty–surrounded the Saracens outside the city walls and melee ensued. Allen kept an arrow to the string of his bow, trained on the chaos below. He stopped firing for fear of hitting his allies, but he kept an eye out for any target he could hit without fear of shooting down the wrong person.

The battle was over faster than any Allen had fought in yet. Within minutes, the wounded were being gathered, the dead buried, and King Richard was angrily demanding a meeting with Saladin.

With the battle lost and Saladin's forces destroyed, negotiations for a peace treaty resumed–this time with little grace on King Richard's part. There was tension on every side as messages were sent back and forth. Still, despite the tensions, a treaty had been finalized within a week's time.

"What was the final outcome of the treaty?" Much asked. Robin had just exited the King's chambers where the treaty was being finalized.

"But we did not do what we set out to do," Allen said.

"Neither side is completely satisfied with this treaty, I think," Robin said. "But it is what it is, for now at least. Until someone decides there needs to be a fourth Crusade. But the monetary drain on the treasuries of the royals in Europe and the lives lost in this war that would potentially have no end–neither side being overwhelmingly larger in number, and every other battle being won by the opposite side–if we did not come to a compromise in this treaty, the Third Crusade might never end."

"So it's done," Much said.

"Yes, I believe it is."

"And we can finally return home."

A pang shot through Allen's heart at Much's comment.

"I don't have a home to return to," Dusty said, voicing precisely what Allen had felt.

"You're coming with us." Robin grinned, throwing his arm around Dusty's shoulders. "You and Allen both are more than welcome in our home."

"Thank you," Dusty said. "I would be glad of that."

"So would I," Allen agreed. "You three are all the family that I have."

There was always William, of course, but Allen hadn't the slightest idea where he might be now–if he'd made it to the Crusades, if he'd died along the way…

It was not long after the peace was finally agreed to that King Richard and his Crusading soldiers were finally loading onto the fleet of ships that had arrived to take them all back to their various homes in Europe. It was a sunny day when Allen and his friends–along with King Richard–boarded their ship to sail for England, but the fair weather did not last and storms soon overtook them.

As the ship pitched violently in the rough waves, Allen and his companion went below deck to wait out the weather. Dusty had never sailed before, let alone during a storm, and was soon losing the contents of her stomach across the floor. Allen could hardly blame her–his own stomach was longing to do the same.

When the ship's erratic movement slowed, Robin suggested they go above deck to see if the storm had passed. Allen allowed Dusty to lean heavily on his arm as they moved toward the ladder that would lead them above deck, and then helped her up the ladder itself. When they emerged from the darkness below, she made her way unsteadily over to the railing at the side of the boat, gripping it with white knuckles.

The dark clouds still hung low overhead, and the waves were not calm yet though they weren't quite as large and violent as they had been. Allen leaned against the rail beside her, looking up at the ominous clouds. "I hope it doesn't start up again."

"You and me both."

There were no other ships in the vicinity and Allen wondered if they'd all gone down in the storm, or if King Richard's boat had been blown off course.

"Look, there's King Richard," Allen commented, catching sight of him not far from them, speaking with the captain of the ship.

"You can't help yourself can you?" Dusty shook her head disapprovingly, but she was smiling. "You always have to eavesdrop."

"You'll find out all sorts of interesting things when you listen to people," Allen replied. "For instance, the captain is saying we're off course. He thinks the nearest port might be Corfu, Greece, but he's not absolutely sure."

"We're lost?"

"This tends to happen to King Richard. I think he's cursed." Allen winked at Dusty, bringing another smile to her face, though the mention of a curse sent a shudder through his heart. His father had always believed Allen's family was cursed, and Allen had little experience to deny such a thought. His entire life was one disaster after another. "Come on, let's tell Robin and Much what we've learned."

As Dusty let go of the railing, she nearly fell. Allen wrapped an arm around her waist to give her support. "Come along, I see Robin and Much."

Allen hurried across the deck, keeping Dusty upright along the way, and then relayed his news to Robin and Much. The latter was not at all pleased with the news.

"I hope it isn't a long stop. I am eager to be home," Much said.

"So am I," Robin agreed. "I need to see Marian's face again. I swear the closer we get to returning home to England, the more desperate I become just to see her smile, to hear her laugh. Do you suppose she missed us terribly?"

173

"I am sure she missed you," Much said.

"I hope so."

As the storm continued to settle, their ship made its way toward the nearest port on what did, indeed, turn out to be the island of Corfu. Once the limping ship docked, King Richard made arrangements to stay at an inn for the night with his four guards, while the captain of the ship and the sailors made their own arrangements for repairs to the hull, mast, sails, and such that had been harmed in the storm.

Once they went ashore and settled into their lodgings, Allen and his companions gathered around a table at the inn and began to dig into a meal with gusto.

"I am rather tired of all my ships being sent off course," King Richard said around a bite.

"Does this happen often?" Dusty asked. "I have never sailed before this, but Allen commented that you might be cursed in this regard."

Allen choked on his drink of ale, sputtering for a moment and sending Dusty a look that clearly meant he hadn't wanted that comment related to King Richard.

King Richard, however, chuckled. "Allen may be right. We were sent off course on our way to the Holy Land as well. I believe Much was almost lost overboard on that adventure..."

"We were above deck when the storm hit," Allen said, leaning across the table and grinning widely as a deep blush spread across Much's face. "The huge waves crashing over the deck and sweeping all but the most hardened sailors off their feet! I'm sure you can picture it. The storm was wild. We'd all begun to run below deck, but Much here noticed Joan was in some trouble, caught up in a wave."

Allen relished telling the dramatic tale, particularly because Much was slowly sinking lower in his seat, blushing, and looking very much like he wanted to disappear. Allen felt such a rush of affection and familiarity watching him–it was not unlike teasing Alice had once felt.

"He ran to help her–very valiant of him–but what he actually succeeded in doing was being washed overboard!" Allen continued his tale, his eyes dancing with mischief. "Joan nearly went overboard, too, but Robin caught her. I'll never forget how he looked, one arm gripping the rail of the ship, his body dangling over the angry ocean, with Joan wrapped in his other arm, hanging on for dear life. And poor Much, practically drowning down below. It was a rather shining moment for our daring Robin of Locksley."

"It wasn't that exciting," Robin said. "I was soaked through, trembling with cold, and straining as I tried not to let go of the ship or Joan. It was actually rather painful, to be honest."

"Your troubles only make the act that much more heroic," Allen said.

"And clearly you managed to hang on and save Joan," Dusty said. "And Much was rescued successfully…"

"Yes, it all turned out quite right," King Richard said. "I am glad, for Robin has been invaluable to me during this war."

When the meal came to an end, everyone retired for some much needed rest. King Richard soon made it clear, however, that he had no intention of sailing the rest of the journey home. Once they'd sailed from Corfu to a nearby port in Italy, King Richard intended to travel by foot. In order to maintain his safety on such a venture, he insisted on going in secret. He called his King's Guard together to demand they all call him Richard and forget he was a king at all. Much protested at this, but the rest could see the wisdom in traveling in secrecy.

175

Part 3

The Imprisonment

Chapter 25

"We cannot stay in one place for too long for fear of drawing attention to ourselves," King Richard said one night as they settled into their rooms at an inn, the snow falling heavily outside and covering the world in white. "So we will live in this village for a handful of weeks and then travel a short distance to another nearby, and so forth. I do not wish to travel great distances in this weather, but I also know we cannot stay in one spot for long."

The group had been traveling for some weeks, keeping King Richard's–or rather, only Richard's now–identity a secret. They traveled by day, and spent the night in one city or another, slowly making their way through Europe. Allen had almost forgotten what true cold could feel like after so long in the warmer climate of the Holy Land, but now the weather began to slowly resemble his childhood in Scotland with the icy winds, freezing rain, and the cold that sank into his bones. It was almost enough to make him homesick.

In one of the villages where they stayed for a handful of weeks, Robin had managed to procure a chess set which he then carried with him for the rest of their journey. As the snow fell outside, the group would gather in one of their rooms, circled up by the hearth to feel the heat of the fire as Robin and Richard played an intense game of chess– and occasionally Allen would try his hand at beating Robin as well. Much and Dusty were usually thick as thieves across the room, discussing Allen knew not what with intensity.

Eventually warm weather returned and their travels grew quicker. One day as Much led them toward a tavern he'd procured rooms in, Richard stopped with his hands on his hips to give the building a once-over.

"I believe you've found us a good place, Much. I wasn't sure our mouse could manage the mission, but you did."

"Thank you, Sire."

Allen instantly reached over to clamp a hand over Much's mouth.

"Much!" Robin glanced around the street at the villagers walking past. "How many times do we have to tell you?"

"I am sorry, it was the slip of the tongue again."

"You have to stop doing that."

Richard placed a hand on Robin's arm. "Let us move inside. We don't need to draw more attention with this argument than his off-hand comment would have on its own."

Allen watched the people in the street, heart pounding in his ears, as his friends made their way inside. No one seemed to be paying any mind to the strangers entering the tavern, but Allen's fear for their secrecy–for the safety of his friends–would not be abated. He hurried inside, impatiently waiting as everyone settled into the rooms Much had procured before turning on him.

"You have to stop doing that. Pay more attention to what you say."

"I do try," Much replied. "It's an old habit and hard to break."

"Don't continue to scold him, Allen," Richard sighed. "He means well."

"Thank you, Your Ma-"

"Much!" Robin and Allen both threw up their hands in exasperation as Richard chuckled.

"My bad." Much sighed, looking truly distraught. "Perhaps I should stop trying to talk to the king at all."

"You mean stop talking to *Richard*," Allen replied with a roll of his eyes. "He's just Richard. Come on, maybe you need to practice. Repeat after me: Richard."

It was Much's turn to roll his eyes. "Thank you for the assistance, but I think I can manage."

"Clearly you can't."

"Allen!" Dusty cut in, "That's enough."

"We will not stay long in this village," Richard said. "The people of...where are we?"

"Scheifling," Robin said.

"Yes, Scheifling. They may or may not have noticed Much's slip, but I wouldn't want to risk staying if they did. We'll leave in the morning. Someone might have heard our mouse calling me 'sire' and I don't want to deal with the consequences if they did."

Early the next morning they set out from the tavern. There were few people in the street so early in the morning–they'd left without so much as a breakfast from the tavern for Richard was eager to be on their way–and those who were up and about paid little attention to the group heading out of town.

They had not gone far from the village when they heard pounding hoofbeats behind them. Allen glanced over his shoulder to see who was in such a hurry and then spun around, drawing his sword. Men on horseback were hurrying after them.

Robin drew his sword as well, as Richard turned to around to see what the commotion was.

"This does not look good."

"There are twenty-seven of them," Allen said, counting the soldiers as they approached. "We're outnumbered by a large margin."

"Doesn't matter," Robin replied. "We defend the king regardless."

"Robin," Richard spoke quietly, his voice firm. "There is no need to die here. We will see what they want. It is possible they are not aware of who we are."

The men galloped forward and soon had the small group surrounded, their weapons drawn. Allen kept a tight grip on his sword as he stepped between the strangers and Richard.

"King Richard the Lion-Heart," the apparent leader of the group called out. "You have been a hard man to find since your disappearance after the end of the Crusade. There is no need to hide your identity any longer. We have orders to arrest you and bring you to Durnstein castle."

"Who gave you such an order?" Robin demanded, his sword still raised, the same as Allen's.

"We come by order of Duke Leopold of Austria, who is most displeased with the King of England."

The swords and spears of those on horseback pressed in around the group. Allen was just beginning to let his mind sink to its place of numbness in preparation for the battle about to begin, but Richard put his hand on Robin's shoulder and shook his head toward Allen.

"There is no need to die today."

With Richard surrendering, there was nothing more to be done. Allen hesitated a moment, but then lowered his blade. Soon enough the soldiers were stealing all of their weapons and binding their hands behind their backs.

The long march to Durnstein castle had begun.

Chapter 26

It was a week before they arrived at Durnstein castle, where they were promptly thrown into a cell in the dungeon. The long hallway on a lower level of the castle was lined with rooms that were used as cells, and it was into one of these that they were all escorted. The cell was roughly six feet across both ways, with stone walls on three sides, along with a dirt floor and an iron gate to shut them in.

Anger coursed through Allen, searing and hot. As if they hadn't had enough trouble in their lives–all of them–now they were rotting in prison. If Much hadn't been so careless about calling Richard 'Sire' on so many occasions; if only he wasn't so self-deprecating and had the barest shred of confidence or self-esteem, they wouldn't have been in this position.

There was nothing to be done about it now. They were locked in a small cell in the dungeon of Durnstein castle and there was little hope of getting out. Allen planted himself in one corner of the cell and refused to even look at Much.

"I am sorry." Much's voice was low and soft. He took a seat along the back wall of the cell, though not directly beside Allen.

"There's nothing to be done about it now." Robin sighed, still standing by the bars of the cell, glaring at the guards at the far end of the dungeon.

Allen crossed his arms. "He could have listened to us in the first place and just called the King 'Richard' like everyone else."

"Leave him be," Dusty said, glaring at Allen. "You've made mistakes, too."

"It's not my fault we're in this prison!"

"Maybe this is where God wants us to be for now, have you thought about that?"

For a moment, silence greeted her question, and then Richard tilted his head to one side as he regarded her. "God? What does he have to do with us being thrown into prison?"

"I believe God is in control of everything that happens to us," Dusty said. "So He has a lot to do with us being thrown into prison. Maybe there is something for us to learn here, maybe He wants us to witness to the prison guards and spread His love here, maybe something far worse would have befallen us if we'd continued on our journey and He is protecting us from whatever it might have been. There are endless possibilities. Maybe whatever this experience turns out to be will strengthen our character in some fashion, or draw us closer in our relationship to the Father." Dusty glanced toward Much and smiled. "Who knows?"

"What are you going on about," Allen asked. "We're not Friars or monks or whatever."

"No, but we're Christians."

Robin shook his head. "Not like you are. You take everything far too seriously."

"Robin–"

"Not now, Dusty." Robin shook his head. "We're stuck in a prison and really ought to be working on how to get out, not arguing over theology that doesn't matter."

"It does matter," Dusty frowned. "It matters more than anything else in this world. Your life depends upon it."

Allen rolled his eyes. "Now really, Dusty, don't be so melodramatic."

Dusty didn't say anything further, lowering her head.

The days that followed passed most unpleasantly. There was little space in the cell–during the day the five of them sat or stood around the edges, trying to stay out of each other's way as much as possible; at night there wasn't enough room for all of them to lay down comfortably, so they would crowd together, laying on their sides close together, or leaning against the cold stone walls and attempting to find rest in that position.

For the most part they were left on their own, their only view of other people coming from the front of the cell where they could see the guards at the end of the hall. There did not appear to be anyone else in the various cells along the hallway.

The light in the dungeon was dim at the best times, and worse if the guards at the end of the hall carried their torches out of sight. The most interesting occurrence each day was the changing of the guards at the end of the hall, but they rarely spoke to the prisoners. Food was brought once or twice a day–maggoty bread, slimy water, nothing worth eating.

And all of it because Much couldn't keep his mouth shut.

With every meager meal placed before them, Allen's frustration with Much grew. Every time he caught sight of a rat scurrying along the floor, or had the indignity of relieving himself in one corner of the cell among his companions, his anger flared.

One day when their rations were brought, Allen stared down at the maggots in his moldy bread and tried to decide how hungry he was. He could see Dusty slowly and methodically flicking the pests out of her piece of bread, but Allen didn't think he could eat his with or without the maggots.

Much seemed less perturbed by his chunk of bread, which only made Allen's frustration flare. He chucked his own sorry meal across the room. The green piece of bread hit Much across the face.

"You can have my portion of that rot," Allen hissed, crossing his arms. "It's your fault we're here."

"Allen!" Dusty chided.

Much glared at Allen, which was remarkably out of character for the meek lad.

Richard sighed heavily, looking about at the group. "This is no one's fault but my own. We are here, not because Much misspoke, but because I alienated Duke Leopold at Acre when I tore down his standard. If the Duke was not angry with me, he would not have seen fit to throw us in prison as we crossed his lands."

"It matters not," Dusty said, "Nothing can be done about it now. Laying blame is not helping anyone."

Allen scoffed at that, but merely crossed his arms and turned away from Much. There was little point in continuing the argument.

Life continued on in the same manner for some weeks, nothing of interest happening during the day except the changing of the guards at the end of the hall, the occasional scurrying of rats, and Allen's perpetual frustration with Much.

And then the Duke of Austria began to visit the prison cell every day or two to ridicule Richard.

"I imagine you'll think twice before insulting another noble in the future," the Duke had said on his second visit.

"You'll regret this!" Robin snapped. "You can't imprison a king and get away with it."

Every time the Duke visited, Richard and the Duke would trade insults, and Robin was often quick to jump into the arguments as well.

186

In one of his gloating sessions, the Duke let it be known that he was holding Richard for ransom and expected to get rich off of the money he stole from England.

One night Allen leaned against the bars at the front of the cell, as far away from the stench in the back corner as he could get. Robin and Much were snoring softly, and Richard was coughing in his sleep, shifting restlessly.

Was this what his life would be until he died?

The lack of food and dignity was almost more than Allen could bear. How was this better than the despair and guilt over losing his entire family? He'd decided somewhere along the Crusades that life was worth living, but his present environment did not give him the confidence to continue believing so. This life was not worth anything at all.

Dusty shifted nearby and Allen turned to her. In the dim light of the dungeon, her dark eyes glimmered–reflecting the slim firelight that came down the hall from where the guards were stationed.

"How long have you been staring at me?" Allen whispered.

Dusty pulled herself into a sitting position carefully, so as not to wake their other companions. She scooted across the floor to sit beside Allen. "A while. You seem perturbed."

"I hate being in this prison."

"We all do."

Allen sighed, leaning his head against the iron bars. "I joined the Crusades so I could get killed."

Silence stretched between them. Allen closed his eyes, unwilling to see judgement or pity in Dusty's eyes. It was the truth; he had wanted to die.

Allen felt her hand come to rest on his cheek and his eyes flew open. In the dim light, he could just make out the compassion and understanding written across her face.

"You wanted to die, and then you met us. Something similar happened to me. I didn't crave death, perhaps, but I created a chasm between me and my past. I severed my connection with who I truly am, which I suppose was a death in a way. And then I stumbled into this family…" Dusty shook her head. "No. I did not stumble upon you. The Lord brought me to you. And suddenly, I could see the beauty in life again, and more than that I began to heal from my past trauma. I am not there yet–not fully healed. These wounds have festered for far too long. But I am learning and growing and healing because of you, Robin, and Much."

Dusty removed her hand from Allen's cheek and curled her fingers around his. Allen squeezed her hand, relishing the connection.

He missed Alice; yet he still had a sister. This was precisely why life was still worth something to him.

"The longer we sit and rot in this prison, the more I feel I made a mistake in not getting myself killed during the war."

"Our circumstances might be terrible right now, but we still have each other." Dusty nodded toward their sleeping companions. "We're all here, alive, together. We can get through this."

A comfortable peace stretched between them, only broken by the gentle snoring of Much and Robin. Dusty was right; for the time being, they were all alive and together. Allen's greatest concern was losing his new family the way he'd lost his old one–but he hadn't lost any of them yet. They were rotting in a prison cell, but they weren't dead.

Not yet.

"Is your frustration at being stuck in this prison of more importance to you than the relationships with your family?"

Allen shifted, letting go of Dusty's hand. "What do you mean?"

"You are angry with Much. I can understand why, to a certain degree. But there is nothing that can be done about the fact that we ended up here. It's done, it's over. It happened. Now you have a choice–preserve your relationship with your brother, or break it."

Allen crossed his arms, glancing toward Much's sleeping form. He was still angry, there was no denying that. Much's inability to have any amount of self-esteem got them into this mess.

Yet Dusty was right; it had happened. There was nothing to be done about it now. He could hate Much, and lose his brother, or he could forgive him and move on.

Allen sighed. "You are probably right."

"I usually am."

"I don't want to lose any of you."

"I know."

"I can't lie and say I'm not upset by what happened, and Much's involvement in it...but he does matter to me."

"Perhaps instead of being angry with him, you can feel compassion for him."

"Compassion?"

"What kind of childhood could he have had that he was raised to believe he has no value? I know some of his story, so I know the answer...I don't know how much he's told you..."

Allen watched her with curiosity, wondering what she was referring to.

Dusty pulled her legs up to her chest, wrapping her arms around her knees. "He struggles with believing he is worth anything, Allen, and that is something to break your heart, not make you angry. It inspires me to encourage him–to prove to him that he does have value to add to my life. He has value to add to yours, too, or you wouldn't have claimed him as your brother."

"You're right."

"I know." Dusty leaned over to playfully push against him and it brought a smile to Allen's face.

"How did you get so wise?"

"Life experience, my friend." Dusty smiled at him through the darkness, the flash of her teeth brightening the darkened cell. "You love Much, I know you do. So forgive him, show him compassion. Give him the grace he will always give to you, no matter how cruelly you treat him."

That brought a flush of shame to Allen's cheeks. Had he been cruel to Much lately? Probably.

Dusty had made her point, and Allen took it to heart. In the days that followed he reined in his hurtful comments and sighs of frustration. He wasn't sure what to say to Much though, so he opted for saying very little.

Chapter 27

One night, after they had been in prison for some months, Allen lay awake long after the others had fallen asleep. Robin was on one side of him and Much the other, as space within the cell was cramped when they laid down to sleep. It was growing increasingly more cramped the longer they stayed there, for the corner of the cell they used to relieve themselves was an ever growing pile that no one wanted to sleep beside.

Allen hated this little cell. He hated the cramped space, hated the stench, hated the darkness. He wanted out. He wanted to see the sun again. To feel the wind on his face.

Even so, his anger toward Much was abating. Much was just as miserable as everyone else, and Allen was well aware that he blamed himself. More than that, Dusty's keen gaze reminded him every day that he should be valuing the love he had for his brother more than hating his situation being stuck in prison.

Allen shifted, trying to find a comfortable way to sleep despite the hard ground and the bodies pressed too close for comfort.

"Allen?"

Much's voice whispered in the darkness and Allen sighed. For a moment, he said nothing, but it was clear Much was awake and aware that Allen was as well. "What do you need?"

"You know I am sorry I got us into this mess."

Allen hesitated; this was the perfect opportunity to put Dusty's wisdom into practice and prove to Much that his friendship mattered more than their circumstances.

"Our companions are right, Much. I suppose this was bound to happen. We were surrounded by enemies and our swift traveling could easily have been suspicious at some point. I know I've been ignoring you and tearing into you by turns, and I am sorry."

Much didn't respond.

"I should not be treating you like this. I have been–I *am*– upset by what has happened. I do not wish to be in prison, I don't want the king in prison. I don't want to die here. But I cannot continue to hold it against you. You are sometimes a foolish little mouse, indeed, but you are a good natured one and don't mean any harm."

Silence stretched in the darkness.

"Let's put it behind us, Much. We should devote our energies to finding a way out of this prison rather than arguing amongst ourselves, after all."

"Do you think we can?"

"If we work together, we will find a way. We survived the Crusades…and if a mouse like you can make it through the war unscathed, anything is possible."

The months continued to pass in relative boredom, only made interesting when the Duke of Austria would come down to visit and ridicule Richard. Dusty took it upon herself to relieve her own utter boredom by writing in the dirt of the floor. The first day she had begun to create the swirling marks in the dirt, Allen leaned forward with curiosity for he couldn't make out what she was doing.

"What are you drawing?" Allen asked.

Dusty took a deep breath, wiping a tear from her cheek. "I am writing."

"Writing what?" Much asked.

"Scripture."

Allen felt a flash of anger run through him. Dusty and her faith again; why did she insist on believing in a god who clearly never helped her? She'd lost everything, the same as him, and now she was rotting in prison.

"Do you think the next poor prisoner who gets thrown in this cell is going to read it and be blessed?" Allen couldn't keep the sarcasm from his voice.

"No, Allen." Dusty's voice was patient and kind as ever. "I am writing these Scriptures to remind myself of what the Lord says, not someone else."

Robin scooted closer to see what she was writing. "Is that…?"

"Arabic."

"Can you teach me?"

"To read Arabic?"

"Read it, speak it, write it, anything! I picked up a few words in the Holy Land. It could be fun to learn more."

Dusty watched him quietly in the dim light. Amusement at Robin's enthusiasm overtook Allen's frustration as he watched their interaction.

"Come on, Dusty, we have nothing else to entertain us!" Robin grinned and winked. "You know you want to."

"Alright."

And so Dusty began to teach Robin the language of her people. Allen hadn't been as interested in the idea, but because they were all stuck together in that tiny cell, he, Much, and even Richard could not help but learn from her as well. Days passed, and the summer came and went without anything within the cell changing. They could not see the seasons changing, though in winter months the dungeon did grow quite cold.

One day after the Duke had visited to throw insults at Richard and then left them alone again, Robin threw himself rather dramatically across the floor. "I give up!"

"On what?" Richard asked.

"Everything. We'll never get out."

"Nonsense," Richard replied. "The Duke has said he's holding us for ransom, has he not? I believe he is capable of doing something so treacherous as hold a king for ransom. And if he is, my people will pay."

"But your brother is running your kingdom, remember?" Robin let out a heavy sigh. "Even if you have forgotten, I can still hear the voices of those who spoke of the terrible things that were happening in England by the hand of Prince John. I still recall the day you informed me your brother was most likely involved in the murder of my own father!"

"I have not forgotten all the reports," Richard said. "But I do believe the people will pay the ransom. Even if they will not, my mother Queen Eleanor will see to it that we are released. My sister Joan will be equally anxious to get you out of prison."

As winter progressed, the cool stone walls of their cell grew ever more cold. Their breath began to crystallize in front of them, and the five of them took to huddling close together throughout the day and night in a desperate attempt to remain warm.

One day when the guards brought their meager meal that could barely be called food, Allen noticed the single jar of what was meant to be water that the guard brought was in fact frozen solid–there was only hard-packed ice in the jug.

"Will our trials never end?" Allen handed the frozen jar to Robin, who turned it upside down. The ice stayed firmly in place.

194

"Have hope, Allen," Dusty said. "The Lord is watching over us."

"Don't even start," Allen rolled his eyes, but there was less anger behind his words than had been in the past. Allen was tired. Tired of the cold. Tired of hardship. Tired of being angry. He just wanted it all to end.

Dusty snatched the jar from Robin and slammed her fist into the opening. She pulled it up dripping wet, with shards of ice attached to her fingers. She handed the jar to Allen. "It wasn't frozen solid. Only across the top. You give up hope far too easily."

Allen took a sip of the cold water, grimacing as his teeth stung at the temperature.

"I would have figured that out eventually," Robin said when Allen handed him the jar to take a drink. He winked at Dusty.

"I doubt it." Dusty carefully pulled the ice from her fingers and placed it in her mouth.

When the weather grew warmer once more, enough that they could no longer see their own breath in the air, Allen felt a renewed vigor to find a way out of their situation. He and Robin would discuss possible solutions–quietly, so the guards at the end of the hall would not overhear.

"We're too weak to fight our way out of the castle," Robin said. "And anyway, we can't get out of the cell."

"We could potentially overcome the guards who bring our food–that's the only time the cell is ever likely to be unlocked or opened…"

"But again, fighting our way out of the castle? We're malnourished, weak, and haven't got any weapons."

"There has to be a way," Allen insisted.

"I want to find it," Robin agreed. "But I'm not sure what it could be."

"Maybe we could find a way to dig through the back wall. The stones there don't seem as firmly in place as the side walls–and who knows what's on the other side?"

Robin knocked his fist against the stone wall at the back of the cell, and the one to his left. "There's just a cell to the side, but you're right…there might be a way of escape through the back if we could move the stones…"

"It is out of the line of sight of the guards," Allen whispered, his eyes darting toward the iron gate and the hallway of cells beyond it, at the end of which the guards would be standing watch. "We can see them, and they us, only when we're up at the front of the cell.

"But it would take so long," Dusty replied. "And when our meals are brought, and when the Duke visits, we'll be found out."

"We decided fighting our way out was too risky…but we have to do something."

Weeks passed as Allen, Robin, and Dusty debated different methods to get out of prison, none of which seemed possible or likely to succeed upon scrutiny.

One night, Dusty nudged Allen with her foot, and then stared significantly at the back wall of the prison. Allen and Robin moved closer to see what had her interest. There was a great deal of mud squeezing between the different stones, oozing out of the wall.

Allen reached out and wiped his hand across the stones, taking a glob of mud with him.

"It's the moisture," Dusty whispered. "It must have snowed through the winter, and given way to rain now that it's spring. It's softening the earth."

"So we *can* dig," Allen grinned, wiping the mud from his hand across his trousers.

"But we're so far beneath the castle," Robin said thoughtfully, wiping his own hand slowly across the back wall. "If we dig…we'll have miles, perhaps, to dig to the top. Where will all that dirt go? It won't fit in this cell. Once it spills out, the guards will notice…if it doesn't smother and kill us first."

"They'll notice before that, when they bring food and see us digging along the back wall," Dusty sighed.

"But we can try," Allen said. "It's something; it's all we've got."

Robin shrugged. "We can certainly try."

Much shifted closer to the wall, running his own hand through the mud. "We cannot be too deep if the moisture on the surface is affecting this wall."

"It is odd," Robin agreed. "Allen's right; it's our only shot. I'm not so sure it will work, but we have to try something."

Chapter 28

Every night the group began to work on the back wall, loosening the stones and pulling a few out of the muddy wall. Soon they began to sift through the earth wall and find jagged bits of rock they could use as digging tools to carve into the wall where they had removed a few stones. They picked a low section of the wall, one they could easily sit in front of and cover whenever food was brought to the cell or the Duke visited to gloat over their situation.

Richard watched with little interest, slumped against one of the cold stone walls. His cough had grown worse, but Dusty did what she could for him—which wasn't much, given she had no access to medicinal supplies and he could hardly get proper rest or nourishment in his current location.

They worked for several days, until their haphazard carving tools cut through the wall, Robin's hand disappearing for a moment before he pulled it back.

He glanced at Allen, and then the two of them began digging with a vengeance, pushing the earth as much as digging it out until there was a hole large enough for Robin to shove his head through.

His muffled voice came drifting back through the wall.

Allen whacked his arm. "What?"

Robin pulled his muddied head back into the cell. "There's a hallway of sorts, a tunnel."

"A tunnel? That is definitely our way out."

"Why is there a tunnel by the dungeons?" Much asked.

"Castles have plenty of secrets," Robin said, winking at Much. "Ours certainly does, if you recall."

"We have to be quick," Dusty said, glancing over her shoulder at the hallway of cells beyond their own. "We have to carve a big enough hole to fit through, get everyone out, and then get far enough away that we won't be caught once the guards bring our food, realize what's happened, and come after us."

"It's risky, but we can do it," Robin said. "We'll be fast."

Robin immediately started digging again and Allen joined him eagerly. For the first time in a long time, hope blossomed in Allen's chest. Were they truly going to make it out? Not just in wild dreams and schemes that they told each other to stave off despair…but really, truly, escape?

As soon as the hole seemed wide enough to squeeze through Allen pushed his head through to see what Robin had found. It was dark within–far too dark to see much. The dim light of the prison cell was the only source of light within the tunnel, but it was just enough to make out a few feet of hard packed earth on the ground and a wall of dirt across the hall.

"Time to go," Allen said, pulling back inside the prison cell.

"Robin?" Richard shifted into a straighter sitting position, though he was still rather slumped against the wall, a frown on his face.

"Yes, Sire?"

"Your plan is risky."

"We know that, Richard."

"And you know that if you are caught–which is likely–you will undoubtedly be killed by the Duke."

"We are well aware, but we have to get out."

"I am no good to England dead, Robin. I cannot come with you."

"Richard!"

200

"No, do not try to argue with me. I cannot take the risk."

"It is dangerous," Dusty said. "Perhaps if we wait, the ransom will be paid."

Allen crossed his arms. "I refuse to be too afraid to do this. I will not stay in this prison."

"Robin is no use to England–or Marian–dead either," Dusty said. "If we stay, we have no risk of being killed by the Duke."

"Just of dying from the cold, the lack of real nourishing food, the fact we haven't seen the sun in who knows how long," Allen began to tick reasons off of the fingers of one hand, his anger mounting with every item on the list. He finally had hope of freedom, and Richard and Dusty were going to snatch that away from him because they were afraid?

"You have to go, Robin," Richard said. "We heard many terrible reports about what is happening in England. I believe my people are suffering. But I cannot leave here and risk it. I will wait for the ransom. Yet I cannot leave my people to their fate, whatever it is. You have to go."

"Richard–"

"No, Robin. Do not try to change my mind. Just go. I'm entrusting England to you. Keep my people safe."

Robin hesitated, but the loud guffaw from one of the guards stationed at the end of the hall set everyone's hearts racing, and Allen immediately pushed through the hole that had been created in the back of the cell.

Allen walked carefully across the tunnel to the opposite side, running his hand along the muddied wall. If the tunnel was entirely earth, there was a chance the whole tunnel might collapse on them. That wasn't enough to scare Allen into going back into the prison cell though.

Robin squeezed through the small opening after Allen, squinting around the dark tunnel.

"Where to?" Allen asked as Much clambered out of the hole.

Robin seemed to be considering both directions of the tunnel that ran along the backside of the dungeon.

"We have to hurry," Dusty said as she scrambled out of the dimly lit cell. "Who knows how soon the guards will notice what has transpired."

"Where are we?" Much asked.

"In a passageway in the castle?" Robin shrugged. "The wall is clearly the back of our cell, the whole tunnel seems to be encased in dirt…there's no stone work on the walls or floor that I can see or touch."

"Where does it lead is a better question," Dusty said.

"We will find out when we follow it," Robin replied. He took the lead, and Much walked close behind him, reaching forward to put his hand on Robin's shoulder. Dusty followed them, so Allen took up the rear, putting his own hand on Dusty's shoulder so as not to lose her in the darkness. As soon as Robin led them away from the dungeon, the dim light disappeared and they were encased in nothing but darkness and silence.

Leaving Richard behind did not seem like a great idea, but Allen was eager to be free and nothing was going to make him go back into that prison cell. If Richard wanted to rot there, that was his choice.

Allen kept a firm grip on Dusty's shoulder, his only anchor to his friends in the sea of blackness that he now traversed through. He could faintly hear the footfalls of his friends, but otherwise silence reigned in the tunnel.

They had no idea where the tunnel might lead, or what they might find at the end of it. It was entirely possible they'd just doomed themselves to getting lost in a maze underground, and they would die of starvation or perhaps a cave in.

But they were no longer in that tiny, stinking, cell. They were moving, and for the first time in a year, Allen had real hope.

Chapter 29

After a time, the pitch-black darkness they had been traveling through slowly began to lighten until Allen could make out the shape of Dusty's head in front of him. Her hair had been growing long while in prison, with no way to trim it. In truth, all of them had longer hair than usual, and full beards too–disgusting beards full of dirt and grime and who knew what all. Allen suddenly realized more than anything else, he wanted a bath, followed by a good meal and a nap.

As the tunnel slowly began to become visible around them, Allen could see a glimmer of light further up the tunnel past the heads of his friends. Robin's steps quickened, and so did everyone else's. Slowly, the light grew brighter until they reached the source of the it; torches were lit and hanging in sconces along the wall at what appeared to be the end of their current tunnel. Passages branched off in several directions, most of them lit with torches, and here the dirt floor gave way to a stone pavement.

"I think we've come to the portion of these tunnels people actually use," Dusty commented.

"For what purpose though?" Allen asked.

"Back home, where Much and I are from, there's a castle that is filled with secret passages," Robin said. "They were originally built for the nobility to have ways to escape if their fortress was overrun. I imagine these hold a similar purpose for the Duke."

"Which way do we go?" Much asked.

Robin shrugged and started walking, throwing his hands to either side. "I'm sure this leads somewhere."

As Robin began walking down a random stone-paved path, Allen and the others hurried after him. They no longer walked single file with their hands on each other's shoulders, because they could see quite well by the light of the evenly spaced torches hanging along the walls. The passage sloped gently upward, and before long it stopped at a door.

Robin paused, glanced silently as his companions, and raised a finger to his lips. Then he tried the handle.

Allen held his breath, his palms growing sweaty.

It was unlocked.

Robin pushed the door inward and Allen instinctively reached for his sword at his waist–though there was nothing there. Unarmed, malnourished…what would they do if there were soldiers or nobles or literally anyone inside that room?

Robin glanced past the door as he slid it open, and then he visibly relaxed. He looked over his shoulder long enough to wink and then disappeared inside. Much hurried after him, and Allen was only a step behind.

Past the door was a small room with no furnishings, smaller than the cell they'd been kept in. Robin was already at the other side of the room pushing open another door. The second door led into a hallway. It was wide, well-lit, with a stone floor and many wooden doors on either side at various intervals.

"I think we're in the actual castle," Dusty whispered.

Robin nodded, putting a hand to his lips again to suggest they remain silent. He began moving down the hallway, and the others followed after him.

Allen could feel his heart pounding wildly inside his chest as his palms grew increasingly more sweaty. They had no idea where they were going or who they might meet along the way. Robin moved confidently and the rest followed him through hallway after hallway, but Allen's sense of unease was growing with every step.

Judging by the grey light of dawn creeping through the windows they passed, it was quite early in the morning. That might account for the relatively empty hallways–the nobles would still be in bed. The few individuals Allen and the others did see as they moved through the castle, they saw from a distance–at the end of hallways or in rooms with doors slightly ajar. Allen would press against a wall or duck into another hallway whenever he caught sight of anyone–it wouldn't be too hard for someone to guess that the refuse-covered group dressed in rags did not, in fact, belong inside the castle.

To Allen's relief, it wasn't too difficult for the group to keep out of sight until they found a door that led out to the courtyard of the castle.

Allen eyed the courtyard, the castle walls, everything that he could see from their vantage point just inside the doorway. There didn't appear to be any obvious soldiers stationed nearby, though there was a guardhouse at the gate at the far end of the courtyard that they would have to pass in order to exit.

Slowly, Robin slipped out of the castle and crept along the wall around the courtyard, trying to stay out of sight of anyone who might be looking but there was very little cover for them to truly hide. Allen took a deep breath to steady his rapidly beating heart, and then followed his friend.

When they reached the guardhouse beside the gate, Robin ducked low to avoid windows, and slowly crept along the ground. He raised himself slightly, peeked in the nearest window, and then grinned and glanced back toward the others. Robin mimed sleeping gestures toward them, still grinning, and then stood up and sprinted past the guardhouse.

Allen's heart leapt to his throat, but no shouts followed, and no guards went running after Robin.

Much sprinted past the gate and into freedom a moment later and suddenly Allen couldn't wait–he sprang to his feet, running as fast as his tired, unused muscles would allow. As soon as he was free of the castle courtyard, Allen could feel the panic at being followed warring with the joy of being free. Both spurred him onward as he continued running after Robin and Much, Dusty at his side. He ran and ran until he could run no more.

Robin led them toward an outcropping of trees and Allen bent over, his hands on his knees as he gasped for air. Much collapsed onto the ground wheezing, and Allen dropped to the ground beside him.

"What's...the...plan..." Allen panted, trying to get words out despite his inability to breathe properly.

"We have no money, no food," Dusty glanced around at the group as they all settled down after their wild run. "We're weak and malnourished. What *is* the plan, Robin?"

"We go home."

"Yes, that much is obvious. But how do you plan to do that?"

"Very carefully," Robin said. He looked around at the trees and then shrugged. "We press forward. Maybe we can get work in a village in exchange for food and lodging, and then we keep traveling onward."

"And if we get arrested because the Duke sends people after us?" Dusty raised an eyebrow. "Or if we get arrested because the village we beg for work in doesn't take kindly to vagabonds dressed in refuse-covered rags?"

"We'll deal with the situations as they arise," Robin said. "As it stands right now…we can sit in this bit of trees until we starve to death, we can go back to the castle and turn ourselves in, or we can press forward. I vote for the latter."

"Hear, hear," Allen raised a tired fist into the air. He didn't have the energy to speak with conviction, and his arm dropped lifelessly back to the ground as he lay backward, stretching his tired form across the ground. "Just…after a brief break, please."

Chapter 30

Eventually Robin insisted they keep moving and Allen forced himself onto his unsteady feet. He followed Robin as well as he could, though his hands had begun to shake from the exertion of running–he hadn't used his muscles or strained his lungs in such a manner in over a year, since before being thrown in prison, and his body was rebelling. The lack of proper food over the past year didn't help. His stomach seemed to be gnawing on itself as he struggled to stay upright following Robin and the others. His vision swam and the world spun occasionally, but somehow he stayed on his feet.

Robin kept them moving across the countryside for a few hours until they came in sight of a town. There were a number of buildings clustered close together along several streets, with a small wall surrounding most of the town–apart from the backside that was pressed against a crag. The group paused while still a distance from the town and Robin stared at it with his hands on his hips.

"Do we go in?" Allen asked as Robin continued to stare at the distant town. The idea of a bath, a meal, and a long nap was growing in Allen's mind, and Robin's hesitation irked him.

"We reek," Robin replied with a frown. "Dusty was right; we'll be no better than street scum to anyone of prestige. We'll get thrown out."

"It is always possible there will be people of compassion," Dusty said. "If there is an abbey or monastery we could start there."

Robin continued to study the distant town. Allen shifted from one foot to the other, ordering his body to stay upright. It would not do to faint from hunger and exhaustion and be carried into town.

"Let's go in," Robin said at last. "We can't just stand here all day."

He set off toward the road to the left of them that led toward the gate into town. Allen moved to follow, Dusty at his side. She and Robin didn't seem nearly as ready to collapse as Allen felt. They were filthy, sure, but neither looked on the point of fainting. He glanced toward Much and felt some reassurance that he looked dead on his feet as well.

They reached the road within a few minutes, and made their way toward the city itself. When they entered, there was a handful of people–merchants, nobles, farmers–moving about the streets on their own business. All of them sent sharp stares toward the vagabonds entering their town, and Allen grew more self-conscious of his filthy and ragged looks even as he swayed on unsteady feet.

Robin gave a wave and moved to speak to a man nearby, but the man hurriedly turned aside and the other people in the street seemed eager to ignore interaction with the group as well.

"We're disgusting and look ridiculous," Allen sighed, scratching his beard.

Soon, however, a tall man, muscular, with a sword at his hip approached the group. He demanded something in a harsh language Allen did not understand, but Robin stepped forward and conversed with him for a few minutes. Both seemed wary but passionate in their discussion, though Allen hadn't the faintest idea what they might have been saying.

Suddenly, however, the man switched to speaking in French–a language Allen did know, having been raised a noble and living with both English and Frenchman during the Crusades.

"If you are Crusaders; that remains to be determined. In any event, I am Isenbern, the younger son of Count Jodok. I have charge over this town and surrounding lands, and I do respect the Crusaders, if that is indeed who you are."

"What can we do to assure you of our honesty?" Robin asked.

Isenbern studied him for a moment, his nose wrinkling. "I'm not taking you into my home just yet, so I'll ask questions here. What is your name?"

"I am Robin, Earl of Locksey. This is my servant Much, and my traveling companions, Allen and Dusty."

Isenbern nodded slowly, crossing his arms.

"Much and I met Allen in the city of Dover, just before we set out on the Crusades. We traveled to Sicily, Cyprus, and eventually to Acre where we joined the fight in the Holy Land."

Isenbern seemed reluctant still, but he uncrossed his arms and turned and began walking down the street. That seemed all the invitation they were going to get. Robin hurried forward to walk beside him while Allen and the others followed behind.

Robin continued to regale their new acquaintance with tales of the war in the Holy Land, trying to impress upon him that the group truly were Crusaders returning home. Allen jumped in to add additions to his stories occasionally, trying to be as persuasive as possible. This man was his current hope for a meal, a bath, and a nap–not necessarily in that order. He'd do anything to convince him that they were trustworthy enough to allow into his house.

When they reached a large manor on the end of a street, Isenbern paused. "I would like to continue this discussion once you are...less disgusting. I'll send my servant out who can take you through the servant quarters to get you washed up, and then you can join me in the house proper."

Isenbern disappeared inside the front door.

"This is going easier than I thought it might," Robin said with a satisfied grin.

"Assuming he does send his servant for us, and assuming he doesn't decide to kill us once we're inside," Allen said, considering all the ways this could go horribly wrong. "and assuming–"

"Okay, okay," Robin held up his hands. "Be alert, of course. Though without weapons I suppose there's only so much we can do if he is going to try and have us killed."

A young man exited the house a moment later, wrinkling his nose as he drew close to them. "You are far worse than he described," he said. Then he waved for them to follow him and began walking around the manor.

Allen followed without hesitation; he was wary, but he was also weary, hungry, and desirous of being–as Isenbern had described it–less disgusting.

The servant led them to the back of the house and through a simple door. He then took them down a narrow hallway and then into a small room with a simple wooden tub.

"There. It's got fresh water. If it needs changing after each of you, fine. Knock on the door. I've got Bernhard boiling more water as we speak. Christoph will be waiting for the knock and get Bernhard and the water for you. There's clothes," the young man gestured toward a table near the wooden tub that had four sets of clothes laid out side by side. "Once you're relatively clean and dressed, I'll take you to the master."

"Thank you, uh…your name?" Robin asked.

"Friedrich. My father has run of the household, and I will once he's dead." And with that, Friedrich left the room and pulled the door shut behind him.

"Pleasant fellow," Allen commented.

"I'll wait outside," Dusty said, glancing at the tub and then at the rest of them.

"Oh, Dusty, we can wait," Robin replied, already moving toward the hallway. "You go first. Come on." Robin grabbed Allen with one hand and Much with the other and dragged them toward the door. "Let us know when you're through."

In the hall stood another young person around their age, presumably the Christoph who was meant to fetch water for them.

"Are you already in need of fresh water?" he asked.

"No," Robin replied. "We just decided to bathe in more privacy."

They only waited in the hall with Christoph for a few minutes before Dusty appeared at the door. Her skin was clean, the smell was gone, and her dark hair had gentle waves in it as it fell pleasantly to her shoulders. There was a smile playing about her mouth, and her dark eyes held a bit of sparkle. Allen was rather taken aback by how pretty she seemed; she'd passed for a man so easily for so many years but just now she looked every bit a woman.

"Who's next?" Dusty asked. "Also, I need my hair cut."

"We need a shave, too," Robin commented, rubbing his chin. Robin turned to Christoph, "Could you help with that?"

Christoph glanced between Robin and Dusty, his eyes widening. "Uh, yeah, I can get a shaving kit…and, uh…sorry, my lady," Christoph awkwardly bowed to Dusty. "I didn't…I mean…Friedrich said there were four men…"

Dusty smiled. "Yes, that is rather the point."

Christoph stared a moment longer before he started, shook himself, and moved off down the hall, presumably in search of the

215

shaving kit and some implement to cut Dusty's hair. Bernhard brought fresh water for each bath, and Cristoph returned with a shaving kit to remove the unnecessarily long beards, along with a knife for Dusty's hair.

Allen leaned against the wall in the hallway, hoping it would keep him upright until it was his turn for a bath. Dusty sat down and calmly began chopping her beautiful hair off as Christoph watched with confusion and concern.

Robin soon exited the washroom, freshly shaved, cleaned, and bright-eyed. Allen hurried inside, waiting impatiently as Bernhard changed out the water–he'd thought about jumping straight in without fresh water, but Robin had left it a strange dark brown and it did not look refreshing at all.

When he finally eased into the steaming tub of fresh water, Allen could feel every aching muscle groaning with pleasure at the feel of the heat. Slowly, his body began to truly relax for the first time since he left Scotland.

After enjoying the moment for a while, Allen began to scrub the dirt, refuse, and other grime off of his skin. Before too long, he'd made the water as equally disgusting and brown as Robin had. But soon enough he himself was clean–his skin, his hair, his beard. After a quick trim to the year's worth of growth on his face, Allen felt like a free man once more.

His stomach growled loudly, and his hands shook as he pulled on the clothes Isenbern's servants had left out for his use. Now that he was clean, and in a place that seemed to promise real food for the first time in too long, his hunger was coming to the forefront of his mind.

Once they were all clean, shaved, and Dusty's hair was cropped short once more, Christoph fetched Friedrich who in turn led them through several corridors away from the servants' part of the house and into the nobility portion. The rooms were wider, ceilings higher, and furniture far more ornate in this part of the manor.

Friedrich led them into a wide room with a large hearth, with several chairs pulled around him–wooden chairs with pillows piled in them to make them more comfortable, as well as a low couch; there was a wooden desk, and several bookcases along the walls. It reminded Allen of his father's study.

Lord Isenbern was sitting by the low fire–far smaller than it could have been given the proportion of the hearth as a whole.

"Ah, I can almost see the Earl in you," he said to Robin as they entered the room. "Come, sit." He waved to the chairs by the fire, and they all sat down.

"I have been informed that one of your number is, in fact, a girl. I apologize, my lady, for your treatment in this house thus far."

Dusty shook her head. "I am used to far worse, Lord Isenbern. And I am not a lady–my parents were no more nobility than Much's, but I appreciate your concern. As it is, we have found it safer on our travels to let the world believe I am not a woman, so if you would be so kind as to keep our secret…"

Isenbern dipped his head. "As you wish, my lady." Then turning to Robin, "Now, tell me about your travels and battles during the Crusade."

Robin and Allen delighted Lord Isenbern with their tales for some time, and as they talked, more of his servants appeared bringing platters of food along with a small wooden table upon which the food was placed.

Allen let Robin take over the storytelling completely and buried himself in the boiled beef, minced apples, and fresh bread. Allen had almost forgotten what fresh bread could taste like, and he closed his eyes as it melted into his tongue. He ate with zeal, not bothering to temper himself to avoid upsetting his stomach as Robin continued to speak with Isenbern.

"You have convinced me to let you show off your skill," Isenbern said to Robin as everyone began to slow their eating–their stomachs having their fill for the first time in far too long. "I wish to see your archery."

He sent for Friedrich, and informed him to bring a bow and meet them outside, and then Isenbern led them to the back of the manor where the sloping hillside provided a grassy enclosed area for them.

A bow was brought, and Lord Isenbern pointed out various targets for Robin to shoot at–all of which he hit. Allen was impressed; if he'd been given that bow he had no doubt he'd miss entirely from his lack of practice and his ill-used muscles.

"You are as good as you say," Lord Isenbern conceded. "And you speak and hold yourself with the authority of someone well-bred. I am inclined to believe your story, despite your lack of proof."

"I appreciate that," Robin said.

"You can stay here to rest and recuperate," Lord Isenbern said.

"We may need to work here," Robin replied, "as we will need to accrue funds for our further travels."

"I'm sure something can be arranged," Lord Isenbern agreed.

They stayed with Lord Isenbern for several weeks–Robin, Allen, and Much joining the ranks of the town's guards who patrolled along the outer wall of the city to watch for intruders. Dusty helped the sick among the townspeople and earned the most affection of all of them.

Once they'd earned enough from Lord Isenbern's generosity, they set off on their travels again equipped this time with money, clean clothes, and freshly commissioned and purchased weapons of their choice from the town's blacksmith.

At the next village it was easier to convince the people that they were, indeed, soldiers returning from the Crusades because they were no longer covered in their own refuse and emaciated from lack of proper food.

Part 4

The Betrayal

Chapter 31

As the white cliffs of Dover came into view on the horizon, tears welled up in Allen's eyes. He glanced toward the sky, blinking rapidly. He didn't need to break down returning to a country that was not even his own.

But when he'd been in Dover last, he'd been setting out to get himself killed–running from the pain and horror of his past. Now he was coming home with new friends–new family–and a fresh desire to live. He hadn't healed from his losses, perhaps, but he didn't want to die, that much was certain. It was such a stark difference from when he'd left Dover that he couldn't help but feel overwhelmed by his return.

Once the group had disembarked from their ship, Robin moved away from the dock and knelt in the road for a moment, scooping up a small handful of dirt and letting it sift through his fingers.

"Planning on kneeling there all day?" Allen asked.

Robin grinned up at him, letting the rest of the dirt fall from his hand. "I can hardly believe we're in England again."

Allen glanced at their other companions; Much had tears in his eyes, but Dusty was merely taking it all in with a curious gaze.

Robin stood, dusting off his hand, and then led the group to a tavern. As Allen followed him, memories came flooding back; he'd chosen a tavern at random when arriving in Dover all those years before, and he hadn't cared to take in his surroundings, but now as Robin led him toward the same door he'd first entered so long ago Allen felt his heart constrict.

As they passed through the door into the familiar common room, Allen paused, taking in the tables scattered about, the stools gathered at the bar near the kitchen. That was where he'd met Robin and Much for the first time; that was where everything had changed, though he hadn't known it yet.

There were only a few people in the common room; Robin gathered the group at a table to order some food after procuring rooms. When the tavern keeper brought plates of food, it was merely a simple loaf of bread and a chunk of cheese.

"Sorry I don't have real meat as yet, but I can fry a few fish if you need it," the tavern keeper said softly. He did not seem to recognize Allen, Robin, or Much.

"Why the meager fare?" Robin asked, taking a bite out of the bread.

The innkeeper filled their mugs of ale and spoke softly, "It is Prince John and his men. He has replaced almost every sheriff in England with ruthless men of his own. The taxes are unbearably high and we all suffer for it."

Allen's heart sank. The rumors that King Richard had heard during the Crusades, the possibility that Prince John was responsible in some way for the death of Robin's father–it all came rushing back to him. What had they come home to? "Surely there is justice somewhere?"

The tavern keeper glanced nervously over his shoulder at the other customers in the room. "If you can't pay the taxes, you'll be hung."

"Surely not!" Much gasped.

"If things continue as they are," the tavern keeper said. "The Prince will have no more subjects left to tax."

"Is no one doing anything about it?" Robin asked.

"There are some who fight it," the man replied. "But they never live long. Here at the coast…you'll find more people leaving England as coming here. People are trying to get away from Prince John's ruthless reign."

The rumors the group had been hearing in the Holy Land and as they traveled abroad on their way home were true: England was a mess.

"We are hoping for a speedy return to our home in Nottingham," Robin said. "Could you direct me to the nearest livery where I can procure horses?"

"Horses?" The tavern keeper raised his eyebrows. "Where have you been that you think there are horses to be found?"

"Not in England, clearly," Robin replied. "Listen, it's been a long few years. I am sorry for your troubles, and I aim to do what I can about them for King Richard's sake. Don't worry about the horses, but if you can spare us some provisions for our travel that would be much appreciated."

"I don't have much," the man said. "But I can gather a bit for you, I suppose. Being Crusaders, and all…"

"Thank you."

They finished their meal quietly, Allen's mind swirling with the news the tavern keeper had related. During their unfortunate stay in Durnstein prison and then their blissful escape, Allen had forgotten that they might return to more upheaval and violence. And then there was the fact that Robin had promised King Richard before leaving him in that Austrian prison that he would take care of the people of England. Seeing their suffering firsthand now, Allen had no doubt that Robin would try and do something to help. What that would turn out to be,

Allen didn't know. But whatever it was, he would stay at his brother's side.

Robin made arrangements for provisions to take along on their journey to his childhood home and plans were made for their trip to begin at dawn. Allen had vague memories of visiting Nottingham for the grand Fair held there every year at some point in his childhood, but he couldn't remember the city distinctly. He was curious to return. Meeting the famous Lady Marian piqued his interest the most, although in many ways he was jealous of Robin.

He missed waking up beside his wife, missed having someone that he could share his heart and soul with. Robin had someone waiting for him, someone to return home to…

As they traveled across England, the suffering became ever more prominent. No one had food to spare, and Allen was shocked to see children scurrying about the streets of various cities and villages with their tiny bones protruding from their skinny bodies. They were as malnourished as Allen and his friends had been in Durnstien castle! Allen also noticed many gallows built in every city and village they passed through–proclamations from authorities declared the dead to be traitors and outlaws, but the darker whispers in the taverns was that they had opposed Prince John and his lackeys and had therefore been killed.

Yet with horror also came rumors of a group of men who were fighting the injustice. The closer Allen and his friends got to Nottinghamshire–Robin's own home–the more cheerful the people were whom they encountered. There were men who were going to stop the Prince and his sheriffs, they said. The Men of the Night.

Along with the Men of the Night came stories of a man known only as the Hooded Rescuer–a man who stopped executions and brought food to the poor. Allen and Robin were keenly interested in discovering who all of these men were.

After a few weeks of travel, the group finally arrived outside of Nottingham. Robin and Much hurriedly led them to the village of Wetherby in their search for Lady Marian. It was a quiet little village; the houses along the streets were relatively small, with thatched roofs. In front of some of the houses were small gardens, and in some a few chickens strutted about.

Toward the end of the street a young woman was leaning against the wall of her home, stringing a bow in her hand. She was short, with dark hair that fell straight past her shoulders, like a chocolate waterfall. Robin stopped walking when he saw her.

Allen watched his friend's face closely. That woman must be the infamous Marian, because there was no mistaking the love on Robin's face. Robin's eyes began to dance and then suddenly he darted forward, scooping Marian into his arms and swinging her around.

"Did you miss me, Marian darling?"

Much moved forward, stopping a few feet from them, but Allen held back from the reunion. Dusty stayed beside him, watching with her keen and curious eyes.

Robin set Marian on the ground and she looked up at him silently. Her took her hand and clasped it to his heart just as the door of the house opened and a young man leaned against the door frame.

"Who's this?" the newcomer asked.

Robin dropped Marian's hand as Marian said, "Will Scarlett, this is Robin of Locksley."

"The Earl?" the stranger asked.

Robin bowed stiffly to the young man named Will. "One and the same."

Allen felt a flash of anger and humiliation on Robin's behalf–
had Lady Marian not waited for him after all?

Robin was speaking to Marian again. "I was sorry to hear of my
father's death. I wish I could have been here."

"We were sorry for it, too. And you *should* have been here.
Your father's death was one of the first things that spurred me into
action."

"Ah. I wanted to speak to you about that. My comrades and I
have heard tales of this Hooded Rescuer and the 'men of the night' in
Nottinghamshire who seem to know the Sheriff's every move." Robin
gestured toward Much, Allen, and Dusty. "You remember Much,
Marian? This is Allen, a brother in arms."

Allen moved forward. "It is a pleasure to meet you, Lady
Marian. We've heard a great deal about you."

Allen winked at Robin and was rewarded with a shove, and
then Robin placed a hand on Dusty's shoulder. "And this is Dusty, our
master healer."

Marian ignored both Dusty and Allen, and moved forward to
hug Much instead. "It's good to see you."

"You, as well, Lady Marian," Much replied.

"Now, about these rumors," Robin said.

"Rumors?" Marian asked.

"Even when he only tells his most trusted servant Sir Guy of
Gisbourne in the darkest chambers of the castle, rumors say these
mysterious heroes still know what the Sheriff and Gisbourne are
planning and stop them. This has given rise to a belief among the
superstitious that they can, in fact, read his mind." Robin winked at
Marian as he continued, "Now I know perfectly well how one might
obtain such secret information, and I also know only a few people know

of the castle's secrets. Now two of those people have been away from England, which to my knowledge leaves you, Mark, and your father. Have you been helping them?"

"Helping us?" Will Scarlett laughed from the doorway. "She's one of us. You, sir, are addressing the leader of these 'men of the night'."

"Truly?" Robin asked.

"Truly," Marian replied to Robin. "You doubt I could do such a thing? It wasn't as though there was anyone else around to take care of the suffering people."

"Well it is a surprise," Robin said, "but not so shocking. You've always been a protector. Who is the Hooded Rescuer then, or do you and your companion," he gestured toward Will, "take turns under the mask?"

The way Robin mentioned *her companion* made Allen uneasy. It was clear his friend was jealous.

"No, that's Mark."

"Remarkable," Robin grinned. "Where is your father?"

"In custody, as he has been for a year. I've only been able to see him for the briefest moments when spying in the castle. Mark hasn't seen him at all. My father is ill, Robin."

"I am sorry," Robin frowned. "One of my friends has great knowledge of healing, as I said. Dusty's remarkable."

"I'm afraid the Sheriff isn't inclined to let my father have visitors of any nature, let alone physicians." Marian glanced down the street and then said, "You've all been introduced to Will Scarlett, my right hand, now meet my brother–the famed Hooded Rescuer, and the last member of our crew, Little John."

Marian gestured behind her and Allen saw two men walking down the dirt path that constituted a road in Wetherby. One was rather average sized and bore a resemblance to Marian, while the other was an extremely tall, muscular man–both carried parcels covered in cloth.

As they approached the group outside Marian's home, Robin's eyes widened. "Little John? Why didn't you name him Mountain John?"

"We thought about it," the young man who looked like Marian grinned as he drew near, setting aside his parcels, and then running forward to hug Much. Given Much's self-deprecating attitude Allen was surprised he'd received such affectionate greetings from both Marian and her brother. Dusty had hinted that night in Durnstein castle that Much's childhood had left him feeling unloved and undervalued, but that was not what Allen was witnessing in Marian and Mark.

"Where have you been off to Mark?" Robin asked as he received his own hug.

"Nottingham. We went to Marcus to collect some weapons we commissioned."

"Marcus?"

"Don't you remember him?" Marian asked. "Of course you don't. You never notice anyone but yourself."

"Marian!" Robin laughed, though Allen could hear the strain in his voice.

"What? Marcus is one of the blacksmith's in Nottingham. We used to play at his house as children if you recall."

"I do remember, I just couldn't place the name at first."

Marian shrugged. "It doesn't matter. Are you in a hurry to return to Locksley or can you stay for dinner?"

"We can definitely stay for dinner."

Robin re-introduced Dusty and Allen to Mark and Little John and then Marian ushered everyone inside the house. The front room was small, with a hearth along one wall and a simple table with chairs around it; there were doors around the various walls that likely led to more rooms and the kitchen, though the group didn't go farther than the front room that night. The group swapped stories from the Crusades and the rebellion effort in England.

Allen sat back and watched with fascination as Robin's eyes never left Marian's face, and while Marian ignored him, Mark ate up every word that he spoke.

Robin was most intrigued by Will's account of their camp in Sherwood, leaning forward eagerly as Will spoke.

"We couldn't stay with Marian and Mark here in Wetherby without drawing suspicion. The same held true for Nottingham. We were both already outlawed in our home shires, and once we came here and began helping Marian's crew, it was too dangerous for the group for us to remain in the open. We risked exposing everyone. We do visit, as often as we can, for we have plenty of information to pass along between us as we plan our various exploits. But we live in Sherwood Forest."

"There ought to be a way," Robin sat thinking, "...if we learn the secrets of Sherwood Forest the way we did of the castle, and make camp deep in its heart..."

"What are you thinking, Robin?" Marian asked.

"He's thinking," Dusty answered in his stead, "he'll help you set up a more stable camp in Sherwood. Many caravans pass through the Sherwood road carrying the taxes supposedly collected for the king's ransom. The Sheriff here seems to have Prince John's ear and his favor, for most of the taxes seem to gather here and line his pockets

231

before being shipped to London. If we knew the forest well enough, we might be able to way-lay the caravans, relieve them of their unjust shipments, and escape into the thick of the woods where no one could track us."

"We'd be a flash in the night," Robin said. "They wouldn't know what hit them."

"You must let me come with you," Mark said. "I can help! I'd love to be a part of the Sherwood gang."

"I do not know, Mark…"

"You cannot now say that I am too young," Mark laughed. "I have been fighting the Sheriff's men without you."

"You seem to already have a crew here," Allen said. "Would you abandon them?"

"Wouldn't it be better if we all worked together?" Mark replied. "We know Nottingham, we know the Sheriff. If you set up camp with Will and Little John and start raiding caravans, we can work in tandem to the benefit of the people of England."

"That's a decision for our leader, isn't it?" Will said, giving Mark a sharp glance.

"He's right," Marian said. "I appreciate the loyalty, Will, but we might as well join forces. It's not different than when you and Little John came to join Mark and I."

"I will return to Locksley," Robin said. "I might be able to assist as the Earl of Locksley as much as raiding the caravans."

"So you stay in Locksley, Marian in Wetherby, and the rest of us live in the forest?" Allen sighed. "I was so looking forward to an extended stay on an actual bed."

Much laughed. "Allen is the biggest complainer you will find in the king's army."

232

"I like beds!" Allen protested. "There's nothing wrong with that."

It was late that night when Robin finally led Allen, Much, and Dusty toward Locksley.

Allen had hoped his days of violence were over, but the people here were in need and he knew Robin would want to take care of them as he'd promised King Richard he'd do exactly that. Seeing the starving children and the swinging bodies of presumed innocents was enough for Allen to agree that joining that fight seemed a good idea. They had found the Men of the Night and the Hooded Rescuer and joining forces to better help the people of England was the most obvious and effective way for Robin to keep his promise to King Richard.

Chapter 32

The moon was obscured by clouds, and it was a relatively dark walk as Allen followed Robin across the rolling hills. Before too long, however, lighted windows appeared, and they were passing through the village of Locksley. Allen was eager to arrive so he could curl up in a bed and sleep–they'd been traveling a long time, and before that was imprisonment and the war…prior to that he'd lost everything the night of the fire. He was exhausted. And apparently he was about to start a new fight alongside Robin and the others, so he wanted more than anything else to just sleep.

Once they passed through the village, they followed the winding road to the manor itself. Lights glimmered in a few windows, but for the most part it appeared dark, the shadow of the house looming up in the darkness in front of them.

"Nice house," Allen commented, his voice breaking the silence between them. It was far larger than his own home had been before the fire.

Robin chuckled as he moved forward to knock. Nothing seemed to happen at first, so he pounded his fist with more gusto.

The door swung open and an old servant stood there. "Who goes there?"

"Your master," Robin said, stepping forward and pushing past the old man into the front room. There was a fire lit in the hearth, lighting the whole of it with a warm glow.

"Master Robin!" The servant bowed, tears in his eyes as his surprise gave way to recognition. "You're home!"

"I am, indeed. I'll need my room ready for the night, as well as three guest bedrooms for my companions here. By the way, Much no longer works for me. He's a free man, so treat him as such."

The servant glanced toward Much with a quizzical look.

"Let us know when the rooms are ready for us," Robin said. "We'll be in the kitchen, assuming that's where Sarah is."

"I imagine she is, sir."

Robin hurried through the house with Much on his heels, and Allen and Dusty followed after them.

As soon as Robin entered the kitchen–a spacious room–he ran forward toward a woman seated at a small table on one side of the room.

"Sarah!"

She turned at the sound of his voice, and her face brightened. Allen's heart felt wrenched from his chest as he watched the middle-aged woman rise from the table, affectionately throwing her arms around Robin. A moment later she was caressing Much's cheek in the gentle sort of way Allen's own mother would have held his.

When their joyous reunion was through, Robin gestured toward the doorway where Allen and Dusty both stood, watching. "We brought friends."

"Oh, guests." The woman–presumably the Sarah that Robin had mentioned upon entering the house–straightened. "I'll have Matthew see to rooms–"

"Already done," Robin kissed her cheek. "This is Allen of the Dale, and Dusty."

"Pleasure to meet you," Allen gave a little bow from the doorway, but Dusty moved forward and hugged the woman. Allen

236

ached for such an embrace though the woman was a stranger to him–he wanted to feel the love of a mother once more.

Sarah ran her hand affectionately through Much's hair and Allen could feel tears filling his eyes. "I was so worried…worried my boys would never come home…and then the Earl died…"

"I was wondering about that." Robin sighed, a darkness clouded his usual cheerful countenance. "We have heard rumors that his death was not…natural."

Sarah crossed her arms. "It most certainly wasn't. It was that wretched Prince John and his servants."

"Have they done any more harm to our household, Sarah?" Robin asked.

"No. But I don't like them. The Sheriff is a terrible man. He hangs people for the fun of it. He almost hung Sir Godfrey! But the outlaws were able to stop that. I can't imagine how, but we're all grateful for it. You know Sir Godfrey has always been a beloved Sheriff of our shire, until the Prince deposed him and put his own wretched man in his place."

"Sir Godfrey was almost hung?" Robin asked. "I'd heard he was in prison?"

Allen stood stiffly in the doorway as Robin's conversation with Sarah continued. It wasn't that he didn't care about the rumors surrounding the death of Robin's father or that he didn't want to know what was happening in Nottingham–this place he was apparently going to call home. But Allen was unsteady on his feet from exhaustion and he only wanted to be allowed a bed for the night–especially given that Robin was threatening to move them to the forest to live among Marian's outlaw crew.

237

"But enough of serious talk," Sarah's voice pierced through the fog of Allen's tired mind. "You all must be famished after your journey! Let me get you something cooked up right quick, and then you can head to bed."

Sarah began to bustle about the kitchen with Much at her side as Robin, Dusty, and Allen found seats at the table where Sarah had been seated upon their arrival. Allen looked around the room, taking in the shelves full of utensils and food, the long table that dominated the center of the room–much larger than the one where he now sat with his friends–and the clay oven sitting beside a massive hearth.

It was more spacious and well-stocked than Florie's kitchen had been, but even so it brought a flood of memories to Allen's mind. Sitting at the table in Florie's kitchen as he strung beads together to create a necklace for Alice...she'd wanted a silver necklace for her birthday, but she'd been only four and father had refused such an extravagance. Allen, perhaps seven or eight at the time, had gone down to the stream and collected all of the grey rocks that he could find. With Florie's help he'd made beads of them and strung them together for Alice's silver necklace. It was probably a sorry sight in truth, but Allen had been determined and Alice had been overjoyed, throwing her arms around him with a shout of glee when she'd seen it.

Allen shifted in his seat. Much was working cheerfully beside Sarah to prepare a meal for them, while Robin and Dusty chatted amiably at the table beside him. Allen blinked rapidly, whether to chase away tears or the sleep that threatened to overtake him, he wasn't sure. Perhaps both.

He looked about the kitchen again, imagining the smaller and far more homier one from his memories...he thought of the way Florie used to ruffled his hair gently like Sarah had done to Much only

238

minutes ago, though Florie's demeanor was ever gruff and bossy…the way William would flirt with Florie; Allen could not help but wonder yet again why the two of them never married.

Allen turned aside to hide from Robin and Dusty as he surreptitiously wiped the tears from his cheeks.

Eventually food was brought and Sarah stood guard over the group, making sure everyone ate a decent amount. Eventually the older servant–Matthew–came to the kitchen to tell Robin rooms had been prepared, and Allen was at last granted his wish for sleep.

Chapter 33

The next day Will and Little John took Allen, Robin, Much, and Dusty to their camp in the woods to show them how they'd been living. It was a simple set-up; two roughly put-together tents propped up under the trees some distance from the main road that cut through Sherwood Forest. There was a burnt patch of grass and dirt where they had a fire occasionally, but there was little else to their make-shift camp.

"This is hardly an ideal spot to create a well established camp," Robin commented. "It's too close to the Sherwood road. If we set up a large, functional camp here, we'll be noticed. We need to go deeper into the woods."

Will shrugged. "We basically just sleep here. If we need to go deeper to suit your purposes, then so be it. Lead the way."

Robin and Dusty took the lead, pushing through the forest and undergrowth with the rest of the group following them as they searched for a better place to house the growing number of people fighting the injustice in Nottingham and the rest of England.

As they walked, they began discussing the various things they would need in order to establish a more proper base of operations; shelters of some kind to live in, supplies and provisions.

"We usually visit Marian and get supplies from her," Will said. "We visit every few days for that purpose, as well as to exchange information or plan rescues."

Robin shook his head. "We cannot continue to take supplies from Marian. The less we do through her, the better. I don't want her getting hurt."

"She's led us well this past year," Little John growled.

"Yes, I know," Robin replied. "But I'm here now, so she doesn't need to worry about it. She can gather information in the castle if she sees fit to do so, but there is no reason for us to expose her unnecessarily. We need to be careful."

"You are rather protective of her," Will commented.

"Yes, I am. She is the love of my life and I will not see her hurt or in trouble. I will do everything in my power to avoid it."

Allen could understand Robin's protective feelings–he would have done anything to keep Eri out of harm's way.

He *should have* done anything.

Allen winced, his hands balling into fists at his side as he followed the rest of the group across a fallen log that formed a sort of bridge over a small stream. He hadn't done anything to protect Eri. He could vividly remember the way he'd lain in the wet grass letting the rain put out the flames on his clothes before he'd remembered that his wife might still be inside the inferno.

He'd failed Eri.

He'd failed all of them.

Will and Little John seemed annoyed at Robin's protectiveness over Marian, but Allen felt his friend was perfectly in the right. He should do whatever was necessary to keep the woman he loved safe.

The rest of the week was busy. Allen, Will, and Little John built huts for everyone to live in, as well as one to store supplies. Robin, Much, and Mark were busy carrying supplies to the camp from Locksley and the market in Nottingham. Robin also had to make some public appearances with the nobles in Nottingham to let it be known he'd returned home. Dusty stayed in Wetherby with Marian and they sewed new clothes for the gang, with lots of greens and browns so as to blend into the forest.

242

Marian soon heard of a caravan of treasure–made up of taxes extorted from the people–passing through the Sherwood road on its way to Nottingham and the Sheriff–a Sir John who had replaced Marian's father as the sheriff once it became clear that Sir Godfrey would not play by Prince John's new rules.

"What do you think?" Allen asked, hands on his hips as he watched Robin walking along the road. The king's road cut through the massive forest of Sherwood, twisting and turning its way through the trees and around the hills and boulders within its borders. When Marian brought news of the caravan that would be passing through with treasure, Robin decided they would ambush it.

It was their first foray into the rebellion. Allen and Robin had left the meadow where the camp was taking shape and had gone to the Sherwood Road to scout out the best place for an ambush.

"I believe this could work," Robin said. "The bend in the road up there will block our ambush from their view until it is too late."

"There's also the spot further east," Allen said, walking over to stand beside Robin. "The road was narrower there–less room for escape or turning around to flee our attack. They'd have to run into the trees."

Robin nodded. "I like both the spots you've found, but this one is better."

"Are we shooting to kill."

"Obviously."

Allen nodded, trying not to let Robin see how much that unsettled him. He would never get used to seeing corpses. Especially not ones that he himself was responsible for.

"I might leave at least one survivor to take news to the Sheriff," Robin said. "Let him know he has enemies now."

"He already has enemies. We didn't start this rebellion, we're merely helping."

Robin shrugged. "They haven't stolen his money right out from under his nose. It will be good, I think, for the Sheriff to hear of it."

The following day, Robin and Allen brought everyone to the place and they chose hiding spots while Robin instructed them to follow his signal–a sharp whistling sound–for the ambush. Robin had also created a second note for retreat, but Allen knew he had no desire to ever use it.

Within minutes they were dispersing off of the road and to their respective hiding places. Allen leaned his shoulder into the tree beside him for support, running his hands lightly over his bow. This was the part that was less fun. Killing. He didn't relish fighting as he once had, and he certainly wasn't looking to die anymore.

But he'd seen the starving children and the dead hanging all across England, and he was willing to fight against that happening to anyone else.

The caravan rolled slowly into sight, coming down the dusty path. The soldiers accompanying it were laughing and talking loudly. They were not prepared; that much was good.

When the high piercing whistle filled the air, Allen leapt from behind his tree, raised his bow and took aim. As soon as he'd let fly the arrow, he turned away, unable to watch the soldier fall.

The dead soldier might not be evil at all, but merely guarding the caravan as a means to keep his own family fed and Allen didn't want to think about that. Each person who fell under the perfect aim of his arrows made him wince, and he found himself sinking into his place of numbness and nothingness so he wouldn't have to see their faces as they died.

But when the bodies dropped, he couldn't help seeing his own family laying–charred and blackened–across the Scottish moors.

It did not take long for the gang to dispatch the few soldiers guarding the caravan, much to Allen's relief. Robin caught hold of the reins of the only survivor. "I thank you for your generous donation to King Richard."

"You...you wouldn't dare!" the soldier sputtered.

"Oh but we would," Robin replied.

Dusty, Will, and Little John jumped onto the carts and began to drive them off the road, Allen moved forward and grabbed one of the large wooden chests that had been carried by several men rather than driven on one of the carts. He couldn't lift it on his own, so he dragged it awkwardly off of the road. He could still hear the conversation that Robin was having with the soldier.

"Who are you?" the soldier demanded.

"No one special," Robin said. "Most people call me Robin."

"I'll remember you, Robin of the Hood! You'll hang for this."

Robin sent the soldier back to Nottingham with the expectation he'd inform the Sheriff he now had someone to answer to when stealing excessive taxes from his subjects, and then assisted with taking the treasure back to the camp.

Once everyone was there, Dusty insisted they pray and thank God for their successes.

Allen felt a flare of frustration at her suggestion. "Is that really necessary, Dusty?"

"You may not think so, Allen, but I do."

"I see no reason why we can't," Will said. "Robin?"

"Whatever," Robin replied shrugging. 'I don't care."

So Dusty knelt and prayed.

"Now, on to more important business," Allen said. "What are we to do with the horses and carts we've just acquired?"

"We can take the carts apart," Will said, "and use the wood to finish building our huts."

"And we will give the horses to some deserving farmer," Robin said.

"Can't we keep them?" Allen asked. "They could be useful."

"But we would have to feed and stable them," Will said. "I do not think that would be wise."

"I don't think so either," Robin said. And so that was decided.

The next day, the Sheriff put up proclamations declaring that Robin of the Hood was an outlaw and anyone aiding him would be labeled such as well.

Allen and Dusty were soon introduced to the secret passageways of Nottingham. Robin had hinted at the secrets that the castle held many times–during their travel to Nottingham he'd assumed that's where the Men of the Night were getting their information, and he was right. He took Allen and Dusty into the city one day to show them how to reach the secret passageways.

They entered a bakery on the street jutted up against the castle walls. The baker seemed to know Robin well. As Robin walked to the back of the shop and slid open the secret door in the wall, Allen watched with fascination.

Slipping into the darkness behind his brother, he said, "Why does the baker let you in?"

"He's a good man."

"That's not an answer."

Once Dusty was inside the passage, Robin slid the door closed again. Darkness consumed them. The only sound was that of their breathing.

But then Robin's voice broke the stillness. "He is loyal to King Richard–and he knew my father, knows Marian's father who used to be the sheriff of Nottingham. Marian and I…and Much and Mark…we would explore the castle as kids. We used to run through his bakery all the time going in and out of the castle. He's fond of us, and more than that he's eager to fight for justice."

"I imagine we'll find many such allies," Dusty said.

"Indeed. Now listen, once we're inside the castle it's imperative that you stay as quiet as possible. Every sound is likely to amplify and echo in the stone passages. It's going to be dark almost the entire time, so you'll need to keep a hand on the wall. I'll bring you back every day until you learn the passages by heart. Much and I have the advantage of having grown up in these secret passages."

"Along with having us visit, you might draw us a map of some kind that we can study," Allen suggested.

Robin agreed.

Allen soon discovered that it wasn't only the sounds inside the passage that could be heard–it was those within the castle themselves. There were slits in the stone at various places where they could listen to conversations within different rooms–and there were doorways that slid or swung open depending on their location within the castle. Spying on the Sheriff and his right hand–Sir Guy of Gisbourne–was easy.

For several days Robin would take Dusty and Allen into the cool stone passages and they would wander the darkness inside the very walls of the castle. In the evening they would gather together as Robin used a stick to draw in the dirt, showing the various passages and secret doorways that led into the castle. Allen wasn't sure how quickly he and Dusty were going to pick up on the secrets, but he did his best.

Every day one or another member of Robin's gang would spend their time in the passageways listening for news of caravans of treasure or unjust executions. The news was then relayed to Robin who would plan an ambush or escape as was necessary. A portion of the treasure collected was given back to the people, and Robin and his new gang spent a lot of their time traveling around handing out money. The rest of the money was sent to Duke Leopold of Austria to pay for King Richard's ransom so he could return eventually and put Prince John in his place.

Chapter 34

As the days passed, Robin and Will were often seen making new arrows while in the camp, and Dusty would spend many days gathering plants and herbs for her healing purposes, many of which she kept on her belt at all times in case she would need them. Whenever someone heard of a scheme of the Sheriff, Robin and Allen would spend the evening at the fireside in the camp discussing the best ways they might deal with the problems that arose.

One day the gang split in two—with Robin taking half of them to distribute money to the poor and needy while Allen led the others in an attempt to rescue a man who was being hung in a village south of Nottingham.

Allen tapped his fingers against his sword hilt as he leaned against the rough wood of the wall behind him. The scream of the woman being dragged to her execution filled the air and Allen peered around the building.

A soldier was forcing the woman to her knees in front of Sir Guy of Gisbourne, the Sheriff's favorite lackey. He was a tall man, with long dark hair. He almost always wore leather dyed black as the shadows from whence he likely sprang. More soldiers were gathered around, holding the tearful and indignant villagers at bay.

Gisbourne pulled his sword from its sheath and Allen pursed his lips together, letting out the high piercing whistle that Robin used as a signal.

At the sound, Will began to fire arrows from his hiding place on the roof of one of the buildings across the village. The soldier by the woman dropped dead, as did others around him.

Little John let out a ferocious yell and charged into the throng of soldiers, swinging his quarter staff wildly. Allen ran after him, his eyes on Gisbourne.

Gisbourne's sword met his with a decisive clash. The man's dark eyes were hard as flint. His arm moved with power and precision as he brought his blade toward Allen again and again. Allen was forced into the defensive, blocking Gisbourne's attacks with little room to spare.

He was good. More than good, he was probably the best swordsmen Allen had fought, and that included William.

Gisbourne's furious blows came without slowing and Allen realized he was being backed into a corner by the wall. He glanced past Gisbourne's shoulder to see the villagers were scattering and the woman was nowhere to be seen–Little John had done his job and gotten her out. Will was still firing arrows from the rooftop at the last of the soldiers in the area.

Allen's back hit the wall of the house behind him and he grunted. Gisbourne's sword came at him yet again, but Allen dropped to the ground, rolling in an undignified manner away from his foe and then springing to his feet and sprinting down the street.

"Running, outlaw? Coward!"

Allen ignored the taunts and kept running till he was free of the village. He sprinted over the hills to the place he'd planned ahead of time to meet Little John and Will. Little John was there with the woman–so Allen made sure she had the pouch of money they had brought as well as directions to the first tavern she should hide at. Robin and the gang had been crafting a sort of pathway from England to the coast and also to Scotland–depending on where people wanted to go–so that after rescuing someone from the Sheriff or Gisbourne they could

250

send them to safety. There were plenty of people in England willing to help save the innocent; once the woman was on her way, Will appeared.

"The soldiers?" Allen asked.

"Dead."

"Gisbourne?"

"Escaped."

"He always does."

"He nearly had you," Will commented.

Allen nodded. "Indeed."

As the weeks passed the gang fell into a rhythm, spying in Nottingham, then ambushing caravans and stopping executions when necessary. There were also plenty of days spent distributing what they had gathered to the inhabitants of Nottingham and the surrounding villages.

After a particularly lucrative raid, Allen dropped a jeweled chest onto the wooden floor of their supply hut with a loud thud. He stood back and surveyed the various chests around him. "Robin...we look wealthy."

Chests that were filled to the brim with gold and jewels were stacked around the storage hut in no particular order, with piles of sacks sitting beside and on top of the chests, filled with more treasure as well. Spare weapons from the blacksmith–Marcus–were hanging on one wall, and Dusty had a stash of herbs and spices hanging to dry on the other wall.

Much leaned around the doorway of the supply hut and grinned. "We *do* look rather wealthy."

"We need a lot," Robin said, stepping up between Allen and Much and slinging his arms around both their shoulders. "We have an entire country to feed and clothe, not to mention we're paying off the ransom for King Richard. We need all the gold we can get."

"Allen!" Will's voice called from across the clearing and Much, Allen, and Robin turned around. Will was just entering the camp, his arms full with a rather heavy looking bundle covered in cloth.

"What is it?" Robin asked.

"I've got the rest of the supplies so Little John and Allen can finish building their forge."

"Forge!" Robin glanced between Allen and Will with a grin. "I didn't realize we were building a town here."

Allen shook his head. "We aren't. But you and Will are constantly making extra arrows and bows; Little John and I thought we'd craft a few swords and daggers, too."

"We have Marcus for that," Much said.

"True, but it could become dangerous at some point to keep smuggling weapons from Marcus," Allen replied. "Little John and I thought it best we be prepared in case of that emergency."

"That's not a bad idea," Robin said.

"We don't have an army to equip," Much said. "Why would we need so many weapons?"

"You never know," Allen said. "We might recruit men for our gang. If we're saving the entire country, we will need some help. As Robin once said during our long adventures abroad, you can't do anything substantial with only a handful of men."

"Are we getting help, Robin?" Much asked.

Robin shrugged. "Who knows? But Allen is right; we are too small of a group to save all of England."

The meadow where they lived continued to take shape as huts were finished, the forge was built, and the place began to take on the feeling of a home despite being little more than a break in the thick forest of trees.

It soon became clear to the Sheriff–and most of the nobles of Nottingham–that the recently returned Earl of Locksley and the fast-becoming-famous outlaw Robin Hood had appeared at the same time and were likely the same person. At that point, it became dangerous for Robin and Much to live at or visit Locksley and they took to staying in camp as much as everyone else did.

Chapter 35

Allen pressed his ear to the cold stone wall, right where the nearly invisible crack was located. He was inside one of the secret passages in Nottingham castle, gathering information for the rest of the gang. The dark passages were still a bit of a maze to him–he couldn't traverse them with the ease that Robin, Much, Marian, and Mark could. Even Will and Little John had an easier time having been doing it for several years now.

There was no light inside the secret tunnels, and the only sound was the sound of his own breathing. He was still learning where cracks were located that peered into rooms, and where doors were located that entered the castle itself.

To his relief, the Sheriff and Gisbourne kept to the Great Hall and the dining room most days, so he didn't need to have the entire castle's secret passages memorized in order to be useful to the gang when it was his turn to spy on their enemies.

The room he was currently peering into was the Great Hall, where the Sheriff and Gisbourne made most of their plans. There was silence on the other side of the wall though, and Allen decided to risk checking.

He slowly pushed the secret door open the tiniest bit and peered into the room. Definitely empty.

They were probably in Nottingham Square, preparing for the Fair. The Nottingham Fair was world renowned and was taking place tomorrow. Merchants from around the world had been arriving all week bringing their own wares to sell, and this evening on his way to the castle Allen had seen that they were beginning to set up their booths in Nottingham Square.

There was also an influx of visitors from various places around the world, people traveling from miles around to come see the spectacle that the Fair was, with all the exotic things to buy, the singers and dancers for entertainment, and even the horse races and archery tournaments that anyone was able to participate in.

Allen knew he'd gone to the Fair as a child, but he had no recollection of the event, so he was as interested in the Fair as anyone else.

Before leaving the castle, Allen wound his way through several hidden passages until he was down in the dungeon. He generally got lost on this route once or twice, but he always tried to visit Marian's father Sir Godfrey when he was in the castle so he could tell Marian and Mark how he was doing.

He couldn't speak to him, due to the guards patrolling the dungeons, but he watched him from the hidden passage for a minute or two to ascertain whether or not his health was improving. Marian would want to know.

The old man sat on his little mattress in his small cell, his stringy grey hair falling around his weathered, wrinkled face. His shoulders were slumped, and he stared at his hands with no evident desire to do anything. He seemed entirely defeated, as usual. He was still thin, too, but that wasn't new.

After deciding Sir Godfrey seemed about the same as always, Allen left the castle through one of the secret entrances and then traversed the streets of Nottingham. He had his cloak tight about him and the hood up and covering his face as that was how they all tended to travel through Nottingham so as not to be seen. The people of

Nottingham were beginning to recognize members of Robin Hood's gang–and of course most knew exactly who Robin was–and most were eager to help hide them from the Sheriff's men.

One day, early on, Allen had been in Nottingham Square when Gisbourne came marching through the market. He was headed straight toward where Allen had been. Allen had been peering around eagerly for a hiding place when the people near him had enveloped him in a throng of gossip and laughter. At first he'd been confused, but then Gisbourne had marched straight on by. Ever since that day, the crowds would press around the gang if they were in Nottingham Square when the Sheriff's men or Gisbourne walked through, shielding them from unwelcome eyes. Or if they were in a more empty side street, the people there might try to cause a distraction or disturbance so that Allen could slip away without detection. He knew the people were doing the same for the other members of the gang. There was little love for the Sheriff or Gisbourne in Nottingham.

This week it was even easier to move through Nottingham without attracting attention because of the many visitors. The streets were flooded with people.

Allen caught sight of Gisbourne, dressed nearly all in black leather as he so often was, with his greasy black hair hanging over his eyes. He was backhanding a woman across the face on a side street not far from the market in Nottingham Square.

Allen winced, and his anger flared. He moved quickly down the street in their direction. Gisbourne spoke harshly to the woman and then turned and stomped down the street. Allen reached the woman a moment later.

She was elderly, with wrinkled skin and watery eyes. She was rubbing her cheek gently, as though to soothe the pain.

"Are you alright?" Allen asked softly, coming up behind her.

"That isn't the first time that young rascal has struck me," the woman replied, grinning at Allen. She was missing several teeth, but her eyes were bright and piercing. "I like to talk back to him. Someone needs to keep him in line, after all. He doesn't appreciate it, is all."

Allen smiled. He liked this spunky old lady. "You need to be careful. Gisbourne is dangerous."

"No, child. He's a hurting soul, that's all." The old woman patted Allen's arm. "You run along and tell that Robin Hood that old Tibb says thank you. You sweet things are doing so much for us."

"I'll tell him."

Tibb patted his arm again. "Get on now, go save the world. I can deal with the young rascal."

"You should still be careful."

"He's hurt, so he hurts." Tibb shrugged her frail shoulders. "I'll keep reprimanding him as his mother should until it gets through his thick skull."

Allen shook his head, but he couldn't help smiling at the woman. She was feisty. Despite the missing teeth and tattered clothes, she did seem more than capable of handling herself.

The next day, Robin and Much went to the Fair so Robin could keep an eye on Marian. It seemed Gisbourne had invited her to accompany him to the festivities and Robin was more than a little jealous.

Allen sat outside his hut sharpening his sword as Dusty mixed her dried herbs together near the supply hut and Will watched her from where he leaned against his own hut.

"You're missing out," Will commented.

258

"I will visit this famous Fair in a year when I am not a hunted outlaw," Dusty replied, not looking up from her work.

"What about you, Allen?" Will asked.

"I don't know, Will…I'm interested in the Fair. I've gone before, when I was a child, but I don't remember it. Still, it is dangerous to spend time in Nottingham. It's different when we're on a mission, but just wandering around? That's reckless. And given this is Robin we're talking about, and the woman he loves will be on the arm of another man–not just any man, but one of our biggest threats…he's bound to be reckless."

"Not that you aren't reckless, too," Dusty laughed. "You're as bad as Robin."

Allen smiled. "Possibly. Still, I agree with you, Dusty. It will be more enjoyable to visit the Fair when I'm not an outlaw."

When Robin and Much returned that evening, Robin was in high spirits. He came into the camp practically waltzing along and he was whistling, too. The rest of the gang had gathered around the fire ring for the night to await their return.

"How was the Fair?" Will asked with a grin as Robin and Much sat down around the fire.

"Entertaining, as it always is," Robin said. "I always loved it as a child."

"Was Marian in any danger?" Allen asked, brushing his shoulder into Robin's with a laugh.

"She was in grave danger," Robin groaned rather dramatically. "That man has his eye on my Marian and I do not like it."

Allen and Little John both laughed at that.

"She'd never think of anyone but you, Robin," Much said.

"I know," Robin said. "Did you see the way she looked at him when he wasn't paying attention? I've never seen more disgust on her face."

"Does she ever look at you that way?" Allen asked, and Robin immediately whacked his arm.

"No, she doesn't. But I may have seen her glance in your direction with that look on her face."

Will threw back his head and laughed.

"You wound me, Robin," Allen chuckled. "I'll never forget this."

"You sound truly heartbroken," Robin rolled his eyes. "I'm sick with remorse."

A few weeks later, Allen found himself far south of Nottingham in a small town called Berkshire. Robin had sent the members of the gang to spread money and provisions to towns beyond Nottingham, and Allen was his chosen companion that day. Together Allen and Robin wandered the streets of Berkshire, going house to house handing out the food and money they had brought to the inhabitants.

The people Allen saw in the town were frail and thin, too many bones protruding from their skin, their cheeks sunken. They reminded Allen of his own appearance after a year in Durnstein prison.

"Are we making a difference, Robin?" Allen asked as they walked away from a woman they'd just delivered money and food to. She had six children, all of whom looked malnourished. Her husband had been hung recently for failure to pay taxes, and the gang had not been able to rescue him. There were only so many of them, and they could not be everywhere at once. The people in Nottingham were fairly well looked after, but the rest of England? Allen wasn't so sure.

"We're helping, Allen. We're doing all we can."

"But everywhere people are still starving, still dying."

"There's only so much we can do." Robin shoved a hand through his blond hair, his blue eyes darkening. Allen recognized the strain and longing in his voice. "I wish there was more, but…we're doing everything we possibly can. We stop as many wrongful deaths as we are able, we feed as many people as we can. What else is there, Allen?"

"I don't know. I just feel like it isn't enough…"

These people didn't deserve the lot in life they had been given. It made him angry just thinking about it. No one should be forced to die of starvation or watch their husband swinging lifeless from the gallows.

Or watch his entire family burn to a crisp.

Robin and Allen continued down the street, passing out the rest of the provisions and money that they had brought. People seemed grateful, but Allen didn't feel like they were worthy of the thanks and praise that they were given.

During the winter months it became even more imperative that the gang spread food around the country to the people who were starving at the best of times. Travel, however, had become more difficult and weeks would go by between trips beyond Nottingham. The extended breaks due to the inclement weather did not help Allen's feelings of inadequacy.

Chapter 36

The weeks continued to pass as the gang traveled far and wide, bringing money to the poorest of England. The Sheriff of Nottingham attempted to hang people who angered him and was foiled again and again by Robin Hood's gang. Occasionally the gang would miss an execution and someone would die–and far more often than Allen liked to think about, people in towns beyond Nottingham were dying at the hands of their own corrupt leaders and the gang was never there for them.

They weren't saving them. They weren't saving anyone.

He couldn't save them.

He wasn't a hero.

The gang continued to raid any of the caravans of treasure that passed through Sherwood, but the Sheriff grew tired of this and started to send his caravans on different routes. Sometimes the gang got wind of this and could still intercept the money, sometime the Sheriff received his ill-gotten treasure.

One day Allen found himself with the rest of the gang on a road outside of the village of Leicester some miles south of Nottingham, hastily setting up an ambush for the treasure that would be coming by.

"We'll hit the ambush as we always do," Robin said as he stood on the road, surveying the foliage around it. "There's less cover, but we can manage with the ditch here at the curve in the road, and there's enough bushes over there to make something work."

"Similar set up as always?" Will asked.

"It hasn't failed us yet," Robin replied. "You and Allen go over there," Robin said as he began pointing to various spots off the road and calling out names of the gang to assign them to a hiding spot.

Allen took up position in the ditch beside the road with Will at his side. They both pulled out their bows and prepared to wait for the caravan to arrive. They didn't have to wait long; soon enough, the creaking of wheels and laughter of men drifted through the air.

Allen pressed himself flat along the ground, holding his bow lightly in his hands. In another instant, Robin's sharp whistle pierced the air and Allen flipped up onto his knees, letting his first arrow fly.

A soldier dropped to the ground, Allen's arrow protruding from his neck.

Allen fired arrow after arrow as Will did the same beside him. Dusty began to dance through the soldiers with her daggers while Little John let out his war cry and charged with his quarter staff.

The road was full of chaos a moment later and Allen drifted into his place of numbness as the dead piled up around them.

A small shriek soon rent the air and Allen spun around, searching for the child who might have made such a sound. A second later he caught sight of a soldier climbing up the embankment further down the road, dragging a small child with him. He held a knife to the child's throat, and there was a thin line of blood already trickling down the small boy's neck.

Robin stepped into the road, arrow trained on the soldier. "You let the boy go, and I might let you live."

"If you fire at me, this boy dies with me."

"My arrows fly faster than the muscles in your wrist could twitch."

"Try me."

Robin glared at the soldier. Allen held his breath, his heart pounding wildly in his chest. Could Robin kill the soldier before the child died?

All fighting along the road seemed to have stopped as everyone's attention turned to Robin and the soldier threatening the child. Allen kept his bow in his hand, but Much dropped his as he watched the exchange.

"I and my surviving comrades are taking this treasure into town. We're keeping this little play-actor with us. Wanted to be a part of Robin Hood's band of outlaws?" The soldier tightened the knife at the child's throat and the child let out a whimper. "He gets treated like one. If you don't let us go, I will kill him. If you follow us or attack us on our route, I will kill him. The Sheriff of Nottingham will likely kill him once we arrive safely, but who's to say? Maybe he'll be lenient, despite him being caught fraternizing with Robin Hood in the middle of an act of treason."

"He's just a kid," Dusty called out from further down the road, her voice wavering with fear. "Let him be, please."

"You can have one of us," Will offered. "Let the child go."

Robin still had his arrow taut to his bowstring, aimed at the soldier, his eyes flashing with fire. Allen wished he'd just shoot and get it over with. He could kill him! He was the best shot in England.

The soldier began moving, keeping the boy in front of him and between himself and Robin, the knife still firmly pressed in place. He called out orders to the other surviving soldiers to start leading the horses pulling the carts down the road. They slowly moved to do so, eyeing the gang warily. Allen was tempted to shoot them, but if Robin wasn't going to then he couldn't break rank.

Robin kept his bow aloft, but he didn't fire, and he didn't say anything else as he watched the boy being dragged down the road, knife to his throat.

Much moved to stand beside him as the carts began to wheel by. "What do we do?"

"If we attack the other soldiers, he'll kill that boy." Robin finally lowered his bow as the last carts began to pass by with the remaining soldiers that hadn't been killed in the fighting.

"Robin?" Dusty stepped up beside him on his other side.

"I don't know." Robin flung his bow across the road and ran a hand through his hair with a groan. "I don't know!"

"We can take 'em," Little John growled. "Get the jump on him."

"He's not going to let that kid go," Will said. "If we try another ambush or attack, he'll slit the kid's throat."

"If we let him take that child back to the Sheriff, the Sheriff will not be kind to him," Dusty said. "He'll never see his family again. We have to save him."

"We're going to save him," Robin said. "I don't know how, but we're getting that kid back to his family, and we're getting the Sheriff's treasure. Just let me think…"

Robin began to pace down the road and Allen resisted the urge to shake him. They needed to go after the soldiers now, while they were still in sight! The kid wouldn't live if he was taken to the Sheriff, and the treasure was needed to keep feeding the people of England that they were barely saving as it was. Robin's delay was tormenting Allen.

The caravan of soldiers disappeared into the horizon down the road.

Eventually Robin started walking. He had not given a clue as to what his plan was, but Allen followed after him, eager to save the child and the treasure.

They were headed toward the village where they'd stabled their horses–borrowed from Marcus–before they'd set up the ambush. But before they reached the village, a man came running toward them.

"Robin Hood!"

"We know," Robin sighed.

"You've heard? You have to return to Nottingham at once!" The young man ran up to them, his breathing labored and his eyes wild. "The Sheriff is hanging six children!"

"Hanging children?" Much asked.

Robin shook his head as though to clear it. "Six? Now?"

"Lady Marian sent word, she's trying to reach you. It may be too late, already!"

"When is the Sheriff hanging children?" Will asked.

"At dawn," the villager replied. "Or so said the message from Lady Marian."

"We're too far from Nottingham to arrive before dawn," Little John commented.

Dusty turned aside, kneeling on the road. Allen wondered if she was praying and his hands balled into fists at his side. Her god wasn't going to save anyone.

"We have to go," Allen said, his anxiety and anger pulsing through his veins. "We can't let six kids hang."

"We can't get there in time to help," Little John said.

"And we have a kid here who needs help," Robin said. "If we run off to Nottingham, who knows what becomes of that little boy?"

"But six kids are being hung!" Allen began to pace. "We can't let that happen."

"We can't do anything," Little John repeated.

"If we hurry we might make it by morning!" Allen said. "Not if we stand here arguing, of course, but if we leave and we don't stop all night…we might make it."

"But that still leaves the question of our own hostage kid," Robin said. "He's our priority. Marian and Marcus can figure out something for the Nottingham kids."

"What if they don't?" Allen asked.

"What if we leave to save them and our kid is killed instead?" Robin replied.

"Saving six over one…if it's down to math, Robin…"

"It's never down to math!" Will snapped, glaring at Allen. "All seven of the children in question matter. All seven lives are valuable. But Little John is right, it's not about saving the six or the one. It's about possibly, maybe, potentially being able to arrive in time to do something for the six, or to do something for the one we have right in front of us."

Robin sighed, his fingers curling into fists.

"We find a way to save our kid," Robin said. "We save the kid, get the treasure, and then make haste for Nottingham."

"We'll be too late," Allen said, crossing his arms as his heart sank into his boots.

"We'll likely be too late for the Nottingham kids either way," Robin replied. "We don't have to be late for the kid who's only a few miles down the road. Now let's move! We need to catch up to that caravan and make a plan."

Chapter 37

Before long, the gang had retrieved their horses from Leicester and were riding after the caravan. Robin took Much and Mark and rode off to the right of the road, while Allen led Dusty, Will, and Little John to the left. They stayed far enough from the road to hopefully not draw the attention of the soldiers as they caught up to them. Allen thought it was a stupid plan, but Robin was insistent.

Allen dug his heels into the sides of his mount, leaning low over the horse's neck, trying desperately to keep the bodies of his family from swimming into his vision. It had been a while since they had, but now with the prospect of six children swinging from nooses in Nottingham and this kid they were chasing after potentially having his throat cut...

Allen tangled a hand into the horse's mane, forcing his mind away from death. He tried to sink into his safe place of not feeling anything, but it wasn't working.

Seven children were going to die that day.

And there was nothing Allen could do to save any of them. Allen kept his eyes on the distant road on the horizon. Before long, he caught sight of a bit of dust on the horizon that might be evidence of the caravan moving down the road.

Allen spurred his horse into a faster gallop, Will keeping pace beside him as they raced forward, trying to outstrip the caravan while still far enough away so as not to be seen.

Just as it seemed they were drawing level with what Allen assumed was the caravan in the distance, he saw something to give him a little hope.

"Trees!" Allen swiveled in his saddle to catch everyone's eyes as he pointed to the right. Allen turned his horse to the right, heading diagonally across the open field toward the trees, still hoping the caravan wouldn't be close enough to see them.

The moment Allen was under cover of the trees he leapt from his horse, slinging its reins around a tree branch and sprinting toward the road. He whipped his bow from his back and collapsed against a tree near the road, looking for any sign of the caravan. It seemed they'd successfully outstripped them–not surprising given they were on galloping horses and the caravan was pulling heavy treasure-laden carts and wagons.

Allen closed his eyes, taking a moment to breathe, trying to still his pounding heart. He hoped Robin, Much, and Mark had seen the trees from their side of the road and would ambush from there as well.

Robin's plan had been to get the kid while the rest of the group dealt with the other soldiers, but if Robin wasn't here, then Allen assumed that job would fall to him.

Allen wiped a sweaty palm down his trousers, his heart loudly beating in his ears.

If it was down to him to save the kid…the kid was doomed.

The sound of wheels caught his attention and his eyes snapped open. Ever so slowly the carts and soldiers came into view, inching along the road toward Allen and the others. The soldiers all had weapons drawn and were eyeing the trees warily. Perhaps they had seen the gang after all–or perhaps they were merely wary due to the previous ambush.

Suddenly Robin's high note pierced the air and Allen sagged into the tree beside him, feeling instant relief. In another moment, Allen was firing arrow after arrow toward the soldiers.

270

Little John let out a roar and went charging out into the road in his maniacal fashion, and Allen kept firing arrows into the chaos. More arrows were flying from both sides of the road; Allen was sure the whole gang had made it to the trees.

Allen saw Robin sprinting toward a cart near the front of the caravan as Mark and Will joined Little John in the midst of the fray, their swords flashing. Allen grabbed another arrow from his quiver, taking quick aim and letting it fly as another soldier dropped to the ground.

"We've got the kid!" Little John's voice echoed above the noise of the fighting. "Do we stay for the treasure?"

"We have six kids in Nottingham to deal with!" Dusty's shout carried across the din of the swordfighting.

"And we've got the treasure right here!" Little John shouted back, using his brute strength to knock aside several soldiers unfortunate enough to be within his reach.

Allen ignored the argument, his heart in his toes–the kids were where he wanted to go, but he couldn't say it. They were probably too late already. So he focused on what he could do–shoot down the soldiers right in front of him.

"I vote we leave the treasure and race for Nottingham!" Much's voice cried from across the road. "We could be too late as it is, why waste time!"

"I agree!" Will call out.

"We have to go now!" Dusty yelled.

"Get a move on!" Robin's voice suddenly joined the shouting match.

Robin's voice held more command than Dusty's, at least to Allen's mind. He snapped his bow onto his back and sprinted back through the trees toward his horse. As soon as he was mounted he spurred the horse into a gallop away from the trees. As he broke free of the outcropping, he caught sight of Robin and the others hurrying along the road as well and he adjusted course to race along beside them.

"The soldiers will be slow on foot," Robin said as the group came together, still racing forward. "Even if they unhitch the carts to use the horses to give chase, that will take time. We have a head start, let's get to Sherwood as fast as we can."

"Sherwood or Nottingham?" Dusty asked.

"Wetherby," Robin called, spurring his horse into a faster gait. "If Marian isn't there, we'll go to Nottingham to see if we're too late, and then convene at the camp."

Allen couldn't speak around the terror lodged in his throat. He couldn't stop picturing those six young bodies swinging in the air.

Duncan's tiny infant form, burnt to a crisp, wavered for a moment in front of his eyes but Allen shoved it away, leaning low over his horse as he raced toward the village of Wetherby. It would be hours before they arrived–they would never make it in time.

They rode through the night, and with every pound of the horse's hooves on the road Allen's despair grew.

Chapter 38

Allen's thoughts were dark and filled with corpses as the sun began to rise. The darkness deepened as the day lengthened. When Wetherby came into view in the distance, he was filled with dread.

Robin led them straight to Marian's home, but no one appeared to be there. Allen sat back in his saddle, straining to catch his breath. His horse was practically wheezing beneath him from the long run, his flanks covered in thick globs of sweat. Allen was sure the insides of his thighs had been rubbed raw from the long gallop.

Robin patted his own horse's neck gently and glanced at the rest of the group who had remained mounted when he'd gotten down to pound on Marian's door. The child they'd rescued was still sitting in Robin's saddle, his eyes wide and hands trembling.

"We can't all ride into Nottingham in this state; we'll draw attention. I'll go and see if there's bodies swinging in Nottingham Square. Meet me back at the camp. Take the kid with you."

"We'll wait to hear the news," Dusty said. "We'll meet you on the road between Nottingham and Sherwood."

Robin handed the reins of his horse to Much. "Alright. I'll see you soon."

Dusty led the group away from the village of Wetherby and toward the main road that led out of Nottingham, keeping out of sight of the city.

"We're too late."

"Don't say that, Much," Allen snapped. He agreed with Much, but he didn't want to think about it. "We don't know what happened."

"The children were to be hanged at dawn," Little John sighed. "It's past dawn, and we weren't here. Much is right. We're too late."

The boy they'd rescued started crying. "It's alright." Much said. "You're safe."

"And we'll get you home soon," Dusty said, guiding her horse over so she could reach out and brush the child's tears away. "Just as soon as we get all this sorted, we'll get you back to your parents. Don't worry."

"Robin's coming!" Mark said, causing everyone to turn and look down the road. Robin was indeed approaching.

"The kids?" Dusty asked, her voice unsteady in a way Dusty's rarely ever was.

"No executions. Marcus doesn't know what went down specifically, but the kids aren't dead. The Sheriff hanged some of his soldiers this morning; they're still swinging in Nottingham Square."

"The soldiers are, but the kids aren't?" Will asked.

Robin shrugged, pulling himself into his saddle behind the boy. "That's what I saw and what Marcus confirmed. I didn't see Marian. If she's not in Wetherby or Nottingham, she's probably at the camp. Let's go see what she has to say."

When the gang rode into camp, Marian was indeed sitting at the fireplace. She looked up as they came into the clearing, and then ran over to Robin and threw herself into his arms as he dismounted.

"Robin! So much has happened, I don't even know where to begin!"

"Start with the children," Robin said, helping the boy off of his horse as everyone dismounted and gathered around Marian.

"The Sheriff was going to hang six kids because he was angry with their parents. You were all gone, and I didn't know what to do. I tried to talk to Gisbourne; I asked him to let them go, but he refused."

"Of course he did," Robin said. "What did you expect?"

"Wait, Robin, I wasn't finished." Marian crossed her arms. "When I went to the Square, fully expecting to see the children hanging, the Sheriff was hanging his guards instead. From his angry ranting, I managed to make out that the children had escaped and he was hanging the guards who were keeping watch over them."

"I did see the dead soldiers," Robin said.

"But what about the children," Dusty interjected. "What happened? Where are they?"

"Sir Guy–Gisbourne–came to see me late last night. He told me he'd taken the children from custody and brought them to the edge of Sherwood. He didn't know what to do with them so he asked me to bring them to you. He figured you could keep the children safe here, and Robin…" Marian bit her lip.

"What?" Robin asked even as Dusty and Will exclaimed "The children are here?"

"Gisbourne proposed after he rescued the children…"

"He what?!" Robin's eyebrows hit his hairline. Little John coughed to cover his laughter as Will dropped the bow he'd been holding. Allen glanced between Robin and Marian, still reeling from the idea that the children were alive and hardly able to comprehend what Marian had just said.

"Gisbourne proposed?" Robin asked.

"Yes," Marian said.

"And you said?"

"No! Obviously I said no. Really, Robin, why would you ask that? Sir Guy of Gisbourne is a wretched, cruel man. Why would I marry him?"

"I'm relieved you feel that way."

"I was worried after I refused him that he'd take the children back and go through with the Sheriff's plan to hang them...but he didn't."

"I'm rather surprised at that, but I'm glad. And of course we'll keep the children! They're here now?" Robin asked as the group moved toward the fireplace and seated themselves on the logs circled around it. The boy they'd rescued sat between Much and Robin, watching the conversation unfold with wide, confused eyes.

"Yes, they're sleeping in the huts; they had a long night."

"I'm sure they did," Robin agreed. "I'm surprised Gisbourne even rescued them, but to let them go even after your refusal? What a man wouldn't do for Marian." Robin bent and kissed Marian's cheek with a wink.

"Sir Guy might not be as vile as people say," Dusty commented. "Or at the very least, he does have a conscience and does struggle with the choices that he makes."

Allen shook his head, considering the vile things he'd seen Gisbourne do in the past. "Don't count on it. He did this for Marian, not for any other reason. His conscience is not getting to him."

"You don't know that," Dusty replied.

Will placed a gentle hand on Dusty's shoulder. "He's evil, Dusty. Don't try to make a saint out of him."

"I don't make saints," Dusty replied. "I am only suggesting he is not fully evil, even as none of us are fully good. Only God can clothe us in any righteousness. We're all the worst of sinners before Him."

"I'd say we're better than Sir Guy of Gisbourne any day," Robin replied.

"Robin…" Dusty sighed.

Robin held up his hands to silence her. "Don't start. We all know how you feel. We don't need another lecture."

Little John steered the conversation away from Dusty before the argument could extend further. "Did Gisbourne not speak of anything else, Marian? He knows you are connected to our gang, that could mean trouble for you."

"I know," Marian replied, her gaze turning on Little John. "But he didn't say anything about it after we fought."

"He didn't mention Mark?" Little John pressed.

"Why would he ask about me?" Mark asked.

"I'm sure they've noticed you are never home," Little John replied.

"What Gisbourne will do with his information that Marian does indeed know who we are remains to be seen," Will said. "It might be too dangerous for her to continue living in Wetherby."

"We'll have to keep watch," Robin said. "Gisbourne knows she's helping us, if he came to her directly in order to get the children to us for safety…"

Marian pushed against his shoulder in a playful manner. "Don't look so grave. I will be fine."

"We'll keep an eye on Wetherby anyway," Robin replied.

"You do that," Marian said, kissing his cheek. "I need to get home anyway. Gisbourne might come back today."

"If he does, we'll be there," Robin said.

Marian gave him a last look and then slipped out of the camp.

"Little John, keep an eye on her today, will you?" Robin said.

Little John rose, grabbing his quarter staff from where he'd set it beside his hut. "Nothing will harm her today."

Little John soon left the camp to follow after Marian.

Much rose from the fire and went to his kitchen, just as the kids Gisbourne had rescued for Marian's sake started to poke their heads out of the huts around the camp. Dusty and Will gestured them over, and they hesitantly joined the group at the fire.

There were six of them in total. As the gang asked questions of the oldest ones to ascertain who they were and such-like, it became clear that the six children were cousins. Seven-year-old Beth, six-year-old John, and four-year-old Peter were the children of one man while ten-year-old William, eight-year old Sarah, and five-year-old Rachel were the children of his brother. It was their fathers who had angered the Sheriff, but he'd arrested them to prove a point and scare the rest of Nottingham.

"Being in the prison was scary," William said, his brow furrowing. He turned to Will. "Have you been to prison?"

"I haven't…I'm sorry it was scary."

"I didn't like it," William said simply.

"I'd imagine not."

Little Rachel, the five year old, crawled into Will's lap as Much began to scoop eggs and sausages onto plates and hand them out to the gang and the children. The little girl stared up into Will's face after scrambling onto his lap. "Are you nice?"

"I don't know, little lady," Will winked, brushing a wayward curl out of her face. "Am I?"

Rachel tilted her small head to one side, seeming to study his face. "I think so."

Allen shook his head with a laugh. "Don't be fooled, Rachel. You're only five, so maybe you can't see the truth, but Will is a–"

Dusty's elbow connected with Allen's ribs and cut off whatever he'd been about to say as he shied away from her with a wince and nearly dropped his plate of food.

Will raised his eyebrows. "I'm a what, Allen?"

Allen shrugged, glancing at Dusty. "I don't know. Nothing."

278

Robin laughed. "Don't worry, Rachel. Despite the silliness of our group, we're actually very nice, I promise."

Once everyone had eaten, Robin entrusted the kid from Leicester to Much to return him to his family while they figured out future sleeping arrangements now that they were housing six children. In the end it was decided that each member of the gang would have one kid live in their hut. The oldest boy, William, was to be Allen's bunkmate.

Given his name and his proximity to Nottingham, Allen couldn't help but think of his old friend William. He'd heard stories of how William had ended up in Scotland decades ago; he'd been a page to a knight of Nottingham. The knight had fallen in love with a Scottish lassie and followed her home to Scotland to marry her–that knight, and the Scottish lass in question, were Allen's grandparents on his mother's side. As he watched young William getting ready for bed, Allen couldn't help wondering what had become of *his* William after he'd set off for the Crusades. He was probably dead.

Chapter 39

The next morning when Robin handed out assignments for the day–spying in Nottingham, distributing food and money, watching over Marian's home in Wetherby in case Gisbourne retaliated in some fashion–Allen was told to stay in the camp and watch over the six children.

"You want me to play nursemaid?" Allen crossed his arms, raising his eyebrows at Robin.

"Someone has to." Robin shrugged. "We can't leave them alone, they're kids. We'll take turns every day, rotating who has to keep an eye on them. Today is your day. Deal with it."

Allen wasn't impressed, but Robin was in charge and he'd followed him through far worse than being a nanny. He wasn't going to argue.

The children were rather subdued and quiet through much of the day. The oldest girls took charge of the youngest toddlers, leaving little for Allen to do but make sure no one died. A difficult prospect for him, if he was honest. The curse saw to that.

Allen sat on one of the log benches by the fire ring, his head resting in the palm of his hands as his elbows pressed into his legs. He was bored.

William came and sat beside him. "I'm sorry you have to be stuck with us instead of saving people."

Allen glanced at him, and then at the group of children gathered across the clearing who seemed to be lost in a fit of giggles.

"I could tell Robin I'm old enough to watch my own family."

Allen shook his head, sitting up and slinging an arm around young William's shoulders. "Robin wouldn't agree to it."

"I'm almost a man."

"You're ten. Did you know Robin refused to let Mark–you know Mark? Lady Marian's brother, the Hooded Rescuer, famed hero of Nottingham?–Robin wouldn't let him come fight in the Crusades when he was fourteen. At least, that's the story I've been told. He's fairly protective of young folks."

"I could do it." William crossed his arms, sitting up straight and jutting out his chin.

Allen chuckled. "I'm sure you could. And it would be nice to be doing something other than watching the little ones today...but I'm telling you, Robin won't go for it. You're also going to find he's incredibly stubborn. You can't change his mind. Only Much could–or Marian, I suppose."

William sagged a bit. "I don't want to be an inconvenience to Robin Hood or his gang."

Allen studied young William and then turned toward the group of children giggling across the clearing, his heart squeezing in his chest. Would Duncan have been like this? Full of life and fun? What would his laughter have sounded like? Would he have looked up at Allen with the adoring gaze that young William always gave Robin?

Allen clenched his teeth together. His son would never get a chance to be anything, because he'd been burned to a crisp as an infant. It wasn't fair.

Allen wasn't going to let anything like that happen to these children. He might be annoyed that he had to watch them instead of doing something he felt would be more useful to the cause, but he wasn't going to let anything happen to the children. Ever.

"You're fine, kid. This is what we do–take care of people."

"You didn't want to."

"No I didn't. Don't, really. But it's true; this is in line with what we do, what we stand for."

Later that night, Allen was shocked to see Much dragging Mark into camp. He let go as they entered the clearing and Mark shoved away from him, turning to glare at Much.

"What's going on?" Allen asked. He was sitting at the fire ring with the children circled around him as an angry Mark and a harried looking Much moved toward them.

"Gisbourne burned the house in Wetherby and has taken Marian captive," Much said.

Allen's knees buckled and his legs turned to noodles as Much's words sank in.

Her home was burned…

Florie's unseeing eyes seemed to be staring up at Allen. He tried to shake his head to clear it, but her face wouldn't budge.

His son, tiny and charred…his wife burned to a crisp…his parents…

"Robin said Mark isn't to leave the camp until he comes back, in case he does something stupid in retaliation."

Allen crossed his arms and studied Mark, trying to keep his own emotions from surfacing as Mark glared at Much.

"You said Marian…"

"Is taken captive," Much said. "She's okay, for now."

Finally, Mark gave up on the glaring match with Much and plopped onto a bench. "If anything happens to Marian because I wasn't there to help her…"

"Robin Hood will keep her safe," young William declared.

Some of the children resumed their playing in the open area of the meadow, while young William settled onto the log beside Mark and tried to convince him that Robin Hood could do anything, including protecting the woman that he loved.

Mark remained tense, but he didn't try to fight Much as he settled onto the log next to Allen, watching Mark carefully from across the fire.

"Eventful day, I guess," Allen said, watching Mark's brooding face.

"Things just get worse and worse," Much sighed. "First the botched raid and the hostage situation, then the children nearly getting hanged, and now Marian's taken captive and her home is burned to the ground...I feel something terrible is coming."

"Or maybe the disasters have run their course and things will settle down again," Allen suggested, though he didn't believe it. He was cursed.

Maybe he should get away from the gang and that would help them.

As they waited for Robin to return with news, the rest of the gang began to trickle back into camp. Much and Mark let them in on what had happened in Wetherby, and they all waited for Robin's return with trepidation. The children were eventually put to bed, and then the gang gathered around the fire ring to wait.

Allen's palms were sweaty, his heart pounding rapidly in his chest. Marian wasn't dead, that much was a relief. But taken captive by the Sheriff and Gisbourne, both of whom seemed vindictive and unpredictable...it wasn't a good situation.

Allen didn't know Marian well, but she was Robin's beloved and that made her family. Which meant her dying was definitely not an option.

The first inkling that Robin was returning to camp was the sound of his cheerful whistling. Mark was on his feet instantly even before Robin strode into the clearing. "Where's Marian? Why are you so happy?"

Robin came to join the circle around the fire ring. "Sit down, Mark. She's alive, she's fine." Mark sank back onto the log-bench with a sigh as Robin continued, "She's under house arrest and has a personal guard to tail her wherever she goes within the castle. It will be difficult to see her, but not impossible. Her room is, in fact, one of the many that has a door directly into the secret passages."

"That's a relief," Mark said. Allen thought that was the understatement of the century. "But it doesn't explain your whistling! Why didn't you get her out as long as there's a passage that leads right to her room?"

"She wants to stay to be near your father, and also to pick up information from the Sheriff and Gisbourne that we might not be able to get simply from the secret passages. They don't connect to every room in the castle, it is possible there are plots and schemes that we miss, that she will now be able to hear about and help us foil."

"That's all well and good, but still not enough reasons to be whistling for," Mark said.

"No, I suppose they aren't. But Marian told me this evening she loved me, and that's enough to get me to whistle."

"We all saw that coming," Mark said with a roll of his eyes, still seeming unsatisfied by Robin's report.

The release of tension washing over Allen as his memories of charred bodies was replaced with the knowledge that Marian was safe–at least for now–caused laughter to bubble up and escape him at Robin's pronouncement that Marian loved him, and Mark's unimpressed attitude.

"It might have been obvious," Allen said as his laughter subsided, "but our poor Robin has been worried sick."

Robin opened his mouth as though to say something and then snapped it shut again, shaking his head silently.

With the news that Marian was safe for the present, Allen was able to retire to bed with some sense of calm.

Unfortunately, his sleeping mind brought forth every image of his dead family that it could conjure–some memories of the brief glimpses he'd gotten of their corpses, some the detailed workings of his imagination.

Allen awoke screaming Eri's name only to find young William bending over him, shaking his shoulders, his eyes wide and terrified.

"Allen?"

"I'm okay, kid. I'm okay. Just a nightmare."

After convincing William to go back to sleep, Allen lay awake, staring at the ceiling of his hut. He wasn't about to go back to sleep. He didn't trust his own mind.

Chapter 40

Marian was not content to stay inside the castle walls while she was under house arrest with the Sheriff, and so she began to sneak out through the secret passages–mostly at night, when she wouldn't be missed. She had a constant guard at the castle, but he slept outside her door when she retired for the night, so she could easily slip into the secret passages through the hidden door in her room and exit the castle without drawing attention to her absence. She would visit the camp, training with Robin to improve her skills with various weapons. Mark also had a Hooded Rescuer disguise made for her to match his own so when she chose to move through the streets of Nottingham to help people she would not be recognized.

Young William was inspired by her dedication and Will soon took up teaching him how to use a bow.

"Is this going to be a useful pastime?" Allen asked as Will and young William moved across the clearing from the rest of the group gathered at the fire one evening.

"You said yourself that we need more recruits for our rebellion if we're going to save England," Will called back, throwing Allen a wink.

"He has a point," Robin laughed.

"I wasn't thinking we'd recruit ten-year-olds."

"He's strong and able," Will said. "And brave, too."

Young William beamed under such praise, but Allen's uneasiness did not abate. What they did was dangerous, and he had no desire for a child to be placed in such violent situations as they often found themselves. Particularly not a child he'd promised himself he would protect.

"Will makes a strong case for our new recruit." Little John nodded slowly, rubbing his chin thoughtfully.

"He's far too young to join us," Allen insisted, worry for the child brewing in his chest.

"He's been in the Sheriff's prison," Will replied. "Have you?"

"Not in the Sheriff's prison, no, but I have been imprisoned several other places." Allen remembered vividly the indignity, the starvation, the horror of being imprisoned. The mere idea of such a thing occurring to young William–or any of the children–sent shivers of dread rolling down his back.

"Then you know the kind of courage it takes to survive that ordeal. Come on, William," Will slung his arm around the boy's shoulders. "Just ignore Allen."

"That's what we all do," Mark chimed in with a laugh.

As time went on, Sir Godfrey's health took a turn for the worse. Both Marian and Mark were extremely worried about him. Allen hated to see his friends so distraught, so he went to Robin.

"Is there nothing we can do, Robin? Can't we get him out of the dungeon?" The two of them were near the edge of camp, the moon pale and cold in the sky above them. Most of the camp had gone to bed, but Allen had cornered Robin before he could retire for the night.

"I have been trying to think of a way to rescue him," Robin said.

"And?"

288

"Anything I have thought of would be risky and nearly impossible." Robin shoved a hand through his hair and shrugged.

"Can we sneak Dusty into the castle to help him? She might be able to heal him."

"I've thought of that as well, Allen. But I don't see how we can get her to his cell without being seen or with enough time to actually heal him before getting caught or getting out."

"We have to do something! He's dying."

"You don't think I want to help him? I've known Sir Godfrey since I was a boy, he practically raised me alongside my own father! He's also Marian's father…I love him. I don't need you to tell me how desperate his situation is. But I can't get to him to help him right now. I've been trying. There's nothing to do."

Allen wasn't satisfied, but he didn't push Robin any further. Robin was right; he did know and love Sir Godfrey more than Allen could, which meant he would be even more desperate to find a solution than Allen currently was. He'd figure something out eventually.

As the days continued to pass, the Sheriff began to send companies of soldiers into Sherwood Forest when no caravans were expected. The gang came across them wandering through the underbrush far from the road, and Robin came to believe the Sheriff was doing his best to find the camp. Despite his best efforts, the Sheriff never found the camp and the gang continued to raid his caravans and stop his executions.

One day while in the secret passages in Nottingham Castle, Allen moved carefully through the dark tunnel, placing each foot gingerly so as not to make any sound that would echo across the cold stone floor and walls. His hand was on the wall beside him, giving him an anchor to reality in the sea of black. Suddenly he heard Gisbourne's voice coming muffled through the wall and he moved closer to the stone, his hand gently sliding over the cool surface until it found the crack he could use to spy on the room beyond.

Pressing his ear over the crack, he strained to hear the conversation beyond the wall.

"…I need him dead now, Gisbourne!"

"You will have to be patient, sir."

The Sheriff and Gisbourne were plotting yet another murder. Allen held his breath, trying to hear past his own breathing and the sound of his heartbeat to catch more of the conversation.

"We'll have to do it soon," the Sheriff said.

"I agree. But not hanging. He'll only be rescued."

"That wouldn't happen if your soldiers weren't so incompetent!"

"I believe we should simply kill him in his sleep. One of the guards could do it easily enough. He's old and weak."

"Well make it happen then. The sooner the better."

Allen waited for information, something he could report to Robin so they could save whomever the Sheriff and Gisbourne wanted to kill in their sleep, but the conversation appeared to be over. He could hear Gisbourne's boots against the stone floor fading as he marched out of the room.

When Allen returned to camp that night, he reported the incomplete plot to Robin, but having no idea who the intended victim was there wasn't much they could do about it. There weren't enough of them to stand guard at every single house in Nottingham where an old man might live. Despite this, however, they never heard of anyone being murdered in their sleep. Robin suspected they hadn't followed through with it, but Allen thought perhaps they were merely biding their time. Gisbourne had told the Sheriff to be patient, whatever that might mean.

One day Mark came striding into camp after a visit to Nottingham with a spring in his step as he strode over to the group gathered around the fire.

"What did you do?" Will chuckled, eyeing Mark's grinning face.

"Me? Nothing."

After a moment's silence, Mark shrugged. "Father should be on the mend soon."

"How do you know?" Robin asked, leaning forward and sharply studying Mark's face.

"Because the physician is seeing to him."

"Will the Sheriff allow that?" Much asked.

"Of course he will, because Sir Guy of Gisbourne is going to send for him."

"Gisbourne!" Allen leaned forward, his eyebrows hitting his hairline. Why would Gisbourne send for a physician for Sir Godfrey?

"Yes." Mark shrugged, cool as a cucumber. "I made Marian go and…ask for his help."

"Marian and Gisbourne still aren't speaking to each other, are they?" Robin asked. "Last I heard they couldn't speak without arguing so they'd resorted to stony silence."

"Well…" Mark sighed dramatically, but his eyes were barely holding in his laughter. "You won't like this, Robin, but I told Marian to charm him into helping!"

"Mark!" Much was aghast, but Robin only burst out laughing.

"Poor man! No one should be tortured in such a way."

Allen didn't care how help had come to Sir Godfrey, as long as he had a chance to get better. Marian and Mark wouldn't lose their beloved father, and everyone could stop worrying about him. Allen didn't care by what means the miracle had been accomplished; it was good news.

Chapter 41

Allen scrambled up a tree, swinging himself into a low hanging branch as Robin called out, "Be careful, everyone!"

Ambushing the Sheriff's caravans was almost mundane these days—Robin would whistle, they'd shoot down the soldiers, maybe engage in a sword fight, and then carry off the treasure triumphantly.

As the caravan rolled into sight around the curve in the road that cut through the forest, Allen crouched low, nocking an arrow to the string and taking aim. He breathed deeply, willing himself to remain calm as he let his mind drift out of any awareness of the deaths he was about to inflict.

By the time Robin's whistle filled the air, the leading cart was directly beneath Allen. He let off a single arrow and then swung from the branch, kicking the driver below him off of the cart. His companions were shooting arrows into the soldiers, or jumping up onto carts and beginning to drive them off the road to take them to the camp, depending on what job Robin had given them before the raid began.

Allen jumped off the cart and blocked a punch from the driver who had scrambled to his feet. The driver pulled a dagger from his belt and Allen cast aside his bow and unsheathed his sword to block the blade as it came close to his heart.

The driver stepped back and paused.

For a moment, Allen thought he was giving up.

And then Allen felt himself tugged backwards and up into the air from behind. The driver grinned at him, his eyes full of malice. Allen was pulled onto a horse in front of someone. He writhed and wriggled trying to break free, but the arm around his waist seemed to be

293

made of iron. The pressure of a vise-like grip on his wrist had him releasing his sword with a cry of pain.

"Allen!"

Allen heard his friends calling after him and he struggled against the muscled arms that held him on the horse.

The cold bite of a knife kissed his throat. Allen froze.

"Don't move," a voice hissed in his ear.

Gisbourne.

Allen tried to elbow Gisbourne's ribs but the knife at his throat pierced his skin and Allen froze again. He could feel the trickle of blood sliding down his neck as Gisbourne held him firmly in place.

If he fought, he'd die. So Allen didn't fight.

Gisbourne urged his mount into a gallop, which unnerved Allen. The knife at his throat was held in a firm grip, but the pounding of the hooves and the jolting of both Gisbourne and Allen as a result meant the blade bit into his skin more than once.

Gisbourne carried him back to Nottingham and then dragged him into the castle courtyard. Several soldiers came running toward them and Gisbourne handed Allen over.

As soon as Gisbourne's knife was away from his neck, Allen tried to wriggle out of reach of the other soldiers, but one punched his face as another kicked him in the gut and Allen doubled over in pain, dropping to the cobblestone courtyard as another soldier began to bind his hands behind his back.

"Take him to the dungeon. It's about time we had another inmate."

"Not that we'll have the other one much longer," one of the soldiers muttered.

"Quiet!" Gisbourne barked.

The soldiers took Allen down to the dungeon and threw him in a cell. Allen slumped onto the bunk against the far wall and sighed, putting his head into his hands.

"It's not so bad down here," a voice to his left said. Then he coughed.

Allen looked over. Sir Godfrey was there in the cell next to him. He was pale, and his grey hair was sticking to his head. Sweat was beading on his face.

"Sir Godfrey!"

"Do I know you, lad?" Sir Godfrey asked, struggling to sit up.

"No, but I work with Robin Hood."

"Do you?" Sir Godfrey asked.

"Yes, sir. Don't worry, Robin will get us out of here."

"I doubt that."

"He will. Robin can do anything."

"You aren't going to save England, you know that? You children aren't going to save England."

"We aren't children," Allen snapped.

Sir Godfrey didn't respond. He leaned his head against the stone wall and sighed heavily, closing his eyes. He looked old and weak. Perhaps that was why the soldier upstairs had said he wouldn't be here much longer.

Allen didn't know him well, but he was Marian's father. He couldn't die. Marian and Robin would be devastated.

Allen studied the man for a moment and then bolted to his feet.

The plot!

Gisbourne was planning on killing someone old and weak in their sleep. No one had died yet…but Sir Godfrey…he could be the victim! Allen wasn't sure, but the more he thought about it, the more he suspected that was the case.

Sir Godfrey was the previous sheriff of Nottingham; he was beloved by the people. He was a symbol of hope–it would make sense to kill him off. The Sheriff had nearly hung him once before according to Marian and then had changed his mind after the initial hanging had been stopped by Marian, Mark, Will, and Little John.

And of course there was Marian herself–fiery, unafraid. She was undoubtedly a thorn in the Sheriff's side and on top of everything else, the people of Nottingham adored her. She wasn't afraid of the Sheriff or Gisbourne, and she'd been fighting to end their injustice longer than anyone. Even under house arrest, she snuck out to be the Hooded Rescuer with Mark. She'd organized the original rebellion in Nottingham, though the Sheriff likely didn't know that. Still, killing her father seemed a brilliant way to get her to give up, to stop fighting. The more Allen thought about it, the more sense it made.

A minute later several soldiers entered the dungeon and came to Allen's cell. "Sir Guy wishes to speak to you."

One of the soldiers unlocked the cell and dragged Allen forward. They made sure his hands were bound once more before they led him out of the dungeons and through several corridors in the castle. Having only traversed the castle through the secret passages, Allen wasn't entirely sure what part of the castle they were in.

When they stopped to knock on a door, Gisbourne's gruff voice called for them to enter. He was leaning against the far wall of the room as the soldiers shoved Allen inside. Beside him was a desk with a chest sitting on it.

The two soldiers left, shutting the door behind them. Gisbourne tilted his head to one side, studying Allen as his hand seemed to almost caress the lid of the chest on the desk beside him.

"I am Sir Guy of Gisbourne."

"I know who you are," Allen spat.

"I believe your name is…Allen?" Gisbourne had a frown on his face, and his dark eyes were intense as they searched Allen's face.

"Yes."

"Where did you meet Robin Hood?"

"In…" Allen had almost said in Dover, but caught himself. "Why does that matter to you?"

"Strange sounding name," Gisbourne smirked. "I am not sure I know where that is located."

"Ha. Ha. You're amusing." Allen rolled his eyes.

"Thank you. Now, I need you to answer my questions."

Gisbourne straightened off of the wall where he'd been casually leaning, his eyes dark and flashing.

"Or what?" Allen asked. He wasn't afraid of Gisbourne, although he probably should have been.

"You'll die."

"I'm so scared," Allen said sarcastically.

Gisbourne's frown deepened. "I need information."

"Do you?"

"And I am going to get that information from you."

"Are you?"

Gisbourne walked around Allen, studying him carefully, his hand resting on the hilt of his sword at his waist.

"Where is Robin Hood's camp?"

"In Sherwood."

"I know that much," Gisbourne snapped.

"That's all I can tell you."

"How does Robin Hood know everything that he knows?"

"He's an intelligent man."

"How does he get his information? How does he know where we are sending treasure, when we are hanging someone…how does he know?" Gisbourne's face was growing more red with every question.

"He has spies, of course."

"Yes, I figured as much. Are you one of them?"

"Occasionally."

"But his spies…how do they learn their information? Who are they bribing?"

The idea that the gang used bribes was amusing to Allen, but he refrained from laughing. "Really, Gisbourne, not everyone works for money. None of your precious soldiers have betrayed the Sheriff. We don't need to work through them. We have eyes and ears without them."

"Where?" Gisbourne demanded.

"In the…" Allen stopped. He had almost said in the walls. That would have been far too obvious. He needed to watch his tongue, lose his confident attitude.

"In the what?"

Allen didn't respond.

"Allen, I don't think you quite understand what is happening here." Gisbourne stopped in front of him, whipping out a dagger and pressing the sharp blade into Allen's chin. "You have this one night to answer my questions, and tomorrow you die."

Allen pressed his lips together, keeping eye contact with Gisbourne. He'd already said too much. He could feel his anger growing, that white hot fury that coursed through his veins. He might do something stupid if he opened his mouth, so he firmly kept it closed.

"Of course, if you cooperate I might be able to postpone your death…for a time."

"Kill me," Allen snapped. "Go ahead. I don't care. I won't betray Robin."

Gisbourne stepped back, sheathing his dagger as he moved toward the desk and the small chest on it. "I could pay you a large sum of money…"

Allen wanted to punch the smug look on Gisbourne's face as he opened the chest next to him. It was filled with gold coins. Gisbourne began to run his hand through the coins, picking a few up and letting them drop one at a time back into the pile.

Clink. Clink. Clink.

Allen was unimpressed. They had more money than that back at the camp if his only desire had been to get rich.

"I am willing to work with you, Allen, if only you are willing to work with me."

"To work with a servant of Prince John? A friend of the dreaded Sheriff? You must be joking."

"Isn't there anything you will give me information for? Anything at all?"

"No."

"That is a pity." Gisbourne snapped the chest shut. "I suppose you'll just have to go back to your cell…I'm afraid we don't have better accommodations for outlaws than the dungeon."

Thinking of the dungeon brought Sir Godrey back to Allen's mind, and along with it came the plot he'd overheard.

Sir Godfrey was wasting away; he was probably dying anyway. But what if that was because Gisbourne was poisoning him?

What if…what if Allen could convince Gisbourne not to do it?

He could save Sir Godfrey.

He hadn't been able to save his own parents, to save Florie. He couldn't save Alice. Or Eri. Or his infant son.

But perhaps, just maybe, he could save Sir Godfrey. For Marian. For Mark. They wouldn't have to lose him the way that Allen had lost his own family.

"I…" Allen hesitated, but Gisbourne's eyes were boring into his now. He stepped forward menacingly, eagerly.

Allen could just imagine how distraught Marian and Mark would be if their father died. He'd heard Robin say Sir Godfrey had been a second father to him–he had to keep them all from that devastating pain that he himself felt on a daily basis.

"Well?" Gisbourne asked. "I'm listening."

Protecting his friends from the grief that consumed him was a worthy cause, but Allen wasn't sure the plot was about Sir Godfrey at all. Before he chose to propose a deal with Gisbourne to save the man's life, he needed to know. Yet he couldn't come right out and ask Gisbourne about it.

"Sir Godfrey…"

"Yes? What about him?" Gisbourne barked.

There was only one way to find out if his suspicions were correct.

"You and the Sheriff are planning to kill him."

"Are we?" Gisbourne tried to sound nonchalant, but his face twitched, if only for a moment, and Allen was convinced he was right.

"Yes, you are. But you aren't going to hang him, are you? You're going to murder him in his sleep. Very bad natured of you, I must say."

Gisbourne just stared at him.

Allen thought of Marian, Robin's beloved, suffering the loss of her father. He thought of how upset Robin would be, both over Sir Godfrey's death and over Marian's grief.

"I don't care if you kill me, if you offer me a sea of riches...I won't betray Robin. But..."

"But?"

"I can't believe I'm saying this," Allen said. "But...for her..."

"Her? Who?"

"If you promise me, absolutely promise me, that Sir Godfrey will not be harmed, I will help you. I will give you the information that you need."

Chapter 42

Allen was returned to his cell, and he laid down on the little mattress to stare up at the ceiling. Sir Godrey was curled up on his own bed in the cell next to him, shivering slightly as though he had the chills. Allen wondered how sick he was; if he died from his illness, the promise from Gisbourne to keep him alive would be moot.

Allen covered his face with his hands and groaned. Had he really agreed to spy on Robin? He wasn't sure he could even follow through on such a promise. But Marian would be devastated if her father died–Allen understood that grief, that horror. He couldn't let that happen to her, to Robin. He just couldn't.

But betraying Robin?

It would be worth it if Gisbourne kept up his end of the deal and kept Sir Godfrey alive. If Marian and Robin didn't lose him, then it would be worth it. It had to be.

As Allen lay contemplating his life choices, he heard soft footsteps. Turning toward the door of his cell he saw Will and Mark sneaking toward the far end of the dungeon to attack the guards.

A moment later a metal-clad guard hit the stone floor with a loud crash.

"You could have caught him!" Little John hissed as he moved out of the secret passageway and into the dungeons. Much and Robin were close behind him. Allen rolled to his feet and strolled over to the barred door of his cell, leaning against it as he watched his friends.

Robin grabbed the keys from one of the unconscious soldiers and moved toward Allen's cell. "We're getting you out of here."

"Thanks."

"Anytime." Robin winked. "We'll always be here when you need us. Do try not to get kidnapped by Gisbourne again."

Allen curled his hands into fists for a moment, his heart pounding. *We'll always be here when you need us.* Was he really going to betray Robin for a measly promise from Gisbourne–a man who was hardly known for keeping his word–to keep a deathly ill man safe and alive?

"Enough joking around, we need to get out before more guards come or these wake up," Little John said.

Robin moved to unlock Sir Godfrey's cell as Allen stepped out of his own.

"No," Sir Godfrey waved a weak hand from where he sat on the little bed at the back of his cell. "I'm not going with you."

"Sir Godfrey–"

"Absolutely not." He shook his head firmly as Robin continued to fiddle with the lock on his cell.

"Father!" Mark grabbed the bars of the cell door that Robin was unlocking. "You have to come with us!"

"I won't leave here just to die in the forest," Sir Godfrey said.

"We have a healer in our group," Mark insisted, reaching for the keys from Robin, as though he could unlock the door faster than Robin. "If she could just see to you, you'd feel better. I'm sure of it."

"Go," Sir Godfrey said. "I am not leaving, but you must. More soldiers will come eventually. You do not want to be caught, or to have the secret passageways discovered. Get out."

Robin glanced toward the unconscious soldiers in the doorway and sighed. "If we're going, we have to go. Sir Godfrey, I do wish you would change your mind."

"I won't."

"Father!" Mark started to unlock the cell, but Robin snatched the keys from his hand. "We don't have time to argue, or to drag your father bodily from his cell. Marian will keep looking after him. Now come on."

"Robin–"

"Move!" Robin tossed the keys toward the sleeping soldiers and dragged Mark by his arm back toward the opening of the secret passage. The others began to follow, except for Much who stood staring at Sir Godfrey.

"Much!" Allen whacked his shoulder. "Come on. Robin says it's time to go, so it's time to go."

"Of course."

Much dutifully followed Allen into the secret passage, but he turned around as Allen slid the secret door in the wall shut.

"Are we making the right choice? Leaving him, I mean?"

"The choice is made, right or wrong," Allen replied bitterly.

He was going to betray his friends, his family, to keep Sir Godfrey alive. Mark was distraught at leaving him, how much more would he be so if his father were murdered?

The gang made their way through the varied passages back to the exit at the back of the castle, then moved along the outside of the city walls until they were beyond Nottingham and could cross the fields and forest to their camp. The entire way, Allen's feet felt weighed down as though someone had tied giant rocks to his ankles. He'd made his decision, and for Sir Godfrey's sake–for Marian, Mark, and Robin–he was willing to go through with it.

The idea that Robin would not understand, that he would not forgive him if or when he found out sent a shudder of dread through Allen. He had to do this–he had to do whatever he could to save

305

Robin's beloved from the type of pain that he himself felt on a daily basis. No one deserved to be tortured in the way that Allen was; he had to do this. He had to.

Dusty greeted Allen with a hug, which in no way alleviated the guilt pressing on his mind. "You have no idea how glad I am to see you."

"I am grateful to have limited this trip to prison to a single night and not a full year," Allen replied.

He hadn't told Gisbourne anything–yet. Once he did, what would Dusty think of him? She was, after all, the moral one of the group. Would his sister-by-choice despise him? He wasn't sure he could bear that.

"I am equally glad you weren't stuck there for a year." Dusty gave him another swift hug and Allen felt his heart drop to his toes. Dusty's affection and trust was scalding; it was almost more than Allen could bear, but...

Sir Godfrey's life was at stake. It was worth it.

In the days that followed, Allen found it difficult to maintain eye contact with his friends, though he hadn't actually shared damning information with Gisbourne yet. He knew he would–for Sir Godfrey's sake, for Marian's–but it hadn't happened yet so his rising guilt annoyed him.

And then one night Robin returned to the camp in a fury after the children had all gone to bed. He stormed into camp, kicking away a loose stone and flinging himself onto the ground outside his hut.

"What is wrong with you?" Will asked from his place at the fire ring where everyone was gathered.

"The passageways are being closed up! The Sheriff has discovered the secrets of Nottingham castle. I couldn't get in. He's blocking some off, and having others guarded..."

"So you didn't see Marian?" Mark asked.

"I went in through the stables. It was trickier than the secret passages because I could have been seen at any moment, but I got there."

"Does Marian have any idea about why the Sheriff found the passages?" Little John asked.

Robin picked himself up and came to join the group by the fire. "No...but I do. How could he have learned of them?"

"They have always been there for anyone to run across, Robin," Dusty said. "It should not have taken the Sheriff as long as it did to discover them."

Allen avoided Robin the rest of the night and soon retired to his hut to be away from the group. He lay in the darkness, listening to young William sleeping beside him and trying to convince himself that the Sheriff finding the passages wasn't his fault.

He hadn't told Gisbourne or the Sheriff about the secret passageways, despite promising to share information to Gisbourne. Even so, Allen felt terrible; his entire body seemed to burn with shame, hotter than his anger had ever been.

Could he go through with this?

Allen conjured up the unwelcome image of his parents' charred corpses, his hands clenching into fists at the mental sight. He let his anguish roil inside him, the hot tears scalding his cheeks. His whole body shuddered as he thought of Alice, of Eri...of baby Duncan.

Allen took a shaky breath, his limbs trembling as his tears intensified.

This is how Marian would feel. How Robin would feel.

He had to save Sir Godfrey, for their sake, whether they ever understood or forgave him. He had to save them.

Chapter 43

Allen hesitated, his fingers curled tightly around the door latch. Could he do this?

He was standing outside a tavern on the edge of Nottingham, about to truly betray his family for the first time.

Allen closed his eyes, picturing Florie's unseeing eyes and the way he'd felt when he'd tripped over her body in that fire all those years ago. He let the horror and anguish flood his veins as tears pricked his eyelids.

This, this is is what he was saving Robin from.

Allen straightened, pushing open the door and hurrying across the common room toward a room at the back. Gisbourne's lackey–a soldier named Andrew–had approached Allen in Nottingham Square to tell him Gisbourne was ready to meet. Allen didn't know how long Gisbourne's lackey had waited in Nottingham Square, scouring the crowds for a glimpse of Allen, but once Allen got the news he'd hurried here to the tavern.

But what was he going to tell Gisbourne?

Allen slipped into a storage room at the back of the tavern. Gisbourne apparently had an arrangement with the proprietor–which probably meant he'd threatened his life or that of his family in order to use his space. It wasn't ideal, but Sir Godfrey's life was at stake.

The room was empty but for the shelves filled with blankets, candles, and various items. There were also a handful of crates and barrels pushed into corners of the room. Allen seated himself on one of the barrels and waited.

He had plenty of time to second guess his decision, as it took Gisbourne nearly an hour to arrive. Allen nearly left on more than one occasion, but he forced himself to remember the pain of his own grief to remind him why he was doing this.

"Well?" Gisbourne barked as he pushed open the door to the storage room, his eyes flashing.

"How is Sir Godfrey?"

"Safe from the Sheriff." Gisbourne crossed his arms, leaning against the door he'd shut behind him. "I can't promise you he won't die of sickness though."

Allen stood slowly, resisting the urge to wring his hands together.

"Information." Gisbourne raised an eyebrow, studying Allen with a harsh gaze. "What do you have for me?"

Allen took a deep breath, keeping Sir Godfrey's frail form and his own family's corpses at the forefront of his mind. "The caravan going through Sherwood tomorrow, we'll be ambushing it."

"Obviously." Gisbourne pushed off the door and strode across the small space in one long step, grabbing Allen by the collar of his shirt. "Where will the ambush be? How will it be executed? And how did you get the information about that caravan in the first place?"

Allen barely maintained eye contact with Gisbourne as he answered his last question. "Robin still has spies, with or without the secret passages."

"Who are they?"

"I wouldn't know."

"I have reason to believe you are his right hand."

"I'm not. His childhood best friend is who he confides in the most, and then there's Will Scarlett."

"The outlaw from Middlesborough."

"That's the one."

Gisbourne's face was too close for comfort, his dark eyes burning into Allen's. "He's still working with Robin Hood?"

"Everyone is. Most inhabitants of the city will tell Robin whatever he wants to know."

"Who? Who tells Robin Hood things?"

"Everyone. I don't have names."

"Who talks to you? How do you know what you do?"

"When people share information with members of the gang, they come home and share that with everyone else. I don't know who all is passing information to everyone."

Gisbourne shoved Allen and he hit the back wall, wincing at the flare of pain in his back.

"You are rather useless. Perhaps Sir Godfrey doesn't need my protection after all."

"I can't tell you what I don't know!"

"Fine. Tell me about the ambush."

Allen only hesitated for a moment before he explained exactly how the ambush was going to play out. All the while, the sick feeling in his stomach kept growing and growing. This was wrong. So, so wrong.

But Sir Godfrey…Marian…he had no choice.

Once Allen had finished explaining the details of Robin's plan for the ambush, Gisbourne thanked him and left. Allen stood alone in the storage closet for a few minutes. If Gisbourne knew what they were doing tomorrow, how would he counter-attack? Had Allen put the people that he loved in danger?

311

Allen slowly made his way back to camp, taking as long as possible to get there. He didn't want to have to interact with anyone, to pretend he hadn't betrayed them all.

That night Allen couldn't sleep–flames and screams and Florie's unseeing eyes had him tossing and turning until dawn.

The next morning as the gang set out for Sherwood Road, Allen kept silent. The others were talking and laughing, discussing the upcoming raid and teasing one another. They were rather good at their ambushes and rarely failed. The Sheriff was incompetent and his men reflected that, so ease and confidence permeated the air as the group set up their ambush.

Allen felt too sick to say a word.

He took his place behind a tree and waited, the pit in his stomach growing. He didn't know what Gisbourne would do with the information that he had given him. He might have sent word for the caravan to take a different road entirely. He might send more guards than usual to protect the caravan, knowing it would be ambushed–he likely would have told the soldiers where to expect the ambush.

In a few minutes, the first of the wagons came into view. Allen gripped his bow tightly in his sweaty palms, his heart beating a wild dance in his chest.

There were more guards than usual, but that wasn't too out of the ordinary. With all the caravans being raided, the Sheriff and Gisbourne often added to the number of soldiers protecting their ill-gotten treasure.

As the caravan drew closer, Allen waited for Robin's signal, the sharp whistle that would tell the group it was time to ambush.

It never came.

312

As the wagons drew close, the guards broke off from the caravan and headed straight toward each hiding place. Allen tensed, watching in horror as the soldiers ran for his friends. If anyone got hurt…

Arrows began to fly, swords were drawn; the guards were prepared for this and more soldiers began to run for the hiding places. Everyone was forced to fight for their lives, apart from Allen. He watched with horror for a moment, and then snatched an arrow from his quiver and took aim, shooting down a soldier swinging his sword toward Dusty.

Robin's retreat whistle–a sound so rarely used that the gang teased they wouldn't know what it meant if he ever used it–rent the air. Allen took off sprinting away from the failed caravan toward the camp, praying his friends would also make it out alive.

He needed them to be okay–saving Robin and Marian from the pain of losing Sir Godfrey was one thing, but being the cause of killing his own family?

And would they have noticed that the soldiers didn't attack him?

As his friends fell into step with him on their way to the camp–all of them looking winded and harried, Allen couldn't help but ask, "How did they know where we were?"

"They were obviously informed," Robin replied, his eyes flashing. His jaw was tight, his hands curled into fists at his side, and his eyes were burning hotter than Allen had ever seen before.   When the group moodily arrived at the camp, Robin stormed off to his hut after glaring at them all. The others slowly made their way to their own huts.

Allen sat down in the doorway of his hut, watching the silent camp. Much cooked dinner without saying a word to the children gathered around him. The rest of the gang remained brooding in their own huts.

"Do you think it's true?" young William came to sit on the ground beside Allen, his innocent eyes wide and full of tears. "Is there a traitor?"

Allen winced.

"I know it's a terrible thought, but Robin said–"

"No. I don't believe anyone in this gang would wish harm on the others."

Young William nodded. "You can't win every fight; that's all it was, right?"

Allen nodded, his mouth dry as he lied to this boy who looked up to him, who believed in him.

The children all ate together but alone with Much that night, and then Mark joined them by the fire to eat as well. Allen contemplated joining the group, but how could he? He was the cause of their discomfort and confusion right now. They didn't know that, but it was the truth. He couldn't face them.

When Dusty emerged from her hut to join the group eating around the fire, Mark got up and returned to his without speaking a word to her. No one else made an appearance until after Dusty had gone back to her own hut. After she was gone, Little John came out to eat.

Allen sat watching it all with a sinking heart. This was his fault. None of them trusted each other because they suspected someone was betraying the group, someone had told the Sheriff and Gisbourne where they would be hiding.

Allen's shoulders slumped as shame washed over him.

314

Was this worth it?

He wasn't so sure.

In the weeks that followed, the distrust continued. Much cooked for everyone, but they took their meals separately. Hardly a word was spoken between them during the day. Allen had never seen Robin so angry. He glared at everyone, and snapped when spoken to, even if it was Much talking to him. The fury in his eyes seemed to burn right through Allen.

Allen returned to the tavern later that week, but he was reluctant to do so. His family was falling apart because of him, and Sir Godfrey was dying from his illness regardless of whether or not Gisbourne protected him from the Sheriff.

Still, when Gisbourne arrived and demanded information Allen forced himself to think of the overwhelming grief that had nearly destroyed him when his own family had died–reminding himself how Marian, Mark, and Robin would feel if they lost Sir Godfrey–so that he could get through the ordeal.

Another ambush was ambushed.

The tensions in the camp became even worse. Almost everyone lashed out in anger, snapping at each other and the children, except for Dusty who only became incredibly sad. That was almost worse than the tension and anger. Her dark eyes were full of pain and Allen hated himself for it.

He'd failed his sister Alice and she had died, and now he'd wounded Dusty. It had been hard for her to love again after losing her own family–which Allen understood only too well–and now he'd made that worse.

Chapter 44

Allen's feet dragged along the street as he approached the tavern where he was to meet Gisbourne yet again. His palms were sweaty and his stomach housed what felt like a boulder. He didn't want to do this.

It had seemed right the night he'd agreed to be Gisbourne's spy–saving Marian from the grief he himself had endured seemed so justifiable. And he'd continued to convince himself of that, but now that the gang was fracturing under the weight of the belief that there was a traitor among them, his actions didn't seem so reasonable.

Allen had never been more disgusted with himself, not after he'd failed to save his family. He hadn't set that fateful fire, even if he had failed to pull his family out of it. But this? This was a choice. Every time he saw Dusty's sad eyes, or heard Robin's voice laced with anger and hurt, he felt a wave of self-hatred wash over him. He'd done this– and for what? Sir Godfrey was ill and dying, he couldn't save Marian and Robin from that grief no matter what he did. And the Sheriff and Gisbourne were hardly trust-worthy, they might kill him anyway regardless of whether or not Allen held up his end of the deal.

Allen was an idiot.

He shuddered as he approached the tavern door. Maybe it wasn't too late to back out? He could stop this. Gisbourne couldn't hurt him–he was back with the gang, and he only saw Gisbourne when he willingly showed up to meet with him. He could stop.

"Forget how to open doors?"

Allen turned at the sound of Gisbourne's voice to see him standing just behind him, arms crossed, a scowl on his face. He

317

considered bolting or fighting Gisbourne, but he knew Gisbourne was a better fighter–people said he was the best swordsman in England and Allen had fought him up close before…he was much better than Allen.

"I was lost in thought."

"I'm sure. Get inside. I need information." Gisbourne reached forward and shoved Allen toward the door, and he reluctantly opened it, walking past the people in the common room to the back storage room to tell Gisbourne the plans for the next ambush.

Allen was hardly surprised when the ambush was later ambushed–Gisbourne's soldiers pouring off the road straight toward everyone's hiding places. The wave of self-loathing crashed over him once more. He had to stop this. It was out of control. He couldn't keep putting his family in danger for the slight chance that he could save Sir Godfrey. This was ridiculous.

Allen fired arrow after arrow in quick succession, killing as many soldiers as he could in a desperate attempt to save his friends from his own choices. Everyone was fighting for their lives, and meanwhile the soldiers driving the caravan of treasure were continuing down the road unharmed.

Little John suddenly cried out and Allen spun toward the sound. Little John's quarter staff was rolling out of his hand as a soldier standing over him swung his sword down in a vicious arc.

Allen was blinded by the searing, white hot anger that coursed through him. He fired an arrow at the soldier, and then another, and another, and another.

Allen sprinted toward Little John, the dead soldier with several arrows sprouting from his chest gasping his last breaths nearby. Allen dropped to his knees beside Little John just as Robin and Will arrived.

318

Crimson blood was staining Little John's shirt as his eyes rolled back in his head.

"Don't die!" Allen hissed, pressing his hands to the area where the blood seemed to be coming from.

"We have to get him to Dusty," Will said.

Much came scurrying over. "Most of the soldiers have been dealt with, but the treasure is gone."

"I'm going to kill someone," Robin grunted through clenched teeth, pulling Little John to his feet. Little John let out a cry of pain as Robin draped one of Little John's arms over his shoulders as Will stepped forward and took Little John's other arm.

The sound of approaching footsteps had Allen whirling back toward the road in time to see a few more soldiers hurrying their way. Allen let his arrows fly, dropping them one by one. Much stood beside him, his bow arm working as fast as Allen's to kill the soldiers while Robin and Will carried Little John away from the fight. Mark snuck up behind the group of soldiers while they were distracted by Allen and Much, and began to cut them down from behind with his sword.

Allen's heart seemed to be pounding from his throat rather than his chest, and he could feel tears pricking his eyelids but he shook them away. He needed his vision so he could aim at the soldiers in the road.

Little John was dying because of him.

The shame and self-loathing that washed over Allen was so heavy his knees nearly buckled beneath him, but he forced himself to stay upright, focusing on his anger instead. Gisbourne had sent soldiers to kill Allen's family, and Allen was intent on killing every last one of them.

As soon as every soldier was dead, Allen, Mark, and Much ran for the camp.

As they burst into the clearing, Dusty was directing Robin and Will to lay Little John in her hut. She saw the rest of the group approaching and started barking orders.

"Much, boil me some water. Allen, get my spare bandages from the storage hut. Will, get this shirt off so I can see what I'm doing."

Allen sprinted for the storage hut, shoving the door open as his eyes bounced around the shelves trying to remember where Dusty kept her bandages. He saw them and sprang forward, yanking a handful off the shelf and destroying the perfectly neat rows Dusty had made.

Little John was going to die.

Allen was going to kill himself.

As Allen ran back to Dusty's hut, she and Robin were bent over Little John–who was now shirtless–both pressing their hands against his wound to staunch the flow of blood.

Allen hesitated in the doorway of the hut unsure what to do, but when Dusty saw him she reached for the bandages and Allen passed them to her.

As her hands came away from Little John's chest, Allen got his first glimpse at the jagged edges of the wound gushing crimson. Little John groaned, seemingly barely conscious.

Allen backed away from the doorway and sank to the ground, covering his head in his hands.

He did this.

Allen was barely aware of Dusty's whispered conversations with Robin and Will, hardly noticed when Much ran over with boiling water. Despite his eyes being closed, all he could see was the wound spouting crimson like a morbid fountain. It was an image he didn't think he'd ever get out of his head.

Florie's unseeing eyes danced behind the gushing of Little John's wounds, and then the charred corpse of his infant son. Allen shuddered, pressing his palms into his eyes, trying to force the visions away.

"What's the verdict?" Little John's voice was soft and weak, but it was clear as a bell and Allen's head snapped up, his eyes searching the scene inside the hut. Little John's eyes were blinking slowly as he looked at Dusty who still worked quietly, bandaging his wound.

"You'll live," Dusty said. At her pronouncement, Allen groaned, collapsing forward onto the ground.

Little John wasn't going to die.

"Keep an eye on him, Dusty," Robin said. "I'm going to Nottingham to talk to Marian."

Much had gathered the children on the other side of the meadow while Dusty continued to work, applying herbs and going about her healing business that Allen didn't truly understand. Will stayed in the hut with her, watching her work. Allen went to his hut, sinking onto his bed with tears slipping down his cheeks.

Little John was going to live.

But even so, Allen had caused this. It was his fault. He'd told Gisbourne the plan for the ambush and look what had happened! This had to stop. He had to find a way to stop. How could he allow his own family to die like this? Sir Godfrey or not, this was wrong. It was all so messed up.

Once Robin returned from Nottingham, he gathered the group around the fire ring, sending the children to the far side of the meadow away from them. Allen could see young William watching with interest as the adults gathered around the fire, though.

"I have asked Marian to keep an eye on things in Nottingham," Robin said. His voice was calm but laced with fire and it sent a shudder through Allen. "Whoever is informing the Sheriff will be caught, and I will kill him."

That was fine; Allen was planning on killing himself anyway.

"Him," Mark repeated, glancing toward Dusty.

"I do not believe that Dusty would do this to me," Robin said.

"None of the rest of us would do this either," Will snapped, his voice ice cold.

"Obviously someone has!" Robin growled. "Little John nearly died today because of the coward who betrayed me! I expect to kill whoever has done this."

Robin stormed away from the group, and Allen felt a wave of heat hit his cheeks.

This was all his fault.

Allen retreated to his hut, the guilt gnawing at his stomach.

Robin hated him. He hated himself.

What was he going to do now?

Chapter 45

The tension within the camp had dissipated while Little John was dying and everyone had worked together with Dusty to save him, but as soon as the crisis was over the tension mounted. It was far worse than before Little John's near-death experience. The anger coursing through the camp was palpable, and no one spent time with anyone else unless absolutely necessary because trust had withered completely.

They had a right to be so wary. Their friend and brother had betrayed them to the point of almost getting them killed. Allen didn't blame any of them for their reaction. He wished he was less of a coward and could simply tell them that it was him. Then they could return to each other for support even if they killed him or kicked him out of the camp.

But he was too cowardly to speak up. He cringed when Robin was in the camp, shooting furious glares at everyone. He shied away from Dusty's sad eyes, and Will's distrustful ones. He couldn't look any of them in the eye anymore, to be honest.

He had to stop. Whenever he wandered through Nottingham and caught sight of Andrew–Gisbourne's lackey–he would hide. If Andrew was looking for him, he'd want to take him to meet Gisbourne and then Allen would be forced to choose to betray the group or die. At this point, he'd rather die. The damage was done. Even if he never spoke to Gisbourne again, the gang was fracturing from the weight of the knowledge that one of their group had betrayed them. Little John had nearly died; that wouldn't change even if Allen stopped.

He couldn't fix it. He'd already broken them.

But he could avoid Gisbourne at all costs and hopefully avoid ever sharing pertinent information again.

One day as Allen was walking through Nottingham Square, someone grabbed his shoulders and pulled him to the side behind a fruit stand. Allen reached for his sword but the hands left his shoulder and he saw Andrew standing beside him.

"Where have you been?"Andrew was looking around the market and not at Allen at all.

"Helping people…spreading a little hope to the people your master crushes beneath his boot."

Andrew crossed his arms, turning to look at Allen now. "I know. I don't begrudge you the good you and Robin Hood and the rest do here in Nottingham, and the rest of England. I'm…well, in truth, I'm on your side. But right now I'm here for Gisbourne. He wants to meet today."

Allen sighed. "Today?"

"Yes."

"Alright…I'll be at the tavern."

Andrew nodded and moved away through the crowded market. Allen wasn't sure what to make of him. He'd just admitted he was supportive of the gang's efforts…and yet he still seemed to willingly work for Gisbourne. That didn't make sense, but it was possible he was being coerced in some fashion. Allen didn't know Andrew well, he didn't know his situation or if he had family or had been threatened in any way. He knew nothing about him other than that he was Gisbourne's lackey.

Allen made his way to the tavern, but he knew he couldn't do it, couldn't betray the gang. Not again.

324

Instead of going to the storage room to wait for Gisbourne, he spoke to the tavern keeper, giving him a pouch of money he'd had on his belt–meant to be used to give to the needy of Nottingham–telling the tavern keeper to give it to Gisbourne as a show of faith that he was still willing to work with him, though in truth he meant to never do such a thing again.

That night when Robin returned to camp after a visit to Nottingham, he stomped into the clearing with a storm brewing on his face. He gathered the group at the fire, and Allen watched the fury on his friend's face with trepidation. Did he know the truth?

"I spoke to Marian," Robin said, the heat in his voice reaching across the distance between them and searing Allen's heart.

Silence greeted his pronouncement. Allen shifted on the log bench, peering at Robin's face and trying to read what he saw there.

The silence stretched on until it was finally broken when little Rachel began whimpering and Will pulled the girl into his lap.

"What did you find out?" Will asked.

"Nothing I didn't already know. Marian followed Gisbourne to a tavern where he apparently meets his informant, and she overheard Gisbourne speaking with the tavern keeper."

Allen shuddered. Marian had nearly caught him at the tavern!

"What did they say?" Little John growled, leaning forward. He was on the mend, though still healing from the wounds that he'd received as a result of Allen's betrayal. Allen glanced between Little John and Robin, his heart pounding.

"Nothing of importance," Robin said.

"Then why are you telling us?" Allen asked, trying and probably failing to keep his fear out of his voice.

"Because Marian said they were speaking of a 'him' which means that I was correct in saying Dusty would never betray me. It's one of you men…and I will never forget this."

With that, Robin rose and stomped off to his hut. Allen watched him go, a weight settling in his stomach.

He did this. He deserved Robin's hatred.

Heat filled his cheeks as anger seared his veins; he hated himself.

Allen rose, leaving the circle of his friends without a word and shutting himself into his hut. What was he going to do? The idea of telling Robin that it was all his fault flitted across his mind, but Allen quickly rejected that. He'd be despised and cast out if his friends knew the truth.

He hadn't done what he did to hurt them, he had done it to save a life but that wouldn't matter. He could see that now, but it was too late to take it back. All he could do now was change his behavior and do what he could to be worthy of trust.

But telling them about his former betrayal? He couldn't. He'd lose them. Robin, Much, and Dusty were the only reason he hadn't given into his desire to die in the Crusades. He couldn't give them up; he needed them.

Days passed, and the tension in the group that Allen had created remained. He never visited the tavern or spoke with Gisbourne, and he did his best to help his friends and protect them during caravan raids. He wasn't going to betray them again.

But the damage was done. Everyone continued to eat their meals separately and refused to speak to each other most days. Robin would assign tasks to the gang each day, but the group no longer traveled beyond Nottingham to help the innocent or stop executions.

They didn't trust one another to have each other's backs in a fight, and it was Allen's fault.

They didn't understand that Allen *would* have their back, that he would do anything–absolutely anything–to protect them.

He'd broken the gang. That much was clear.

The Nottingham Fair came and went but no one within the gang seemed remotely interested. A week later, Robin stormed into the camp and shut himself into his hut. Slowly, one by one, the members of the gang made their way to the fire. Robin would come out eventually, and they all wanted to know what he'd heard. Even Allen couldn't stay away. He sat slightly apart from the others, clenching and unclenching his fists.

This was it. He was sure of it. Robin was going to kill him.

"Allen!" Robin's voice, so full of ice and fury, exploded from his hut as Robin slammed his door open and marched toward the group gathered around the fire.

"Yes, Robin?"

"You better start running now if you expect to live."

"Robin?" Will looked from Robin to Allen, but Allen refused to meet his gaze. "What do you mean?"

Robin drew his sword as he came toward the group. "I mean it, Allen."

Little John shifted and Allen shied away from him. "He's the traitor?"

Robin kept his gaze on Allen as he strode forward, sword raised. "Yes."

Mark spun toward Allen. "I hate you."

Allen winced, but he couldn't blame him.

"No." Dusty's whispered horror cut through Allen's heart. He couldn't look at her, he couldn't look at any of them. He lowered his head, waiting for Robin's sword to end his life–he certainly deserved it.

He heard Little John's growl and then felt strong arms jerk him off of the log bench. Allen opened his eyes in time to see Robin and the others in the gang running after Little John as Allen was carried to the edge of camp.

Suddenly he was flying through the air, and in another moment he slammed into the ground. Pain shot through his side.

Allen scrambled to his feet as he heard Little John's thundering foot falls. He was going to kill him.

A moment before Allen had been ready to face Robin's wrath, but just now all he could think about was survival so he took off running. He could hear Little John crashing through the underbrush behind him, but Allen was smaller and quicker. The darkness under the trees came to his advantage as well—as the moonlight could barely filter through the thick tangle of branches overhead–he slipped in and out of sight among the shadows around tree trunks. Until he was sure that he'd lost Little John.

Chapter 46

Every step seemed to deaden Allen's feeling as he ran. He wasn't sure anymore if Little John or Robin or any of the others were chasing after him. It didn't matter.

He'd destroyed his family. Maybe he'd thought that he had to, but it hardly mattered anymore. He'd lost everything, precisely what he'd been fighting not to do ever since he met Robin and Much.

He expected to see flashes of Eri or baby Duncan or Alice as his mind swirled with guilt, but didn't. He didn't see the faces of the friends he had betrayed either. The farther he ran from Sherwood Forest, the quieter his mind became.

Allen slowed his running as the city of Nottingham came into view. He paused for a moment, his hands on his hips, trying to catch his breath. The stars and moon were shining overhead, blissfully unaware of the turmoil that ought to have been filling Allen's soul.

It wasn't though.

He was numb.

The question now, was where to go? He thought he'd surely be dead when Robin found him out, but since he was still alive he needed a place to go. He could leave Nottingham and get far away from the gang, but he didn't truly want to leave them. If he tried to stay at a tavern in Nottingham it was likely one of the gang might still try to kill him. The safest bet was going to the castle.

Allen started walking again. The city gates were closed, but he pounded on the guard door until someone answered.

"What business do you have?" A soldier cracked open the small door set into the larger gate. He looked a bit disheveled, as though he'd been sleeping.

"I need to speak with Sir Guy of Gisbourne. I am a friend of his. It is urgent."

The soldier studied him silently for a moment and then shut the door.

"Wait!" Allen began to pound on the door some more.

Nothing happened.

Allen slumped against the door, easing to the ground and staring up at the moon. How had it all come to this? Gisbourne wasn't a good man, he wasn't likely to care about Allen's plight.

And what was Allen going to do in the castle?

Allen tried to think about the gang, tried to conjure the pain and guilt, but nothing came. The only emotion he seemed able to muster was a desire to survive the night.

Suddenly the door opened, and several soldiers began to exit the city. Allen started to stand, and then several rough hands pulled him to his feet and jerked his arms behind his back to bind him.

"No, wait! I'm a friend of Gisbourne!"

They ignored him and bound him anyway, before dragging him into the city and down the empty streets. Nottingham was rather eerie at night to Allen's eyes. A ghost town, devoid of the life and love that usually lived there...

Eventually they arrived at the castle and the soldiers led him through the courtyard and into the castle itself, leading him down to the lower levels and then to the dungeon.

Allen couldn't help but wonder if this was Gisbourne's doing. He'd told the man at the gate he needed to speak to Gisbourne, and then he'd been left outside. Maybe the man had reported to Gisbourne and he didn't care, telling his men to throw Allen in prison.

Or maybe they just decided to do that on their own.

It didn't matter.

Allen was shoved into a cell and then the soldiers retreated. Allen sank onto the small mattress at the back of his cell and studied his surroundings in the dim light of the dungeon. It wasn't his first visit here, and nothing seemed to have changed. Sir Godfrey was sleeping in the cell next door, pale and sweaty and looking like death already.

Allen rolled onto his back and stared up at the ceiling. Would Gisbourne and the Sheriff execute him because he was an outlaw?

He would deserve it, undoubtedly. He'd betrayed the gang, he didn't deserve life.

Allen couldn't conjure the painful images of his dead family, or of the family he'd betrayed. His mind was numb, but he could convince his mind to sleep either.

As morning dawned, the doors to the dungeon creaked open and Gisbourne came striding in. "I heard you came for a visit."

Allen sat up, unsure what to say. His eyes were dry and his head ached from the lack of sleep he'd gotten the night before.

Gisbourne leaned against the bars of Allen's cell, his dark eyes flickering with emotion that Allen couldn't place. "You were discovered?"

"Yes."

"That is unfortunate." Gisbourne stepped away from the cell, crossing his arms. "My source of information is gone…"

"I might still be useful."

Gisbourne sighed and then chuckled. "Useful? I doubt it. But in any event, you should meet the Sheriff. He'll decide what to do with you."

Gisbourne whipped a key out of his pocket and unlocked the cell. Allen moved forward to exit, and Gisbourne grabbed his arm and jerked him the rest of the way. Allen winced; the wrench on his arm would leave a bruise no doubt.

They walked in silence through the castle corridors until they came to the Great Hall where the Sheriff was sitting on his little throne.

The Sheriff's eyebrows hit his hairline as they walked in.

"Gisbourne?"

"Sir, this is Allen, our informant."

"Allen?" The Sheriff tilted his head to one side, considering him. "It's good to meet you, I suppose. You've been most helpful. What is he doing here, Gisbourne?"

"He was discovered and thrown out of the outlaws' camp."

"What? We've lost our spy?!" The Sheriff leaned forward, gripping the arms of his chair as his eyes flashed with anger.

"He is at your disposal, Sheriff." Gisbourne crossed his arms. "He did suggest he would like to be made useful even if he cannot be our informant."

"Fine. He'll help you, of course. I don't need him."

Gisbourne grunted.

Allen met Gisbourne's cold gaze, but before he could say anything a new voice spoke.

"Allen?"

Allen spun around. "Marian!"

She stood in the doorway, her eyes wide and sparking with anger. A million emotions seemed to cross her face before she clenched her jaw shut. The numb shell around Allen broke as he watched the horror and pain and hatred in her eyes.

An ache began to fill his chest and he curled his hands into fists at his sides, trying to keep out the guilt and shame.

The Sheriff stood. "Marian, my dear. Why don't I introduce you to our newest recruit? He was apparently thrown out of Robin Hood's camp."

"Literally. Little John threw me."

"So he's taken refuge with us," the Sheriff added. "Poor fellow."

Marian spun on her heel and left the Great Hall. Allen took half a step after her, but Gisbourne grabbed his arm. "We have much to discuss if you are going to live here and work for me directly."

Allen wanted nothing more than to follow Marian and try and explain why he'd done what he had done, but Gisbourne took him to his own room to give him a rundown on what would be expected of him. Attending executions to ensure they were carried out without interruption from the gang, collecting taxes with whatever force was necessary, informing the Sheriff of any rebellious individuals who needed punishment. In short, everything Allen had been fighting against since coming to England in the first place.

He didn't want to do any of it. He wanted to find Marian and tell her why he'd betrayed Robin.

After Gisbourne had given Allen a long list of duties, he'd shown him to a room in the castle. As soon as Allen was left alone, he went in search of Marian's room. He knew he'd found the right place when he found Andrew. He was sitting in the hallway outside her closed door.

"Is Marian in there?"

Andrew glanced up and then stood. "Yes. I doubt she'd want a visit, though. She's not fond of you these days."

"Did she tell you that?"

"She doesn't speak to me at all if she can help it."

Allen reached out hesitantly and knocked, but heard no response. "Marian?"

333

Andrew stepped to the opposite side of the hallway and simply watched.

Allen's heart was heavy as he knocked again.

"Marian, please." He needed her to understand...

There was no response from within Marian's room. Maybe she was sleeping, but more likely she was too angry to speak to him.

"Marian...I'd like to explain."

"Explain?!" The door burst open and Marian stood there, glowering at him. "Explain? You...you...just get out, Allen!"

Marian started to slam her door shut again, but Allen pushed forward through the gap before she snapped the door shut.

"Marian, I have to tell you. Please."

Marian crossed her arms. "Nothing you say will make me hate you any less."

Allen sighed. "I know, Marian. I can't change that, but I want to explain why I did what I did."

"There isn't a good reason, Allen. You betrayed your friend, and all of us. You nearly got Little John and the rest of them killed!"

"I know," Allen sighed. The weight of his guilt and shame pressed down on his chest like a boulder. "It all got so out of hand...I was so proud to fight for England, for the king. But even more so to come home and fight for Robin here. He's like a brother to me, Marian."

"Which is why you betrayed him I suppose," Marian snapped.

"Sir Guy..." How could he explain? Even he knew how stupid his reasoning would sound.

"Offered you money."

Allen frowned and shook his head. How could she think he would be so low as to betray Robin for money? "No. I wouldn't betray Robin for such a thing; I wouldn't take money."

"What did you take?"

"A promise."

"A promise?" Marian asked indignantly.

334

"The Sheriff was planning—"

"The Sheriff is always planning something, Allen!"

Allen shook his head. "This was different. When he does things in the open, we can stop him. This time was different. He was planning to kill your father."

Marian took a step back, studying Allen. His heart skipped a beat. Would she believe him?

"The Sheriff wasn't going to hang him, he was just going to have him murdered in his cell while he slept. For the brief space of time I was here, when I was captured…Sir Guy questioned me that night, offered me my life if I betrayed all of you. Sir Guy was going to kill me unless I joined him, but my own life was nothing. I would gladly die for Robin and England, and I had told Sir Guy as much. I told him I wouldn't help him, he could kill me, it didn't matter."

"Then why did you help him?"

"I had heard of the Sheriff's plan and I knew how much it would hurt you, Marian, and through you, Robin. So I told Sir Guy he could kill me and I wouldn't care. He could dangle money in my face, I wouldn't care. But if he would promise to keep your father safe, I would help him. So here we are."

Marian was silent.

"Marian?"

She shook her head. "I have to think. Get out."

"Alright, I'll go. I know…I can't turn back now. I'm on the side I hate…but it is almost worth it to keep you from pain."

"Is it, Allen? I'm not proud of you. Nor am I grateful. I don't forgive you."

"If you had been hurt, it would have hurt Robin. I couldn't let that happen."

"Your betrayal hurt worse, Allen."

Her words were a knife slicing through his heart. He knew she was right. He hated himself for the choices that he had made. If he could do it over again…but he couldn't. Robin would never forgive him and left a cold chill in his body.

Allen left Marian to mull over his explanation and returned to his own room. His hands began to shake and he stumbled over to his bed and collapsed into it, curling into a ball and letting the weight of his guilt drown him as tears poured from his eyes and his shoulders shook with his sobs.

A few days later, the Sheriff summoned Allen to the Great Hall. He sat on his throne, glowering at Allen and at Gisbourne who was also present. "We have to get rid of these pests! Since you are no longer in Robin Hood's camp picking up valuable information we have no clue when or where he will strike. He's getting away with my money! And ruining my executions!"

The Sheriff rose from his chair and began to pace in front of it, grumbling to himself.

"We need to get him once and for all," Gisbourne said. "Attack him where he'll least expect it, in his own territory."

"Meaning what?" Allen asked.

"We need to attack him at the source."

"You want me to take you to the camp?" Allen asked. There was no way he was leading Gisbourne and his soldiers directly to Robin. "I can't."

"Are you forgetting who you work for now?" the Sheriff growled.

Allen shook his head. "No. It's just that…I promised Robin…"

Not to mention that he loved Robin and his other friends, he didn't want them getting hurt by his choices any longer. He already hated himself for betraying Robin, taking the Sheriff or Gisbourne to the camp was out of the question. He was only here so he could stay alive while remaining in Nottingham to be close to his friends.

The Sheriff laughed. "There's no need to worry about that. No one keeps promises, and no one but a fool would expect us to."

Allen glanced at Gisbourne. Was Gisbourne's promise to protect Sir Godfrey a true one? Would he continue to protect Marian's father if Allen continued to earn his favor? Not that it mattered. The promise he'd elicited from Gisbourne had not been worth betraying Robin. Allen understood that now.

But Robin already hated him. He was never going to forgive him. And the Sheriff would likely kill him if he didn't go along with their wishes…

After a long pause Allen finally spoke. "It's quite a ride and they have an alarm, traps…"

"We'll take plenty of soldiers," Gisbourne said. "Robin only has a small band does he not?"

Allen nodded slowly, and the Sheriff insisted they begin their assault on the outlaws' camp immediately.

Chapter 47

Gisbourne gathered a company of soldiers in the courtyard and Allen saddled one of the horses from the Sheriff's stables. His movements were slow and precise as he mulled over what to do. Gisbourne had a temper–he'd burned down Marian's house after professing to love her–so it would be best for Allen's own survival if he didn't do anything to anger him. That meant going along with this terrible scheme. But the truth was that Allen wanted nothing more than to protect Robin and the others that he loved.

He'd hurt them, and they would not forgive him for what he'd done, but he couldn't let them die. They were justified in their hatred of him.

As Allen led his horse into the courtyard where Gisbourne was giving orders to the soldiers, the Sheriff waved at them from the top step. "Come back with the outlaws' heads."

"We will, sir." Gisbourne gave a quick bow to the Sheriff before he disappeared inside the castle.

Allen desperately hoped that they would not, in fact, come back with anyone's head.

Marian soon appeared in the courtyard and ran over to Gisbourne.

Allen swung into his saddle and watched as Marian pleaded with Gisbourne to let her visit a physician for her father. Allen was certain it was a ploy; Marian could warn Robin. The gang would be ready for any attack.

Allen held his breath as Gisbourne mulled over Marian's request. "I'll send a servant."

"I'd rather go myself."

"Marian, I can't trust you to do that."

"I'll come back to the castle. Please?"

"Promise me you will return to the castle immediately."

"I will return."

"I don't know, Marian."

Gisbourne remained indecisive and Allen watched with fascination as Marian began to cry, tears slipping softly down her cheeks, her voice wavering as she spoke again, "Guy, please."

"Fine. We'll escort you to the physician's."

"Thank you."

Allen caught Marian's eyes and tried to convey how grateful he was that she was going to warn Robin. She glared in his direction and then ignored him the rest of the walk to the physician's home.

When they reached the physician's, Gisbourne stopped. "Do you need my assistance?"

"No," Marian said, moving away from the line of soldiers. "I'll be fine."

"Go straight back to the castle, Marian."

As Gisbourne, Allen, and the soldiers continued on their way out of the city of Nottingham, Allen could only hope that Marian's visit to the physician was, in truth, a ploy and that she had a plan to get to the camp and warn the others.

Even if she did not, Allen wasn't going to lead Gisbourne to Robin. He'd take him to a different part of the forest and go in the most round-about way he could think of. Gisbourne wouldn't believe he didn't know the way to the camp, so he had to make it believable and yet find a way to avoid going to the camp without alerting Gisbourne to his motives and getting himself killed.

As they entered the forest, Gisbourne pulled his mount to a halt and all the soldiers behind him pulled to a stop.

"Where is the camp?"

"Follow me." Allen urged his horse forward. He kept to the main road at first, hoping against hope that Marian would go directly to the camp and warn everyone. If she wasn't doing that, if he'd misread her desire to visit a physician without an escort, he wasn't sure what he would do. He didn't have a plan to keep his friends safe, but he knew he couldn't take Gisbourne to the camp.

Eventually Allen led Gisbourne and the others away from the road, his palms sweaty and his heart racing. Every crunch of leaves and twigs beneath his horse's hooves seemed to echo loudly in Allen's ears. How many of the gang would be in the camp? It varied from day to day. And would those who were present hear the company of soldiers and come out to fight? Allen knew he couldn't go to the camp itself–not for anything–but he hoped the gang would be able to ambush them–either because they heard them coming or because Marian did, in fact, warn them. It didn't matter the reason why, he just needed the gang to attack first.

"How much further?" Sir Guy barked after they'd been wandering the woods for quite some time.

"It is still a ways off," Allen said.

They trotted on in silence for a few more minutes. Allen glanced at Gisbourne, wondering what he might do if Allen led him in circles all day. He'd burned Marian's home, but he'd also rescued the children right out from under the Sheriff's nose. He wasn't entirely evil. He had a violent temper, that much was true, but Allen wondered if he wasn't simply a misguided man like himself, making choices and then regretting them afterward.

He had easily given in to Marian's tears and let her go to the physician. It seemed he still cared for her. Allen could sympathize with acting rashly and immediately regretting it, but having no real way to take it back or make things better.

Suddenly, Allen heard the unmistakable twang of a bowstring. He ducked low in his saddle, bringing his face close to his mount's head so as not to be an easy target as arrows began to fly from the surrounding trees.

A few soldiers fell from their saddles and horses started rearing in fright.

"I thought you said we had a ways to go!" Gisbourne shouted at Allen.

"We do!" Allen tried not to show how pleased he was that the gang had gotten the drop on them.

"Someone must have warned them! The Sheriff won't like this!"

Gisbourne swung his mount around, racing out of the ambush. Allen followed him, with Andrew hurrying along nearby. A few of the other soldiers followed, though more and more dropped from their saddles with arrows protruding from their chests and necks.

When they returned to Nottingham, alone and without the rest of the soldiers, Gisbourne was reluctant to inform the Sheriff. Allen could understand why, as within moments of hearing the unfortunate news, the Sheriff punched Gisbourne in the face. He stumbled backward for a moment and then straightened, his face impassive.

"How did they know to ambush you?"

The Sheriff spun toward Allen, his eyes flashing as he raised his fist. Allen took a step backward, raising his hands in a placating manner. "I don't know. Perhaps they heard us coming? I was with Gisbourne the whole time, I couldn't have informed them what we were doing!"

The Sheriff sighed. "Fine."

He continued to lecture Gisbourne on the failed attempt to kill Robin and the other outlaws. When Allen finally had a spare moment, he escaped to his room and threw himself on his bed.

That was a narrow escape. Allen didn't want to think about what would have happened or what he would have done to keep Gisbourne satisfied if the gang hadn't ambushed them.

The next day, as Allen was walking down one of the many hallways in the castle, he felt the hair on his neck rise. Was someone watching him? He listened closely without slowing his steps. Yes...yes, someone was definitely following him.

Allen detoured from his path, and headed for the kitchens. He was still a distance from the busy room when a boot connected with his back and he fell onto his hands and knees.

Allen scrambled to his feet, turning around. He'd barely turned to face his assailant when a fist connected with his nose and he reeled backwards.

His assailant grabbed him and shoved him against the wall, bringing a knife to his throat. Allen's gaze met Robin's sharp blue eyes and his heart plummeted into his boots.

"I told you I'd kill you," Robin hissed.

"Robin, please..."

"Shut up! You disgust me. You know that?"

"I do." The knife pricked his skin and Allen could feel a trickle of blood sliding down his neck. He closed his eyes, waiting for Robin to slice his throat.

"I hate you."

Allen winced. This was Robin. His friend. His brother.

And Allen had betrayed him.

He wished Robin would end his life already, the hesitation was torture.

"Robin!" Allen's eyes snapped open at the sound of Marian's voice. She came running toward them with a horrified look on her face.

"Marian." Robin sighed. "Leave us alone."

"No, Robin." Marian grabbed Robin's arm.

"Marian, he can't live. We've talked about this. You know why he has to die." Robin pressed the knife into Allen's throat and Allen winced at the sharp pain, though he didn't try to pull away from the blade.

"Robin." Marian was pulling on his arm, her eyes pleading and serious. Why was she begging for Allen's life? They barely knew each other, and he'd betrayed the man she loved.

Robin loosened his grip on Allen.

"He won't betray me. I won't get hurt, Robin. Please, just let him go."

"I can't."

"Robin, please, please. Just let him go."

After a moment Robin stepped back. He lowered the knife and sighed heavily.

Allen rubbed his throat. "Thank you, Marian."

Marian glared at Allen. "I didn't do it for you."

Robin shoved a hand through his hair, glaring at Allen and then turning to Marian with a look of mingled frustration and love.

"You need to get out of here before the Sheriff or Gisbourne finds you!"

Robin kissed her cheek, shoving his blade into his belt and then running down the hallway and out of sight.

Allen reached up to his throat to feel the cut there and pressed his palm against the flow of blood. There wasn't much; Robin had not cut him deeply–physically at least. Though Allen's very soul felt rent in half.

Marian grabbed Allen's arm. "We're even. I don't forgive you for betraying the gang, but I can't hate you for trying to save my father.

Now I've saved you–saved Robin's soul from regret and pain. We're done."

Allen wanted to tell her he wouldn't betray anyone again. He hated himself already, there was no way he was doing this a second time. But he said nothing as Marian spun on her heel and marched away.

Chapter 48

The next few weeks blurred together. Allen followed Gisbourne around Nottingham as he collected taxes and brought people to the dungeon who couldn't pay. Marian always got wind of the latter and informed the gang of any executions whenever Robin had the chance to visit her.

Spending so much time with Gisbourne and Andrew, Allen began to wonder if he was right about his suspicions. Gisbourne didn't seem to enjoy or relish the violence he sometimes inflicted, and he seemed eager to appease Marian though he wouldn't come right out and say as much. And Andrew appeared to be more than simply his lackey–he was his friend.

Andrew was a decent man, if anyone working for the Sheriff could be called such. He was polite and kind as far as Allen could see, and he did not pretend he wasn't appalled at some of the things that the Sheriff and Gisbourne chose to do. That kind of person would hardly be friends with the likes of Gisbourne if the latter were truly evil.

One day, Allen was sitting in his room, staring out the window at the courtyard below where the Sheriff's men were training. It was evening, the sun was setting over Sherwood Forest on the horizon. There had been a commotion in the castle earlier but Allen had not been informed as to what had happened.

He watched the soldiers down below sparring together, each fight reminding him of training on *The Barbara* with Robin. He had barely been learning to open up and care about Robin and Much back then, still drowning in the horrors of his family's deaths. Now he was a traitor, hated by those he loved.

A knock sounded at the door. Allen sighed, reluctantly rising from his chair by the window and going to open the door.

Andrew was standing outside his room, wringing his hands.

"Andrew? Does Sir Guy need me?"

"No. I thought you should know what had happened."

"What? The commotion earlier?"

"Someone has died."

Allen felt his throat constrict. He hated it when people died. "Who?"

"Sir Godfrey."

"Oh no." Allen closed his eyes, hoping to shut out the pain as flashes of Florie and Eri and Alice flickered across his mind. "The Sheriff's plot?"

"No."

"His sickness?" Allen opened his eyes.

"No. He attempted to escape. Somehow he ended up stabbed through the heart."

Stabbed through the heart. "No...no, no, no..." Allen backed away from Andrew. "Marian?"

"She is...distressed." Andrew sighed, running a hand over his eyes for a moment. "Sir Guy has been with her. He's planning a funeral for the late sheriff. The current Sheriff is...not pleased with that idea, but Sir Guy insisted."

"Thank you for telling me, Andrew."

"Of course."

Allen sighed as Andrew shut the door and left him in peace.

Sir Godfrey was dead. That would be a harsh blow for Marian and Mark. For Robin, too. And probably for Much, come to think of it.

It wasn't fair, this life. It wasn't fair at all.

348

Allen wanted to be angry, but he was too worn out to feel anger. He sank onto his bed as an ache filled his throat and burned behind his eyes. The tears just kept coming. He wept for Sir Godfrey, for Marian, for Mark.

He wept for all the soldiers he'd had to kill over the past few years. Sinking into his place of numbness during a fight did not remove the memories of the violence that he inflicted. He could see every crimson wound he'd created, see every corpse dropping to the ground.

Allen curled into a ball on his bed, covering his face with his hands.

He wept for Dusty and the way she'd lost her family as he had. Wept for how alone she'd felt for so long, for the struggle she still fought to this day to open up and be vulnerable with the people she loved.

Allen gasped for air as the tears came in a torrential downpour with no intention of slowing or stopping.

He wept for his father, his mother. The people who had raised him but had not been given the chance to see their grandson grow up.

Allen's shoulders shook as he screamed into his pillow, trying to muffle the sounds of his sobs as the tears refused to abate.

He wept for Florie and her love for William that was never allowed to blossom to fruition.

For Alice. The green eyes that would never sparkle again. The mischief she would never conjure, the laughter she would never feel again.

Allen was shaking, his whole body trembling as his grief drowned him in tears.

For Eri.

349

For baby Duncan. For the life that Allen had been robbed of, raising his son with his wife at his side.

Hours later, when he had no more tears to cry, Allen lay awake with a roaring headache and a sick heart. After all the suffering he had caused within the gang in an attempt to keep Sir Godfrey alive, he'd died anyway.

After her father's funeral that Gisbourne arranged in spite of the Sheriff's protests, Marian disappeared from Nottingham. Allen knew she'd gone to the camp. Where else would she be?

A few weeks later, Allen was leaning against the ramparts over the castle courtyard, looking down in the city streets below. Andrew stood beside him, looking up at the deep blue sky filled with white puffs of clouds. The Sheriff and Gisbourne were expecting a shipment of treasure and Allen and Andrew had been sent to watch for it.

"What are the odds the treasure gets here, do you suppose?" Andrew asked, casually leaning against the stone wall and grinning at Allen.

"Slim."

"How do you manage it?"

Allen winced. "I'm not about to give you specifics."

Andrew's grin faltered. "I didn't mean to imply…I'm not digging for information. I am glad Robin Hood and the rest of you feed and clothe the needy, both here in Nottingham and in the rest of England."

"You seem to be on the wrong side of this war."

"So do you."

Allen nodded. He couldn't argue with that.

"So why are you?" Andrew watched him closely, his brow furrowing as he waited for an answer.

Allen shrugged. "I thought protecting the people I loved from grief was more important than protecting their trust and their lives. I was wrong."

"You regret passing information to Guy."

"I do."

Andrew glanced toward the city, studying the rooftops nearby. "I understand your desire to protect Marian from heartache. Unfortunately, her father died anyway."

"You know why I did what I did?" Allen studied Andrew's face. "How?"

"Guy. He tells me…well, everything. I asked you how you ended up on the corrupt side of this war; if you asked me the same question, my answer would be simple: Guy and I grew up together. He is my brother, and I love him. I don't agree with his choices, and I don't approve of his actions most days…but somewhere below the ruthless, cruel man is the boy I grew up with. I see glimpses of him sometimes– the sweetness, the gentleness, the kindness. It is buried deep, but Marian brings it to the surface more and more. I will stand by him and hope to win his heart back from the darkness until the day he dies."

Allen smiled. "I have a friend like you…Much. He grew up with Robin, and I imagine no matter what Robin does, Much will always stand by him."

A lone soldier came riding up the cobblestone street toward the castle courtyard.

Andrew grinned. "One soldier is not a good sign. We'll undoubtedly be informing Guy and the Sheriff that Robin Hood successfully stole the treasure and can feed more hungry souls."

"You don't sound the least upset by that fact." Allen headed for the stone stairs that would lead him back down into the courtyard just as the guards at the gate were swinging it wide for the rider to enter.

"I'm not sorry for it," Andrew said, following behind him. "I have always supported the outlaws' work, and Guy knows it."

As the soldier dismounted and a stable boy ran over to deal with his horse, Allen approached. "No treasure?"

"There was an ambush." The soldier trembled from head to toe, his eyes wide and wild. He appeared to be little more than a child, perhaps fourteen or fifteen. How he ended up in the service of the Sheriff, Allen could only guess.

"Well come along, we have to tell the Sheriff."

Allen and Andrew led the soldier into the castle and then to the Great Hall where Gisbourne and the Sheriff were waiting.

The Sheriff was furious at the news. "You lost my taxes?! Again? How many times will we let that outlaw steal our money?" The Sheriff took a threatening step toward the young soldier.

"I only escaped with my life!" The soldier said, his voice timid and shaky, but then he puffed out his chest. "But I did kill one of the outlaws!"

Allen thought he might faint. Had he heard that correctly?

Not one of his friends. *Please, no.*

"Perfect!" the Sheriff clapped his hands. "This deserves celebration…a feast!"

"Do you have the body to prove it?" Gisbourne asked. "A soldier once told us he had killed Little John, but it turned out he'd only wounded him and the outlaw was soon back in business."

The soldier looked devastated. "No, I don't have the body. I barely left with my life."

"You are one of the lucky ones you know," Gisbourne told him. "Not many come away from the outlaws' raids at all."

The Sheriff sighed. "Gisbourne is probably right. Without a body we can't have a celebration...what a pity..." The Sheriff collapsed into his throne, his shoulders slumping. He was sulking in disappointment, but all Allen could feel was relief.

"What happened?" Allen asked, moving toward the young soldier. "Why do you think you killed one of them?"

"I shot him. The arrow hit his heart and then I ran, because we were outnumbered and overwhelmed."

"You ran?" The Sheriff jumped to his feet. "Gisbourne. Hang him."

"No, please!" The soldier began to protest, but Gisbourne grabbed his arm and dragged him from the room.

Allen glanced at Andrew. His face was calm and impassive, but Allen could see the turmoil in his eyes. He didn't approve...but it didn't appear he was going to say or do anything about it.

Allen went to his room, his heart heavy over the idea of the young soldier being hung–although if he'd still been with the gang, he probably would have killed the kid himself during the raid. That's how it worked.

Allen wished he had more time to talk to the soldier, to question who had been shot and how bad the wound looked. His hands shook and he clasped them together to still their trembling. Even if someone had been hurt, Dusty was there; there was no greater healer in any land.

Chapter 49

Winter set in and the weather turned bitterly cold. Icy drafts whistled through the stone passages in the castle as snow fell outside. At least in the castle there was easy access to roaring fires, fur blankets, and warm food from the kitchen. It was cold but not nearly as miserable as spending winter in the camp in Sherwood.

One day, Allen was in the stables grooming his horse after a ride. He'd gone riding over the snow-covered hills to clear his head for a bit and to be free of the Sheriff's wayward moods.

His hands were stiff as he worked to remove all the tackle from the horse. He needed a warm bath, a hot meal, and then he was going to curl up in front of the hearth in his room.

The large doors at the front of the stable opened, filling the space with the bright light of the sun reflecting off of all the snow and ice in the courtyard. "Allen!"

"Over here, Andrew. What's the matter?"

Andrew hurried through the stables past the stable hands busy at their own work, coming to rest against the door of the stall where Allen was now brushing down his horse.

"It's bad, Allen."

"How bad? The Sheriff is murdering someone?" Allen kept his voice low, barely glancing at Andrew. Neither of them truly wanted to work with the Sheriff, but as long as they valued their lives it was best not to proclaim their dislike to anyone.

"Guy caught the Hooded Rescuer."

Allen's head snapped up. "Mark?"

Allen set aside the brush and moved to exit the stall. Andrew stepped out of his path.

"No, not Mark. Marian."

"Marian!" Allen stopped walking and turned to look at Andrew who stared back with fear in his eyes.

"What's going to happen?"

"Guy is sending a message to the Sheriff...you're supposed to go down to the dungeons and guard her."

"Guy won't let the Sheriff hang her, will he?"

"The Sheriff is in Abingdon...he won't be back until tomorrow...I don't know what Guy will do." Andrew looked distressed, which was exactly how Allen felt.

He hurried down to the dungeons to be with Marian. Surely Sir Guy wouldn't let Marian die. He had once claimed to love Marian.

But so much had happened since then...

Marian glanced up as Allen entered the dungeons. She was in a cell, still dressed in the Hooded Rescuer outfit that Mark and Dusty had constructed for her–simple trousers and shirt, along with a hooded cape and mask. She wasn't wearing the mask at the moment.

"Marian."

She glared at him, not saying a word.

Allen took a seat along the wall opposite her cell. "I'm on guard duty."

"Now won't that just please Robin." Marian rolled her eyes.

Allen winced. It wouldn't please Robin, but Robin was angry enough at Allen over far worse things, this would hardly make a difference.

"Allen, get me out of here."

"I can't do that."

"Why not? You told me you only joined their forces to save my father. Well guess what? He died anyway, so thanks for nothing."

"Even if I rescued you, Robin would never take me back."

"No, he won't. And I'll never trust you either, Allen. You made your choices."

"Then what would be the point?" Allen sighed.

"It's the right thing to do, you imbecile," Marian snapped.

The doors creaked open again and Gisbourne strode into the dungeons.

"Marian." He stopped outside her cell, leaning against the bars and studying her. "Two and a half years ago I wounded the Hooded Rescuer…"

Marian placed her hand on her side. "Yes. I remember. And you'll remember you didn't see me in Nottingham for several weeks after that. You thought I was sad over my father being arrested, if I recall."

Gisbourne sighed. He turned and left the dungeons without another word.

"If he hears a word about Mark…" Marian's voice was sharp as a sword.

"I won't say anything, Marian. Believe me, I've learned my lesson about betraying my friends. It's never happening again."

"I don't believe you. But I will haunt you from the grave if my brother comes to harm."

"He won't. Not because of me. Though if I were you I would lower my voice, or better yet not mention him at all while Gisbourne is near."

"If I were you, I'd shut up altogether," Marian said. "If I'm going to die, I hardly need my last memories to be of an idiot like you trying to give me advice."

Allen crossed his arms, frowning. Through the evening and into the night they sat in stony silence together. Time passed slowly. Allen wasn't sure what he should do or say, if anything. He wanted to believe that Guy wouldn't have her killed–but if Andrew wasn't sure that Guy would come through this time, there was little hope for it.

Eventually morning came and with it came Andrew.

When he entered the dungeons, Marian sat up. Allen glanced between them, his heart pounding. Was this it? Was Marian going to die?

357

Eri's face flickered in front of Allen for a moment and darkness seemed to encircle him. He couldn't let Robin feel that pain; he simply couldn't.

Andrew had a bundle under his arm, but Allen couldn't make out what it was. "Allen, you're needed upstairs. Gisbourne is in his room and expecting you."

Allen got up, and hurried from the dungeons wondering what Guy might have planned.

When he reached Guy's quarters, the door was open. Guy was leaning against his window sill, his face brewing with darkness.

"What's going on?" Allen slipped into the room, looking around as though there would be an obvious answer present.

Guy glanced at him and then returned to his brooding. Allen moved to stand by the hearth, relishing the warmth of the fire. The dungeons had been far too cold for comfort.

The silence stretched until Andrew entered the room and shut the door. "I gave Marian the dress to change into. She seemed a bit surprised by that."

Guy nodded, turning from the window to study Allen. "You are fairly small...do you think you could fit into the Hooded Rescuer disguise?"

"Could I fit into...why?"

"Because I'm going to rescue Marian." Guy said it as though it was the most obvious thing in the world, as though he hadn't once burned her house to the ground. "Here is what I propose we do: the Sheriff will be here tomorrow for the hanging. I will be there to greet the Sheriff. But before anyone is hung you, dressed in Marian's disguise, will appear up on the wall. Create a disturbance and make sure the Sheriff sees you and thinks you are the Hooded Rescuer. Then run out and hide. I will follow with a few soldiers, not find you, and come back to the Sheriff."

"You aren't going to let Marian in on this plan?"

358

"No. I don't know if it will work yet. And if we are caught, we will all hang. I am not going to raise her hopes."

"Very considerate of you." Allen rolled his eyes.

"Do you think this plan will work?" Guy asked, his voice wavering for the first time since Allen had known him. The emotion there surprised Allen.

Andrew nodded. "It might. As long as Allen is good at hiding or you only take soldiers with you to look for him that know what is going on and won't tell the Sheriff."

"And what if the Sheriff shoots me down off the wall?" Allen asked.

"Then you will be dead." Guy shrugged, seemingly unconcerned by the prospect. "But Marian will be free because the Sheriff will believe he's killed the Hooded Rescuer."

Allen nodded slowly. It could work…and saving Marian was worth it. If he died to save her, even better. It might in some small way make up for a portion of his betrayal to the rest of his friends.

"Not for you, Guy, but for Marian. I'll do it. First we have to make sure I can fit into that disguise."

Chapter 50

The sun was rising, casting its warm hues over the quiet world. The morning air was clear and cold as it drifted through the window above him. Allen could hear every beat of his heart, every exhale of breath from his lungs. He crouched at the top of the stone stairway just behind the thick wooden door. He was wearing Marian's disguise, a bow in his hand.

The Sheriff was expected to arrive any moment. It was almost time.

Allen's knees ached from his crouch, but he knew he needed to remain out of sight until the perfect moment. He sincerely hoped this would work.

Would Robin finally forgive him if he died for Marian? Would he forgive himself?

"Drat that Robin Hood!"

Allen heard the Sheriff shout from the courtyard beyond his door. He got to his feet and cracked the door open, peering down into the courtyard below. The Sheriff was marching toward Guy with his usual frown on his face.

"Did the treasure evade you?" Guy asked.

"Are you mocking me, Gisbourne?"

Andrew entered the courtyard with Marian following him, clothed in a dress now instead of the disguise she'd been found in.

"Ah, Marian dear, you're just in time. We're going to hang the Hooded Rescuer."

"I am ready."

Allen set his bow down long enough to wipe his sweaty palms along his trousers as the Sheriff laughed at Marian.

He didn't hear what the Sheriff said as he picked up his bow and pushed open the door. Allen ran out onto the battlements, raising his bow. He didn't take time to aim properly; he let the arrow fly and ran further along the wall.

A glance back told him his arrow had glanced off the ground near the Sheriff's feet.

"What's the Hooded Rescuer doing up there?" the Sheriff shouted. That was enough; they had his attention.

Allen turned and jumped off the wall, to the street below. When he hit the ground his knees buckled and he crashed to the cobblestone, wincing. Pain shot up his legs, but Allen scrambled to his feet and limped past the shops. There was a side gate several shops down that would lead him into the hillside behind the stables.

Allen could hear pounding feet behind him and his heart leaped to his throat. Surely Guy had a plan in place–he hadn't given Allen any more instruction than simply wait on the battlements, draw attention, and run.

If Allen was caught…hung in Marian's place…it wasn't more than he deserved.

Allen pushed through the side gate and made a beeline for the stable doors. Once there he ducked into a horse's stall and stripped out of the Hooded Rescuer disguise. Andrew had left a sack of clothing for him to change into and Allen did so as quickly as he could with his trembling fingers.

Then he stuffed the disguise into the bag and hurried back out into the street with the bag slung over his shoulder.

Guy was near the courtyard gate, speaking to several soldiers. Allen hesitated, his breathing hitching.

The soldiers soon turned from Guy and hurried away. As soon as they had disappeared down the street, Allen moved to join Guy and Andrew by the wall.

"Well done, Allen." Guy gave him a curt nod and spoke in hushed tones. "I think it's going to work. Stay here, outside the wall, until the Sheriff has gone inside. Once he is in the castle, come straight to Marian's room."

With that, Guy and Andrew returned to the courtyard.

Allen waited, hands sweaty, heart pounding. He moved toward the gate, listening. He didn't want to be close enough to see inside–and have the Sheriff see him–but he wanted to know when it would be safe for him to enter.

"Well?" the Sheriff's voice demanded.

"He's gone," Guy said.

Allen heard a loud crack and winced. The Sheriff must have struck Guy. "You have failed me one too many times!"

Allen listened until he heard the Sheriff stomp up the stone stairs and slam the door behind him as he entered the castle. He took a deep breath, and took a tentative step into the courtyard. Only Guy was there.

"Are we going to explain to Marian now?" Allen asked.

"Yes," Guy replied.

"Good. Maybe she'll forgive me now."

"Forgive you?" Guy asked, his eyebrows raising. "Whatever for?"

"Don't you know?"

"I know she hates *me* for betraying her, for burning down her home…" Guy's brows drew together as his eyes darkened.

Allen crossed his arms. "Ever since I betrayed Robin, Marian has been angry with me. I've been angry with myself. I don't know why

363

I stay here. The only reason I helped you at all was because you were going to protect Sir Godfrey. But Sir Godfrey is dead now…so why do I stay on?"

Guy didn't respond, he simply started walking. Allen followed. They went inside and straight to Marian's room.

"I had Andrew return her here," Guy said as they neared the door.

When they entered the room, Marian's face lit up with a bright smile. She half darted forward and then stopped as she said breathlessly, "You saved me?"

Her eyes were only on Guy.

"Hey!" Allen laughed. "Don't I count for something?"

Marian smiled, turning to Allen.

"You both saved me. Thank you…but why?"

"Get rid of that disguise, Allen," Gisbourne said, ignoring her question. "Burn it."

"Yes, sir," Allen said, giving Marian one last glance before he left the room and shut the door behind him.

Allen felt good, for the first time in a long time.

He hurried through the passages to his own room. Once there, he bent over his hearth, studying the little fire the servants had lit there. It wouldn't be enough.

Allen grabbed some of the logs neatly stacked nearby and began to pile them over the flames. He waited for a moment, letting the fire catch hold.

Marian had smiled at him.

Did that mean he was forgiven? Perhaps it was simply the relief of not being hanged, and once she'd had time to consider it rationally she would still find it in her heart to hate him.

Once the fire was burning to his satisfaction, he took Marian's disguise out of the bag and threw it into the fireplace. He stayed kneeling there before the fire, watching the flames slowly take hold of

364

the fabric. Ever so slowly, it began to burn away the evidence of Marian's outlaw crimes.

Could his own crimes be burned away so easily?

He didn't want to be here. Working for the Sheriff, even for Guy. He wanted to be with Robin and Much and his other friends.

But he'd betrayed them. He didn't deserve a second chance with them. Tears pushed their way from his eyes and Allen shoved the palms of his hands against his eyes to hold them back. His breathing became shallow and hitched as he fought off the wave of emotion.

Whether he deserved it or not, he desperately wanted to be allowed back home.

The door to his room opened and Allen turned around, springing to his feet. Robin and Mark were there, closing the door and looking around as if expecting to see a guard jump out at them.

"Robin!" Allen hastily wiped the remnants of his tears from his face. He glanced at the fire and the smoldering cloth still burning there.

"I came to thank you," Robin said. He didn't look particularly pleased despite his words. "You saved Marian."

"I had no choice. It was Marian."

Robin nodded but said nothing.

Mark walked forward and stuck out his hand. Allen hesitated but then shook it gratefully.

"Thanks, Allen. Really." Mark smiled at him, no hint of anger or hatred burning behind his eyes. Only gratitude. "And for the record, I'm not mad at you anymore. You did what you did for my father, and now you've saved my sister. I can't hate you."

"Thank you." Allen took a shuddering breath, hoping he wouldn't start crying again.

Robin crossed his arms. "I'm still angry, just so we're clear."

Allen nodded, wringing his hands together. What was the purpose of this visit? "I understand, Robin. What I did...was unforgivable."

"I am going to offer you a place in the gang again."

Allen stared at him, his hands falling slack at his sides. "What?"

"I said, you can come back. Marian said I should let you…"

"I…I would love to come back…"

"Betray us again, I'll kill you." Robin's eyes flashed, his hand flinching toward his sword hilt and Allen swallowed hard.

"Understood."

There was no need for Robin to fear for that. Allen was done with betrayals.

"Then let's go."

"Now?"

"You can always stay here…" Robin turned around, heading for the door. Mark rolled his eyes.

Allen hurried to grab a few of his clothes and stuff them into a sack, checking the fire one more time when he was done. All evidence of Marian's outlaw antics was gone. All that remained was the ash below the burning logs.

Allen followed his friends as they snuck their way out of the castle and through Nottingham. He hadn't had a chance to speak to Marian, Guy, or Andrew…he hoped the latter would understand and not be angry at his disappearance.

Chapter 51

It was dark beneath the trees, but Allen followed Robin confidently. He'd made his way through this forest in darkness too many times to count; he didn't need the moonlight that remained blocked by the branches overhead.

An owl hooted nearby and Allen took a deep breath.

He was headed home. He didn't deserve it, not in the slightest, but somehow…Robin was letting him back into the gang. Allen was intent on making it up to everyone.

His palms grew sweaty at the thought of seeing Much and Dusty again. What would he say to them?

A glimmer of orange light flickered through the trees ahead of them–they were nearing the camp. Allen slowed his steps, letting Robin and Mark take the lead.

Apart from greeting Much and Dusty after his betrayals, there was also Little John to account for…he'd likely want to have Allen killed.

As Allen thought it, Little John's voice came drifting through the quiet night.

"I do not like him."

"You'll have to get over that," Robin called as he stepped into the clearing. The light from the flames in the firepit lit the faces of Little John, Dusty, Much, and Will. Allen wished it were darker, or that he could slink into camp without an audience. With no trees to block its path now, the moonlight lit up the little meadow, too brightly.

As he followed Robin and Mark across the meadow, he kept his head down, trying not to meet anyone's gaze. Yet even from his peripheral vision he could hardly miss Little John's giant form leaping to his feet.

"Robin?" Will's voice was full of questions.

Every step toward the firepit felt like an eternity. Allen's feet were heavier than stones as he dragged his way over behind Robin.

The children were gathered around the fire, too, Allen could see now. They cowered away from him and closer to Will–their favorite member of the gang.

Robin nonchalantly sat down, helping himself to the meal Much had cooking over the fire. "Allen is once more a part of my gang. You'll have to try and not hold that against him too much."

Little John unashamedly let out a string of curses as he plopped back down onto one of the benches and Mark patted his shoulder in mock sympathy. Allen hesitantly took an empty seat, keeping his eyes on his clasped hands in his lap.

"You're accepting him back just like that?" Dusty asked.

The words cut through Allen like a knife. Dusty–his sister–was the one person he'd thought he could count on to forgive him. She had such strong convictions about Scripture and her faith…that was all about forgiveness, wasn't it? Allen wasn't sure. He'd never paid too much attention to her lectures, but even so…he'd thought she would at least be glad to see him back.

"After what he did today…" Robin shrugged, taking a bit of his pottage. "Besides, Marian told me I had to."

A bowl appeared in front of Allen, and he looked up to see Dusty holding it out for him. He gratefully accepted the food, though he could barely look her in the eye.

"Where is Marian?" Will asked.

368

"She promised Gisbourne she would stay in the castle." Robin let out a sigh, pushing his hand through his hair as he so often did.

"Why would she do that?"

"Out of gratitude, I suppose. But also for us. We need someone on the inside getting information from the Sheriff. Too many people have died because we didn't know what he was planning."

Allen didn't look at anyone as he ate, and before long Will was putting the children to bed and the group around the fire began to disperse.

He was back. One of Robin's gang again. Yet he wasn't sure anyone was truly ready to have him there. He couldn't blame them for that, and yet somehow it still hurt.

Even so…this was where he belonged.

The moment he was done eating, Allen rose and hurried to his hut. The cold welcome, if it could even be called a welcome, was making him uncomfortable.

Allen shut his door firmly and leaned against it, closing his eyes for a moment. His chest constricted as a lump formed in his throat, but he was determined not to cry.

Allen sank onto his bed just as someone knocked on the door and pushed it wide open without waiting for his response. Looking up, Allen saw his sister, in all but blood, standing in his doorway.

"Dusty."

She was silhouetted by the moon behind her, and he couldn't make out her face or expression.

She stepped forward without hesitation and took a seat beside him on the bed. For a moment they were both quiet, but then she said, "Robin accepted you back into camp so easily."

It was the same sentiment she'd expressed to Robin earlier and once more it cut straight through him.

"He isn't entirely happy about it." Allen bit his lip as a tear escaped and slid down his cheek. "I don't blame him."

"He said Marian insisted on it?"

"Yeah…I guess she could see how much I hate myself for everything that happened. Being here isn't helping that feeling."

"Allen…"

"If I could do it all differently, believe me I would."

He dropped his head into his hands, his shoulders slumping as more tears pushed past his fingers.

"I don't hate you, Allen."

"Everyone else does."

"Everyone else is struggling to forgive you for betraying us. Little John almost died because of your actions."

"I know…" Allen groaned into his hands. They couldn't forgive him, and he couldn't hate them for that. He was the one they had every right to hate. But somehow…it still broke his heart.

"Much doesn't hate you, by the way. He and I are both trying to forgive you as our Christ would do as well."

Allen straightened, his hands dropping to his lap. He searched Dusty's face in the dim light. "You forgive me?"

"I'm trying to." Dusty sighed, closing her eyes.

Allen swallowed hard, waiting, hoping…

"You're afraid to lose people."

Allen stiffened. "What?"

"You're like me; you're afraid to lose the people you love. For me, I close off and don't let people get too close. For you…you do outlandish things in an attempt to save them."

She *knew*. Of course she did. She was Dusty, after all. She was the one person in the gang who truly could understand all he had suffered.

Allen relaxed, leaning back against the wall with a deep sigh. "You know me too well."

"I don't think I do. I just put those pieces together in this moment."

Eri's gentle smile flashed through his mind, but it was a balm instead of a dagger. Alice's sparkling green eyes were next, and Allen could feel his heart lifting ever so slightly.

Dusty understood. She'd lost people, too. Maybe there was a better way to handle his fear than he had so far, but even so she knew why he acted as he had. She forgave him.

"You're an idiot, Allen."

Allen winced. "You don't pull any punches, do you?"

"We could have helped you–helped with saving Sir Godfrey. You didn't have to feed information to the Sheriff and Gisbourne."

"I know! I know how terrible I was, that I made the wrong choice. Believe me, Dusty. I know."

"Well...at any rate, I suppose I'm glad you're back."

"Are you?" Allen held his breath, hoping she meant it.

"It means you aren't truly on the Sheriff's side, you thought it was your only choice. I am glad to know you aren't evil."

"Did you think I was?"

"I didn't know what to think."

"Life here is going to be awkward, isn't it?"

"Probably. Just avoid being alone with Little John. He's likely to strangle you in your sleep."

"Well that isn't at all disturbing."

Dusty soon left; Allen didn't press her to stay longer. It was enough that she understood his motives–truly understood them–and was trying to forgive him. And for Allen's part, he would do better. He wouldn't be ruled by his fear. He wouldn't betray his living family or use his dead one as justification for it.

He would be better.

Not long after Dusty had departed, there came another hesitant knock on the door. Allen stared at it, wondering who was coming to talk to him now…Much, perhaps?

The gentle knock sounded again, but whoever it was did not push open the door as Dusty had. Allen stood and swung the door open.

Young William stood outside, his arms crossed as the moon reflected off of his scowling face.

"Oh. William."

Allen took a step away from the door, further into the hut. Young William hesitated, but then the boy stepped inside. He shut the door and leaned heavily against it, eyeing Allen.

"I forgot I had a roommate…I imagine you had the hut to yourself while I was gone."

"I did." Young William crossed his arms.

"I can…go somewhere else. Or…you could move in with Robin?"

"You think you can strut back in here and kick me out of my hut?"

"No, no…I can sleep outside."

Allen would have moved outside immediately, but the boy was still leaning against the door, glaring at him. For a moment, neither spoke.

"Why does Robin trust you now?"

"He doesn't." Allen rubbed his forehead, wondering how to explain everything. "He's angry still…it's just…I saved the life of the woman he loves, and she asked him to bring me back so…he did."

Young William seemed to deflate, the tenseness of his shoulders loosening as his head fell. When he spoke, the bite had gone out of his voice as he whispered in a wavering tone, "why did you do it?"

Allen sat on the edge of the bed, taking a moment to consider how to respond. "I was afraid."

"Of Gisbourne and the Sheriff?"

"No, of people dying. Of Sir Godfrey dying, and how it would tear Marian, Mark, and Robin apart from the insides. I wanted to protect the people I love from grief."

"By betraying them? By almost getting them killed?"

"I know it sounds stupid, kid. I also think it is stupid. I realize I was an idiot. But the truth of it is just as I said. In my own way, I thought I was protecting them from something worse than my betrayal."

"So you don't hate us?"

"Of course not."

His heart squeezing inside his chest, Allen reached out a shaking hand. For a moment, young William didn't move, but then he sank onto the bed beside Allen and let him wrap him in a hug. The boy began to cry into his shoulder.

"I shouldn't have done what I did. I am sorry."

"I thought...you were bad..."

Allen's heart ached. His own son would be only a few years younger than William if he'd lived. As young William wet his shoulder with tears, Allen could feel his own soaking his cheeks.

In the weeks that followed, Robin always paired Allen with Mark or Much whenever he went to distribute food and money, which was probably for the best. Little John wouldn't look at him, much less work with him. If they happened to be in the camp at the same time, Little John often made a point of cracking his knuckles as he glared at Allen. It was a quiet threat, but one Allen could hardly avoid. He wasn't entirely sure Little John wouldn't snap and simply kill him in his sleep one of these days.

Will avoided him, though when they did have occasion to speak to one another it was civil at least. Dusty tried to act normally around him, but the pain in her eyes was enough for Allen to want to avoid her.

Chapter 52

"I wonder how long it'll be before King Richard decides to come home."

Allen glanced at Mark. He was leaning against a tree, one knee drawn up with his arm perched across it lazily. Allen was sprawled in the grass at his feet.

"I don't know."

After saving Marian, Mark had no quarrel with Allen. He was the most natural to be around–Dusty and Much both tried to act normal, but Allen could see the hurt in their eyes and it cut through him. It was easier to spend his time with Mark.

Allen watched the branches of the trees wave gently above him. "Hopefully it won't take much longer. When we first arrived in England, Robin thought it would only be a few months before all was set to rights."

Mark chuckled. "It's been a bit longer than that."

The sounds of Little John's sword whacking into a nearby tree filled the air. Again. And again. Thwack. Thwack. Thwack. Allen could hear the bark of the tree splintering beneath the weight of the sword's strokes.

"Is he practicing for you?"

"Probably."

Apart from Little John's violence against the tree, the atmosphere within the camp was a calm one. The children were already asleep as twilight stole over the camp. Everyone was relaxed. Will and Dusty were near the fire, chatting softly. Even in the low light of dusk, Allen could see Dusty slip her hand into Will's.

It seemed there had been serious developments in the camp while he was away. Allen was glad for Dusty's sake. He let out a sigh.

"What's wrong?" Mark asked.

"Nothing is wrong. That was a sigh of contentment. I'm glad to be back here, a part of the family."

"Even if Little John does ignore you?"

Thwack. Thwack. Little John's sword bit into the tree nearby.

"I deserve some mistreatment. Besides, it isn't Little John I'm hoping will forgive me. It's Robin."

"It might take him a while to get there, if he ever does."

Allen turned his head to the side to see Mark's face better. "I know, but I do hope."

They lapsed into silence.

Allen had fought in the Crusades with Robin–their shared experiences bonding them together in a unique way–but Mark had grown up with him. If he thought Robin wouldn't come around...

Allen closed his eyes, listening to Little John's grunts as he slammed his sword into the tree again and again. He'd likely ruin the sword.

Allen hardly knew Little John–he was sorry for nearly getting the man killed, but he wasn't too distraught over Little John's lack of forgiveness. Will was civil and making an effort, which Allen appreciated, but again, he was not one that Allen couldn't live without.

It was Robin, Dusty, and Much that Allen longed to be on solid footing with once more.

Dusty would get there eventually, Allen was sure of it. She was, after all, the one who always preached forgiveness. She understood his pain, and he knew hers. They'd both lost everyone in horrific ways before they'd met Robin and Much. Still, the pain of the betrayal lingered in her eyes and until it left, Allen wasn't sure he could meet her gaze.

Thwack. Thwack. Little John's grunts filled the air.

Much and Mark were already making leaps and bounds in reconciliation. Allen was grateful to Mark as he had become his most constant companion and friend since the return to the camp. Much was never one to hold a grudge anyway, being the gentle peacekeeper that he was, so it didn't surprise Allen that he was trying to forgive him.

But Robin...Robin was still angry, that was clear. Yet Allen did hope...

Into the stillness in the clearing, Robin suddenly came bursting through the trees."Will!"

Allen propped up on his elbow, watching Robin rush toward Dusty and Will at the fire pit.

"What's wrong?" Will asked.

"We have to go. Now!"

Allen rolled to his feet and tentatively walked toward the group gathering at the fire. Little John stopped attacking the tree at the edge of clearing and Mark strode past Allen, who was in no hurry.

"What is it?" Dusty asked, her dark eyes watching Robin's red face and hurried movements. Allen crossed his arms, almost hugging himself, afraid of what could have put Robin in such a state. Was Marian alright?

"The Sheriff is leaving Nottingham." Robin's hands twitched at his sides and Allen waited, anticipating the worst.

"Where is he going this time?" Mark asked, with far too nonchalant a tone.

"To Austria!"

"Austria?"

Allen's arms dropped to his sides as understanding dawned. The Sheriff was going after the King of England.

"I just spoke to Marian," Robin said, jogging over to the storage hut and starting to throw the extra weapons stashed there out of it and into a pile on the ground. "We have to pack. He's going to Austria to kill the king!"

"When is he leaving?" Allen asked.

"Tomorrow morning. Hurry up, all of you. We have to get there first, we have to leave tonight."

"What is our plan?" Will asked.

"I don't know yet..." Robin paused in his work to shove a hand through his blond hair. "All I know is that we have to beat the Sheriff to Austria and rescue King Richard from Durnstein castle."

"Perhaps the Duke will hand him over if we explain the situation," Dusty said. "After all, we have been paying the ransom all this while."

Robin snorted. "I doubt the Duke will do any such thing."

Robin continued his hurried packing, and everyone moved to help. Allen hurried to his hut to stuff his few changes of clothes into a satchel and then grab his weapons. He tried to be quiet and not wake young William as he worked.

Young William...the children...

Allen glanced down at the sleeping form of the boy, his mind racing. They could hardly leave the children here alone...but they couldn't take them on the mad dash to Austria...they couldn't go back to their families...

Allen hurried out of his hut with his packed supplies, searching the darkness for Robin. He saw him by the storage hut and strode that way. Much and Will were with Robin, and as Allen approached he heard Much say, "Robin...what are we going to do about the children?"

378

Allen slowed his walk, but continued forward, curious what Robin's answer would be. In the candlelit storage hut he saw Will pause in his work to stare at Much, and then glance toward the huts where the children slept.

"We can't leave them alone." Will's voice was filled with horror. Allen knew he'd formed a bond with all of them, taking them under his wing as though they were all his own.

"We have no choice, Will," Robin said. "We have to go *now*. I don't have time to make arrangements for the children; the king is in danger!"

"I can ride to Nottingham," Allen spoke up from behind them.

Robin whirled around, fire flashing in his eyes and Allen flinched. "And what exactly do you plan to do there?"

All activity in the camp seemed to pause as all eyes turned toward Robin and Allen.

"Speak to Marcus." Allen took a step away from Robin, putting his hands up in a placating manner. "He can look after the children while we're gone."

Robin eyed Allen suspiciously and his heart sank. Robin didn't trust him; he couldn't fault him for that, but it stung.

Allen felt pressure on his shoulder and turned to see Dusty standing beside him, her hand on him. "That is a good idea, Allen."

The light shimmering in the dark of her eyes was a balm to the ache in Allen's chest. Dusty trusted him. Dusty turned to face Robin as she continued to speak, "Set up a place where young William can meet Marcus in the woods, not far from here but not in the camp either. No one can know the location of our hideout."

"I'm aware of that," Allen said. "I'd never bring anyone here."

"You did before," Robin snapped, crossing his arms.

"I didn't though. Maybe you didn't notice as you were too busy hating me, but I did not lead Gisbourne here. I told him and the Sheriff I

379

would in order keep my own life, but I was leading him to a different part of the forest when you ambushed us."

"Fine." Robin continued to glare at Allen. "Go to Nottingham, speak to Marcus. But if you aren't back soon enough, we'll just leave without you. You can watch the children in that case."

Will reminded Robin that their quickest way of traveling was by using Marcus' horses, so Allen was given a second task when he left for Nottingham, that of retrieving the horses.

"I'll go with him," Little John said firmly, his voice full of ice.

Allen shuddered. Little John might just kill him on the way and no one here–except Dusty–would bat an eye.

Will went to wake young William and inform him of what was happening as Allen and Little John left the camp. The woods were dark; as soon as they left the clearing the moon disappeared and the light of their fire disappeared behind them. The shadows loomed large and Allen walked with one hand held slightly in front of him, feeling the tree branches as he moved so he wouldn't walk into a tree.

Little John was silent beside him, and Allen had no intention of starting a conversation with the man who wanted him dead. The only thing keeping Allen alive in Little John's presence was undoubtedly the man's respect for Robin. But the slightest provocation might break the tenuous truce.

Once they were free of the forest, the moonlight lit their way to the city. The city gates were closed for the night, and all travelers had to deal with the guards on duty to be let in, which was hardly ideal given the need for the gang to remain secret. But Allen had connections now.

Before they drew too close to the city wall, Allen turned away from the gate the gang usually used and started to walk around the city.

"Where are you going?" Little John growled.

"I can get us in without bothering the guards and getting us caught."

Allen paused, looking over his shoulder at Little John who seemed unconvinced.

"There's a small door that enters the wall in the lower district, unguarded. Andrew showed it to me—it's one way that Sir Guy travels outside the city without attracting attention."

"Oh, a secret door you learned about from your friends?" Little John crossed his arms, rolling his eyes. "That doesn't sound like a trap to me at all."

"Then go your way," Allen said. "We don't have time to argue."

Allen turned and continued on his way to the door Andrew had pointed out to him weeks ago. It wasn't long before he heard Little John's lumbering footsteps behind him.

The door was precisely as he'd expected; unguarded.

Once inside the city walls, the two of them hurried through the empty streets toward Marcus' home. Marcus answered their banging on his door looking disheveled and on edge, a knife in his hand. His hair was in disarray and his eyes bleary as he took them in. "Allen? What...?"

Marcus lowered the knife in his hand.

"We're in a hurry." Allen stepped past him into the house and Little John followed. Marcus glanced into the street and Allen wondered if he was looking for Gisbourne or the Sheriff's soldiers there.

"The Sheriff has a scheme to kill King Richard." Allen said. "The gang is leaving tonight. Can you look after the children?"

"The children?"

"We took in those six kids, remember?" Little John said, leaning against the wall and crossing his arms. "They've lived in the camp since their near execution."

Marcus nodded. "Of course."

They discussed how Marcus might get in touch with young William to ensure the little ones were looked after for however many weeks the gang would be gone.

"What will become of Nottingham in your absence?"

Little John shrugged. "You'll have to look after the people, too, it seems."

"Our travel when we left the king to come to England was several months long," Allen said. "The Sheriff's coffers will undoubtedly fill with his treasure that we can't confiscate because we're gone, but you should be able to keep an eye on executions at least and keep them to a minimum."

"I'll do what I can, but I don't have your resources. Keeping my job is hard enough–I have to supply the Sheriff's men with their weapons, you know, or he'll have me killed and bring in his own blacksmith."

"We know." Little John said. "Be safe, be smart. We'll get back to our work as soon as we can. It is likely there will be less destruction with the Sheriff and Gisbourne traveling abroad. His lackeys won't be as active without his orders."

"Unless he's left them with orders to be as destructive as possible."

"Either way, we can't deal with that. We have a king to save."

"Of course. Godspeed, Little John. Allen. Go save our king."

Marcus gladly gave them access to the horses, and Allen and Little John hurried through Nottingham leading the beasts through the empty streets. Allen knew there were patrols of the Sheriff's men in the city, and his heart pounded loudly in his ears as he waited for them to stumble across the soldiers and have to fight their way out of the city. But they never crossed paths. They reached Gisbourne's secret exit easily enough and hurried back to the camp.

The gang rushed to leave the camp and the flight to Dover began. Their travel to the coast was hurried but uneventful. They did catch sight of the Sheriff's party behind them on more than one occasion, and Robin had snuck back to the Sheriff's camp to scope out the possibility of merely ambushing them on English soil–but they were too heavily guarded. He did discover, however, that Marian was with them.

Why they had brought her, or how she had convinced them to let her come along, piqued the gang's interest. Robin thought perhaps she had a plan for stopping the Sheriff and Gisbourne along the way before they could kill the king.

Chapter 53

The gang crossed the channel without trouble. It was Allen's second time sailing away from English soil and he was not unaware of how different he felt. The last time he'd been completely lost and in despair. He had no purpose and only wanted to die.

Now he was racing to save the King of England, with his family at his side. It was true he'd hurt them and some of them didn't trust him—or even like him—anymore. But he had purpose and he had people he loved and he was running to save a life and not to end his own. As he leaned against the rail to watch the cliffs of Dover disappear in the fog of morning, he breathed deeply, relishing the difference in himself and his life.

They'd left Marcus' horses at a stable in Dover, and once they landed at Calais they procured fresh ones for the ride to Austria. Weeks passed in quick succession as the group hurried across the countryside. It was reminiscent of traveling in secret with the king after the Crusades, except on horseback and with more urgency as the Sheriff and Gisbourne were not far behind them.

The sun was barely cresting over the horizon when Durnstein castle came into view. The group rode toward it for a while, until Robin pulled the group to a halt and dismounted in a patch of trees. The castle loomed in the distance, stark against the brightening sky.

"We'll just have to go in the way we came out." Robin said, eyeing the castle as the horses panted in the reprieve they'd been given.

"Right past the guardhouse?" Much asked.

"It's fool-hardy, but I've got no other options."

"What if they've moved the king?" Allen asked, his mind walking through all the ways Robin's non-existent plan could fail and get them killed. "What if he's not in the same cell, or they blocked up the hole we created? What if–"

"I know it's not a good plan!" Robin shoved a hand through his hair as he glared at Allen. Allen bit his lip; he hadn't meant to anger Robin, he'd been trying to be helpful. There was a time when he and Robin had made the gang's plans together and Allen had always been the one to try and poke holes in the plan in order for Robin to be able to create the most airtight one possible.

"I've got nothing else," Robin said. "We get in there, we hope to find him, and we get out before the Sheriff arrives."

Allen held back the rest of his objections as the rest of the group seemed willing to simply follow Robin and improvise. Little John cracked his knuckles menacingly as he walked past Allen to follow Robin. Allen found it difficult not to read that as a threat.

Allen fell into line behind the others as they crept toward the castle in the dim light of dawn. He and his companions carefully watched the guards pacing on the wall above the courtyard in order to perfectly time their sprints across the open field to the wall of the castle.

Heart pounding in his ears, he held his breath as he pressed his back against the stone wall of the castle, craning his neck to look upward. No faces appeared over the wall to stare down at the group, no shouts of alarm sounded. So far, so good.

Allen and the others began to inch their way along the wall toward the guardhouse–the same one they had run past on their way out of the castle the last time they were here. Allen couldn't see anyone at the gate from where he was at the back of the group with Little John, but he did see Robin and Will dart forward into the courtyard. Seconds later, Dusty and Mark shoved open the door of the guardhouse and ran inside. Much hurried past the gate, whipping his bow from his back and shooting down the soldiers up on the wall before they could notice what was happening and sound an alarm.

Allen peeked into the guardhouse, his sword drawn, but Dusty and Mark were already coming out, leaving three bloodied bodies behind.

There were two dead soldiers in the gateway, presumably what had caused Robin and Will to run forward to begin with.

The group crept past the bodies and ran across the open courtyard–hoping not to be seen from the windows–as Much dispatched the last of the soldiers on the wall.

Little John stayed close beside Allen, breathing down his neck with unspoken threats.

Once inside the front doors of the castle, Robin took the lead and the gang fell into step behind him as they hurried through the corridors. Everything around them was at once recognizable and alien. The escape from the castle was not something Allen was likely to ever forget; he could easily recall stumbling through these very halls, emaciated and filthy and eager for freedom. But he had been focused on escape and not committing the castle to memory. So it felt familiar, sure, but he would have been lost if Robin hadn't been leading the way.

How Robin could remember the path to the tunnels, Allen didn't know but he wasn't going to question his friend. He'd already angered him once today.

Given that it was early in the morning, there were few nobles awake and moving about the castle yet; there were servants scurrying here and there, but Robin always noticed these from his place at the front of the group and paused the gang or directed them into open rooms out of the way before they could be seen, questioned, or caught. Yet as Robin and the others in front of Allen hurried around another corner, voices echoed in the hallway and then immediately stopped.

As Allen stepped around the corner, he saw his friends paused in the hallway and beyond them a group of noblemen who had apparently been conversing before the gang had interrupted their conversation. The men studied Allen's group of friends with curious and suspicious eyes.

"Gentlemen…" one of the nobles said hesitantly. One of the other noble's hands twitched toward their sword hilt.

"Don't kill them," Dusty whispered sharply, in Arabic rather than English.

"What is your business here?" the noble who'd spoken before stepped forward, his eyes on Robin.

"We are here to visit a friend," Robin said easily, his back straightening as he spoke. Robin Hood the outlaw melted into Sir Robin the Earl of Locksley right before Allen's eyes.

Allen inched closer to Dusty, concentrating on all the lessons Dusty had given on her language so he could respond to her in Arabic. "If we don't kill them, they will alert the Duke and other soldiers of our presence."

"They are innocents," she hissed back at him.

"More so than the soldiers we killed?"

Robin was still speaking with the nobles, his voice commanding as it always became when he slipped into his role as the Earl of Locksley. Allen glanced between the strangers, taking in the furrowed brows, dark eyes, deep frowns. They were not buying whatever Robin was selling to them as the truth.

388

"If we don't kill them, word of us being here will spread." Allen put his hand on Dusty's arm ever so gently, hoping she would be convinced.

Much tilted his head toward their whispered conversation and shrugged, meeting Dusty's eyes and then Allen's before he, too, spoke in Arabic. "We can knock them out."

"I agree."

The last statement had come from Robin himself, in Arabic as the rest of the conversation had been. Allen's head snapped forward to his friend just as Robin darted forward and wrapped his arm around one of the noblemen's necks. Apparently, knocking them out was the plan.

The other nobles drew their weapons or cried out in alarm as the rest of the gang followed Robin's lead and rushed forward. Allen lunged at one of the nobles trying to flee down the hallway, tackling him to the ground and then pinning his neck beneath Allen's muscled arm as he blocked the man's airway long enough for him to pass out.

When the man slackened beneath him, Allen let go. He turned around to see who else might need to be dealt with, but was met with only his friends. The rest of the nobles were on the ground; unconscious.

"Let's go." Robin marched away from the men littered across the hallway and the gang hurried after him.

The group made their way through the remainder of the castle to the small room that led into the tunnels beneath. There were a couple soldiers stationed there that were quickly killed. From there, Robin lit a torch and led the way deeper underground. Allen's palms grew sweaty as they made their way into the deeper darkness. He had no desire to get trapped down here again. The year he'd spent in this prison had been harrowing enough; he didn't need to repeat the experience.

The silence that stretched around them pressed down on Allen, sending his heart racing. The only sounds were the footfalls of his friends and the faint crackling of the flame of Robin's torch. Little John's aggressive breathing just behind him sent shivers down Allen's spine.

Allen briefly wondered if the large man intended to kill him during this wild prison escape and simply pass it off as an unfortunate part of their dangerous job. Surely he respected Robin more than that though.

"I think we're getting close." Robin's voice drifted through the tunnel, breaking the silence that had been suffocating Allen.

"How can you tell?" Allen asked. "There's so many branches and passages down here, I'm not convinced we're on the right one."

"I remember the tunnels. I'm not worried about that. I do think we're close. Keep an eye out along the wall for our hole."

"Which likely isn't there anymore."

Robin swung around, the torch in his hand sending the shadows scurrying along the walls. "If you don't want to save King Richard, go home. I didn't want to bring you at all."

Allen winced. "I want to be here, Robin. I only meant it might be harder than you let on."

"I don't need your negativity."

"Enough." Will stepped in between Allen and Robin, glaring at first one and then the other. "We have likely attracted attention with all the soldiers we killed. We don't have time for arguing. Let's keep an eye on the wall for any sign of a hole, whether it is open or plugged up in some fashion. Let's move."

Robin spun on his heel, marching down the hallway as Allen remained standing where he was. The rest of the gang followed after

Robin, while Allen tried to process the argument. He'd started to grow comfortable on this trip—comfortable enough to speak his mind as he would have done before the betrayal, but clearly Robin wasn't in the mood for that. Perhaps he never would be.

A light squeeze on his shoulder as Dusty passed by him brought a small smile to Allen's lips. She, at least, was willing to forgive him and move forward.

Allen followed the others, his eyes on the wall, scanning for any sign of the hole they had dug through their cell the last time they were here.

"I think I found it!" Dusty's voice drifted through the darkness and everyone hurried toward her. Robin held his torch over where Dusty's hand was rubbing the wall. The wall of the tunnel was dirt and rock, seemingly carved directly from the ground and not built, yet there was a large portion of the wall that was discolored.

Much leaned forward, running his hand along the wall. "It's clay."

"That's it." Robin waved his torch over the wall, illuminating the clay portion and how it differed from the wall around it. "They filled it in, but that's it."

"The other side of our cell," Dusty said.

Robin kicked at the clay, but nothing happened. He passed his torch to Much and began to shove his full weight against the wall. Allen was sure it would take more than Robin's determination to break down the clay wall. He also wanted to mention it could be a trap—the king could have been moved, or there could be soldiers in the cell, or any number of things. But he held his tongue, unwilling to anger Robin further.

Will crossed his arms. "Should we have a plan before we break that down?"

"We're getting the king before the Sheriff does," Robin grunted as he strained against the wall.

"What if the king is not in the cell?" Will asked the very questions that had been on the tip of Allen's tongue. "What if he is, but so are a bunch of soldiers? What if it is only soldiers, lying in wait for us?"

"Now you sound like Allen," Robin snapped.

"Allen has a point." Will stepped closer to Robin, laying a hand on his shoulder. "Before we rush in, we need to think this through."

"We've already rushed in." Robin relaxed; still leaning against the wall, but no longer pushing his weight against it with the same ferocity.

"Robin." Will's voice was almost a reprimand, reminiscent of how he spoke to the children when they were out of line.

Robin sighed, and then straightened and crossed his arms. "Okay. Okay. Get your weapons at the ready. Little John, smash this in and then duck out of the way–you're too large to fit through quickly. Dusty and I will dive in, Will and Much can cover us at the hole. Mark, stay clear for your own safety."

"You don't have to be protective of me!" Mark was instantly angry and defensive.

"There's not space for everyone around the small hole we created last time. I doubt when they plugged it up they made it any larger! Just stand aside, please."

Mark grumbled, but he moved a few steps down the tunnel. Allen followed him. It didn't escape his notice that Robin had not said a word to him—no orders, not even a command to stand aside as he'd given to Mark. Nothing.

Much held an arrow at the ready as Little John took Robin's place at the wall and began to kick at the clay with his powerful legs. The rest of the gang drew their weapons and prepared for whatever might come next.

Allen kept his hand on his sword hilt, but he didn't unsheathe it yet.

At first, nothing seemed to happen as Little John kicked at the clay. He grunted as he placed his hands on the wall and leaned forward to give himself leverage as he leveled another kick at the clay.

Suddenly, the wall caved inward.

Little John leapt out of the way as Robin rolled through the hole and Dusty followed him.

The sound of muffled voices drifted through the wall and Allen's hand tightened on the hilt of his sword. But a moment later Robin was clambering out of the hole again and pulling King Richard along behind him. The king was shockingly thin; Allen could count the bones poking through his sunken skin. His hair was matted and tangled and full of mud—or refuse—and his clothes torn to shreds.

He looked terrible.

Much suddenly fired an arrow through the hole as Dusty crawled out of the cell.

Robin pushed the king further down the hallway and the gang began to rush forward, away from whatever danger Much had seen in the dungeon. Allen sprinted along beside them.

Little John took up the rear of the group, brandishing his quarter staff at the few soldiers who were pushing out of the hole to follow after the gang.

Robin led the way back to the castle proper and soon the group was running through brightly lit hallways once more. Dusty and Will spun around to fire arrows at the approaching soldiers that Little John had been attempting to fend off. Allen kept running with Robin, Much, Mark, and the king.

There were more people moving about the castle at this point in the morning, and Allen winced every time they ran past nobles and servants. Too many people knew they were here, increasing the chances they'd get caught with every minute they remained in the castle.

As soon as the group had sprinted across the courtyard, past the bodies they'd dropped earlier that day, and into the open air beyond the castle, the king tried to pull Robin into an embrace.

"We cannot have a reunion here, Your Majesty," Robin snapped, pulling away from him. "We must be on our way."

The group sprinted after Robin back to the trees where they had left their horses. Robin had brought along an extra horse specifically for the king, showing his unwavering belief that the gang would be successful. Once mounted, Robin led the group toward the city of Vienna, stating it would be easier to lose any tail the Duke sent after them if they were in a crowded city rather than running across the open countryside.

Chapter 54

They hadn't traveled far through the mostly empty streets before the distinctive twang of a bow sounded and then the king fell from his horse. Allen's heart leaped to his throat as the rest of the gang pulled their mounts to rough stops and began dismounting. A moment later soldiers began pouring into the street and among them was Gisbourne.

Allen jumped from his horse and unsheathed his sword, spinning around to get a better look at the chaos ensuing all around him.

He'd almost forgotten the Sheriff entirely in the mad dash to get in and out of the castle.

Allen charged into the fray, sword raised as he sliced through one of the soldier's arm's, causing him to drop his sword as blood gushed forth. In his moment of pain, Allen slammed his sword through the man's chest.

As the body fell to the ground in front of him, he let his mind sink to its natural state of numbness as the fight dragged on. He'd grown more accustomed to killing and seeing corpses at his feet, but he didn't relish it and he hated the way it brought forth his memories of his dead family. So he let his mind drift away from his reality as he set to work.

Arrows were flying all around the street and the gang all appeared locked in combat with the Sheriff's men. Allen ducked and dodged through the chaos, entangling himself in one fight after another.

Allen blocked a soldier's blade, their swords striking and the sound ringing out into the noisy hum of the battle around them. As their blades were locked together, Allen felt movement nearby and sidestepped the incoming blade of another soldier, hooking his boot behind the second soldier's knees, kicking backward to trip him. The soldier sprawled in the dirt as Allen's first opponent swung at him again and he was forced to focus on him.

The second soldier struggled to a kneeling position.

As Allen blocked another swing from the first soldier, he simultaneously punched the kneeling soldier in the face and he fell to the dirt once more, this time unconscious.

The Sheriff was nowhere to be seen, but Sir Guy was among the soldiers fighting Robin's gang and Allen was grateful he wasn't near him. He didn't exactly count Sir Guy as a friend, but he was far more than simply an enemy at this point. And Andrew was certainly drifting past the line of friendship.

Allen glanced toward Sir Guy again and saw that he was advancing on the king who was still laying in the dirt. Mark was fending off other soldiers around the king, as Marian suddenly came running from Allen knew not where to stand between Sir Guy and the king. Allen was soon distracted by another soldier and lost sight of Guy and Marian as he blocked, struck, and danced around his opponents.

"Marian!"

Allen could hear the sound of his own haunted memories in Robin's voice. He swung around, fear turning his veins to ice.

Florie's lifeless eyes drifted across his vision, followed quickly by the last view of Eri's face he'd ever seen.

He caught sight of Robin sprinting across the street toward Marian. Sir Guy was backing away from her, his arm bleeding. Marian herself was on the ground, a sword protruding from her chest.

Everything around Allen was fading into blackness.

Guy had killed Marian.

396

Allen wanted to be angry, but at the moment all he could feel was emptiness.

He vaguely heard the Sheriff calling for Guy, and was half aware of the remaining soldiers retreating. All he could see was the blood pooling beneath Marian, seeping outward across the dirt road.

Robin was at her side, as were Mark and Dusty.

Allen stumbled forward, Eri's corpse and Marian's bleeding form swimming in and out of his vision, entwining in a picture of horror. Robin couldn't face this; Robin was pure and compassionate and more in love with Marian than Allen ever could have claimed to be with his own wife. He'd barely been more than a child himself when he'd loved and lost Eri and it had destroyed him.

Robin couldn't...

It wasn't fair.

He noticed Little John pulling Much off the ground, where it seemed he'd fainted.

Marian's head was in Mark's lap, Robin was kneeling beside her with tears coursing down his cheeks as he gently cupped her face in his hands. Dusty and Will were clinging to one another. It seemed Dusty had determined she couldn't save Marian this time...

Little John was holding Much up with a hand on his shoulder. Everyone was crying. Allen grabbed Much's hand, as much to support his tottering friend as to support himself.

Marian, gasping and choking, asked Robin to marry her before she died. Allen didn't think his heart could handle it. Someone was holding onto his heart with an iron grip and squeezing the life out of it. Allen couldn't breathe. He couldn't see either, as hot tears blurred his vision and splashed down his face. This couldn't be happening.

Not to Marian.

Not to Robin.

But it *was* happening.

Much swayed on unsteady feet beside him as though he might faint again and Allen squeezed his hand. "Not now. Stay with us."

Much turned to him with wide, tear-filled eyes.

"She needs all of us right now. Don't faint again."

Robin choked out vows for Marian as her breathing grew more and more shallow.

Even as the old darkness encroached, Allen fought against it. He knew what it was to lose everything and then lose his way; he needed to protect Robin from himself now.

Allen closed his eyes as Marian took her last breath. He felt Much fall to the ground beside him; he'd fainted after all.

The next few days were a blur of agony. King Richard chose to stay in Austria to complete what he called unfinished business. Dusty insisted they bury Marian despite Robin begging that they take her back to England. Allen couldn't eat. He couldn't sleep. The nightmares never stopped.

His tiny son, a blackened corpse.

Alice's shining green eyes void of all life and shimmer.

Eri's smile melting into nothingness.

Marian, blood spooling around her frozen corpse.

Robin with red eyes and knife at his throat.

The journey home seemed a thousand times longer than the journey to Durnstein castle had been. Robin was in a haze, one that Allen understood all too well. It was only a matter of time before he would come out of his stupor and the darkness would consume him. Who would pull him out of it?

For Allen it had been Robin himself–along with Much and Dusty–who had given his life meaning once more. But while Much and Dusty might be a comfort to him, Allen knew that he himself would only serve to anger Robin further. He desperately wanted to help him– he knew what his friend was suffering, he could empathize with that ache far more than most–but how could he help someone who hated him?

When they finally returned to the camp, Allen went straight to his hut and shut himself in. As far as he was aware, everyone else had done the same.

Marian was dead. What were they supposed to do now?

Part 5

The Absolution

Chapter 55

The winter months had melted into spring during the long trip to and from Austria, but the air still held a crisp chill when Allen exited his hut the day after the gang's return. Much and Dusty were sitting around the fire already and Allen made his way over to them. A few birds sang in the trees, but otherwise the forest was still. A heavy morning mist hung over the clearing.

Allen had been surprised to see young William sleeping in a tangle of blankets on the floor of his hut when he'd awoken. He wondered who had fetched the children from where Marcus had been keeping them.

Much had cooked breakfast, and when Allen approached to sit on one of the benches Much quietly handed him a plate of fried eggs and mushrooms.

Marian was dead.

Allen ate in silence. Neither Dusty nor Much seemed inclined to break the quiet of the morning either. Allen's mind was spinning; his emotions warring between grief over Marian, a desperate desire to protect Robin and the others from the darkness he himself had fallen into, and yet an overwhelming ache to avoid doing anything as rash as betrayal again.

Allen closed his eyes for a moment, breathing in the sharp cold air of the morning to clear his head.

The desire to help was overwhelming. He couldn't do anything stupid again–he couldn't!–but he could perhaps start small. Much had been feeding everyone on the journey home even after Marian's death. As soon as Dusty and Much finished eating Allen reached for their plates. "I'll wash up today, Much."

"You don't have to do that." Much seemed reluctant to hand over his plate.

"I know. But you have been working to keep us all fed this whole journey, though I know you haven't been entirely present. You are grieving and you deserve a chance to do so properly. You've known Marian as long as Robin and Mark; this has to be hard on you more than some of the rest of us."

"Thank you."

As Allen set about boiling some water in order to wash up the dishes, Much walked to the edge of the clearing and disappeared. Where he was going, Allen didn't know. But he deserved the chance to grieve Marian so Allen didn't try to stop him.

Will soon joined the circle at the fire; the children had been waking up and gathering around, too.

"Are you hungry?" Dusty asked Will as he slumped onto the ground at her feet, ignoring the benches.

"Not really."

Will's eyes were glazed over, his expression forlorn. Allen hurried over and started scooping some of Much's breakfast onto a plate for him. "You should still eat something."

Will didn't seem inclined to touch the food, so Allen set it on the ground next to him.

The children ate and then moved across the meadow to play quietly and silence fell at the fireside. Allen took a seat near Dusty and watched with satisfaction as Will finally picked up his plate to eat.

As he watched Will slowly chewing, Allen could feel resolve settling in the pit of his stomach. He'd been where they all were now, and he'd let it consume him–that was what he could protect them from. He'd have to be careful to not go too far, as he knew was his natural impulse, but Allen was sure he could manage. He'd focus on small things for now, like washing the dishes for Much and ensuring Will ate.

As soon as Will was finished, Allen jumped up to clean his dishes and then returned to the fireside. Silence stretched, broken only by the children's voices across the meadow and the occasional chirruping bird.

"I can't believe she's gone." Will's voice wavered and his hands shook as he spoke.

"I know." Allen reached down to pick up a stone off the ground, bouncing it from palm to palm. "It doesn't feel right."

"She was so good," Will whispered. "All kindness and compassion."

"And fire and conviction," Allen added. "She was…"

Will nodded in silent agreement to Allen's unfinished sentence.

"She was a good friend," Allen said at last.

A good friend. Robin's beloved. She had been strong and kind and good. And now she was dead.

"Yes, she was," Will agreed. "She took care of us–Little John and I–before you all came back from the Crusades. She was our leader, the heart and soul of our little band back then…I just can't…I can't fathom life going on without her. It isn't right."

Hot tears boiled up and over, splashing down Allen's cheeks. He didn't try to wipe them away.

"I am so sorry that this happened." Dusty said. "Marian was a good woman."

"I wish…" Allen started, and then stopped. He wished Marian was alive. Wished he had been the one to die. Wished he'd been close enough to save her…*something*. Anything other than what had happened.

"We can't play the 'what if' game, Allen," Will said. "It will lead us nowhere fast."

405

"It is too cruel. This isn't fair. I'm the traitor, why wasn't it me? Marian was all goodness!"

Neither Dusty nor Will had an answer for that. Allen sighed.

Silence stretched once more as the three of them softly cried but said nothing. Much came back into camp and joined their circle, studying Dusty's tear-streaked face as he sat down.

"Are you alright?"

"No one is alright anymore," Will said.

"But I will be," Dusty said. "Grief is no small thing, but I know the Lord is in control of this situation. And He knows the pain that we are feeling. He is my great comfort."

Allen shook his head. "I see no reason to turn to him for comfort. If he is all that you say he is, you could have saved her, if he really cared."

"Oh, Allen! He does care," Dusty leaned forward, her eyes full of passion. "He loved Marian more than you or I—or even Robin—ever could. Much like the story of Lazarus, I do believe Jesus is weeping now."

Allen sighed heavily and did not respond. He didn't believe Dusty. Yet there was a calm about her that he could not claim to possess at the moment, so he didn't argue with her. Let her believe what she would if it helped her through this horrible experience. Any relief she could find was surely welcome.

Will reached up and took Dusty's hand in his own. "I am glad that you can find comfort at this time. I feel no comfort, from any quarter."

"Will, if you'd only turn to Jesus. He'd comfort you; He's so willing and ready to do so."

Will shook his head. "We will need to put up a brave front for the children. They will have a hard enough time with the grief that has

406

settled over the camp, without seeing so many grown men and women crying all the time."

"That's a tall order," Allen said.

"Has anyone told the children?" Dusty asked.

"I told them," Much replied. "When they returned from Marcus' home last night."

"When did they get back?" Allen asked.

"Well everyone disappeared into their huts when we arrived yesterday…" Much shrugged. "I met Marcus last night to bring them back here."

Of course he had. Much was always looking out for everyone else. That was precisely what Allen wanted to learn to do–to give relief to Much and everyone else in their grief.

Neither Robin, Mark, nor Little John emerged from their huts that day. Allen helped Much gather food for them which they left just inside the door of each hut. Robin and Mark were both in bed still, wrapped in blankets and ignoring the world. Allen let Much take food to Little John as he still didn't trust the man not to kill him at the slightest provocation.

The next few days passed with little interest. Most of the gang remained in a stupor, other than the children–though they tried to stay out of the way of the adults and kept their games subdued. Finally, however, Will gathered Much, Dusty, and Allen at the firepit for a meeting.

"We have to continue our work. Marian made Robin promise to do so and I think it is fair to say that the promise extends to all of us. Robin isn't likely to do anything about it right now, but the Sheriff is still plotting and people are still suffering."

"What do you propose we do?" Allen asked.

"We are going to Nottingham to keep an eye on things. Dusty, you can continue to travel and distribute food and money. I'll get Little

John out of isolation, and he and Allen will come with me to Nottingham to see what the Sheriff and Gisbourne are up to these days, to try and hear of executions and caravans before they happen. Much... you can look after the children and also do your best to care for Robin and Mark."

Before too long, Allen found himself pushing through the busy streets of Nottingham with Will and Little John at his side. The market in Nottingham Square was as bustling as ever. There were occasional patrols of the Sheriff's men, but they didn't do anything violent or untoward and simply went about their business; there was no sign of Gisbourne or the Sheriff himself.

Little John drifted to one side of the market to be more inconspicuous, leaning up against the wall of a butcher's shop. His size certainly made it more difficult for him to hide, but the people of Nottingham tended to help if they realized Little John was in town by distracting the Sheriff's men whenever they were near.

Will crossed his arms, eyeing the vendors hawking their goods and the people adding to their baskets and Allen followed his gaze. No one had a full basket. And much of the clothing the people wore was thin and ragged. More than one person was too skinny, their bones protruding from their skin in ways they were never meant to. They had had a hard winter with the gang gone abroad. Their money stores must be near to empty by now–the Sheriff's caravans of collected taxes would have been making it to him without Robin Hood's gang stopping them.

"I'm going to try and sneak into the castle," Will said. "We still need a way to gather information."

Since we don't have Marian... Allen shuddered and nodded.

Will strode through the crowd to where Little John was waiting. "Go speak to Marcus, tell him what has happened and ask him to inform us if he hears of anything the Sheriff is planning. Caravans, hangings, plots. We need to stay informed if we're to do any good at all."

"Of course, Will." Little John gave a curt nod and then sauntered off.

"I'll come with you to the castle," Allen offered.

Will studied him, his dark blue eyes flickering with emotion. For a moment, he only studied Allen. The lack of trust seemed palpable to Allen. Then finally Will said, "Alright. I might need you if I run into trouble."

As Allen followed Will out of the busy Square and into the less crowded streets, he clenched his hands into fists at his side. Sneaking into the castle without the secret passages was no easy feat. They could be caught; killed.

And did he want to encounter Gisbourne or Andrew or the Sheriff again?

Certainly not after what Gisbourne had done to Marian.

The two of them slipped outside the city walls and around the town to the top of the hill where the castle was located. The stable doors were open, letting the horses graze on the hillside under the watchful gaze of a few stablehands. Will and Allen strolled nonchalantly into the open stables. Inside there were more servants at work mucking out stalls, but none of them paid much mind to Will and Allen.

Allen glanced toward the stall that housed Gisbourne's stallion, his heart pounding. The horse was there, eyeing him suspiciously, but Gisbourne was not.

At the far end of the stables they paused, peering out into the courtyard. There were soldiers on the walls, marching back and forth and eyeing the streets of Nottingham beyond. None seemed to pay too much mind to the courtyard itself, so Will and Allen sprinted across the courtyard and up the stone steps to the front door. Once they'd slipped inside, they took a moment to breathe, glancing up and down the hallway.

Allen's hands shook and he clasped them behind his back to hide them.

"The last time…" Will shook his head.

"Sir Godfrey died," Allen whispered.

And now Marian was dead, too.

Will crept across the hallway to the doors of the Great Hall that were partially open. Allen followed him, heart pounding in his ears. Inside they could see the Sheriff. He was seated at a large table covered with platters filled with various kinds of food; meat pies, roasted boar, baked fruit. He was gorging on his feast with an unnerving grin.

Hot anger flashed through Allen's chest as a familiar emotion boiled beneath the surface; Allen hated him.

Will turned away and walked down the hall and Allen hurried to keep up with him, his eyes darting down every side corridor and open doorway they passed. There were a few nobles moving about the castle, but Will and Allen never drew too close to anyone or engaged in conversation. They wandered the halls for a few hours, but learned nothing. The Sheriff wasn't scheming; he was merely eating. There weren't many soldiers out and about either, and Gisbourne was nowhere to be found.

"We'll come back tomorrow," Will said as they scurried into the stables once more to sneak out. "We need to keep going like before, helping the people."

In the days that followed, Allen tried to find some sort of sanity. Robin would wander the woods aimlessly most days, and Mark never left his hut for anything, but the rest tried to keep the people of

Nottingham and the rest of England safe from further harm. Dusty traveled alone, distributing food and money to the poor beyond Nottingham. Little John occasionally went on distribution trips of his own or he watched over Nottingham. Much kept everyone fed, especially Robin and Mark who never came to eat at the fire pit when everyone else did. Will and Allen continued to attempt to spy in the castle, though some days the presence of soldiers in the courtyard prevented them from entering the castle at all.

There was no way to know what the Sheriff was planning without being inside the castle, but they couldn't get in. One day Allen was caught by a group of soldiers when he attempted to spy in the castle.

He jerked against their rough hands as he tried to be free of them, but to no avail. He was being dragged to the dungeons once more, and this time it was almost certain the gang couldn't save him.

Suddenly Andrew's voice filled the air. Allen held his breath as Andrew marched up to the group, demanding the soldiers hand him over.

"We're taking him to the dungeons."

"And I've been sent to take him to Gisbourne! You think you have loyalties higher than Sir Guy of Gisbourne? I wonder what he'll do when I tell him who, exactly, defied his orders to bring the prisoner to him directly."

The soldiers let go of Allen. "Don't tell him that!"

The fear in their voices and on their faces was striking–what was Gisbourne like these days?

"We'll come with you–"

"No. You've done enough. I'll escort him myself."

411

Andrew waited until the soldiers were gone before taking his elbow and guiding him back down the hallway.

"Andrew–"

"Shut up. Don't say anything."

Allen bit his lip and waited, wondering what would become of him. He wanted to plead with Andrew not to take him to Gisbourne–the man who'd murdered Marian. If he could kill the woman he claimed to love, what would he do to Allen? But Allen kept his mouth shut.

Allen suddenly realized that Andrew was leading him out of the castle and across the courtyard.

"Andrew–"

"Shut. Up." Andrew didn't look at him, and his voice was a low hiss. Allen complied.

Andrew led him straight past the guards. They didn't stop him– he was, after all, Sir Guy of Gisbourne's right hand. No one wanted to cross him.

Once they were on a street out of sight of the castle, Andrew unbound him and shrugged. "Maybe don't try spying in the castle."

"We need a way to get information."

"Be more careful then."

Andrew turned and walked away without another word.

With Robin out of commission, Will was the undisputed leader of the gang. He took Robin's place reluctantly, but he led them well while Robin was consumed with grief. Sometimes the gang would get wind of a caravan going through Sherwood and Will would make plans for an ambush–Robin and Mark both joined in the raids, if not the planning, but Mark never said a word and it was clear Robin's only intention was to find Gisbourne and kill him.

Allen couldn't blame him for that. If there had been someone to blame for the fire that killed Allen's entire family, he undoubtedly would have sought revenge as well.

The presence of a mysterious archer was felt, as arrows flew during raids to wound the enemy while the gang shot to kill. More than once a well-placed arrow saved the life of Little John, Mark, Robin, and many others when engaged in melee in the road with the Sheriff's soldiers. Whoever the archer was, they were clearly looking out for the gang. Will was insistent the gang find them and get them to join them officially.

"Without Robin, we need all the help we can get." Will sighed, stroking his forehead and frowning. He, Dusty, and Allen were sitting by the fire. Robin had wandered off earlier in the day and hadn't been seen since. Mark was still brooding in his hut as always. Much was entertaining the children across the meadow and Little John was in Nottingham, checking in with Marcus.

"Robin will come around," Dusty said.

"And I can keep an eye out for the mysterious archer," Allen said. "They'd be an asset, for sure, despite their aversion to killing."

Allen dove into the raids with a passion, helping Will organize their ambushes. He needed to make a difference for the people; he needed to make up for past mistakes. So he eagerly jumped in whenever Will needed help–and he cheerfully helped Dusty gather her supplies when she went on her solo trips to pass out food and money beyond Nottingham. He cooked with Much or cleaned up his dishes as often as Much would let him.

It wasn't enough; it would never be enough.

Chapter 56

One day Allen was sitting at Marcus' home in Nottingham waiting for Will to arrive. His leg was nervously bouncing beneath the table and he kept glancing toward the door.

Dusty was seated beside him, her keen eyes watching him. That only served to make him all the more uncomfortable. Everything felt so...wrong...in all of his interactions with the gang. Setting aside that Little John wanted to murder him, he couldn't stand how awkward it was to be around Dusty and Much sometimes. They used to be his family...

Those in the gang who still spied in Nottingham and watched over the people–basically everyone except Robin and Mark–would gather at Marcus' house at the end of the day to share reports of what had been overheard or discovered. Who needed money, who was sick, who had been roughed up by soldiers and might potentially be in danger of an execution. To that end, Dusty and Allen were waiting for Will.

Marcus was out on errands and his wife Lillian was at the market, so it was only Dusty and Allen in the house at the moment.

"Calm down, Allen. We aren't going to get caught here."

Allen tried to still his bouncing leg. "I'm not worried about that. We never get caught..."

"Then why are you so anxious?"

"I'm...I feel out of place."

"Probably because this isn't our home."

"No, not here at this house. I meant in the gang."

"Ah." Dusty rested her elbows on the table, leaning forward. Allen cowered beneath her sharp gaze. "I understand. I am sorry, Allen. I truly am. But this is, to some extent, your own fault."

415

"I know. I betrayed you all. I am sorry. You have no idea how sorry I am. It was pointless, and I never meant it to go so far. I do realize now that there were so many better options to try and save Sir Godfrey that did not involve me betraying you. So please, please forgive me."

"You know you are forgiven."

"Am I? Because no one is treating me like I am a part of this gang. You try, and so does Much, but it isn't the same as it was."

"Did you expect it to be the same after everything that happened? You almost got Little John killed. You broke our trust. You hurt us, Allen. That is going to take time to heal. And now everyone is in pain over Marian, which complicates things…"

"I thought you, out of everyone, would be my advocate."

"I'm not saying that I can't forgive you because I do. I do forgive you. But I was hurt, and that is hard to forget no matter how much I desire to forgive you. You just have to give us time."

"I know…but you have no idea what it is like to be an outcast in the gang. I'm part of you, but I'm not."

"You would not know that feeling either if you had made wiser decisions."

"Do you think I don't know that, Dusty? I was an idiot. And I know I'll never be able to make it up to any of you. But I am sorry…so incredibly sorry."

"Forgiveness is one thing, but trust…trust you are going to have to earn."

"I know…"

Allen sighed. She was right. He couldn't fault her or Much for their wariness around him, or even Little John for his murderous thoughts. Allen had brought this on with his own choices and he had to live with that. But he was going to make it up to them if it killed him.

One night as Will, Little John, and Allen were sitting around the fire–Dusty nearby with the children gathered around her–Much came wandering into the meadow with a young woman at his side. Robin was sitting by his hut, barely caring to glance at Much and the stranger at all.

Allen jumped to his feet just as Will and Little John did the same.

"Much!" Will hurried forward while Little John crossed his arms and scowled at Much and the newcomer. "Who's this?"

Much beamed at Will. "I've found the mysterious archer!"

Allen saw Robin's head snap up then, though he stayed where he was sitting.

"Are you truly the mysterious archer?" Little John asked as Much led the woman and Will over toward the fire.

"Yes." The woman seemed about the same age as the rest of them. She had dark hair that fell gracefully down her back and brilliant blue eyes that shimmered like a jewel.

Dusty stood, leaving the children as they continued to gawk at the newcomer, and came to sit beside the woman as they all settled down on the logs around the fire. "Are you planning on joining us?"

"Well…I hadn't planned on…" the woman glanced toward Robin and then at her toes.

"But you must!" Allen said.

Much nodded. "You have to. All the people fighting for England have to work together."

"It does seem we can do more good when we all work in tandem," Little John agreed.

The woman looked around the group, her eyes darting from one face to another, confusion swirling in her eyes.

"I…I'll pray about it," she finally said.

Dusty grinned. "Now that is a wonderful idea!"

417

Robin rose slowly to his feet and walked toward the group circled by the fire. Will turned to him. "Robin? What do you say to another gang member?"

Robin studied the woman for a minute and then shrugged. "What we really need is a way to get information."

That much was true; it was difficult to spy on the Sheriff when it was so hard to wander the castle without getting caught.

"You need someone on the inside," the woman said.

"Yes. We need someone with the Sheriff and…Gisbourne." The latter name came out in a strangled sort of manner, and Robin turned away from the group.

"I don't know that I want to be on the Sheriff's good side…but I'll see what I can do."

Robin nodded briskly, and then his mouth turned up into something resembling a smile, though it may have been more of a grimace. "If you're going to stay, you'll need to know who we are. I'm Robin, this is Much, Will, Dusty, Little John…and Allen. Mark is in his hut…he'll come out eventually, I'm sure."

Allen tried not to notice the slight hesitation before Robin introduced him.

"I'm Lucy. I've…well, to be honest, I've seen all of you in Nottingham before, and recently I've been stalking your ambushes, so I know who you are."

"We've noticed your presence in our raids," Will said. "You've definitely saved a few of us more than once. The more raids we have, the more soldiers the Sheriff and other lords send with their caravans, the more trouble we have successfully ambushing without falling to harm."

Will absentmindedly rubbed his chest where his own wound had once been, and Dusty reached over to take his hand. Allen had been living in Nottingham castle when Will was injured–he remembered the panic he'd felt when the young soldier had declared he'd killed one of the gang.

"We do appreciate what you've been doing," Little John said. "And it will be good to have eyes and ears in Nottingham again."

And so Lucy became a part of Robin Hood's gang.

Lucy moved in with Marcus and Lillian soon after that. She spent several days visiting various tailors and embroiderers and jewelers in Nottingham, using both money from the gang's storage and the credit of her reputation as a noblewoman so she could look and act the part of a visiting noble and get the Sheriff's attention. Will assumed the Sheriff's pride would dictate that he invite the noble in town to live at the castle and he was right; Lucy hadn't lived with Marcus and Lillian long before the Sheriff extended the invitation.

Allen was grateful for Lucy's presence in the gang simply because it had spurred Robin to action again. He was taking part and seemed to actually care about England again. Lucy joining the gang seemed to jerk Robin out of his stupor. He was still angry and bitter most days, but he helped Will more often and stopped wandering the forest aimlessly.

Chapter 57

A few days after Lucy moved into the castle, Will assigned Much and Allen to distribute food to the villages around Nottingham. With baskets filled from Much's kitchen, they made their way to the village of Locksley first.

"How long has it been since you've visited Sarah?" Allen asked, peering at his friend as they walked over the grassy hillsides toward the village where Much had grown up.

"Nearly eight months," Much said.

The people of Locksley village hurried to their homes as the two men approached, and none came to answer any knocks on the door, so they left parcels of food on people's doorsteps.

"They hid the last time I was here, too," Much said. "They're afraid of Gisbourne's retribution."

After placing food on every doorstep, Much led the way to the manor itself. When they arrived at the manor's backdoor, Sarah was already waiting with the kitchen door open.

"I saw you coming!" She pulled Much into an awkward hug around his basket of food. "Usually our village gets the big fellow…"

"Little John," Allen said.

"That's the one," Sarah nodded. "Come inside, come inside."

Allen followed Much and Sarah into the empty kitchen. The large table that dominated the center had no food in preparation spread across it, there were no servants or cooks bustling about. It hardly felt like the kitchen of a manor at all.

"Has Gisbourne been frightening the village more?" Much asked.

"No. We haven't seen him since before…" Sarah looked at Much and suddenly there were tears welling in her eyes. "Not since before you came back from your trip abroad."

Allen winced.

Not since Marian died…

Gisbourne hadn't been seen by anyone since Marian's death as far as Allen was aware. He hadn't been tormenting anyone in Nottingham, they certainly never caught sight of him marching through the streets anymore. Why? Allen could hardly fathom, but he wondered…he'd gotten to know Gisbourne–Sir Guy–to some degree while living in the castle. He'd grown fairly close to Andrew at any rate, and Andrew knew Sir Guy the best.

Andrew was a good man, and he believed in the goodness in Sir Guy. Allen couldn't help but wonder if the murder of Marian had been entirely intentional or if, like himself, Sir Guy had made mistakes that he now hated himself for.

"I miss seeing her, you know," Sarah said, seating herself in a chair. "She was always so vibrant. And poor master Robin…how is my boy doing?"

"He's grieving," Much said.

"Oh, and her brother…the poor baby. How is he?"

"Not well. He's…he won't talk to anyone."

Sarah nodded. "Poor dears. They'll have to grieve in their own time, in their own way, I imagine. I just want to wrap them both up in a hug, you know? Poor young Mark has lost everyone now, with both parents dead, and now Marian…"

"We're trying to keep an eye on him," Allen said.

Sarah turned toward him, her eyes sharp and unnerving. "Ah, Allen. You came home from the Crusades with my boys, and you are one of the outlaws, too. The one who can't decide which side he is on, yes?"

Allen flushed and looked down at his boots.

"He's with us," Much said.

Allen was grateful for the support, but he still cowered beneath Sarah's gaze.

Sarah stood, moving toward Allen and lifting his chin until he made eye contact with her. "You better be. If I hear you've put my boys in danger again, you'll have me to answer to. Do you understand?"

"Yes, ma'am."

Sarah nodded, seeming satisfied. "Right, you both have a bite to eat before you head out again. And I can refill your baskets so you've plenty of food to hand out to those who can't afford to buy it. Where are you headed next? Wetherby?"

Much grimaced. "Yes."

Wetherby. Marian's home. Allen sighed, watching Much's face. He wished he could have kept Much from the grief clearly written there; the tears in his eyes and the darkness no doubt filling his heart.

Sarah fed them, replenished their baskets with food, and then sent them on their way. Much didn't break down when they visited Wetherby–the residents there did not hide, but came running to hug Much and Allen and accept their gifts. Allen's eyes could not help but stray to the charred ground and broken bits of wood that was all that remained of Marian's childhood home. Sir Guy had burned it, so long ago now, and he'd been tormented by the choice he'd made. No doubt Marian's death weighed heavier on him than the burned home had.

Allen briefly considered sneaking into the castle to find Andrew and ask about Sir Guy's health but decided against it. Sir Guy wasn't his problem; Robin and the gang were.

The return to the camp was met with chaos as the gang was rushing around gathering weapons and supplies for a raid.

"Hurry!" Will called as they walked into camp. "We must be on our way."

"Lucy informed us of a caravan coming through Sherwood," Dusty said, throwing her bow over her shoulder.

"And Gisbourne will be there," Robin said, shoving his freshly sharpened sword into his sheath and buckling his belt around his waist in a tense manner. "I have a chance to avenge Marian. Let's *move*."

Allen felt momentary concern for Sir Guy, but then ran to join the group as they left the camp. The man had murdered Robin's beloved–if Robin wanted revenge, Allen would not stay his hand. He might even help him if it came down to it. Anything to alleviate Robin's pain; anything to assuage his own guilt over betraying his brother.

Allen relentlessly wiped his sweaty palms on his trousers as the gang dispersed to hiding places around the road that passed through Sherwood. They were near a curve in the road hidden behind a large boulder–one of Robin's favorite spots. The gang did their best to switch up their routines so caravans wouldn't know when or where they'd get hit when passing through the massive forest, but this spot happened to be one they often returned to.

Allen had his bow at the ready and soon enough the creaking of wheels indicated the slow approach of treasure-laden wagons.

The moment the caravan rounded the bend, arrows flew and soldiers dropped dead. Allen caught the briefest glance of Sir Guy–dressed in his black leather and riding his black stallion as always–but he fled as soon as the fighting began.

Robin chased after him, breaking away from the raid itself while the rest of the gang dealt with the remaining soldiers. Robin, however, was on foot. Allen watched him fire a few arrows at Sir Guy's retreating form, but he was too quick on his stallion and was out of Robin's range.

The gang returned to the camp in a mixture of emotions. Robin was angry he'd failed to kill Sir Guy. Yet the fact that Lucy's intel had resulted in a successful ambush and less money in the pocket of the Sheriff was a relief–so many caravans had slipped past them in recent weeks, not to mention those that had gone through while the gang was traveling abroad.

Allen began to carry the chests of stolen treasure to the storage hut with Much's help while Little John and Dusty unhitched the horses from the carts to lead them away from the camp and find new owners for them.

Much lifted the chest onto the top of a stack and grinned. "We're getting rich again."

"And we'll give it all away again," Allen replied, dropping his own chest into the hut with a thud.

"I like helping people," Much replied, his voice defensive as he walked back to the carts to grab another large chest.

"So do I, Much. I wasn't meaning to complain."

"Oh."

"Has Mark spoken to you today?" Allen asked as they brought their last load to the storage hut.

"Did he talk to you?" Much spun toward Allen, eyes wide.

"No, no. Don't get your hopes up. He hasn't spoken a word to me or to anyone as far as I can tell. I simply thought if anyone was going to get him to talk again it would be you...or Robin, but he's too bitter himself these days to be much help."

"No, I haven't broken through to Mark either." Much shut the storage hut's door and leaned against it, surveying the camp around them. "I think the sight of Robin closes Mark up even more, because of his connection to Marian."

"I hadn't thought of that, but you may be right. Robin always says you are the most observant little mouse and I am beginning to agree with him. You see everything, don't you?"

"I don't think I do, Allen."

"Regardless of what any of us do or do not see…we have to break Mark from this silence. It can't be healthy."

Much nodded silently. Allen could only hope he would find a way to break through to Mark. Allen knew the torment of losing a beloved sister; he'd do anything to assuage that darkness and despair from Mark's heart and mind.

Alice's sparkling green eyes and ready smile wavered in his mind, both a balm and a curse. Someone needed to keep Mark from the shadows that had consumed Allen.

Chapter 58

Lucy began to spend more time in the camp even when she didn't have news to report. She cooked with Much, went for long walks with Dusty, and assisted Will in training young William with the sword and bow. She also spent a great deal of her time with the other children, playing with them, telling them stories, and taking them for rides on her horse. One evening as she was giving them rides on her horse–borrowed from the Sheriff's stables–the children clambered around her begging for a turn.

"Who's next?" Lucy laughed, having already taken each of them twice around the camp.

"Oh, me!" John said. "I want to go!" He was bouncing up and down in excitement. Lucy's smile flashed–seeming to brighten the whole meadow–as she lifted him into the saddle.

Allen was stretched out on the ground with his head propped on one of the logs that sat by the fire pit. He was watching the children trailing Lucy as she led the horse and John giggled from the saddle.

The camp was empty, the rest of the gang still busy with various activities. Allen breathed a deep sigh, drinking in the calm. There was no Little John to put him on edge, no Robin to bring his guilt boiling to the surface.

"Why do you bother leading them around in circles?" Allen asked, unable to hold in a chuckle. "Surely there are more productive things to be doing."

Lucy grinned, whilst rolling her eyes in Allen's direction. "What are you doing, Allen, except lying around the camp in a lazy fashion." Considering his current position on the ground, Allen couldn't argue with her assessment.

"At least I am exercising, both myself and the horse," Lucy continued, "and entertaining the children besides."

"You've gone in so many circles you are making me dizzy," Allen said.

"Good." Lucy laughed, the sound bringing smiles to most of the children's faces. "That was my plan all along, you know."

Allen grinned. It was so easy to be with Lucy. To forget that the world was a horrible place and everything went wrong.

He hadn't betrayed her.

Their friendship was still fresh and new; unspoiled by Allen's choices and mistakes. He felt at ease with her in a way he couldn't be with any of the others. Despite Dusty and Much and even Will professing to forgive him, despite Robin allowing him back in the gang, he couldn't help but notice the shift in everyone's behavior around him at times. The sadness in Dusty's eyes. The hesitancy in Much's voice. Just the other day Much had assumed Allen didn't even like helping the people of Nottingham. His betrayal had broken everyone's perception of who he truly was—but Lucy could see him. She knew he was the traitor, but she treated him no different than she treated everyone else in the gang that she was becoming fast friends with.

It was remarkable how easily she seemed to fit in with everyone.

After leading a few more children in mindless circles around the camp, Lucy tied the horse to a tree at the edge of the clearing—warning the children not to get too close without her supervision—and came to sit on the ground beside Allen.

"You seem especially lazy today."

Allen quirked an eyebrow up at her from his prone position, a grin spreading across his face. "Lazy? I'm just relaxing after a hard day's work. This is earned rest."

Lucy's blue eyes danced with mischief. "Is it?"

"I would say so, yes."

"You do seem especially at ease though."

"That's you."

Lucy tilted her head to one side, her brow furrowing despite the smile on her face. "Oh?"

Allen lost his own smile and shrugged. He hadn't meant to speak of all he'd been brooding over a moment before, but now the door was open...

"You don't treat me any differently than you do anyone else. I...I can feel the difference spending an afternoon in your presence rather than the others."

Lucy nodded. "They are trying to forgive you though, aren't they? I mean...Robin let you back."

"They're trying, and I can't fault them for any of their reservations. I know I can't. But it's still...uncomfortable at times. And with you? There's nothing. No awkwardness, no hesitation. You don't ask me to do things and then look at me like you aren't sure I'll follow through. You don't study me from across the fire with a face that says you don't know whether or not you should kill me while I sleep."

"Okay, *no one* does that."

"You should watch Little John the next time the two of us are in the same space."

"Well, I am glad that I can be a balm of sorts."

In the weeks that followed, Lucy kept the gang informed of caravans of treasure passing through Sherwood–or taking other random

429

routes when the Sheriff tried to outwit the gang–and she brought news of every execution the Sheriff was planning. Robin took charge in planning ambushes and rescues and Will stepped back from leading the group. It seemed everything was returning to a semblance of normality.

Mark still hadn't spoken to anyone since the return from Austria as far as Allen knew–he certainly wasn't speaking to Allen–and Robin was still angry, but that was to be expected. He was a far more broodish leader than he had been previously, but at least he was leading again and not completely useless. He bounced back to having purpose much faster than Allen had when he'd lost his love–and everyone else–and Allen was glad of it.

Allen didn't want to rest secure in such positive thoughts, however, because surely every time he felt at peace in his life, horror followed.

A few days later, Lucy came riding into camp in the evening. Allen was lounging against one of the log benches again with Will and Dusty sitting near him and Mark sitting across the fire, brooding. It wasn't often that Mark left his hut except to participate in raids and rescues and Allen wasn't oblivious to the fact. Maybe Much had spoken to him; maybe healing was beginning.

Dusty hurried over to greet Lucy. Allen noticed Robin watching from where he sat outside of his hut. Lucy didn't wear her usual smile and Allen wondered what news she had to share.

"Any news from Nottingham?" Dusty asked.

"Who is the Sheriff hanging now?" Allen added.

"The Sheriff isn't hanging anyone." She spoke softly, glancing toward Robin.

"Is there anything of interest happening in Nottingham?" Will asked as Dusty and Lucy joined him on the bench by the fire.

"Well…" Again, Lucy shot a glance toward Robin, this time glancing toward Mark as well. "Sir Guy confronted me today, about helping the outlaws. He suspects I am an informant."

"Oh no!" Dusty shuddered and Will tensed beside her.

Allen shifted position, keeping his eyes on Lucy's face. Would Sir Guy hurt her, as he'd hurt Marian? Or would his better nature prevail for once?

"What happened?" Will asked, leaning forward, his dark blue eyes fixed on Lucy, concern written across his face.

"Nothing happened," Lucy said. "I told him he was right."

"You did what?!" Robin snapped, jumping up to move closer to the conversation. Allen shifted away from him slightly as Robin sat on the bench he'd been lounging against.

"It's alright," Lucy said, throwing up her hands in a placating manner. "He didn't tell the Sheriff. He didn't do anything at all."

"You've blown your cover! Now who is going to be our informant?"

"I am." Lucy frowned at Robin. "Nothing has changed. Guy won't betray me."

"Guy?" Robin's eyebrows shot to his hairline as his voice turned ice cold. "Since when are you so familiar?"

Lucy crossed her arms. "For your information, Sir Guy of Gisbourne and I have been sort of friends for nearly two months." Robin rolled his eyes. "Oh, splendid. Now our informant hasn't only blown her cover, she's also fraternizing with the enemy."

"I live with them, Robin! How can I not?"

"She has a point," Will said.

"I need to get back to Nottingham," Lucy said, standing up. "I only came to let you know what had happened. I am quite thrilled that Guy…Sir Guy…Gisbourne, that is, didn't turn me in."

"Go on then," Robin said. "Run back to Nottingham."

431

The bitterness in Robin's voice sent shivers through Allen. He had every right to hate Sir Guy and to hate that Lucy was feeling kindly toward the man who'd murdered Marian. It was a valid response. But it gave Allen the distinct feeling that he himself would never be forgiven; Lucy's actions brought some hope, however.

If Sir Guy was truly trustworthy–if that was even possible–then surely Allen could be, too. He hadn't fallen so far, he hadn't murdered someone he professed to love. Betrayal was bad, and he knew it now, but if Sir Guy could come back from his choices, surely Allen could, too.

As soon as Lucy was gone Robin turned to Will. "You are keeping an eye on Nottingham tonight. We'll take turns watching out for any news of Lucy being arrested until we're entirely sure this has blown over."

In the days that followed the gang did as Robin requested and took turns staying in Nottingham to keep an eye on Lucy. She wandered the streets of Nottingham passing out food from the castle and visiting the sick much as she had always done, and even rode to the camp on occasion. It seemed Sir Guy had kept her secret.

He'd rescued the children for Marian.

He'd killed Marian.

Allen didn't know what to make of the man.

He hadn't betrayed Lucy's secret, but what would he do next?

Andrew would undoubtedly be grateful for his current behavior and have faith in it continuing, but Andrew was in many ways blind to Sir Guy's worst tendencies–or so Allen thought. It was true that Sir Guy had been known for acts of kindness before–saving Marian, rescuing the children–but that had all been because he was in love with Marian. Was he capable of goodness outside of being in love?

Or, perhaps he *was* in love with Lucy now. Though it had hardly been long enough for anyone to get over Marian's death.

432

Certainly not if he'd truly loved her. Despite killing her, somehow Allen did think his feelings toward her had been anything but genuine.

Chapter 59

As the summer passed, Lucy continued to keep the gang informed of the Sheriff's activities and to discuss Sir Guy's potential for goodness. She didn't often speak of the latter around Robin, who clearly hated every mention of the man's name, but she would speak to Dusty, Much, and Allen about her budding friendship with the man who had murdered Marian. Allen had noticed she'd even stopped using the horses from the Sheriff's stables and rode to camp on Sir Guy's own horse most days.

One day when she came riding into camp on the familiar black stallion, she seemed in an especially cheerful mood. The gang was gathered around the fire pit, though it was still early in the evening and no fire was lit.

"I'm going to test Guy, I think," Lucy said as she seated herself between Robin and Much.

"Don't," Will said. "Please, don't do anything foolish. He's unpredictable and dangerous."

Allen shifted in his seat, picturing Sir Guy burning Marian's home, but freeing the children. Killing Marian, but not turning in Lucy when he found out she worked with Robin Hood. Will was correct; he was entirely unpredictable.

"I'm not afraid of Guy. I trust him."

Robin snorted at Lucy's confident assertion. "You are foolish if you trust Gisbourne."

Lucy shrugged her shoulders. "Then I'm foolish. Regardless, I'm going to ask him to let the children go."

"What?" Much glanced from Lucy to the children playing across the meadow.

"I'm going to ask him to speak to the Sheriff to see if we can get the children pardoned so they can go home to their families."

"That will never work," Robin said.

"Besides, what would camp life be like without them?" Will asked. "I'd miss them."

"They belong with their parents, Will," Lucy said. Her voice was firm and her eyes flashing as she turned toward him. "They need to go home."

"Gisbourne won't help you," Robin said, crossing his arms.

"He might," Allen said, watching Robin's face across the fire. "I think he is capable of great kindness."

"Says the man who betrayed my trust," Robin snapped. "I should have expected you to defend my enemy."

Allen lowered his head. He could feel the heat of shame from his cheeks to his toes. Robin still hadn't forgiven him. He'd hardly forgiven himself for that betrayal either, yet it still cut his heart to pieces every time Robin suggested he was untrustworthy.

"Great kindness from the man who murdered my wife? What nonsense."

Lucy sighed. "I need to go. I'm causing more rifts in this camp than anything else I think."

"It's hardly your fault, Lucy," Will said quietly.

Allen silently agreed. Lucy had nothing to do with Sir Guy killing Marian or with Allen betraying his friends. When it came to the things that caused arguments and tension within the camp, there was plenty of blame to go around, but Lucy had nothing to do with any of it.

Lucy rose and went to mount Sir Guy's horse. Allen wondered if Robin knew what horse she rode, but it was unlikely. He hadn't lived with Sir Guy and probably didn't pay too much attention to the horse the man rode.

"Do you think it will work?" Little John asked as Lucy disappeared into the trees.

"Of course it won't," Robin replied, sighing as he shoved his hand through his hair.

"But these are the children that Sir Guy saved in the first place," Allen said. "Why wouldn't he save them again?"

"He is evil," Robin said. "I think Marian's death has made that perfectly clear."

Mark hastily stood and left the circle to go to his hut. Allen watched him go with a heavy heart. Would Mark ever recover from Marian's death? The likely answer was no. Not that he necessarily should, either. Allen knew what it was to lose a sister. And even to blame oneself for the tragedy.

Yet he had moved on in some ways.

Alice's green eyes and bright smile flashed in his mind and Allen shook his head, pain filling his heart. Moving on with life was not exactly the same as healing. It didn't seem Mark was capable of either. Did that mean that Mark loved his sister more? Allen wasn't sure and he didn't want to think about it.

"From what Lucy has said, Gisbourne is changing for the better," Dusty said, pulling Allen back to the present conversation.

"Marian always brought goodness out of him, too," Robin replied, his eyes flashing. "And that led nowhere. Lucy is going to get herself killed!"

The anger in Robin's voice was also laced with something else that Allen instantly recognized; concern. Robin was worried about Lucy.

Allen was, too, but he had a bit more faith in Sir Guy. It seemed strange, given that Sir Guy had killed Marian. That act alone should have been unforgivable. But then, Allen had betrayed his family and that also ought to be unforgivable. Yet here he was, back in the gang–despite how hard it was for Robin to trust him.

Allen felt a kinship with Sir Guy simply because they were both capable of evil and yet both wanted, in some way, to do good by those they cared about. He wanted–no, he needed–Sir Guy to prove worthy of Lucy's trust because if Sir Guy could come back from such a terrible mistake then surely there was hope.

That night as Allen was drifting to sleep, young William's voice broke through the silence and darkness and jolted him to wakefulness.

"I don't want to leave."

"What?" Allen rolled over, peering into the darkness as though he could see young William despite the lack of light, though he could not find his face in the shadows of the night.

"If Lucy convinces Gisbourne or the Sheriff...I don't want to leave."

"Don't you miss your home and your parents?"

"Yes. But...I want to be here; I want to help." The boy's voice wavered and cracked.

Allen reached out into the darkness until he found his shoulder. He gave the boy a gentle squeeze.

Young William sighed. "You think I'm just a child, but I'm almost a man. I could help you; I could help Robin Hood!"

"If the rebellion lasts long enough for you to be a bit older, I'll gladly accept your help. But for now...if Lucy manages the impossible, it would be good for you to be home."

"Why can't I stay? The little ones can go home."

"You've never been allowed to help in any of our missions. What makes you think you would be now?"

"I...I don't want to go."

438

"I know. But perhaps you could find ways to be useful while living in Nottingham, too. You could watch out for your neighbors. Let Marcus know who is in need of money or who is sick and needs Dusty or Lucy to visit. It's a large city, we can't always be everywhere or know everyone who is in need. You can help, William. Even if Lucy succeeds and you have to go home; you can help."

The boy sighed and Allen gave his shoulder another squeeze.

"I suppose."

"And I'm sure you'll be more glad to be back with your family than you think."

In the end, Lucy did succeed. It was only a few days later that she arrived in camp to say that the Sheriff was publicly pardoning the children. She and Dusty gathered up the children and their meager belongings and took them back to Nottingham. Allen made a promise to young William that he would visit him sometimes.

Will suggested the gang take turns keeping guard near the homes of the children's families for a few weeks to be certain the Sheriff would leave them alone and that it wasn't a trick. Robin agreed. Yet in the days and weeks that followed, the Sheriff never did anything; his soldiers weren't seen near their homes, Sir Guy never visited. There was no retribution or punishment for the execution the children had escaped the year prior.

Chapter 60

Sir Guy doing precisely what Lucy wanted and convincing the Sheriff to pardon the children had a sour effect on Robin. He grew more angry and bitter than he already had been, sending foul looks toward Allen on a daily basis. He seemed almost as murderous as Little John now, though neither acted on the intention so clearly written in their eyes.

One day when Robin was ordering everyone to their duties for the day, he told Allen he had nothing for him to do.

"Are you sure, Robin? I could at least take some money and go distribute it to the villages nearby."

"Not a chance," Robin replied, strapping his bow to his back. "Just stay here."

"There are few of us and so much of England to look after, surely–"

"I said *no!*"

Allen sighed and said nothing more. He watched with a heavy heart as the camp emptied around him.

He was soon alone.

Even the children were gone now, back in Nottingham. He was completely isolated and unwanted. Allen slumped on one of the benches by the fire pit, putting his head in his hands. A moment later, he heard hoofbeats. Looking up, he saw Lucy riding into camp.

"They're all gone," Allen said sullenly as Lucy dismounted. "Robin has given everyone something to do today. Except me."

"I imagine he is used to having to leave one person in camp to watch the children and hasn't gotten used to the idea that he doesn't have to anymore." She sat beside him with a smile on her face and light dancing in her eyes.

She didn't understand.

"He doesn't like to have me help with raids," Allen said. "And he never sends me on missions of my own like he does everyone else. He doesn't trust me. He hasn't completely forgiven me for what I did."

"Do you blame him?"

"No." Allen sighed. He couldn't blame him, but he hated the way he was treated all the same. "But you've forgiven me."

"Your offense wasn't against me."

"No one has completely forgiven me. Not even Dusty."

"You hurt them. Forgiveness is hard, Allen."

"You don't find it so. You'd forgive any one of anything, I'm sure you would."

"I do try to be forgiving, Allen. But it isn't as easy as you think. Sometimes it is very hard. For instance, I would find it difficult to forgive the assassins who killed my father. I don't know who they are, but if I did…if I met them, I don't know that I could be as gracious to them as I am to Sir Guy."

Allen sighed.

"Just continue to prove your worth, Allen. Keep showing how loyal and true you are. You are going to have to re-earn their trust and that will take a great deal of time."

"I know."

"I'll support you, for whatever that is worth…but Robin's opinion of me is not very high."

"Thank you, Lucy. I appreciate your friendship."

She was too generous and kind, but Allen was grateful. He'd destroyed most of his friendships and felt she was the only person he could truly talk to anymore. Dusty and Much certainly tried, and he loved them for it. Mark had been easy to speak to before Marian's death, but he hadn't talked to anyone since the return to England.

A week or so later, Lucy came to the camp to report that the Sheriff was going to hang a man in the village of Abingdon. After she had relayed her news and preparations had begun for rescuing the man, Lucy drew Allen and Dusty aside.

"Something truly wonderful has happened," she said as she led them a short distance across the meadow.

"What is it?" Allen asked.

"Guy told me," Lucy said, her eyes sparkling. "I didn't know about the hanging, but Guy came and told me directly. He knows I'm an informant for Robin Hood's gang, and he told me anyway, knowing what I would do with the information. He's helping us."

"Did he truly do that?" Allen asked, the shock of her revelation running through him.

Lucy nodded, grinning.

"That is crazy!" Allen said. "Good though. I knew he had it in him."

"I can scarcely believe it," Dusty said. "But Allen is right, it is good. Now we have two people on the inside acting as informants. And with Gisbourne being the Sheriff's right hand, we should never miss an execution."

"I'm afraid Robin won't like it," Lucy said, glancing back toward the group gathered around the fire pit. "That's why I didn't tell him. And it would only upset Mark as well."

"I won't tell them," Allen said.

"I will probably tell Will," Dusty said.

Lucy nodded. "I don't want to keep secrets, I just don't want to upset anyone. My friendship with Guy tends to lead to arguments and frustration here in the camp."

Her concern was probably for the best. Robin was still angry, and of course Mark was still silent. Neither of them needed a reminder of Marian or the fact that her killer was now helping them.

One day Will suggested he and Allen pay a visit to Marcus to learn more of his blacksmith work. When the camp had originally been built a forge had been constructed, but it wasn't often used and Will was feeling the itch to learn more. Allen was grateful to be invited on such a journey. It seemed Will, for the time being at least, was in a gracious mood.

Before long, Will and Allen were in Marcus' shop watching him work. Marcus leaned over his forge, his leather apron sweating from the heat as he pulled a molten piece of steel from the fire with a pair of heavy tongs.

A shadow crossed the open door and Allen glanced up to see Lucy standing there.

"Learning tricks to take back to the meadow?" Lucy asked.

Allen grinned. "We'll never match Marcus' skill, but yes. We're trying."

"What is your purpose here?" Marcus asked. "Need a better weapon than your flimsy bow?"

"My bow has served me well, thank you very much," Lucy laughed. "Actually, I need help from the gang."

Allen stepped away from the forge instantly, ready to help.

"What do you need?" Will asked.

"There's important information that Robin needs to know."

"What is the Sheriff planning now?"

"I can't tell you."

Allen tilted his head to one side, his eyebrows raising. "Why not?"

"Because I promised the Sheriff I wouldn't."

"What?!" Allen gawked at Lucy. He heard Marcus sigh.

"Don't be so distressed." Lucy said. "You'll still get the message."

444

"How?" Will asked.

"Sir Guy is in Nottingham Square. He'll tell you what you need to know. *He* didn't promise not to."

Will raised a skeptical eyebrow. "Can we trust him?"

"Yes."

"Robin won't like it."

"He'll have to get over it."

"I don't like it either," Will said, his blue eyes darkening as he stepped toward Lucy. "He cannot be trusted, whatever you and Dusty might think to the contrary."

"He can. He's helped me before, multiple times," Lucy said. "The children going home? Nothing has happened to them. And the execution in Abingdon? You were able to stop that."

Allen nodded along in agreement. "If Sir Guy is helping us, I wouldn't pass up the offer."

"Besides, how else will you get the information he has?" Lucy said.

"From you," Will replied.

"I promised I wouldn't tell."

"Lucy, you're insane. You could just tell us. Don't be ridiculous."

"I am not in the habit of going back on my word. And more than that, the Sheriff is using this as some kind of test. If I can't honestly prove I didn't tell the gang the news, he might do something drastic. So no. I'm not telling you."

"If the Sheriff is testing you, then even Sir Guy giving us the news will tip him off," Will said. "Either way you'd be in trouble."

"I think I can manage the situation, so long as someone talks to Sir Guy and I'm not the one informing Robin."

"I don't think this is wise," Will said. "Apart from the nonsense of not telling us yourself, if the Sheriff is using this as a test perhaps we shouldn't use whatever information you are withholding at all, and let this incident–whatever it is–pass."

"But what if it is an innocent person dying?" Allen asked. He could understand Will's reluctance to deal with Sir Guy, and his fear that it was a trap that Lucy was walking into. But Allen couldn't take that risk. "I'll go talk to Gisbourne."

"Thank you, Allen," Lucy said.

Allen nodded and then strode out of Marcus' shop. As he walked along the cobblestone streets toward the Square, he decided it was probably best he was the one to speak to Sir Guy anyway. He already had a relationship of sorts with him and, next to Lucy, was probably the most accepting of working with the man who'd killed Marian.

Chapter 61

Allen entered Nottingham Square and wandered through the merchant's booths. Men and women were walking about on business of their own, buying necessities, chatting with neighbors. His eyes danced across the people, searching for the familiar black cloak he knew Sir Guy would be wearing.

He saw Old Tibb with her missing teeth and ratty clothes chatting with a young woman. He saw young William following his father into a tailor's shop. A shadow caught his attention and he finally saw who he was looking for. Sir Guy leaning against the wall of the bakery on the far side of the Square. Allen hurried over to him.

"Sir Guy?"

"Allen." Sir Guy studied him from beneath the hood he had pulled up over his dark hair. His dark eyes glittered with secrets Allen couldn't read. "It has been a while since we last spoke."

"Yes it has. The last time was before…"

Marian died.

Sir Guy frowned, his brows pulling together and a storm cloud suddenly brewing on his face though he said nothing.

"Ah…Lucy said you had a message?" Allen crossed his arms, taking an involuntary step away from Sir Guy. "Will did not appreciate her method of getting us information this time…and he doesn't think Robin will either."

"Yes I have a message. There's a caravan coming through Sherwood tomorrow."

"And you're helping us stop it. Why?"

Sir Guy winced and then ran a hand across his face. "Because I am tired of being the villain. And Lucy…"

Allen nodded at the unfinished thought. He understood. "Inspires you to believe the impossible. I know."

The impossible. That Allen could be forgiven and accepted. That he could do better, and be worthy of trust.

Sir Guy and Allen discussed the particulars of the caravan, exactly when it was traveling, how much treasure it had, how large of a guard was going with it, and then Sir Guy returned to the castle and Allen made his way back to Will.

They hurried back to camp together to wait for everyone else to get home from their various activities from the day so that they could share their news. As soon as everyone had returned, they gathered at the fire pit to eat the meal Much prepared and Will related Lucy's news and how Allen had spoken to Sir Guy.

"Perhaps he is simply trying to get close to the gang," Little John said. "Get our guards down so he can kill us, too."

"Lucy knew of the caravan," Will said. "She is the one who came to us and sent Allen to Sir Guy."

"Why?" Robin's frown deepened and Allen resisted the urge to hide.

"Because she made a promise to the Sheriff that she wouldn't tell anyone about it." Allen clasped his hands together, hoping Robin couldn't tell that they were shaking.

"She did what?" Much asked, clearly shocked.

"She promised the Sheriff she wouldn't tell us," Will said.

"So she had us meet with Sir Guy to hear it from him instead."

"That is ridiculous!" Robin said.

"I agree," Will said. "But it's done now, so it hardly matters where we came by the information. We know there's a caravan of unfairly collected taxes coming through Sherwood, so let's plan where we'll ambush it."

Robin and Will discussed the best places along the road to set up an ambush until Lucy came riding into camp. She seated herself

448

beside Dusty, seemingly unaware of the ire that awaited her. Robin glared at her for a moment before shucking a stick into the fire.

"We didn't have to go to him," Robin said. "You could have told us."

"Not after I promised I wouldn't."

"You're playing games with us, Lucy."

"I am not. But seriously, Robin, the Sheriff might decide to get rid of me at any moment–he's certainly suspicious–and then you never would get information from inside the castle."

Allen's focus bounced from the anger on Robin's face to the stubbornness of Lucy's expression wondering what they might do to each other.

"I still say you could have delivered it. We don't need Gisbourne!" Robin's voice was rising, his eyes blazing with anger and fear and pain. "He's entirely untrustworthy. He. Murdered. My. Wife."

"And he's as tormented by it as you are! More, probably, considering…"

Robin stood and Allen was not the only person who flinched. Robin did nothing but storm away from the group, however.

"You didn't expect that to go any differently I hope," Mark said, his voice full of venom as he too glared at Lucy. "You can't trust Gisbourne."

"I know you all think that, and I perfectly understand why–"

"Then why are you so insistent?"

Mark and Little John were glaring daggers at Lucy and Robin was muttering curses from across the meadow.

"Sir Guy has helped us in the past," Dusty said, her voice soothing as she tried to calm everyone down. "He's made mistakes; massive, unforgivable mistakes one might argue. Yet somehow, he still helps us."

"Even so," Little John said, "in this scenario, Lucy could have simply told us herself, using Gisbourne was superfluous. And more than that, if this is a test, a trap, she should have been much more careful and perhaps not told us at all."

"Well next time I'll just keep my information to myself," Lucy huffed.

"If you are going to do something as stupid as tell us you can't talk to us about whatever you find out, you might as well," Mark snapped.

"Well unlike some people, I keep my promises."

Allen flinched. Lucy was the last person he would have expected to lash out in such a way. Robin stormed back toward the group at the fire as Lucy continued railing at Mark. "You're asking me to break my word like it's no big deal. But it is a big deal to me."

Robin spoke up as soon as she stopped. "A promise that was forced out of you–"

"It wasn't forced."

"What?"

"It wasn't forced. I didn't have to promise. I only did because I knew you could still get the information without me telling you."

"Lucy–"

"You still got the information you needed, so why does it matter?"

Robin threw up his hands in disgust and stomped away again, and Mark soon withdrew to his hut as a silence settled over the gang.

"That...went about as expected," Will sighed.

"Guy did give me the news without hesitation," Allen said. "Lucy's right. He is helping us."

"I almost believe it myself," Dusty said. "He hasn't given any indication he'd turn on Lucy."

"*Yet*," Little John growled. "There is, however, the glaring truth that he murdered Marian."

The argument over working with Sir Guy and his evil nature or potential for goodness continued on. Allen tried to stay out of it as much as he could, not wanting the people who didn't trust him to have more reason to hate him. Lucy went round and round in circles with Robin and Little John until she'd had enough. Lucy left the camp in a sour mood, and those she left behind were equally frustrated.

Chapter 62

Life in the camp had fallen into routine once more; Lucy informed them of the Sheriff's schemes and Robin and Will worked together to plan the gang's countermoves. Nottingham remained the safest place in England–the gang didn't travel enough to protect everyone else. They tried–Robin would send them out on missions for weeks at a time, but there was only so much they could do. Executions and brutal beatings took place all across the country that the gang failed to stop, but they did the best that they could.

It wasn't enough in Allen's estimation. He wanted–needed–to do more.

One night Lucy came to the camp with a little old monk in tow.

Robin stood as soon as she entered the meadow. "Lucy, who is this?"

"Friar Tuck," Lucy said, leading the old man over to where everyone had gathered at the fire. "He's a very dear friend of mine. He was a father to me when I was growing up in London."

Robin sat back down as Lucy and Friar Tuck joined the group.

"What brought you to Nottinghamshire?" Will asked.

"Lucy did," Friar Tuck replied. "I have been anxious to see her since she left home so many years ago."

"I told him he could live in the camp, if that's okay, Robin," Lucy said. "I think he'd be safer here."

Robin studied her for a moment. "You don't trust Gisbourne then?"

"I–"

"That's fine. Friar Tuck, you are more than welcome here."

453

Over the next several days Will enlisted help from Little John and Allen in order to gather material to build a hut for Friar Tuck. The friar sat by the fire and watched them work.

Allen's eyes kept straying to the strange little man as he pounded a nail into the wooden plank Little John was holding up. They had nearly finished the third wall of the hut.

"If you can't pay attention to your work you might as well leave us to be productive on our own," Little John growled.

Allen glanced at him and grimaced. "Sorry."

Little John scowled at him.

"I think I can, in fact, manage to spy on our newcomer while also building a hut."

"If you try to start bantering with me I might just take that hammer and ram it into your sorry face."

Allen turned back to his work with a frown.

"Little John, don't threaten Allen." Will's voice held a teasing to it as he walked up to them, carrying more supplies.

"He deserves it."

"Undoubtedly, but you could extend some measure of grace." Will grabbed a hammer and set to work beside Allen.

Will's tone of voice was light, but Allen could hear the seriousness running beneath his teasing. He was sure Little John–who'd known Will much longer–could hear it, too. Allen appreciated Will coming to his defense, but he wasn't afraid of Little John. The man might have wanted to kill him, but he hadn't. Allen believed his threats were empty even if his hatred was real.

Nottingham was soon bursting with merchants and tourists as the time of the Nottingham Fair drew close once more. A year ago Allen had been thrown out of the camp when the truth came out about his

454

betrayals, but now he was fighting to free the people from the cruelty of the Sheriff and others like him alongside his family once more.

Not long after Friar Tuck's arrival, Dusty and Will announced they would like to get married. Friar Tuck agreed to perform the ceremony and before long the two of them were bound together as one. Allen was surprised but pleased by the unforeseen development. Dusty deserved happiness.

Yet watching the two of them brought a pain with it, too. Allen had been quite young when he'd loved Eri, but he'd loved her more than he could express. And he'd lost her.

He missed having someone he could always turn to, always rely on. He missed waking up beside her; seeing her gentle smile and her messy hair and the way she always smelled of heather and flowers and the moors on a rainy morning.

He missed his wife.

So many years had passed, so much life had been lived. He'd been haunted by her death, suppressed his grief. Yet now, watching the happiness of his friends as they vowed to love each other until death, it was Eri's life that made his heart ache. Allen was grateful young William was in Nottingham and no longer sharing a hut with him, because he cried himself to sleep nearly every night, longing to feel his wife in his arms again.

Robin soon assigned Allen to a two week trip to the south of England with Much to help whomever they could. They borrowed horses from Marcus, stocked up on provisions and money–both for themselves and to pass along to the people of England, and then set out on their journey.

They traveled from village to village, handing out supplies to the poor and needy. One day as they walked along, Much said, "I am sorry that I have mistrusted you."

Allen stopped walking, glancing from Much to the ground and then back again. "You have every right not to trust me."

"I know. But I am called to forgiveness and that is what I am trying to offer. Yet I still held onto some misgivings, and I wanted to apologize for that."

"I appreciate that." Allen started walking again and Much fell into step beside him. "What do you mean you are 'called to forgiveness'?"

Much was quiet for a moment before he responded. "Only that living with hatred and revenge is not a life that I want to live."

"Do you think...I mean, would Robin ever forgive me or trust me again?"

"I'm not sure. I'd like to think so...he did let you come back, but...I don't know."

Allen's heart was heavy, but not without hope. "Lucy seems to think even Sir Guy of Gisbourne is redeemable, so I like to believe I can be, too."

Much nodded. "Lucy...I don't know how she does what she does. I could not."

"Working with Sir Guy, you mean?"

"Not just working with him, befriending him, caring about him. I'm not sure I could manage that, no matter how far he turns his life around."

Allen sighed as they continued on to the next village to hand out money. The people they encountered were starving, and in grief. So many people were dying at the hands of the sheriffs of other shires and the gang wasn't traveling enough to help them. They couldn't be everywhere, there weren't enough of them. It became an exhausting and disheartening trip, but eventually their feet turned toward home. As much as they tried to visit other parts of England frequently, it was never enough.

Allen led Much along the edge of Sherwood. They only had a few more miles before they would turn inward and head toward the camp. Allen could feel his heart lighten at the prospect of returning home, but he could tell Much was dragging his sluggish and tired feet behind him.

"One foot in front of the other," Allen encouraged.

"Remember when you were the biggest complainer of the group?"

"Well I haven't heard you complain yet, Much, so that title may well still be mine."

Much grinned. "I was thinking about marching through Palestine."

"Ah, when it rained." Allen rolled his eyes and clutched his chest dramatically. "All that mud to slosh through…nothing could be worse."

The smile that lit Much's face set Allen's heart aglow. Somehow despite the depressing nature of their journey, Allen had managed to find his footing in his friendship with Much once more.

It wasn't long before the last few miles had been traversed and Allen and Much made it to camp. Others were recently returned from their own missions and greetings were exchanged among them before a tear-streaked Lucy interrupted them.

"You were gone…I had no way to tell you…"

Allen took in her wild eyes and the tears creeping down her cheeks and his heart sank.

"Tell us what?" Robin asked.

"The Sheriff went off to burn a village to the ground–barring the inhabitants inside!"

"Oh no…" Dusty closed her eyes, clutching Will's arm. Much knelt to start a fire in the empty ring as everyone else gathered around Lucy.

"I had no way to tell you…and I couldn't stop the Sheriff alone. So I went to Guy but…I don't think he's going to help."

Allen reached out to place a hand on Lucy's arm. "Sir Guy won't let it happen."

"He gave me no assurance of that."

"Perhaps the Sheriff was watching?" Dusty offered.

"Or perhaps," Robin said. "He really is evil."

Allen shook his head. "He is not."

"He is." Mark said quietly.

The gang settled onto the benches around the fire that Much had lit as the conversation continued.

"He's done so much…for both sides," Will said. "How can you even tell one way or the other?"

Allen leaned forward, thinking of the children being pardoned. He wanted to believe that Sir Guy would do something to stop the Sheriff's scheme. He'd been changing for the better, had been helping so much of late…surely he would save the village, too. "But for Lucy–"

"People said he'd do anything for Marian," Robin snapped. "And he *killed* her."

Allen saw Mark wince, his shoulders tensing.

"I can't believe he'd let them die," Lucy said, wringing her hands. "I don't want to believe it…"

"He won't," Allen said firmly.

458

"He most definitely will," Robin said. "Where was the village? We can ride there tonight, see if there are any survivors."

"I don't want to see that," Lucy said with a sigh, but she gave Robin directions nonetheless.

"Mark, Will, Dusty, Little John, Allen...let's go see what there is to see, and help if we can. Much...keep an eye on Lucy."

Allen's gaze darted to Robin's face. Did he just say he wanted Allen to come along?

Allen hurried to grab his weapons and follow Robin and the others as they set off. Much and Lucy were still by the fire with Friar Tuck as they hurried out of the camp.

Chapter 63

The sun was setting as they set out–first to Nottingham for horses from Marcus and then onward to the village in danger. Allen's emotions were spiraling–worry for the innocents who might be harmed, gratefulness to Robin for showing some measure of trust in him; asking him to come along. Concern for Lucy's state of emotions, hope for Sir Guy's choices. He had to be trustworthy–he *had to be.*

Allen leaned low over his horse, gripping the reins tight in his hand as the beast's hooves pounded the ground beneath him. The desperate race to the village was long.

The sun sank and darkness consumed the land. It was a cloudy night, though the moon did its best to peek through the shadows. Before too long the gang crested a hill and a blazing light appeared a few miles ahead of them.

"The village is already burning!" Robin pulled his horse to a hard stop. Allen jerked on his own mount's reins and came to a stop near Robin as the others did the same.

"We're too late," Dusty said, the sadness in her voice unmistakable.

"We can still try and save whomever we can," Robin said. He was watching the growing brightness of the fire. It was still some miles from their position, but the flames were clearly climbing the houses.

"Let's swing wide to the left," Allen said. "We can approach without running into the returning Sheriff."

Robin nodded, breaking into a trot. Allen followed after him with the rest of their companions. Robin led them on a wide path around the village as Allen had suggested. By the time they were approaching the western edge of the village, the smoke was billowing in thick black shadows that obscured the sight of the village and the few stars in the sky. The heat drifted toward them in waves, making the horses skittish.

The flashes of flame flickering from behind the thick black fog of smoke sent shivers through Allen's body. He slipped from his horse and crashed to his knees, pain radiating up his legs as he collapsed to the ground.

He couldn't see anything. His eyes were burning and tears were leaking down his cheeks. The smoke was too thick. The fire was all around him now. There was no escaping it. It ate up Allen's clothes and burned his flesh. Everything went white.

"FLORIE!"

"Allen!"

Hands were shaking his shoulders and the world spun. Allen put out a hand to steady himself and felt someone clasp his fingers in his own.

"Eri?"

There was smoke all around, filling the night sky. But it wasn't raining. It was supposed to be raining…

"Allen?"

Allen's eyes shifted from the flame and smoke-engulfed building in front of him to the woman kneeling beside him, her dark eyes glittering in the light of the fire nearby.

"Dusty?"

"Are you alright? You fell from your horse, and then you were screaming…"

Allen pulled his hand from Dusty's and ran it across his eyes. "I'm…I'm okay."

"Are you sure?"

"I was just…I was…" Allen shuddered as his vivid memories surfaced once more. He struggled to stay with Dusty and not drift into the painful past.

"You lost someone to a fire, before you met us…"

"Yes."

"It's over now. I am sorry for whatever loss and pain you had before; but you are safe now, Allen. You're here. You're loved."

Dusty wrapped an arm around his shoulder and kissed his cheek.

"We found them!" Robin's voice came bellowing out of the darkness behind them. Dusty helped Allen to his feet as Robin approached. "We found the villagers. They weren't inside–they are unharmed and Will, Mark, and Little John are sending them along the route of inns and merchants we've used before who help the innocents we rescue make it to Scotland or the coast."

Robin crossed his arms and studied Allen.

"How long was I…incapacitated?"

"Too long. You were entirely useless. We tried putting out the fire, though we haven't made much headway. We soon realized no one was here though, and we went in search of them. Dusty decided to help you. You were just laying on the ground screaming out names I've never heard you speak before."

"Sorry. I…" Allen hugged himself and looked at his boots.

Robin put a hand on his shoulder. "You told me years ago you'd lost everyone in a fire. I assume that's where your mind went."

"I've never been so overcome by the memories before." Allen shuddered and took a deep breath. He could feel his lungs burning though he hadn't gone close enough to the present fire to have filled

463

them with smoke. It was all a memory, but it was vivid enough he could feel his eyes watering from the sting of the smoke as his lungs struggled to breathe.

"I sometimes think I'm still holding Marian…watching the blood pool beneath her…" Robin crossed his arms. The fire behind Allen lit Robin's face and he could perfectly see the ache in his eyes.

"Memories of losing those we love can be so vivid," Dusty said, her voice soft. She reached out to clasp Robin's hand and then Allen's. "Come on. We should help the refugees on their way and see if we can't get this fire to die down before we head home."

It was early in the morning when they returned to the camp; Much was still sitting up, tending the fire. Dusty went to give him an update on the night's events, and Allen went to his hut to try and sleep.

Instead of sweet repose, he was haunted by the fire that had destroyed his life.

He finally gave up on trying to shake the memories and exited his hut, going to sit by the fire pit where the gang often gathered. Staring in the depths of the bright orange embers Much had left behind did not help.

The gang remained in the camp that day, some sleeping off the night's events, some waiting anxiously for Lucy to come and explain what had happened with the village, but she didn't come.

That night Allen was plagued by the fire. He desperately tried to drag Florie from the flames again and again, but to no avail. He held baby Duncan in his arms, but the boy withered into ashes and slipped through his fingers.

He awoke in a cold sweat.

Allen was morose as he sat with the rest of the gang that morning, eating the breakfast Much had prepared.

Lucy came riding into camp before the gang had finished their meal, a smile on her face. She dismounted and hurried toward them, seating herself between Dusty and Much. "He did it!"

464

"Who did what?" Little John asked.

"I imagine she means the village," Dusty said. She turned toward Lucy, "We found it empty, and later discovered the refugees. We helped them start their travel toward a safer place to live, for now at least."

"That's good," Lucy said.

"How did they know to evacuate?" Much asked.

"Sir Guy. He sent Andrew ahead. He rescued the villagers."

Relief washed over Allen, lifting his mood. "I knew he would. Well...I hoped he would."

"I wish he hadn't," Robin snapped.

"Robin!" Dusty turned her sharp eyes in his direction. "You wish those people had died?"

"No. Of course not. But I wish someone else had rescued them."

"It's much easier to hate him when he's always doing evil," Friar Tuck observed. "If he was evil you would perhaps have grounds to hate him."

"I have perfect grounds to hate that man!"

"Hatred is never the answer, my son. And if you gave up this foolish hatred it would not sting so when he proves his worth."

"He isn't worth anything!" Robin jumped up and stormed away from the group.

Allen sighed. "He'll never change his mind."

"He shouldn't." Mark's eyes flashed toward Allen, daring him to say more. "Gisbourne isn't worth anything. He's a murderer."

Lucy didn't stay long at the camp, once more feeling she brought more strife with her than she meant to.

Allen was sorry she always felt she had to run away due to how angry Robin and Mark were whenever Sir Guy was brought into the conversation. He wished he could speak to her more–he wanted to know what she said to Sir Guy, how she'd influenced him for the better. What was he doing, exactly, to change his behavior after he'd murdered

465

Marian? Allen wanted direction for his own quest to prove himself a changed man.

Chapter 64

One day Robin gathered the gang with urgency, explaining that Lucy had delivered news of an execution taking place in Nottingham.

"She did her usual run-around with who she could tell and who she couldn't based on silly promises made to the Sheriff," Robin said. Allen could hear the exasperation and tiredness in his voice as he spoke. They were gathered in the meadow in Sherwood Forest on a cold morning, a scattering of snow littering the ground at their feet.

"But at least we have the information and we can plan a rescue. We'll have to leave now, however. She was urgent that it was happening today, within a few hours' time."

Allen went to his hut to fetch his sword and bow, strapping his weapons on with fingers stiff from the cold and then he followed the rest of the gang out of the camp. During the long walk through the trees and then over the fields toward the city of Nottingham, Robin and Will gave out assignments for the coming mission.

Much would be waiting with Marcus' horses on a street not too far from Nottingham Square for a quick escape while the rest of the gang disrupted the execution. Robin didn't know what it would look like–hanging, beheading, or something else–as Lucy had had very little information for them. They were playing it by ear.

"Allen, your only job is to get the girl, get her on a horse, and get out of there as fast as possible."

The gang dispersed before they reached the city, some slipping in the front gates with other merchants and farmers and travelers on the road, while Allen took Mark and Much and snuck into the city via the secret door that Andrew had shown him so long ago.

The streets grew more and more congested the closer they drew to the Square. Much rushed off toward Marcus' home to collect the horses while Mark slipped into the crowd in the Square and disappeared from Allen's view. Allen pushed through the people, inching closer and closer to the center of the Square.

Over the heads of the people gathered he could see two platforms had been erected. On one stood the Sheriff, Sir Guy, Lucy, and a few other nobles and soldiers. On the other stood the executioner and his chopping block.

There was a restlessness to the crowd and murmurs scattered about the place. Allen saw young William near the platform, scowling at the Sheriff. He hoped the boy wouldn't do anything foolish.

The low hum of dissatisfaction suddenly burst into angry shouts. Allen strained to see over the bald head of the man in front of him. Soon enough, soldiers were shoving the people aside to create a pathway through which they dragged a young woman toward her death.

Her hands were bound, but her head was held high and her chin set stubbornly.

The soldiers dragged her up the steps of the platform and forced her to her knees in front of the chopping block. They roughly pulled aside her straw colored hair to reveal her slender neck.

Allen bounced on his toes, waiting for the signal.

The soldiers left the platform and the executioner stepped forward. He raised his axe high above his head, preparing to bring it down on the young woman's neck.

Allen clenched his fists. Robin would stop the execution–he had to.

The people around Allen were pushing and shoving against each other as they railed at the Sheriff. The glint of sunlight on the blade of the axe sent a shiver through Allen.

Suddenly the executioner dropped the axe, an arrow protruding from his chest. He stumbled backwards and off the platform.

Allen sprinted forward, shoving through the people in front of him to reach the platform. He trusted the rest of the gang would do their jobs to distract the soldiers and occupy the Sheriff's attention.

Allen ducked under the blade of a soldier near the platform and then sprang upward, grabbing the edge of the platform and using it to vault himself onto it. He dropped to his knees behind the young woman.

"Hold still." He drew a knife from his belt and began to cut the bonds holding the girl's hands behind her back.

She glanced over her shoulder at him, grinning, and when her blue eyes met his gaze his heart skipped a beat.

"I knew Robin Hood would come."

"Follow me," Allen responded, taking her hands and leading her to the edge of the platform. There was chaos beneath them as soldiers fought the gang and the citizens of Nottingham brave enough to join the fray. Little John cleared a swath of ground with his quarter staff and a ferocious growl and Allen took that opportunity to jump off of the platform with the young woman. They ran, hand in hand, through the jostling crowd. People fell in behind them, forming a human wall as the Sheriff's soldiers began to cut them down with swords and bows.

Allen glanced over his shoulder once to see the horror they were fleeing, and then focused on getting the woman out of Nottingham Square and to the side street where Much was waiting with horses.

"Get on a horse and follow me!" Allen said to the woman. He took a set of reins from Much's hand and swung himself into a saddle, watching to be sure the woman would do the same. Soon the two of them were galloping down the street as more of the gang rushed toward Much and their escape.

They raced through the nearly empty streets of Nottingham and plowed past the soldiers at the city gate, galloping over the hills with the rest of the gang close behind.

When they were out of sight of the city, Robin slowed their pace and introduced everyone to the woman they had rescued.

"Lucy and I met Ida before, when we saved her family from a few of the Sheriff's men."

"I do appreciate you saving my life today," Ida said. Something in her eyes caught Allen's attention again–there was a fire there in the depths of her cool blue eyes. The contrast stirred something in his chest.

"It was our pleasure," Robin replied. "This is what we do, after all."

"Yes, and I'd like to be a part of that, as I mentioned the last time we met."

Robin grinned. "I can't say no. You don't have a choice this time; you can't go home."

Allen held his breath. She was going to join the gang?

Chapter 65

It was a frosty morning as the gang gathered around the fire the next day. There was a slight dusting of snow on the ground and the trees surrounding the camp were covered in a sparkling white cloak.

"Oh this weather," Allen moaned as he joined the group at the fire, pulling his cloak tightly about him.

Ida handed him a plate of warm food. Allen was struck by the way her sky blue eyes twinkled. He quickly turned from her and focused on the food. She and Much seemed to be sharing the kitchen duties for the morning and the gang was teasing Much about her cooking being better than his. Into the midst of this banter, Lucy arrived.

"It's wonderful to see you again, Ida. Though I wish our meetings would stop being under such dire circumstances."

"I feel quite honored to be a part of Robin Hood's gang," Ida said. "Though unofficially. I'd like to help as much as I can. I'm good with a dagger. And until the country is back in order you'll meet a lot of people under dire circumstances."

"We wouldn't have had time to plan your rescue if Lucy hadn't told me about your execution," Will said.

"Then I am beholden to you," Ida said to Lucy.

Lucy shook her head. "That's just what we do."

"I want to help with that," Ida said.

"Then we'll find ways to include you," Robin said.

"Good."

Mark stood and moved away from the group around the breakfast fire. After a moment, Lucy followed him. They seemed to have a heated conversation. Allen watched with interest; Mark had slowly been coming out of his shell of silence, but he rarely had much to say.

"How is Mark doing these days?" Allen asked no one in particular.

"Well he speaks now," Robin said, following Allen's gaze to where Mark and Lucy were speaking across the meadow. "I think you can see for yourself how he's doing, Allen. It's obviously still a struggle. It is for me, too."

"We all still carry that grief," Little John said. He crossed his arms and glared at Allen, as though Allen didn't also miss Marian.

"We were all devastated to hear of Lady Marian's death," Ida said quietly. "All of Nottingham was horrified. Her father was our beloved sheriff before Prince John replaced him–his death was a tragedy. Lady Marian brought us hope in the darkness, even before the rest of you banded together. We all loved her…"

The sincerity in her voice and her eyes caught Allen's attention once more and he studied her quietly as the conversation moved on. From what he had seen in the few hours he had known her, she seemed kind and fierce. Both qualities he readily admired.

Allen looked at his hands, trying to still the wild beating of his heart.

He'd only felt this way once before…when he'd met Eri. He'd decided the day he met her that he wanted to marry her, and he had. It hadn't ended well, but it had undoubtedly been the happiest period of his life.

Allen bit his cheek, drawing blood. As the metallic taste filled his mouth he forced his thoughts away from his dead wife and away from the beautiful woman sitting near him. He'd never given thought to falling in love again, and he wasn't about to start.

472

There were far more pressing things at hand.

The Sheriff needed to be dealt with. King Richard needed to come home. And anyway…though he didn't know her well, Allen knew with certainty that Ida deserved a better man. Not a traitor.

Chapter 66

Allen assisted Robin, Will, and Little John in gathering supplies and building another hut for Ida's use. Lucy teased they were creating a village in the middle of Sherwood Forest, and she wasn't entirely wrong. Ida cheerfully joined in the work of building her hut, declaring she was in no mood to let the men do all the work.

As the days passed, she seemed to fit into the gang perfectly, as if she'd always been a part of their group. She was playful and outspoken and joined in the banter that often existed between Robin, Will, and others. She also eagerly jumped into the work, helping to distribute food and money alongside everyone else.

One evening as Allen huddled close to Much's fire to ward off the cold of the evening, Ida approached with a mischievous grin.

"I know a better way to keep warm."

"Oh?"

"Train with me. A fight will get your blood boiling."

Allen studied Ida's determined face and laughing eyes. "The farmer's daughter wants to train with a battle-hardened warrior?"

"Oh is that what you are?"

"I'll have you know I fought and survived King Richard's Holy Crusade."

"I survived the Sheriff."

"I rescued you from the Sheriff, if I recall."

Ida shrugged, pulling two daggers from her belt and flipping them in the air, casually catching them by the handles again. "Alright then. I'll just go get Little John to train with me…"

Allen stood. "There's no need for that."

They moved away from the fire pit and the huts to an open part of the meadow. There was snow on the ground and in the trees, and the sun was setting over the forest. The sky was a pastel masterpiece of soft pinks and purples and oranges and the snow sparkled and danced as it reflected the colors back.

Allen crossed his arms, studying Ida. "So what would you like to do, exactly?"

"Spar." She flipped a dagger in her hand again, throwing him a wink.

Allen drew his sword from its sheath and planted his feet. Ida grinned.

A moment later she darted forward, one dagger extended forward. Allen stepped to the side to avoid her, not even bothering to use his sword to deflect her attack as her arm swung past the empty air where he had been standing.

He was going to make a snarky comment, but she didn't even hesitate, spinning on the spot with her arm extended again. Allen reacted instinctively, raising his blade to throw her smaller one off its course.

As his sword and her dagger moved together, her other hand suddenly sprang forward with her second blade.

Allen dropped a hand from his sword and caught her wrist, her dagger inches from his belly.

"Trying to gut me?"

Ida grinned. Allen kept a firm grip on her wrist, but her other arm was free of his sword now and she brought it back toward his chest.

They were too close together, Allen realized. As her dagger cut toward his shoulder he let go of her wrist and took a large step backward. Her blade sliced the air once more.

Allen raised his sword, glaring at the tiny blades in her hands.

"I haven't fought an opponent with only daggers before."

"You're doing better than Little John did." Ida let out a low chuckle, though her eyes stayed on Allen's face as the two of them circled each other. The twinkle in the ice blue of her eyes melted his heart again, but he tried to ignore it.

Ida sprang forward, attacking with first one blade and then the other and Allen's sword cut back and forth in precise movements blocking each of her blows one after the other. Soon they were both sweating despite the frigid evening air.

Allen caught sight of Much and Dusty watching their sparring from the fireside, but he ignored them and focused on the feisty woman with blades trying to cut him.

Ida's grin grew the longer she failed to get past Allen's defenses.

"You might be as good as your arrogance suggested."

"I definitely am." Allen could feel a grin to match hers tugging at the corners of his mouth.

Little John came lumbering into camp, finished with whatever mission he'd had for the day–distributing blankets and food probably, as that was the gang's main priority during winter months. He paused to watch Allen and Ida for a moment.

The obvious audience seemed to fuel Ida's determination. She came at Allen with furious blows, her eyes dancing as he sidestepped around her. Sometimes he'd deflect her blades with his sword, sometimes he'd merely move out of reach. Always, he stayed on the defense.

It was clear Ida didn't realize how easy it would be for him to use his sword to his advantage. The blade was far longer than her measly daggers. One well placed swing and she'd be unable to block his blow. He could cut her down easily.

But it was far more fun to stay on the defensive and let her get close to him again and again, her eyes flashing with stubbornness and enjoyment. She was loving this, that much was obvious.

Little John crossed his arms. "If you manage to kill him, I might just marry you."

Ida hesitated in her attack, pausing to throw Little John a disparaging look. "If and when *I* choose to marry, I'll find my own husband, thank you. And anyway, I have no intention of killing one of Robin Hood's famed heroes."

"I wouldn't call the traitor a hero."

Allen lowered his blade, shame flooding his body.

Ida's arms dropped to her sides as her eyes darted from Allen's face to Little John's and back again.

"Oh."

"I…" Allen swallowed. Little John chuckled maliciously and walked past them toward the fire pit where Much and Dusty were still sitting. Ida gave Allen an appraising look.

"I made mistakes a while ago…but I've been back with the gang for nearly a year. I wouldn't betray any of them; they're my family."

"You're him though? You're the one who was working with Gisbourne and the Sheriff…I remember seeing you with Gisbourne in Nottingham!" The light seemed to have left Ida's eyes altogether, although that may have been due to the fact the sun was nearly set and darkness was settling over the whole meadow.

"I did…work with them. It was over a year ago and it was short-lived and my reasons, though misguided, were actually to help Sir Godfrey."

Ida sheathed her daggers and crossed her arms. "You're the traitor."

"I'm…I was, but I'm not anymore."

"You think you can come back from something like that?"

Ida shook her head and marched away from him, over to the fire. Allen watched her sit herself beside Little John. He watched the group by the fire for a few minutes and then went to his hut to be alone.

Their friendship had barely begun and now she hated him like everyone else did. His offense hadn't been against her, and so many of his friendships were already healing, it simply wasn't fair for her to hold his mistakes against him.

And yet.

478

He *was* the traitor and he *had* nearly gotten Little John killed. He had hurt Robin, betrayed his trust.

He'd been entertaining thoughts, however fleeting, of courting Ida but all thoughts of romance fled from his mind. He was a traitor; she deserved better. He knew that.

Chapter 67

Allen was sitting at the fire pit, studying the flames that licked the logs Much was adding to the already burning pile. He tried not to let his mind wander to another fire and the bodies it consumed, but it was a difficult task.

Suddenly Lucy burst into the camp, shouting Ida's name. She was pale and there were tears on her cheeks.

"What's wrong?" Ida stepped toward her.

Lucy was wringing her hands as more tears slipped from her eyes. "The Sheriff...Sir Guy..."

"What?" Ida asked again, crossing her arms and clearly impatient. Allen stood to move closer. The rest of the gang seemed to think that was a good idea, for soon they were all circled around the two women. Allen had never seen Lucy so distraught, not even when she'd thought Sir Guy was going to burn a village to the ground.

"Sir Guy didn't know what the Sheriff was planning or he would have told me..."

"What did the Sheriff do?" Robin asked, crossing his arms.

"He burned Ida's farm!"

Allen's heart leaped to his throat, flashes of dragging Florie's body from the flames and seeing his charred family laid out across the Scottish moors filled his vision.

"Where is her family?" Allen asked, hoping against hope that it was only the farm that had been burned. "We can give them money to rebuild, we can–"

"You can't." Lucy was shaking her head, more tears pouring from her eyes.

"Why not?" Much asked, his voice wavering as though he already knew the answer.

"Because the Sheriff burned them with the farm…Ida, I am so sorry!"

There was a long silence. Ida's face grew pale as the snow that covered the ground. Allen could feel a weight as heavy as a mountain boulder filling his chest.

"How do you know?" Ida's voice was low but calm as she met Lucy's gaze.

Lucy tentatively reached out to touch her shoulder. "When Sir Guy found out what had happened, he came to me–"

"A little late," Little John snapped.

"Yes, but he didn't know sooner!" Lucy threw up her trembling hands in a panic. "He was distraught, Ida, believe me. If he'd known, he would have told me."

"I don't believe it." Ida jerked away from Lucy's touch as she reached out to comfort her.

"But he was! And so am I, Ida. Your mother and little brother…" Lucy shook herself, seeming to remember something. "Your father. Your father is alive, he's in the castle dungeon right now, set to be executed later this week."

"You could have led with that," Little John said.

"My father!" Ida turned her desperate eyes toward Robin. "We have to save him!"

"Of course we will," Robin said. "Ida, don't worry. We can handle this."

"Why did he do it?" Will asked.

"That hardly matters," Ida said, her hands coming to rest on the hilts of her daggers at her waist. "The Sheriff is vile."

"He was frustrated," Lucy said. "He's angry that he can't find Ida after her failed execution and he needed a way to retaliate…"

"So he killed my mother and baby brother." Ida shook her head, tears beginning to fall from her eyes. She jerked away when Dusty reached out to hug her. "We need to get my father out of the Sheriff's clutches as soon as possible, Robin."

"Let's go to Nottingham and see what we can do," Robin agreed.

And so the gang did exactly that. They stayed in Nottingham, some near the castle walls, some in Nottingham Square, some speaking with Marcus. They learned nothing, however, of when or where Ida's father might be executed.

The next day Robin gave out assignments as usual, suggesting he'd stay at the camp in case Lucy visited with news of Ida's father. "There are still people who need our help–especially now that winter is upon us. If Lucy learns anything, she'll come tell me. The rest of you can help the rest of our people."

Ida was reluctant to obey, but she acquiesced.

As they'd left the camp, Ida dejectedly said, "This is my fault."

She'd spoken almost under her breath, as though to herself, but Allen fell into step beside her all the same. "No, it isn't."

Ida's head snapped toward him, anger radiated from her. Allen almost stepped away from her but he steeled himself against her frustration and pressed onward.

"It was the Sheriff, plain and simple. It isn't your fault."

"He's angry he can't find me after my rescue. My family died because I was saved; my father is going to die…"

"The blame for the murder of your family lies entirely with the Sheriff. You had no hand in it; don't carry that weight. We'll figure out

483

how we're going to rescue your father the moment we know the Sheriff's plans. Lucy will see to that."

Ida didn't say anything else and Allen didn't press her. They parted ways after reaching the edge of the forest to go about their separate missions.

Allen could not keep thoughts of Ida's tear-streaked face from his mind as he passed out blankets in the villages around Nottingham. His vivid imagination supplied him with horrifying images of her mother and young brother burning alive the way his own family had.

When he and the rest of the gang returned to the camp that evening, Robin informed them that Ida's father was already safe.

"He's here!" Ida asked, looking around eagerly.

"He's sleeping in my hut right now," Robin said. "I think he was exhausted from his near execution today."

"You saved him?"

Robin nodded and Ida threw her arms around his neck. "Thank you!"

As Much and Ida set about cooking up dinner for the group, Robin shot Much a look and then wandered off toward the other side of the meadow.

"I'll be right back," Much said, getting up to follow Robin.

Allen watched the two of them for a moment, and then turned his attention to Ida.

"I am glad your father is safe."

"So am I." Ida's eyes met his for the briefest moment and then she turned away from him.

She wouldn't forgive him for his past mistakes. But perhaps she was right; what he had done was unforgivable.

That evening Ida's father, Robert, joined them around the fire for supper. He hardly spoke, and the look in his eyes was remarkably reminiscent of Mark. Allen didn't blame him. His wife and son had been killed and his home burned to the ground.

Allen knew only too well what that felt like.

Chapter 68

One clear cold day, Allen found himself wandering the woods, wondering when all the madness was going to end. Visions of the fire that killed Ida's family–a fire he hadn't witnessed–plagued his dreams, and his waking hours were filled with memories of his own family and the ordeal he had gone through.

The only reprieve to his dark thoughts was the knowledge that his relationships were being restored. Robin was beginning to trust him again. Dusty and Much forgave him. He'd never known Will too deeply, but they seemed to have restored their civil friendship–due in no small part to Dusty's influence, Allen was sure.

Little John would never forgive him, and Allen was sorry for it, but he hadn't been close to Little John so though he felt shame at what he had done that had led to harm he wasn't too concerned about reconciling with Little John in particular.

Allen paused by a frozen stream. The snowy ground led down to a slick bank and then ice encrusted water. The center of the stream was still free flowing, but the ice was encroaching from both sides, seeking to still the movement or so it seemed.

Allen's eyes lifted from the water slowly being trapped and alighted on Ida. She was alone, sitting on a fallen log and staring into the icy depth of the water.

Allen approached her, aware of every crunch of his boots in the snow. She didn't acknowledge him, even when he drew close and sat down on the log beside her.

He'd thought at first that she was focused on the water, but now that he was close he could tell that her eyes were not focused on anything. There was a vague and distant look to them; she was lost in thought. Her shoulders were slumped forward as she leaned her elbows on her knees, her hair falling out of a simple braid.

She looked defeated.

They sat in silence for a while until Allen broke the stillness. "It is hard to keep up, isn't it?"

"What?" Ida turned toward him, her sky blue eyes lacking their usual luster.

"The fire—the anger—it carries you for a time, but when it leaves, it is hard to keep up the facade that you're alright, that you're unbothered. That you have purpose. That you even care about living at all."

"And you would know this, because?"

"That's the story of my life." Allen closed his eyes, trying to hold back the rising tide of emotion sweeping up from his gut. His family, dead. His guilt, consuming. "The only way I lived for a while. It gave me something to feel. Because otherwise—without the anger—all was numb."

"What happened?" Ida asked, her voice barely above a whisper. The darkness in her eyes mirrored the darkness of his own soul.

Allen sighed.

He'd never told anyone. Not truly. He had mentioned the loss of his family before, to Robin and Much and Dusty. But he hadn't told them the details, hadn't opened his raw wounds and showed them his heart.

Could he talk about it?

"My family died," Allen said finally. "Much like yours. There was a fire."

"I should have been there," Ida said. Her voice wavered as her lower lip trembled. A single tear slipped down her cheek. "My mother and brother would not have been burned to a crisp if I had been there."

"You don't know that. I *was* there when my family died, and I wasn't able to save them."

Allen shuddered, remembering the corpses he couldn't bear to look at, remembering the weight of Florie's body as he dragged her from the flames.

"That must have been horrible," Ida said softly. "How…how do you keep going?"

"I let the anger carry me for a while…but I wanted to die. I found myself a new purpose, which for me was the Crusades. Dying in the Crusades."

"You didn't die though."

"No. I met Robin and Much and Dusty and they gave me hope that I could move forward, start again."

"Being a part of Robin's gang–saving other people's mothers and brothers–that's what I want to do. That's what motivates me now."

"Keep reminding yourself what your purpose is. I won't say it gets easier. It doesn't. I'm still haunted by my fire. Some days…I can still feel the heat of the flames, I can feel the fire burning my skin, I can see…I can…" Allen swallowed hard.

Ida reached out and brushed a tear from his cheek. "My pain is unbearable, heightened by my imagination of what could have been… but you had to truly see it. The charred corpse I imagine my brother to be, you saw that with…whomever."

"My parents. My sister…"

Ida slipped her hand into Allen's, her fingers curling around his. "I am sorry."

489

"And I am more sorry for your loss than you could possibly know. I *understand* precisely how dark your grief is. I have been there. I am there, even still. I would not wish this fate on my worst enemy."

They lapsed into silence, the only sound that of the stream struggling to keep pushing forward in spite of the ever mounting ice above it.

"If nothing else, I have my father." Ida took a deep breath. "I'll be alright, I think."

Ida's father Robert was a restless man. Not that Allen could fault him for it–Allen knew the horrors of losing a wife and son to the flames. Robert spent his days pacing the camp or lying listlessly in Ida's hut. He hardly talked to anyone apart from Ida.

And then one night, he disappeared.

"He left me a note," Ida said quietly when the gang gathered around the fire to partake of Much's supper. "He's gone to find King Richard."

"What good will that do?" Lucy asked.

"None," Ida said with a sigh. "I expect he won't find the king; he'll perish on the journey."

"Do not think such gloomy thoughts," Dusty chided. "He merely needs some time to himself. He is grieving, as are you. Let him do so in the way that he needs. He'll come back to you."

"How can you be certain?"

"Because Robin and Mark came back to us," Will said.

Allen wasn't so sure. Robin might have been healing, but Mark still barely spoke to anyone unless he had to. He was still as angry and bitter as ever.

And more to the point, Allen had never recovered. He'd never healed; he was still haunted. He'd certainly never gone home to

Scotland, to Edinburgh. Never sought out William, even to discover if he was alive or had perished in the Crusades.

"We're both grieving," Ida said, looking from Dusty to Will. "You say he needs time to mourn, to heal. That he'll come back to me when he's ready. But I'm grieving, too! And I *need* him."

Allen reached out to clasp her hand. "You have all of us, Ida. Anything you need. We're a family here and we will be your strength in this storm."

Chapter 69

One wintry day, Lucy came riding into camp to request her little monk friend join her in Nottingham, to live at the castle instead of in the camp. The gang was gathered around the fire, and they all turned to Lucy with curiosity.

"Why?" Will asked.

"Because…" Lucy glanced at Robin. "Well…because Sir Guy has come to know the Lord as Dusty and I do, and I believe it would be best to put him in the wise hands of Friar Tuck rather than leave him alone, adrift in a stormy sea."

Robin crossed his arms but said nothing.

Dusty smiled at Lucy. "That is wonderful news for Gisbourne."

"Wonderful? Gisbourne?" Little John asked. His scowl sent a shiver through Allen. "I do not think those two words belong together."

"Little John…" Lucy began and then stopped.

"What, Lucy?" Robin asked.

"It's just that…no one is perfect."

"We haven't murdered anyone," Little John growled.

"I beg to differ," Lucy said firmly. "What about all those soldiers you've killed?"

"They deserved it."

"One could easily argue we all deserve death and judgment," Dusty put in.

"And why would you assume they deserve it?" Lucy asked. "Because they work for the Sheriff? First of all, that doesn't make them evil. You don't know their stories, why they work for him or what desperate circumstances drove them to do what they do. And secondly, you might have noticed I never shoot to kill because I do believe

493

Scripture when it tells us not to. Death is death, regardless of *why* you choose to kill someone."

Ida rolled her eyes. "This is absurd. We aren't discussing the philosophical questions behind our morality within the gang. We're discussing Gisbourne. He's evil."

"No." Allen said. "I don't think he is."

Ida sent him a disdainful look. An expression that said 'you *would* think that, given you're the traitor.'

Perhaps he had imagined that much in her eyes, but whether it was real or imagined the sharp look had occurred and it stung. Whatever she meant by it.

"Regardless of what any of you think about Sir Guy," Lucy turned to Friar Tuck, "Will you come to Nottingham sometimes?"

Friar Tuck smiled. "Of course, daughter. You need only ask."

"Thank you."

Lucy helped him collect his things and soon the two of them left the camp together. Allen wasn't sure what to make of it. He didn't truly understand Dusty's faith–the faith Lucy shared and now apparently so did Sir Guy.

Ida stormed out of the camp soon after Lucy and Friar Tuck had left. Allen hesitated a moment, hopeful that Dusty or Much would notice–they always noticed when people were in crises and needed a shoulder to cry on or an ear to vent to.

But neither of them moved to follow her.

Allen rose and slowly walked toward the edge of the meadow. The sun was setting and darkness was filling the forest. The frigid air of the day was turning truly freezing now.

Allen took a deep breath, letting the cold air fill his lungs for a moment. He took a step forward and then another, his eyes scanning the darkness for any sign of Ida. She was upset and needed someone.

Maybe she'd prefer that someone wasn't him, but he wouldn't let her wallow in her darkness alone.

William hadn't let Allen be alone, and it had undoubtedly saved his life.

It was only a few minutes before Allen heard the tramping of feet. He followed the noise until he saw Ida pacing in the snow beneath a great oak tree. Beneath the trees the dwindling sunlight could hardly shine, so she was little more than shadow. But he could see the light reflecting in her blue eyes.

She saw him coming and paused in her pacing. "This is getting ridiculous! Gisbourne helping us, Lucy befriending him...he *killed* my family!"

"That was the Sheriff," Allen said, coming to stand in front of her.

"Don't you dare take his side!" Ida reached out and shoved his shoulder, hard. Allen took a step back as Ida began pacing again. "He's hurt so many people! How could Lucy be so naive as to think he's on our side?"

"She has a knack for seeing the best of people."

"I think she sees what she wants to see," Ida responded sourly. "She's so..." Ida waved her hand vaguely and spun on her heel marching toward Allen before she turned and trudged back the other way. Ida seemed at a loss for the right word to describe what she thought of Lucy, but clearly it wasn't good.

"She may be a bit naive," Allen said. "And definitely gracious and forgiving beyond the point of sanity, for which I am personally grateful. I think she's strong, too, Ida. And more than that she's kind, and good."

"The perfect saint." Ida rolled her eyes as she came to a stop in front of him. He could only just make out her face in the dim light. "That's what you all seem to think. Perfect Lucy can do no wrong."

"I'm sure she has faults; everyone does."

"And yet!"

"I think your grief is what is making you so angry with Sir Guy."

"That, and the fact that he is entirely evil."

Allen sighed.

Ida returned to pacing and Allen said nothing. It was perhaps best to let her work out her frustration before trying to continue the conversation. Her anger wasn't unfounded. Sir Guy had gone so far as to murder Marian. He wasn't innocent. Yet Lucy's radical forgiveness was something Allen desperately wanted and needed in his own life and he could not find it in his heart to begrudge Sir Guy the same.

When Ida's pace slowed down, and the stomping stopped, Allen spoke again. "Tell me about your family, Ida."

Ida stood still.

It started to snow. Fluffy white flakes pushing through the branches overhead and falling into Allen's hair, onto Ida's shoulders.

"What do you want to know?" Her voice was soft, hesitant. Raw.

"Everything." Allen stepped forward, reaching out to clasp her hand gently.

"Well…" Ida took a deep breath. "You've met my father. He's a good man. He was always strong, worked hard. Until he abandoned me…"

Allen squeezed her hand, hoping she might draw some comfort from him.

496

"My mother…" Ida pulled her hand from Allen's grasp. She wrapped her arms around her torso and shuddered and Allen knew it wasn't because of the cold. "My mother was gentle. She loved my father and me and my brother so much. But she was afraid. My father was, too, sometimes. When Prince John took over England and everything went downhill…I always wanted to fight, but they were content to hide. Maybe if I'd hidden with them, the Sheriff wouldn't have taken notice of us and killed my family."

"Their deaths are not on you." Allen stepped forward, wrapping an arm around her shoulders.

"I know. It's the Sheriff. I hate him." There were tears in Ida's eyes, and she shivered. Allen wrapped his other arm around her and hugged her tight. He wanted to keep out the cold and pain and the haunting memories that would plague her for the rest of her life. He wanted to keep everything away from her.

"I'm sorry, Ida. I truly am."

Ida relaxed into his embrace, crying into his shoulder for a time. But after a few moments, Ida stepped back, pulling out of his arms. She sniffed and then turned her sharp eyes toward him. "What about your family?"

Allen froze.

"My family?"

"You said you lost them, the way I did. To a fire. Tell me about them. I think…in some twisted way, I think it helps to hear I am not alone in this suffering. You've felt it, too. I need to know, Allen."

Allen closed his eyes, hesitantly creeping the door open to peer into his memories. He would undoubtedly be plagued with nightmares that night but he would trade his sleep for Ida's comfort.

"I had a sister." Allen opened his eyes, staring into what little of the blue of Ida's eyes that he could see in the gathering darkness. "Her name was Alice."

Allen could still see her sparkling green eyes and the curly red hair that framed her dimpled face. He could hear her laughter ringing in his ears.

"She was my whole world. And then the fire…"

"And your parents?"

"They were good people. My mother was sweet, and kind. My father was a good man, if a little paranoid…they died in the fire, too."

"I'm sorry."

"Yeah."

The silence stretched between them. Allen was lost in thought, remembering. Florie's bossiness. Eri's gentleness. Alice's mischief. He missed them all.

"You said your sister was your whole world," Ida said at last. "Well that was my brother for me. John. He was only a child! I hate the Sheriff."

Ida slipped her hand into Allen's once more. "Come on. We're going to freeze if we stay out here much longer. Let's get back to the fireside."

Chapter 70

Nearly a week after Friar Tuck went to live in Nottingham with Lucy and Sir Guy, he visited the camp with news. The winter days were cold and miserable and snow fell nearly every day. The little monk looked far too frail as he hobbled into the camp with a large fur cloak hanging limply off of his shoulders. The gang was gathered close to Much's fire, trying to stay warm as they decompressed from their long day of looking after the frozen English subjects who needed their help.

"Sir Guy has asked Lucy to marry him," the little monk said without preamble as he sat on the end of one of the benches.

"What?" Will and Robin both exclaimed as Much nearly dropped the plate of food he'd been handing to Allen.

"I said–"

"They heard what you said," Allen laughed, taking the plate carefully from Much's hand. "They just can't believe it."

"What did she say?" Robin asked. The way his eyes stayed on Friar Tuck's face with rapt attention did not escape Allen's notice. "Did she agree to marry him?"

"I do not know. She would scarcely speak to me about it, despite having brought it up herself."

"She wouldn't marry Gisbourne," Ida said. "She's foolish enough, but she's not stupid."

"Lucy isn't foolish," Robin snapped.

"You're certain you don't know her answer," Will asked.

"Yes," Friar Tuck said. "I do not know what she told him. We will have to wait for Lucy to tell us herself."

499

"How soon do you think that will be?" Dusty asked. "Her visits to the camp aren't exactly on a strict schedule."

"I do not know," Friar Tuck replied.

"She's not an idiot," Ida insisted. "She wouldn't marry him."

Robin's obvious discomfort was understandable–he wouldn't want any friend of his too close to the man who'd murdered his beloved Marian. Of course he wouldn't want Lucy to marry him. And if Allen's suspicions proved true, that there was something more to his concern, it would make even more sense.

But Ida's disdain for the idea that Lucy could love a man who had made terrible mistakes sliced straight through Allen's heart. Whatever feelings he might harbor for her, she'd never accept him.

And why should she? He was the traitor.

But if Lucy could forgive and love a murderer…surely…

Allen shook his head, trying to rid his mind of the thoughts swirling around inside of him. It didn't matter whether Lucy had agreed to marry Sir Guy or not. It didn't matter that Ida would never love him. It didn't matter.

When Lucy next visited the camp she informed the gang that she had not, in fact, accepted Sir Guy's offer of marriage.

The winter weeks continued onward and the gang fell into routine once more. Friar Tuck and Lucy split their time between Nottingham and the camp, the gang passed out food, blankets, and money to the needy so they could survive the harsh winter months, with Lucy and Dusty visiting those who were sick to facilitate healing.

One day Lucy brought news that the Sheriff was planning yet another execution and so the gang hurried to Nottingham to prepare. Lucy had very little information when she first visited the camp, so they waited at Marcus' house for her to return with more details.

500

Allen leaned against the wall as other members of the gang gathered at the table in Marcus' front room. A knock sounded at the door and Marcus moved to open it.

Andrew was standing just outside.

Allen saw the glint of light on metal as Ida whipped out a dagger and Little John gripped his quarter staff tighter, taking a menacing step toward the door. Allen shoved off the wall to hurry to the door and Much met him there with Robin to welcome Andrew into the room.

"The Sheriff has planned a hanging for Faith and her father," Andrew said without preamble. "The gallows are being constructed in the Square this very night, and they will be hanged in the morning."

Little John didn't lower his staff, nor did Ida sheath her dagger. Andrew stayed near the door, his eyes on Robin and occasionally Allen.

"The Sheriff has set a heavy guard on them in the dungeon to ensure that you all don't rescue them there as you sometimes have in the past, and Guy is there now keeping an eye on them. I'm not sure how you want to pull off the rescue, but I imagine it will be much like the other ones you have done in the past."

"Is that all the information you have?" Little John asked. "How many guards will be accompanying them as they are escorted to the gallows? How many soldiers stationed in the Square, and where precisely? Will the Sheriff be there? How is Gisbourne planning on assisting with this endeavor?"

Andrew clasped his hands behind his back, turning to Little John with a slight bow of deference. "I do have the military reports you will require to station yourselves around the soldiers of the Sheriff."

Andrew relayed the bulk of his information, and Robin and Will began to plan the rescue as they so often did.

Little John, Ida, and even Mark glared at Andrew throughout the discussion. Allen tried to give his unlikely friend a reassuring smile.

501

He knew only too well how uncomfortable it was to be in the room with these people when they didn't trust you.

In order to avoid arousing suspicion, those who would be archers stationed in various buildings located around the Square went to the shops that very night. Robin had chosen Allen to be one of the archers, along with himself, Dusty, and Much.

The Square was empty and dark as they approached, spreading out to the four sides of the open market area. Allen pounded on the door of a baker they knew while Much went to a tailor shop he often used as cover for his archery during executions.

The baker answered Allen's knock with a bleary-eyed look and ruffled hair, as though he'd been in bed–which he probably had been. Allen quickly explained his presence and the baker let him inside. Allen moved through the pleasant smelling shop to the stairs and bounded up them two at a time. He found a window overlooking the square in one of the guest bedrooms above the shop and stationed himself beside it.

Little John, Will, Mark, and Ida would sleep at Marcus' house and then come to the Square in the morning–while Allen and the other archers cut down the soldiers from above, Little John would cause general mayhem, while Mark and Ida fought any soldiers who got in the way of the rescue. Will was going to run for the gallows to free the prisoners and then as their circumstances allowed the gang would break for Sherwood with all haste.

It was a simple enough plan.

Allen leaned against the wall and watched the stars through the window. He wasn't going to sleep–the last thing he needed was to be plagued by nightmares before a fight.

As the grey light of morning began to creep over the city, Allen's eyes shifted from the sky to the market below. Before too long, the Square began to fill with people who'd heard or seen the gallows being constructed and knew an execution was coming. The people came armed with their pitchforks and heavy rocks and stones, and fierce sense of loyalty and justice and Allen loved them for it.

The Sheriff's men soon brought forth the prisoners and Allen drew an arrow from his quiver, fingering the fletching as he waited for Robin to fire the first shot.

As soon as he did, Little John let out a roar down below in the crowds and rushed into the throng of soldiers around the gallows with his quarter staff. Allen chose a target among the soldiers and let an arrow fly. And then another. And another.

He saw Will rush up to the gallows and begin to untie the father and daughter. They soon disappeared into the chaotic crowd. The citizens of Nottingham were rioting and Little John was their battle cry.

Allen waited a few minutes, firing a few more arrows in an attempt to protect the people from any of the soldiers who fought back.

Eventually the chaos began to die down and people ran for their homes as the gang ran for their horses. Allen snapped his bow into place on his back and bounded down the stairs and out of the bakery–he took the back door, rather than the one that opened into the Square–and then hurried through the streets to Marcus' house and the horse that awaited him there.

He urged his horse into a gallop once he was free of the city and hurried to the rendezvous spot just inside Sherwood Forest. Once everyone had arrived, Robin introduced the gang to the father and his daughter.

"I assumed that you were Robin Hood," the girl–Faith–said. "Sir Guy told us last night while we were in the dungeons that you would not fail to rescue us."

"Gisbourne told you that?" Ida asked.

"Yes, he did."

"You are welcome to live with us," Robin said. "Or we can send you on your way to Scotland via our secret route of loyal subjects."

"Thank you," Faith's father said. "But tell me, this Gisbourne fellow, is he not as bad as people say? My daughter and Gisbourne spoke much during our stay in the Sheriff's dungeon. I had been under the impression based on the many tales told among the inhabitants of this country that he is a wretched man and your mortal enemy. How can it be that he would assure us, calm our fears, as though he were helping you?"

Robin sighed before he spoke. "It is complicated. He was a wretched man, and most definitely my bitter enemy, but…things have changed. He has changed; I have changed. We are working together to save England, though I don't particularly like him."

Faith suggested that she and her father would appreciate the gang's hospitality rather than running to Scotland, and so Robin led everyone back to camp.

Chapter 71

Faith was a gentle spirit. She didn't fight or know the use of any of the weapons that the gang used on a daily basis. She did, however, eagerly join in helping in the ways that she could–distributing food and money to the poor and visiting the sick alongside the healers of the group; Lucy and Dusty.

One frosty day after the turn of the new year, Allen and Ida were paired together and sent off on a distribution mission. As they walked along the ice covered streets of a village to the south of Nottingham, Ida sighed heavily.

"What's wrong?" Allen shifted the weight of the sack slung over his shoulder–it carried a hundred smaller sacks inside, each filled with coins. They had far to go yet before their day would be done. Ida had a large basket under her arm filled with bundles of bread and cheese.

"Nothing's exactly wrong, Allen. I'm just annoyed."

"With what?"

"Faith."

"Faith? She seems quite sweet."

They stopped at a house and knocked on the door. When there was no response, they left a bag of coins and a bundle of food on the step and then moved on.

"Oh I won't deny that she's sweet. Much enjoys her help in the kitchen, too, but she's…pathetic."

"That's a bit harsh, isn't it?"

"She's never used a weapon. Not once."

"Not everyone is a fighter."

"Yeah, but she's just so…weak. Afraid. I don't know."

They stopped at the next house and knocked. A frail middle-aged woman answered the door timidly, but when she saw who was on her front step she smiled widely. She accepted their gifts with tears and insisted on hugging them both before they moved on to the next house.

"Don't let it bother you, Ida. She's not you, and she never will be."

Ida's blue eyes caught his for a moment and then she turned away. "Her father is helping in the caravan raids. She could bother to try and help."

"I don't think you're ever going to convince Faith to take up arms. Let it go. She's helping distribute money and food to the poor, so it isn't as though she's doing nothing."

They stopped at another house, and then another, before Ida said anything else. At last, she stopped walking and turned to face him. "I find it hard to trust people."

"I hadn't noticed."

Ida rolled her eyes. "I mean it. When I found out you were the traitor…I almost couldn't be your friend. I certainly didn't *want* to be. But then my mother and brother died and my father abandoned me and you were the one person who looked after me, who understood. I was practically forced to accept your friendship and I must say, I hated it."

"That's not at all offensive." Allen tried to keep his voice light, but he wasn't sure he succeeded.

"I'm terrified of betrayal, Allen. And you…well, you represent it." Ida shrugged. "Gisbourne came to our town a vile man, but then he grew close to Lady Marian and he changed his ways. He became a kinder person. And then he burned her house to the ground! And then he

506

tried to convince her he was changing again…and then he killed her. And now he's gone all soft on Lucy, and she's falling for that routine."

"I don't think it's an act this time. To be honest, I don't think it was an act with Marian. I think he has a temper and his emotions are raw and unpredictable at times. I don't think his goodness was any more fake or real than his more evil actions."

"Every time you defend him, I trust you less."

Allen winced.

"I don't say that to hurt you. I say that because…well, because I *want* to trust you. You are the one person I can talk to, the one who gets it. You are my strength and comfort since my father abandoned me. I can't lose that–you–so don't let me. Don't scare me off with your love of a murderer, or betray me, or…" Ida waved her hand in a vague gesture. "I don't know. Just don't."

Allen dropped his heavy sack of coins to the street and took Ida's basket from her, setting it down, before he took her hands in his. "I'm never going to betray anyone that I care about, ever again. I can promise you that."

"I want to believe that."

"As long as we're being frank…I'm afraid to give in to these growing feelings that I have for you, too. I loved before…I lost my wife. I don't think I told you that. The fire, that night when I lost everyone…it took my wife. My…my son."

Ida's eyes filled with tears as she met his gaze and Allen swallowed over the lump growing in his throat.

"I am so sorry."

"So am I. I don't bring this up for more sympathy…it's just… I'm afraid to care about you. To lose someone else that I love…"

"I'm terrified of trusting you, and you're afraid to care about me at all."

"We're a mess."

Ida smiled through her tears. "Well. I won't argue with that. I suppose the best we can do is try to move forward."

Allen nodded. "I agree."

Ida brushed away her tears roughly, almost impatiently, and then reached up to gingerly wipe the tears from Allen's cheeks. "So… you think you're falling in love with me, huh?"

Allen chuckled even as the heat of embarrassment flushed his cheeks. "I…maybe."

Ida grinned. "I do have that effect on men."

Winter passed away and spring came once more. The flowers bloomed, the trees donned their green leaves once more, and life in the camp continued in a simple manner. Lucy or Sir Guy would inform the gang when the Sheriff began to plot something, and they would stop it. Faith was quiet and peaceful and preferred wandering through Sherwood Forest collecting flowers to braid through her hair than fighting alongside the gang as her father chose to do. Ida found her distasteful, the rest of the gang thought she was sweet.

And so the year wore on.

Chapter 72

Allen drew his sword along his whetstone with tedious precision, relishing the sound of his blade sharpening beneath his hand. Spring was in the air. He hadn't had a nightmare in weeks. He and Ida didn't often speak of their grief or the fires that consumed their families, but when they did he could still sleep through the night. Talking with Ida seemed to be the healing balm he needed all these years.

They spoke of other things, too. And they sparred together as often as Allen could manage–Ida was growing into a fearsome warrior in her own right, and Allen grew exhausted when battered with her determination and ferocity. But he loved every second of it.

They didn't speak of their fears or the tentative feelings that they opened up about that day they'd been distributing money and food to the needy. They skirted around their vulnerability with practiced ease. Yet they were comfortable in each other's presence and Allen even dared to hope he might truly be happy for the first time since losing everything.

As he leaned against his hut sharpening his sword, he could hear Much banging about his kitchen not too far away. Will was sitting by the fire lost in conversation with Dusty–his wife. It was a pleasant day, all things considered, and Allen breathed it in with the strange sensation of peace and hope brewing in his chest.

It wasn't to last.

Little John came crashing into the camp with a frenzied look in his eye. "Robin!"

"Robin isn't here," Will said from where he sat by the fire.

Allen set aside his whetstone, watching Little John hurry toward Will. Will cocked his head to one side. "Actually…wasn't Robin with you distributing money in Nottingham?"

Little John's hands were shaking and his eyes darted around in a panicked manner. "Robin was caught!"

Allen heard the soapy splash of a dish falling into the bucket Much washed his dishes in. Will stood up, his eyes intense as he stepped toward Little John. "How? When?"

"We were separated in Nottingham, in order to reach more families today. He was caught by the Sheriff's men…I don't know how. I wasn't there. One of the citizens of Nottingham came running to tell me. I saw Robin being dragged into the castle courtyard…"

Allen's heart sank. Not Robin . Not his friend, his brother! How could Robin, the best soldier of all of them, get caught?

"We have to rescue him," Allen said, jumping to his feet and hurrying over to them.

"He's being beheaded…at dawn." Little John said, his frightened eyes meeting Allen's gaze without any of his normal animosity.

"Beheaded!" Much gasped from behind them. Allen glanced over his shoulder to see Much wrap his arms around himself and rock back and forth. "No, no, no, no…"

"Much, calm down," Dusty's voice was gentle but firm as she laid a hand on his arm. "We must all remain calm or we will be of no use to Robin. Little John! Return to Nottingham and keep watch. We will meet at Marcus' once the whole gang is aware of what has happened, and we will figure out what to do."

"Gather your weapons," Will said.

"I'll deal with Much," Dusty replied, kissing his cheek.

Allen fetched his sword and bow and then hurried from the camp with Little John and Will. As soon as they arrived at the blacksmith's house the discussion of what to be done about Robin's

510

execution began. Dusty soon dragged a forlorn Much into the house and then Mark and Ida made their way into Marcus' front room. Soon everyone but Faith was there–she had said she would stay in the camp to pray. What good that might do, Allen didn't know; he was far too concerned for Robin to care what method his friends chose to employ that night.

Anything that might help was welcome. Let her pray if she wanted to.

"This execution will be more heavily guarded," Ida said. "It's *Robin Hood*. The Sheriff will not be willing to let him go so easily."

"We will have to be extra careful," Dusty said.

"What if he doesn't execute him in the Square?" Little John asked. "What if he takes into account how often and easily we stop his executions, and he chooses to do it inside the castle courtyard? We can't get in there like we used to…"

"There's always the stable," Allen said. "But Ida's right, there will be far more guards than usual."

"We can do this, Allen." Will shot him a look of equal panic and determination. "We have to do this."

As darkness began to fall outside, Marcus' wife Lillian brought food to the group. Some of the gang began to eat, though Allen noticed Much simply stared at the food on his plate.

A knock sounded on the door and Much jumped, knocking over the mug of ale Lillian had put before him. She came hurrying over with a towel as Marcus opened the front door a crack.

"Can…can I help you?" Marcus asked, his voice cracking slightly.

Allen peered around the door and was not surprised when his friends reached for their weapons. Little John was on his feet with his quarter staff held threateningly forward; Will, and Mark had their swords in their hands, and even Dusty had drawn hers. They were on edge, and Allen could understand why.

Robin was caught, and now Sir Guy of Gisbourne was standing outside Marcus' door.

Marcus stepped aside as Sir Guy and Andrew entered the room.

"You have no need for fear," Sir Guy said. "We're here because we need your help."

Silence greeted his words.

Allen wanted to believe Sir Guy and Andrew meant no harm– but Robin was in their dungeon. A quick glance showed Ida beside him with her daggers in her hands and ice in her eyes.

Sir Guy sighed. "Please. You can trust us. We aren't just doing this for Robin Hood. Lady Lucy has been thrown into the dungeon with Robin and is going to be executed with him at dawn. We need your help if we are going to rescue them."

"Lucy!" Dusty gasped, her sword lowering to her side.

"Whatever you are going to do, do it quickly," Sir Guy said. "We only have one night to plan this rescue."

Sir Guy stepped forward, causing Little John and Ida to swing their weapons forward in a defensive stance. Allen put a hand on Ida's arm, hoping to calm her down. He hadn't drawn his own weapon–Lucy trusted Sir Guy, and if Allen was going to have any real hope of his own redemption he *needed* to believe that she was right.

"I know we haven't had the best dealings between us in the past," Sir Guy said patiently, eyeing the swords raised toward him, "but I need the gang's help. We have to save Robin and Lucy."

Will stepped in front of Ida and Little John. "We are rather good at that. But this execution is going to be more heavily guarded is it not?"

Sir Guy nodded.

"We'll need to know all the details, where guards are stationed and so forth. And to get away, we're going to need fast horses."

Marcus spoke up. "You can borrow mine, as usual."

"I can supply the rest," Sir Guy said. "The Sheriff will expect me to be with him for the most part so Andrew will have to be our messenger."

Will nodded. "We'll be here; Andrew can bring us whatever information you think will help."

Andrew nodded. "I'll do what I can."

Little John stepped up behind Will, glowering at Sir Guy. "I don't trust you."

"But Lucy believes in him," Will said, giving Little John a sharp look, "and that is enough for us."

Allen whole-heartedly agreed.

Will turned back to Sir Guy. "You should definitely stay in the castle. With Lucy coming to the camp after this we're going to need someone on the inside collecting the information she has been. That would be you now, I assume, so it would be best if you didn't draw suspicion now."

Sir Guy nodded. "I am willing to gather information for you. Andrew and I will go back to the castle for now and learn all we can about the execution. Don't fail."

With that, he turned on his heel and marched out, Andrew following after him. Marcus closed his door and the gang's weapons finally lowered, Ida slumping into her seat at the table with a sigh.

"Gisbourne wants to save Robin?" Ida shook her head. "Now that is remarkable."

"It's not Robin," Little John said, starting to pace beside the table. "It's Lucy."

Much moved to a corner of the room, sinking down to the floor and drawing his knees close to his chest.

"It doesn't matter why he's helping," Will said. "The main point is that he and his lackey are going to supply us with the information we need."

As the hours passed, Andrew visited to relay news. The gang shared their ideas for ways to interrupt the execution, and Andrew returned to the castle to relate them to Sir Guy.

"What happens if Gisbourne really has been playing Lucy all this time?" Little John asked. "He has all of us in one spot tonight and could easily siege Marcus' home and kill us tonight. And now he knows about Marcus, too, whose involvement we've been trying to keep secret all this time."

No one had an answer for him. Andrew returned a short while later with more information from Gisbourne, and so the night progressed with Andrew going back and forth many times between the castle and Marcus's home carrying information.

Much had been rather uselessly cowering in the corner of the room throughout the night. Allen could sympathize with his panic–it was Robin, after all. Dusty went to speak with him and soon the two of them rejoined the group at the table.

"Where are we with the plan?" Much asked.

Chapter 73

The execution will be in the Square," Will said. "The Sheriff wants to make a big deal out of it."

"We'll deal with it as we have all the others," Little John added. "Will and Ida will shoot down those who attempt to kill Robin and Lucy while the rest of you deal with the other soldiers and Andrew and I will get Robin and Lucy out of harm's way."

Much shook his head. "I'll shoot down the executioners with Will."

"You've been a wreck," Ida said, crossing her arms. "No offense, but we don't need shaky hands and violent emotions attempting to save Robin Hood."

"I'm a better shot than you are," Much said, his voice surprisingly calm and confident. "Will and I are the best options for archers with both Lucy and Robin out of commission."

Allen nodded; he wasn't wrong.

"You've been brooding in that corner–"

"I have years of experience as an outlaw that you do not," Much cut in before Ida could finish her thought. "Having only recently joined our crew. I was a soldier for more years before that, seeing real combat in the Holy Land while you were still mucking out your father's stalls. I can do this."

Will nodded. "He's right; he is the next best archer, and we need the best focused on saving Robin and Lucy."

Early the next morning the gang positioned themselves around Nottingham Square as the crowd began to gather. The Square was more packed than it usually was, people standing shoulder to shoulder and

515

leaving almost no room to maneuver through the masses. Apparently all of Nottinghamshire was coming to see Robin Hood's execution.

There were soldiers everywhere, too. Some stationed near the platform that held the execution blocks, some scattered among the crowd.

The Sheriff's soldiers soon formed a line, shoving people out of their way to open a path for the Sheriff and his entourage to enter the Square and take their place on the raised dais opposite the execution. The crowd was in a fury, people hurling insults at the Sheriff and spitting at the soldiers.

Only a minute later the soldiers lined the pathway that had been created, separating the people from the men who dragged Robin and Lucy toward their deaths.

Allen gripped his sword, his heart pounding as his palms grew sweaty. What if they failed?

The Sheriff called for silence and an eerie quiet settled over Nottingham Square. A gentle breeze ruffled the banners that were hung over the Sheriff's platform.

"Now, Robin Hood. What do you have to say?" The Sheriff stood above the crowd, his arms held out to either side and a maniacal grin plastered on his face. "The Great Robin Hood is about to die…does he have any last words?"

"A few," Robin called back, lifting his head to stare down the Sheriff.

Allen shook his head, wishing Robin wouldn't anger the Sheriff even further by being his usual sarcastic self. The man was about to be beheaded, for goodness sake. Didn't he know how to hold his tongue?

"Do tell," the Sheriff laughed. "If you want to plead for your life, I'm listening."

"Sorry to disappoint you, Sheriff." Robin's voice rang out clear and cold in the quiet that had settled over the Square. "But I don't want to plead for my life."

"Then what do you want to say, you dirty, terrible, outrageous, traitorous…"

"Alright, Sheriff. You win. You can do what you like with me. But let Lucy go."

"Proceed with the execution!" the Sheriff bellowed.

The guards pushed Robin's head down over the wooden block in front of him and more did the same to Lucy. Allen held his breath, praying to Dusty's god that he didn't believe in that Much and Will would shoot straight and true.

Two axes swung upward into the air and Allen resisted the urge to close his eyes.

Suddenly the twang of bowstrings was heard in the silent Square and the guards dropped dead, their axes falling to the platform uselessly.

Allen rushed toward the platform then, drawing his sword on the first soldier he came near and cutting out the man's legs from beneath him. As the man fell into the crowd, the people began to kick and punch him and Allen left him to their fate while he rushed onward.

The rest of the gang were undoubtedly doing the same work, fighting the Sheriff's men and hoping Robin and Lucy would get away before anyone died. The angry and restless crowd set to work beside them—some with their bare hands, some with weapons they'd brought from home.

As soon as it was clear Robin and Lucy were free, Allen ducked and dodged his way through the crowd to freedom, fleeing the Square and the chaos there. He ran through the streets of Nottingham, across the hills, and through the trees of Sherwood Forest without stopping for a single moment. As he pushed his way past the last underbrush into the camp, his frightened eyes landed on Robin and Lucy and relief flooded his being.

He doubled over, gasping for air, a smile on his face. The rest of the gang gathered around and Lucy thanked them earnestly.

Will hugged her. "We couldn't live without you."

"But you would have left me to the wolves, I suppose," Robin said with a laugh.

Much swung his arm over Robin's shoulders. "Oh no. We would have rescued you either way."

Later that day as they sat around the fire pit discussing the future, Much looked toward Robin with wide and frightened eyes.

"I suppose we will have to go directly to Gisbourne now..."

"It's alright, Much," Robin said. "Gisbourne may be a great help. And we can go through Andrew as well; that would be more to my personal liking."

"Andrew will be more than willing to help," Lucy said. "He has already been acting as a middle man for Sir Guy, myself, and the gang when he needed to."

Lucy moved to the camp permanently after that. Allen wasn't sorry to have her around more often–he'd always found Lucy's company to be a comfort. And since the gang still had spies within the Sheriff's inner circle, the loss of Lucy inside the castle was not as devastating to the people of Nottingham as it had been when Marian had come to live in the camp and the gang had been left without any method of spying on the Sheriff.

Chapter 74

A few days later, Allen and Ida were sitting at Marcus'
table, cool drinks in their hands courtesy of Lillian. They'd been
distributing money in Nottingham; they'd been at it all day, and stopped
by Marcus' home for a break before they returned to camp for the night.

Ida shook her head, scowling into her drink.

"What?"

"I can't believe our lives these days. Getting help from
Gisbourne. He's our main informant now."

"And Andrew."

"Right. We're working with the enemy…who somehow,
someway, aren't the enemy anymore?"

"It is strange."

"Worse than strange. I keep waiting for something to happen.
Like when Gisbourne burned Marian's home to the ground–or straight
up murdered her. He's our only link to the castle, to the Sheriff, these
days. What if he leads us straight into a trap?"

"You don't have to be so cynical."

Ida shot him a sharp look. "Of course you trust him implicitly."

Allen winced. "I am not going to betray you any more than Sir
Guy will betray the gang."

"Neither of those statements gives me great comfort."

Allen sighed. He'd thought they were passed this, but the more
the gang was forced to work with Sir Guy and Andrew, the more Ida
seemed to distrust Allen. It was hardly fair.

Yet he had been the traitor. He wasn't worthy of her. He didn't
want to betray her, and he believed that he wouldn't…but could

someone ever truly make amends for past mistakes to such a degree? Could a traitor ever be truly trustworthy ever again?

"There haven't been as many raids on caravans lately, what if Gisbourne isn't telling us when the Sheriff brings his money through a different route."

"We'd still hear about it if that was the case. You can't sneak an entire caravan of treasure through the streets of Nottingham."

"I suppose not."

"I think the Sheriff has given up. There aren't as many attempts at executions these days either."

"Good. Maybe one of these days we'll catch him off guard and kill him."

"Maybe King Richard will come home finally. If he does, your father should come home, too."

"If my father ever found King Richard at all. I haven't heard from him since he left." Ida took a long drink and then shrugged.

"You're worried about him."

"Of course I am. He's all I have left of family, outside of the gang. But he abandoned me."

"He was—"

"Don't you dare defend him."

"Sorry." Allen took a sip of his drink to buy some time and then he cleared his throat. "But I understand him, Ida."

"And I don't? I lost my mother and brother when he lost his wife and son. I still miss them!" Sadness and anger battled for dominance on her face. Ida sighed as tears starting to form in her sky blue eyes. "Do you still miss your family?"

"Of course." Allen reached across the table to take her hand in his. "Every day."

"What were they like?"

Allen took a deep breath, thinking about his family. He was surprised to find he didn't mind letting the memories rise to the surface. "My father was a superstitious man. He used to believe that our clan was cursed."

"Clan?"

"Yeah. I'm from Scotland, originally. Duncan of the Logan clan was my father."

"Your a Scot?! You don't sound like it."

Allen sighed, scratching his chin for a moment with his free hand. "Yeah…there was an English knight that raised me and my sister alongside my parents. He was rather old–I think he'd raised my father, too. Anyway…I admired him a great deal as a child and I mimicked his manner of speech. I lost my accent quite young. My sister was horrified. So was my father."

"And your father thought you were cursed?"

"Yes. Apparently whenever a baby was born in our clan, either the baby or the mother would die. It was the Logan curse. Never would both survive. But Alice and I were healthy babies, and my mother didn't die."

"So no curse after all," Ida said with a tiny smile.

"I don't know…" Allen said slowly. "Alice and I lived but… then the whole family died in a terrible fire…"

Ida's eyes darkened. "So perhaps the curse was real after all."

"Indeed." Allen sighed. His heart squeezed in his chest as he thought of his parents and his sister and the others who had died that day.

"We had a cook, who was more family than servant…her name was Florie. She was a bossy, no-nonsense lady. A second mother to me

521

and Alice. She and William–the English knight…I think they loved each other, though they never married. She died in that fire."

"That's horrible."

Allen took a deep breath. "I dragged her from the flames that night…I can still remember…"

Ida squeezed his hand before he could get too lost in the horrors of that night.

"I hate that you had to live through that."

"So do I."

Closing his eyes, Allen started picturing Eri's shining eyes and shy smile, with her one little dimple in her cheek. "I…I miss my wife. I've never told anyone about her…not Robin or Much or Dusty."

"What was she like?"

Allen sighed heavily, letting his mind wander of the bittersweet memories of Eri and his youth.

"Sweet, gentle, shy…the opposite of you, really." Allen gave Ida a lopsided grin and shrugged. "Her name was Eri."

"You truly did lose everyone, didn't you?"

"Not everyone. William didn't die in the fire. He joined the Crusades and I never heard from him after that."

"That's awful, Allen. I thought my predicament was bad."

"It *is* bad. Your mother and brother were murdered. That's about as bad as life gets."

Ida nodded, tears dangling on her lashes.

Despite Ida's frustration with her father abandoning her, Allen couldn't find it in his heart to blame the man; he knew only too well what it was to lose a son and wife in a fire.

Allen sucked in a breath as he thought about his son. Tiny, and wrinkled, with his big eyes, gurgling happily in Eri's arms.

"I had a son."

Ida squeezed his hand, her eyes full of tears.

"He was only an infant. He died in that fire."

"Oh, Allen!" Ida stood and moved around the table, wrapping Allen in a hug. He relished the comfort of her embrace.

"His name was Duncan, after my father."

Ida kissed his cheek. "I don't know how to express how awful I feel for you."

Allen reached up to wipe the tears from her cheek. "We've been through a lot, you and I…but we found each other."

Chapter 75

The gang continued to distribute money and food around Nottingham. Robin would send them out in pairs to travel beyond their own shire to feed the hungry of England beyond their shire, too. Dusty and Will usually traveled together; Ida was almost always Allen's companion. By choice or by Robin's design, Allen didn't know. He didn't mind; he enjoyed every moment he could spend with her.

Sir Guy and Andrew kept the gang informed of the Sheriff's schemes, but there were few executions to be had as the Sheriff seemed dejected by how often he lost. And then the news came that King Richard had finally returned home. Rumors began to spread that he'd gathered support abroad–from his mother Queen Eleanor of Aquitaine or from his relations in Saxony. No one knew particulars, but everyone whispered that the King of England was home and his army was sweeping across the land, supplanting Prince John's ruling nobles with men of his own.

"Do you think it's true?" Ida asked as she and Allen stood in the market in Nottingham. It was a bustling day. People were unafraid of the Sheriff these days, and the news of King Richard coming only heightened their brazenness in the face of the Sheriff's cruelty.

"I'm sure it is."

"He'll deal with the Sheriff and Gisbourne no doubt, and life can finally return to some measure of normality."

"Sir Guy has been helping us for weeks now; surely it would not be fair–"

"To imprison the man who murdered Lady Marian? Are we about to have this discussion *again*?" Ida's sky blue eyes were flashing with her ire.

Allen sighed, crossing his arms and surveying the people nearby before he spoke. "I know you don't forgive him. I know–"

"Forgive?! He murdered Lady Marian. Nothing he does now will make up for his past."

Allen winced. "Is that how you view me, Ida? Nothing I do can overcome my past mistakes. I'm the traitor. That's it."

Ida shook her head. "I didn't say that."

"You did."

"Well maybe I do feel that way." Ida shrugged, looking away from him. "I don't know..."

"I thought we'd agreed to trust each other."

"I don't think I realized you were the sort of man to forgive murder."

"What sort of man is that? You respect Robin, and he's working with Sir Guy with civility."

"Because he *has* to."

"I don't think–"

"I. Don't. Care." Ida whirled toward him, grabbing his arm. "Can we drop it? I said before that I *wanted* to trust you, not that I do. The more you defend murderers the more afraid of you I become and I don't want that."

Allen sighed. "What do you want me to say? I know Sir Guy; not well, perhaps, but I do know him. He's–"

"If you say 'a good man' I might just kill you right now."

Allen shrugged. "Then I won't say it. He's done horrible, unforgivable things. So have I. I don't blame those who hate him–or

526

hate me–but I am immeasurably grateful to people like Lucy who can find it in their hearts to forgive us anyway."

"Oh of course. Perfect Lucy can forgive you, why can't Ida?" She rolled her eyes, crossing her arms and turning away again.

They returned to the camp separately that day, as Ida wanted space to think and Allen didn't know how to broach the conversation again without angering her.

He didn't want to walk on eggshells with the woman he was growing to care for so dearly. He shouldn't be afraid to express his opinion to her. And yet, she shouldn't have to be afraid of him and his potential for stupid decisions that led to betrayal.

Yet here they both were.

In a few short weeks, word came that King Richard was arriving any day. The Sheriff and his lackeys holed up in the castle for fear of him–though some fled the city altogether–and the gang began to walk more freely through the streets of Nottingham. And then a company of the King's men arrived and arrested the Sheriff, Sir Guy, Andrew, and everyone who had been connected to the Sheriff during Prince John's rebellion.

One day Allen found himself decorating every door frame and windowsill in Nottingham with Lucy at his side. It hadn't been his idea, but when she'd turned to him with her bright smile and sparkling eyes he could hardly say no.

"Why are we doing this again?" Allen asked. He looked from the flowers in his hand to the ropes of flowers hanging from every window and door along the street in Nottingham, and then glanced toward Lucy. She had a large basket full of flowers hanging off of one arm as she carefully hung a wreath in a nearby window.

"Because!" Lucy laughed. "The king will be here tomorrow, and we have to have everything dressed up. This is a grand occasion! We're celebrating."

"With flowers."

"Just put them up, Allen."

Allen grinned. "Why did you talk me into this?"

"Because everyone is helping dress up Nottingham in one way or another."

"Except Gisbourne," Allen frowned. "I can't believe they threw him in prison with all the others."

"I know," Lucy paused in her work, turning toward Allen. "But maybe…"

"King Richard will let him go? I doubt it. I hope so, but I doubt it."

King Richard rode into Nottingham later that day in a great parade–he rode on his horse in full armor, with a crimson cape blowing in the breeze behind him and a soldier beside him carrying his banner. The people gathered in Nottingham from the city, the nearby villages, the farms, and even from other cities and towns across England, and all were cheering and laughing and singing and crying. He took up residence in the castle and prepared to hold trial against his enemies.

He sat in the Great Hall with his advisors and other lords, and all of Robin's gang with him as he held trial for weeks after his arrival. Allen, Robin, Much, and Dusty had been a part of his Royal Guard, and he trusted them implicitly. He trusted Robin most of all, and wanted him present during every trial.

Hour by hour, his soldiers brought forward one after another of the soldiers, sheriffs and other lords and lowlifes who had helped Prince John against him. Prince John himself, along with many of his most trusted allies, were banished from England.

One day after sitting for hours in the Great Hall listening to King Richard pass judgment, Allen sought solitude up on the battlements overlooking the city. He leaned against the stone parapet and sighed.

Sir Guy and Andrew hadn't been brought forth yet, but it was coming. They would undoubtedly be given the same treatment–banishment or death. Those seemed to be King Richard's favorite choices.

Ida stepped up beside him. "It's a glorious day, isn't it?"

Allen glanced up at the blue sky and the bright sun shining down on the city. "I suppose it is."

"Suppose? The King of England is here–I, a farmer's lowly daughter, have met him. He thanked me personally for my help in saving his people! And now he's giving justice to our enemies. It is a good day, Allen."

"I don't disagree with all of that."

"Then why the long face."

"You won't understand and it will only upset you."

Ida studied him for a moment, her brows drawing together. And then comprehension lit her face, closely followed by anger. "Are you *concerned* for that murderer again? What is wrong with you?"

"He and I are similar in so many ways. If he can't have redemption, neither can I."

"Then I guess you can't! Because Sir Guy of Gisbourne is a wretched man and I, for one, am eager to see him swinging from the gallows. Or better yet, getting his head chopped off."

"Ida!"

"I mean it!"

Allen sighed. "Let's not go over this again."

"What else is there to discuss? You sympathize with the man who killed Robin's wife! And now you get all too friendly with the woman he loves in the absence of Marian."

"I beg your pardon?" Allen jerked away from Ida as though she'd slapped him.

"She just bats her eyelashes and you leap to do whatever she pleases, don't you? You did spend hours together putting flowers all over Nottingham."

"She's my friend, she wanted to–"

"How am I supposed to believe you? Maybe she is your friend. Maybe you love her. I wouldn't know because you aren't trustworthy, are you? You defend murderers. What does that make you?"

Allen crossed his arms, anger and confusion swirling in his chest. She was jealous of Lucy? That was absurd. Her anger at Gisbourne was justifiable but it broke Allen's heart. He'd meant what he said: if Gisbourne wasn't worthy of redemption, how could Allen be?

"Why do you bother to continue speaking to me if you think so little of me?" Allen took another step away from Ida. "Just move on. Go back to your farm–you can now. King Richard is home, the outlaws are no longer needed. Leave me to my fate, such as it is."

"I–"

Allen didn't wait to hear what Ida would say next, he simply stormed past her back into the castle.

Sir Guy was one of the last to be tried. When he was brought forward, Lucy left the room. She was closer to him than any of the rest of them and Allen assumed she couldn't bear to see what was going to become of him. Allen was nervous, too. He certainly didn't want Sir Guy to be executed, but what were the chances that King Richard would pardon him? None.

King Richard sentenced Sir Guy of Gisbourne to death.

Allen hung his head. If word reached King Richard of Allen's betrayals, of his own involvement with Sir Guy, would he be killed too? He probably deserved it. He'd nearly gotten Little John killed.

But then Robin stepped forward. Allen's heart leaped to his throat. He glanced at Ida, who was frowning, her arms crossed as she slumped into her seat in disgust.

Robin asked for the king's mercy, explaining how Sir Guy had helped the gang in the last few months. Allen held his breath the whole time. Would King Richard's implicit trust in Robin be enough?

Allen stared at his friend, amazed at how eloquently he pleaded for Sir Guy's life. He was there when Sir Guy killed Marian…he'd seen Robin fall apart. Allen didn't think he could ever be so gracious to someone who murdered Eri…or Ida.

"Robin, you have done so much for my people," King Richard said. He stroked his bearded chin, eyeing both Robin and Sir Guy thoughtfully. "You are so dear a friend of my own…alright, Gisbourne. You have a full pardon for your past crimes. But you shall not receive any special treatment should you break the law henceforth.

Sir Guy was free.

Allen's entire being seemed to relax, letting loose a tension he hadn't known he'd been holding. Sir Guy had done it; he'd managed to turn his life around and not only receive a pardon from the king but also from Robin himself–from the man whose wife he'd killed.

Allen could feel a smile tugging at the corner of his mouth.

Chapter 76

Allen stood on the stone steps leading down into the courtyard, wondering where to go now. Sir Guy was pardoned, the last of the Sheriff's men had been dealt with. Sir Guy and Robin had managed to get a pardon for Andrew as well before the trials were over.

Ida exited the castle and came to stand next to him, crossing her arms and not looking at him. "So Gisbourne is pardoned."

"He did help us, Ida."

"He also killed a lot of people."

"I know."

"I can't believe Robin has actually forgiven him." She sounded truly disappointed in that fact.

"It is strange. Yet it is a remarkable thing, too. It's a good thing, Ida."

"I disagree."

"I know you do."

Ida turned toward him, her eyes meeting his finally. "I think you're right. I can't trust you not to be your past self–and you can't be bothered to stay in a conversation with me when it gets heated. If you abandon me so easily in an argument, how can I know you'd remain at my side for anything more pertinent?"

"Ida–"

"No. We're through."

Ida marched down the stone steps. Allen watched her cross the courtyard and pass the gates into the city beyond.

He couldn't blame her for her fears. He'd never deserved her in the first place.

Once the trials were officially over, King Richard declared a time of feasting and celebration. Tables were set up outside Nottingham, piled high with food, for the people's enjoyment. As for King Richard himself, his nobles, and Robin Hood and the gang, they adjourned to Nottingham castle where their own feast awaited them.

Laughter filled the Great Hall as outlandish stories of the gang's exploits were told to the king and his entourage. Music and entertainment was provided.

Allen couldn't enjoy any of it.

Sir Guy might have been pardoned, but Ida was lost to him and somehow he knew it was no more than he deserved. He hadn't done anything good with his life.

He pushed a meat pie around his plate with his spoon as he considered the choices that had brought him here. Failing to save his family. Betraying his friends. Pushing Ida away with his desperate clinging to Sir Guy's redemption.

His father was undoubtedly right; he was cursed.

That night Allen tossed and turned in the featherbed in the room he was offered at the castle. The rest of the gang were in rooms nearby– they were living in Nottingham now instead of the forest. It might have been an improvement, but Allen couldn't tell.

Eri's trusting eyes stared at him from the darkness.

"Surely ye can put it out."

The flames leaped from the hearth into his heart and Allen closed his eyes. But that did nothing to dispel the memories.

The thick black smoke issuing from the kitchen seemed to fill the space around him. He was shouting Florie's name, running for the kitchen and leaving Eri behind.

He'd left her there, with his infant son. He'd abandoned her to fire.

Allen groaned, springing from his bed and pacing over to the window. He threw it open and leaned out into the cool night air. The chill breeze sent a shiver through him as it caressed the cold sweat on his skin. His nightshirt was clinging to him; Allen hadn't realized how sweaty he'd become.

He tried to shake off the memories, staring at the stars, at the city below.

He paced his room for a time, but Eri's last words to him kept echoing in his mind.

"Surely ye can put it out."

He couldn't. He didn't.

The fire had won; Eri had died. He failed her. Failed their son.

Now he was failing Ida.

Allen sank into a chair by the empty hearth in his room, wondering if he'd ever be free of the ghosts from his past.

It wasn't his fault. He knew that; he had tried to save Florie, tried to save his family. He hadn't set that fire, hadn't wanted any of them to get hurt.

And Ida…surely he wasn't wrong to want to extend grace both to Sir Guy and to himself. Lucy did it, Robin chose to do it. It seemed a virtue and not a flaw. It was not Allen's fault that Ida could not see it so.

She was afraid of him–afraid that he'd abandon her. But she'd been the one to push him away.

Allen stood, moving to the window again and breathing in the night air. He could not fault her for her fear, but he didn't have to leave her in it. Robin had chosen to forgive the man who'd murdered Marian–

535

and Allen suspected it was due to his love for Lucy. He made that difficult choice for her sake.

Allen squared his shoulders, nodding to himself. He could love Ida, prove to her that he wasn't going anywhere. She might push him away in her fear but she needed his friendship–she'd said so herself. She'd told him before how much she wanted him in her life, that she didn't want to give in to her fear of betrayal. So Allen would see the bold aspect of who she was, and he would remind her of it. He would stay at her side despite her fear until he assuaged it altogether.

He could be trustworthy.

He had to be.

Chapter 77

King Richard held various games and tournaments during his stay in Nottingham. The feasts continued for days and the people celebrated their freedom and the king's return. On one day there was an archery contest–which, of course, Robin won. On another day there was jousting. Allen walked toward the make-shift raised wooden benches that had been erected to view the jousting, his eyes scanning the faces of those who watched.

Two horses stamped impatiently at each end of the open space, the lists. A long, low pole extended from one end of the field to the other as a fence between the jousters. In a flash, a signal was given and both horses and their riders charged toward each other separated by nothing but the rail between them. With the pounding of their hoofbeats in his ears, Allen caught sight of Ida.

She was near the top of the raised seats, leaning forward eagerly as the jousters drew close to one another, their lances crossing dangerously near to each other as they attempted to unseat their opponent.

Allen climbed the steps quickly and took a seat beside Ida.

She didn't look at him until after one of the knights tumbled from his horse and cheer went up from the watching nobles and villagers.

"What are you doing?" Ida asked, still not looking at him.

"Watching the joust."

"You could sit anywhere."

"I want to sit by you."

"We decided we're not courting each other."

"I've decided that is the worst idea we've ever had."

Ida snorted, remaining focused on the joust as a new rider took the place of the fallen knight who could be seen dusting himself off as he walked his horse out of the lists.

She didn't say anything else, so Allen stayed where he was, watching the jousting and enjoying being close to Ida. It was small, just sitting beside her, but it was his first step and she didn't tell him to leave.

For over an hour he sat there and enjoyed the jousts while Ida pointedly ignored him. When the jousting was done for the day the crowds dispersed—some to their homes and some to the feasting tables that King Richard kept full for the people to consume throughout the day. Allen felt a twinge of sympathy for the servants who had to cook and carry the food to those tables.

As Ida stepped toward the edge of the raised seats, Allen jumped down and held out his hand for her. She rolled her eyes, but she accepted his support as she stepped down.

"Hungry?"

"I'm not letting you escort me to the feast," Ida said. She crossed her arms and quirked an eyebrow at him. "What part of 'I don't trust you' do you not understand?"

"Oh I understood; I choose to believe I can change your mind on that point."

"Good luck with that."

She turned and walked away from him, but not before he saw the hint of a smile playing about her lips.

That night Allen dreamt of Eri once more. Her dimpled smile, her gentle touch. He awoke feeling refreshed instead of tormented and he lay in his bed for sometime, not wanting to spoil the feeling.

The feasting came to a close when King Richard departed Nottingham. Slowly, life began to shift back into normal. But what was normal for Allen?

He'd been an outlaw. Before that he'd been a Crusader. Before that he'd been a Scotsman with a wife and family and lands to his name.

Allen didn't think he could go back there, to truly face the memories and his home, and anyway, Ida was here in Nottingham. She, for her part, returned to her family farm. Her father had not been heard from since his disappearance, but she took to rebuilding her farm.

A week after King Richard's departure, Allen strode across the hills and fields toward Ida's farm. She'd gathered the men and women that had worked the farm before the Sheriff burned it, and they were beginning their work—first, rebuilding the house and barns and then tending to the fields and seeing what damage had been done there. It would take years, probably, to get the farm fully functioning once more but Ida was determined.

And Allen went to her farm every day to help where he could.

As he approached, Ida was directing the men and women already there as they raised the four walls of what was to become her house.

Allen jogged forward, coming to a stop beside her. "Where can I help?"

"You've been stalking my farm for weeks, Allen of the Dale. Can you not give it a rest?"

"Only if you truly wish me to leave."

Ida's blue eyes met his as the slightest blush creeped into her cheeks. "I don't wish that."

Allen grinned. "Then where can I be of use?"

Ida gave him a hammer and sent him to the line of folks building her house. He was glad to be of use–it was intense labor and he left her farm every day with muscles sore and aching. But he left with smiles from Ida, despite her protestations, and he went home to pleasant dreams.

After a few hours of work, Ida gathered everyone to eat and rest for a while.

Allen plopped onto the ground beside her, leaning back to soak in the sun that was shining down on them.

"You meant it, didn't you?"

Allen glanced at Ida. "Meant what?"

"That you won't leave me unless I want you to."

Allen sat up, giving Ida his full attention. "Yes. I do mean it."

"You've been pursuing me…trying to convince me you won't abandon me or betray me."

"You know me, Ida. You know my heart beats for you– whatever you need from me, I will supply it."

Ida shook her head. "What a strange man you turned out to be."

"How so?"

"The man I have the most faith in, the one I rely on and turn to for strength and comfort…is the traitor." Ida shrugged. "I cannot fathom how such a thing came to be."

Allen continued to visit Ida daily, helping her rebuild and start to work her farm again. The rest of the gang was at work, too, taking down the huts in the forest and re-purposing the supplies there. One day Ida and Allen joined the rest in packing up what remained of the camp.

They set to work gathering what remained of the treasure in the storage hut in order to take it to Nottingham and add it to the treasury there. King Richard was going to appoint Robin as the Sheriff of

Nottinghamshire and he intended to continue using the king's ransom for the good of the people. King Richard had no objection.

"I'll miss this place," Ida said thoughtfully as she hefted a chest filled with gold coins onto the wagon they'd brought to the camp for that purpose.

"In some way, I think I will, too. Since losing my family, I never lived in any one place for long. During the Crusades we were always on the move...this was the one place I was finally stable."

The two walked back toward the storage hut to grab more chests of treasure.

"This place was formative for me." Ida sighed, resting her hand on the wall of the hut. "I didn't live here long–certainly not as long as the rest of the gang–but...I almost died, my family did die...my father ran away. And I was able to fight for people, to stop injustice... everything about my life here changed me. And I met you."

"I hope that wasn't a bad thing."

Ida shook her head, lifting another heavy chest and exiting the storage hut. Allen grabbed another chest and hurried after her.

"I'm going to focus on rebuilding the farm," Ida said, hefting the heavy chest into the wagon. "Hopefully my father will come home soon and help me. What about you? Returning to Scotland?"

"Never. This is where my family is."

"I'm glad. I wouldn't want to lose you, Allen." Ida smiled at him and Allen's legs went weak. "I know we haven't known each other for even a year yet, but I'm quite fond of you."

"When you aren't angry with me."

"Yes, well, that tends to happen."

Allen dropped his chest into the wagon and then leaned against it. "I don't mean to be troublesome."

541

"You have interesting ideas of forgiveness…but I suppose I could forgive you for that."

"Thank you."

"Well…" Ida grinned, skipping back toward the storage hut. Allen followed.

Ida hefted another chest off the floor and Allen followed suit, though his eyes remained on Ida's face. "Well…what?"

Ida laughed. "I *have* to forgive you because I'm planning on marrying you."

Allen dropped the chest he had been holding. It landed on his foot with a clatter of coins and Allen winced, jumping backwards and hopping up and down for a second. Ida began to laugh. She laughed and laughed until tears ran down her face.

Allen leaned against the wall, rubbing his bruised foot but grinning at Ida. He couldn't help but laugh with her.

When they both caught their breath, Ida punched his shoulder.

"That was not how you were supposed to respond."

"Sorry. You just surprised me."

"I meant what I said. I'm going to marry you whether you like it or not."

Allen grinned. "Do it. I have no objections."

Epilogue

"Ida did indeed marry Allen." Aunt Lucy smiled as her story came to a close.

Robin felt a warmth fill his chest as he looked at his daughter. Mari-Lu was leaning into Aunt Lucy's side, half asleep. Her eyes drooped, almost closed, and a sweet smile curled her lips upward. Young Edmund had laid down halfway through the story, with his head on Lucy's lap.

"It was sad," Mari-Lu said dreamily, her voice soft. "But it ended happy."

"They always do," Edmund replied, shifting in Aunt Lucy's lap.

"Well…" Aunt Lucy glanced toward Robin and he smiled at his grandmother. "I think it's time for bed."

Mari-Lu groaned softly, causing Aunt Lucy to laugh. "You can barely keep your eyes open, little one."

Mari-Lu gave a sleepy, non-committal grunt.

"Come on," Aunt Lucy prodded Mari-Lu gently until she sat up.

Robin rose from the table, listening to the wind still howling outside of his house. He scooped up his daughter and kissed her cheek. "Come on, little one."

His wife Marian collected little Edmund and together they made sure the children were tucked in and sleeping upstairs before returning to sit by the fireplace with Aunt Lucy.

Robin knelt by the hearth. The flames of the fire were nearly gone, leaving glowing embers in their place. He carefully added logs to the fire and prodded them with a metal poker until the fire caught once more.

A sigh sounded behind him. Robin looked at Aunt Lucy. She was leaning back in her chair, her eyes closed.

"As tired as the children?" Robin asked.

Aunt Lucy's eyes flickered open. "It is getting harder to tell these stories."

Robin moved to sit beside Aunt Lucy, taking her frail hand in his. "You don't have to oblige them."

"I do." Aunt Lucy's tired blue eyes met Robin's for a moment before the elderly woman lay her head on his shoulder. "I might be out of breath…and emotionally drained. But I do have to keep telling these stories until I can trust someone else to the task."

"Mari-Lu would do it eagerly."

"I know." Aunt Lucy was quiet for a time but then she spoke again. "I am old, little Robin."

"Don't say such things."

"Nearly eighty years…" Aunt Lucy sighed. "It's been nearly a decade since my Robin passed. I miss my family."

"You still have us."

"And I love you. But I am tired. There is no getting around that fact. It is time for someone else to carry the truth of what happened to our family into the future. I do believe your little Mari-Lu should be that person. She will keep the histories of our family safe, and share them with passion and joy to new generations."

Acknowledgments

As with every story that I write, I did not take this journey alone. I have compiled a list (probably not exhaustive) of the wonderful people who helped me get this story from idea phase to published novel...twice. The following thank you's are due to folks who helped with the original publication AND those who assisted on the rewritten version—a few amazing individuals who did both.

Always a heartfelt thank you to my parents for their support of my dreams.

Rebekah, for her willingness to read the worst of my drafts even when her schedule doesn't truly have the time for it. Also for staying up until 1am editing chapter 1 with me this time around.

Elizabeth Hutchinson, for being the most gracious and brilliant editor and helping me keep track of characters (counting is hard...)

My remarkable Critique Partner Ellie, for doing her best to keep up with my mad dash to the finish line haha. Your perspective on Allen's beginnings, and your sharp eye for commas, are always a lifesaver.

My writing group Quill and Cup, without whom I would not have had the motivation, accountability, and enthusiasm for finishing the rewrites of this series of books so quickly. For every time one of you said, "Oh, poor Allen" or "What have you done to him now?" at the start of a prickle. For every "I can't wait to read Allen's book" I will be forever grateful. This one was a doozy, but you all made it possible. I could never name you all, but you know who you are. Most especially my 9am and 3pm hedgies. THANK YOU

Benjamin, for being Mark's advocate and making sure I never forget him.

Susannah Schmidt, for her critiques on the OG version of the book.

Sarah Loewen, for her editing assistance on the OG version of the book.

And of course, Jesus, without whom I wouldn't be writing any stories at all. He gave me my passion for writing and helps me bring each story to fruition. I could never thank Him enough for all He has done for me.

www.ingramcontent.com/pod-product-compliance
Lightning Source LLC
Chambersburg PA
CBHW051930020726
47501CB00001B/62